Praise for Jennifer Hillier

"Hillier's third thriller fairly shudders with tension. [She] sends her reader into a labyrinth of creepy twists and grotesque turns. . . . The secrets of the past refuse to keep quiet in this disquieting, taut thriller."

—*Kirkus Reviews*, on *The Butcher*

"As she ably proved in her debut (*Creep*, 2011), [Hillier] has a fine knack for creating hideous killers. This time she turns the formula whodunit on its head. . . . A tense, suspenseful, thoroughly creepy thriller."

—*Booklist*, on *The Butcher*

"Once I got started I couldn't stop reading, and I confess to having sweaty palms a few times. A thrill ride that will have your attention from start to finish! This one is 4.5 stars."

—*Suspense Magazine*, on *The Butcher*

"Hillier writes beautifully horrific stories. . . . Readers will be immersed until the final page, thanks to the velocity at which this unique thriller is told."

—*RT Reviews* (Top Pick), on *The Butcher*

"[A] rapid-fire thriller of dark, unsettling proportions with some very surprising twists. With the turn of each new page, the suspenseful plot is tense and gripping . . . a skillfully penned tale of murder and cover-up that will keep readers enthralled until the powerful finish. Thriller fans should not miss *The Butcher*!"

—*Fresh Fiction*

"Top-of-the-line writing . . . You better call in sick, because you're not going anywhere until you finish reading it. Oh, and you might want to lock the door, too. Just to be safe."

—Jeffery Deaver, *New York Times* bestselling author, on *Creep*

"I was engrossed on page one, couldn't put the book down, and breathless at the ending. Be prepared for late-night reading. Then sleep with the lights on—if you can. This one blew me away."

—Robert Dugoni, #1 *New York Times* bestselling author, on *Freak*

JENNIFER HILLIER

WONDERLAND

POCKET BOOKS

NEW YORK   LONDON   TORONTO   SYDNEY   NEW DELHI

Pocket Books
An Imprint of Simon & Schuster, Inc.
1230 Avenue of the Americas
New York, NY 10020

This book is a work of fiction. Any references to historical events, real people, or real places are used fictitiously. Other names, characters, places, and events are products of the author's imagination, and any resemblance to actual events or places or persons, living or dead, is entirely coincidental.

This Pocket Books paperback edition April 2023

POCKET and colophon are registered trademarks of Simon & Schuster, Inc.

For information about special discounts for bulk purchases, please contact Simon & Schuster Special Sales at 1-866-506-1949 or business@simonandschuster.com.

The Simon & Schuster Speakers Bureau can bring authors to your live event. For more information or to book an event, contact the Simon & Schuster Speakers Bureau at 1-866-248-3049 or visit our website at www.simonspeakers.com.

Interior design by Davina Mock-Maniscalco

Manufactured in the United States of America

10 9 8 7 6 5 4 3 2 1

ISBN 978-1-6680-1217-8
ISBN 978-1-5011-1518-9 (ebook)

For Maddox John
(the best kid I've ever known)
and
for Kobe
(the best cat I ever had)

Recipient(s): All Wonderland Staff

Sender: Nick Bishop

Subject: Welcome to Wonderland!

Dear Wonder Worker,

Welcome to Wonderland! We are most pleased to have you on board with us this summer. It will be quite the ride! We pride ourselves on being in the Top 100 Places to Work for Young People in the Pacific Northwest, which is why so many of our Wonder Workers are excited to come back again, summer after summer.

Working at Wonderland will provide you with opportunities to work in customer service, food preparation, electronics, mechanics, ground maintenance, landscaping, theater and performance, ticket sales, and management. Many of our Wonder Workers have gone on to careers in sales, accounting, teaching, and even entertainment. With Wonderland on your résumé, there's no telling where you can go in the world. The sky's the limit!

    I heartily welcome you
into our team of dynamic young
professionals. I have no doubt
you will have the best summer of
your life! That's the Wonderland
way!

Yours sincerely,
Nick Bishop
Owner, Wonderland Amusement
Park, Inc.

ONE

The sky was just beginning to change from night to day as Blake Dozier snuck into Wonderland. It was pretty easy to do, as long as you were willing to cut through the densely wooded forest that bordered Wonderland's south end, which could be kind of spooky if you were easily spooked. At 5 a.m., the only person scheduled to be at the park was Glenn Hovey, a creepy security guard of questionable intelligence who was likely watching porn instead of the monitors inside the office. Security at Wonderland was a joke. Most of the cameras didn't work, and the ones that did fed crappy footage to the computers. Nevertheless, Blake kept out of sight as best he could, just in case "Lovey Hovey," as the Wonder Workers had nicknamed him, was watching.

Wonderland didn't open for another five hours, but Blake was on a mission. He'd been thinking about it for weeks, and if he pulled this off, he'd be able to leave the park knowing he'd accomplished at least one cool thing. Today was his last day at Wonderland. In fact, he'd already quit—he just hadn't told anybody yet.

But soon, everybody would know.

He'd decided at the last minute that his Wonder Worker uniform would be appropriate for this morning's undertaking. The signature purple golf shirt and khaki shorts, ugly and universally despised by every employee forced to wear them, would be the ultimate fuck-you. Especially if the picture went viral. Which he expected it would. Because that was the point.

He made his way down the Avenue, the name for the main path that ran the length of the park. Wonderland felt like a completely different place with nobody around. Other than the Wonder Wheel, which always stayed lit, it was dim and quiet. No excited kids, no tired parents. Nobody in a purple shirt making cotton candy or hot dogs at the various food carts dotted throughout the park. No whooshing from the Legion of Doom roller coaster, no whirring from the Giant Octopus ride. The Spinning Sombrero, which played "Living la Vida Loca" and "Bamboleo" at full volume during business hours, was eerily silent, its swings drooping listlessly from the giant steel Mexican hat to which they were attached. The electronic dog outside the Hot Diggity hot dog stand wasn't barking. The dancing neon cat on top of the Tiny Tom Donuts hut wasn't doing the twist.

The park, normally a sea of moving bodies and noise and energy, was totally inanimate. It felt . . . dead.

Blake figured he had at least an hour before Lovey Hovey would be out in his golf cart checking for trespassers, assuming the security guard even would. He debated whether to take a shortcut through Elm Street, where all the scary attractions were, then decided against it. Too spooky.

Blake had only been inside the Clown Museum once, but once had been enough. The attraction, one of the originals from when the park opened back in the 1980s, was creepy as fuck. It featured more than just wax clowns; the Clown Museum also show-cased wax movie stars, wax cartoon characters, and, in a separate room called the Dollhouse, an exten-sive collection of antique porcelain dolls.

Dolls, for fuck's sake. Weren't dolls just miniature replicas of little girls? And with their white faces and glass eyes, they looked like *dead* little girls. Apparently the mother of the original owner of Wonderland used to collect them and she'd left them all to the park when she died. Blake didn't get the appeal of any of the horror attractions—the House of Horrors was, in his opinion, genuinely terrifying, and the Cirque de Sang (which was French for "blood circus" and featured a different show each day) wasn't his cup of tea, either—but Elm Street supposedly did mad business the entire month of October leading up to Halloween.

No, sir, not his thing. Blake continued past Elm Street, staying focused on his destination. The Wonder Wheel was at the very south end of the midway, all fourteen stories of it, sparkling and bright. It was the second-largest Ferris wheel in the Pacific Northwest, and remained largely unchanged over the past three decades. Under the burgeoning orange sky, its silhouette was majestic.

The first time Blake had ever gone on the Wonder Wheel he was seven years old. That was eleven years ago, but the memory was tattooed into his brain, fresh and colorful as if it had happened yesterday. It had been the first time he'd ever been up so high, the first time he'd ever seen Puget Sound from up above, the first time he'd ever felt scared and exhilarated at exactly the same time. The people down below had looked so small, like the figurines his mother collected and displayed in her curio cabinet before she died.

Blake had loved Wonderland ever since then. He'd loved it so much that his widowed, workaholic father had bought him a season pass to the park the year he turned twelve. From June to September, Wonderland was Blake's second home. It was the one place he was never lonely, never neglected, never sad.

When he was old enough, he applied for a job. Wonderland employed over a thousand Wonder Workers during the busy summer season, and he was exactly the candidate they were looking for—clean-cut, enthusiastic, and willing to start at the bottom. Blake's first summer as a Wonder Worker had been magical. He was earning his own money in the same place he used to pay to spend time in. And he had a plan. First Wonder Worker while in high school, then team leader during college, then manager of his own division after graduation. Someday, maybe, he'd be running the place. Because why not, right? At Wonderland, anything was possible.

Including love.

At least, Blake had thought it was love. Now he wasn't so sure. What had started last summer as the best sex of his life (okay, the *only* sex of his life) had turned sour a few weeks back. While Bianca had pretended to be supportive of his plans to work his way up at the park, it turned out that she actually hadn't expected him to stick around. When he'd told her that he'd deferred his acceptance to Puget Sound State University till the following September so he could spend more time with her, their relationship changed. She became cool, distant, uninterested. Seemingly overnight, she'd gone from wanting him all the time—in her office, in the maintenance room, *in the food court public bathroom, for fuck's sake*—to avoiding eye contact whenever they ran into each other. It had been fun, she said, but it was over. Her feelings had changed, and it was time for them both to move on. She'd said it with no compassion, no sadness, no remorse. She encouraged him to go to college, reminding him that it would be awkward for them to run into each other every day. But he'd already deferred his college acceptance. *For her*.

He didn't know what he did or didn't do. It didn't matter what he said or didn't say. It didn't matter how much he begged. She was finished with him, and there was no changing her mind. She'd used Blake, and while he couldn't say that it was all bad because the sex had been off-the-hook amazing, it wasn't fair. Bianca had all the power, because she was the person in charge. He was just the lowly Wonder Worker, and that's all he would ever be to her.

Seeing her at work every day was excruciating. She barely acknowledged him now. Never mind the sweet things she'd said to him before, never mind the way she had done things to his body he'd only seen in pornos . . . it was like the relationship had never happened. The prime gigs he'd had while in her good graces disappeared, and his assigned tasks were becoming more menial and degrading with every shift. Hell, he'd spent the last week cleaning the toilets inside the very same bathroom where they used to fuck.

She wanted Blake gone from her precious park? Fine, he was gone. But not before this one last thing.

He approached the Wonder Wheel and gazed up at it. Measuring 150 feet high, it was no longer the largest Ferris wheel in the Pacific Northwest (that place of honor belonged to the Great Wheel in downtown Seattle). But it was the oldest, and with its primary-colored gondolas and thirty-year-old sign in circus-themed lettering, it had a certain retro charm that the Great Wheel couldn't match.

The wheel was locked, as all the rides were right now. And as with all the rides, it required a key to get it moving, which Blake didn't have. But that didn't matter, because his plan wasn't to turn the wheel on and take a ride.

His plan was to climb it.

He'd spent a good chunk of his life around this wheel, and he knew he could do it. The Wonder Wheel was made of steel, and there were zigzagging bars between each pair of spokes, turning them into ladders. Climbing a ladder sounded easy in theory, but the bars of the Ferris wheel were five feet apart and tilted, which meant he'd be doing an awkward pull-up in between each one. And then, once he reached the center point of the wheel, he'd have to maneuver his way around it to continue on to the top. But it could be done, sure as shit, though he was pretty sure that nobody had ever tried it before.

But that was the thing about being an urban free climber. Creativity mattered. Blake had been free climbing for the past three years, and he'd climbed all sorts of structures, from apartment buildings to office buildings to construction cranes, posting his accomplishments on Facebook, Twitter, and Instagram in order to get the kudos and street cred he deserved. *Pics or it didn't happen, bro.* The Wonder Wheel would add to his list of accomplishments nicely, and would be a fitting end to his employment at the park. Not to mention, it would horrify *her* that he had dared to climb her precious fucking wheel. The thought made him smile.

Taking a deep breath, he took a moment to ensure his iPhone was securely in its case, which it was. The case was attached to a lanyard that he'd then clipped to his belt. Slipping the phone into his pocket, he began to climb.

The dampness of the air created a thin film of moisture on the bars of the Ferris wheel, which made it slippery. Taking his time, he focused on each of his movements, doing his best not to look directly at the bright lights dotting each of the spokes. He also made a point not to look down. You never looked down, not until you reached the top and could savor the victory of the climb. Hundreds of hours of both free climbing and traditional climbing had taught him this.

Unlike traditional climbing, however, he was not belayed. There was no harness around his waist, no rope to save him if he slipped. That was what made this endeavor so risky, so crazy, and so totally awesome.

It took him almost thirty minutes to reach the top, but when he finally did, he knew immediately it had all been worth it. Keeping one foot balanced on the bar, he wrapped his other leg around the spoke. Once he was secure and had his balance, he finally allowed himself to gaze down at Wonderland and the Pacific Ocean. From fourteen stories up, he could see everything. Morning had broken and the sun was now over the horizon. Everything looked warm and gold, and with the early rays of sunshine on his face, he felt like Superman. The world was always beautiful if you could just climb high enough.

Reaching for his phone, Blake unclipped the lanyard and hooked it around the bar nearest his head. He shortened it so the phone wouldn't be swinging around, and then opened the camera app on the phone. It took a moment to angle himself into the right position and figure out where his head and arms needed to be to get the shot he wanted. Turning on the timer, he set it to thirty seconds and got into position.

Keeping one leg planted on the bar and the other wrapped around the spoke, he leaned way back, arms outstretched to show he wasn't holding on to anything. Then he stuck out his middle finger and smiled right into the camera. It was important to capture the gloriousness of this moment.

He snapped a few selfies in that position, then grabbed the spoke again. Most of the pictures turned out fine, but there was one that was the clear winner. In it, he looked like a free-climbing god. The light was just right on his face, and beneath him was Wonderland, and the Pacific Ocean, sparkling.

A few taps on his phone and the photo was uploaded

to all his social media accounts. He even went one step further and made it his profile picture on Facebook. At this time of the morning, it would be awhile before the comments and "likes" started coming in, but he knew the photo was impressive. He could already imagine what his friends would say. He also knew what Wonderland's management would say, especially about his middle finger, and the thought made him grin.

Because *fuck you, Bianca*.

As he was clipping his phone back to his belt, a movement below caught his eye. There was a golf cart gunning through the midway, heading straight for the Wonder Wheel. *Shit*. Lovey Hovey wasn't rubbing one out in the security office like he should have been, and Blake was about to get caught. He thought he'd left himself enough time to climb back down, but apparently the security guard had decided that today, of all days, he was actually going do his job.

Goddammit. What was Blake supposed to do now? If word of an arrest got out before people had the chance to see his picture in their social media feeds, it would ruin the impact of what he'd done. And the impact was everything.

The golf cart stopped at the base of the Wonder Wheel and someone got out. Blake was assuming it was Lovey Hovey, but from this high up, the person seemed smaller, somehow. Glenn Hovey was slow and overweight, and this person didn't seem to be either of those things.

Okay, already, Blake thought. *Get the fuck of here, asshole. Go.*

But the person didn't leave. Blake watched as whomever it was moved closer to the base of the wheel. And then suddenly, without warning, the Wonder Wheel's music began to play. A nondescript, tinkly carnival melody that Blake had heard countless times began to blast through the speakers inside the carriages. In the silence and stillness of the early morning, the sudden noise was jarring. He dropped his phone to grab the steel spoke with both hands. Luckily the iPhone was still attached to the lanyard, and it dangled from his belt.

And then the wheel began to turn.

The movement was slow, only a few inches in a couple of seconds, but the rotation was enough to kill Blake's balance. His left foot, resting on a skinny, slanted bar slick with moisture, slipped off and dangled in the air. Panic set in. The sudden weight of the unanchored limb, combined with the continuing rotation of the wheel, caused his sweaty left hand to lose its grip. A second later, his right hand slipped, too.

Oh shit oh shit I'm going to fall . . .

He took one last swipe at the pole, but he missed, his fingers clawing at the air, grasping at nothing.

TWO

Vanessa Castro had fallen asleep beside the stranger, which she didn't think was possible for her to do. She wasn't comfortable in strange beds, and that included hotel rooms, her friends' guest rooms, and the beds of men she'd only met a few hours ago.

The sun was up and she could see a sliver of light peeking through the bedroom window where the curtains didn't quite meet. Her bed mate was snoring beside her. She was glad he was sleeping, because she could make her escape without the usual awkward goodbye, which would include one of them saying something like "I'll call you" or "We should have dinner sometime." Things people said to each other when they had no intention of calling or having dinner. Things people said to each other the morning after the night before.

He'd said his name was Oz, but she didn't know if that was true, and it really didn't matter. She'd given him her middle name, Lynn. They'd hit it off immediately after he approached her at the bar, and she knew within ten minutes that he was there for the same reason she was. Just on the outskirts of town, the Tango Tavern was a well-known pickup spot, the place you went specifically to meet new people you might never see again for small talk, craft beer, and whatever else might follow.

They'd avoided the usual getting-to-know-you questions like "Where are you from?" and "Where do you work?" and instead spent the first half of the evening sitting on bar stools, staying carefully impersonal. The Seahawks, the Mariners, and the Sounders were included in the conversation, which flowed more naturally with each beer they drank. He'd been impressed with her football knowledge, less so with her baseball and soccer knowledge, and when those topics dried up, their conversation had shifted to Wonderland. He regaled her with stories about the early days, back before it was bought by Nick Bishop, the park's current owner. Oz clearly thought highly of Bishop, whom he referred to as a friend, and not so highly of Jack Shaw, the original owner and founder of the park, and a man most people in Seaside had hated.

It was safe to assume that Oz currently worked for the park in some capacity—a lot of people in Seaside did—but he never confirmed it and she didn't ask. He was a few years older than Vanessa, maybe midforties, but his confidence and easy smile made him seem younger.

After exactly three Ninkasi IPAs each, he picked up the tab and invited her back to his place for more drinks. She accepted without hesitation. The ease with which he'd extended the invitation suggested that he'd done this a time or two before, and the ease with which she'd accepted probably told him the same thing. Again, it didn't matter. All she wanted was not to be alone tonight in the new house, with memories of the past jammed into boxes she had yet to unpack. It was why she'd thrown on a pair of high heels with her jeans, and why she was wearing her one good Victoria's Secret push-up bra underneath her low-cut top. Oz only lived three blocks away, and though they should have walked over due to their level of inebriation, the cool night air would have sobered them up. Neither of them wanted that. Besides, bringing her car made for a quicker getaway in the morning.

They had sex twice. The first time was on his living room sofa after two shots of Patrón, and it was the ripping-off-your-clothes kind of sex, sloppy and hard and fast. The second time was a bit later, in his bedroom, and they both took their time. If he was married, there was no evidence of it anywhere, not that she was looking too closely. He wasn't wearing a wedding ring, and that was good enough for her.

Vanessa watched him sleep a moment longer. Even in the minimal light of the bedroom with one side of his face pushed into the pillow, she could see the chiseled angles of his jaw, the curve of his lips, the strong shape of his brow. That, too, was unusual. In her experience, most princes turned out to be frogs once the beer goggles were off. This was a guy she would have been attracted to sober. She wondered if he'd feel the same about her—he'd certainly been complimentary about her dark hair, dark eyes, and curvy build the night before—but she wasn't planning on sticking around to find out.

She eased out of bed, careful not to joggle the mattress. Dressing quickly and quietly in the dark, she slipped out of the bedroom with a small sigh of relief. Her high heels were in one hand and her purse was in the other as she tiptoed down the stairs and out the door in her bare feet.

This was the last time she would do this. Once the kids joined her on the weekend, she was done with strange beds and strange men. Her grief would have to manifest itself in a different way.

Driving home, she couldn't help but compare Seaside to Seattle. Dubbed the "Wonder of Washington," according to the sign at the side of the freeway as you drove in, Seaside was picturesque. Small enough to be charming, but large enough to have all the amenities, it was safe, clean, and right on the Pacific Ocean. And it was home to Wonderland, the Northwest's largest amusement park.

Turning onto Main Street, she could clearly see the silhouette of the Wonder Wheel and the roller coasters, though they were two miles away. Because of Wonderland, all the local businesses did well, and not just in the summer, but all year-round. Seaside had money, and lots of it. And it spared no expense in ensuring that everything always looked pretty.

Which it did. The downtown, with its mature oak trees casting dappling shadows on the sidewalks and its old-fashioned store signs, looked like something out of a postcard. In fact, you could buy postcards in almost every shop in the downtown stretch that featured photos of all the shops in the downtown stretch. Seaside relished in its own aesthetic appeal.

It hadn't always been like this. In the midnineties, back when Wonderland was still called World of Wonder, the town hadn't exactly been flourishing. The accusations against Jack Shaw were no longer being ignored, and Shaw had finally been charged with multiple counts of sexual abuse. His accusers were several young men who'd worked for him in the eighties. The ugliness of the whole thing had tainted Seaside, but right before the trial was set to begin, Shaw died.

By then, the amusement park—and Seaside as a whole—had dried up. Many of the privately owned businesses downtown, hanging by a thread over the summer, were closed and boarded up by winter. Families moved away; tourists spent their dollars elsewhere. Vanessa had spent one fabulous summer between high school and college working at Wonderland, and during her time as a Wonder Worker, the park had never been more than half full on its busiest day.

Still, she'd enjoyed her time in Seaside tremendously. It was the first time she'd ever been away from home. Wonderland had been her first real job, where she'd learned to make cotton candy and caramel apples. Shabby though it was in those days, Seaside was the first place she'd fallen in love. Marcus, a local boy with shaggy hair and a Harley, had brought her to the beach the night of July Fourth to watch the fireworks. They'd shared a joint, talked all night, and then he'd taken her virginity in the sand as the sun came up. That summer had been the first and last time Vanessa had ever felt like she was exactly where she wanted to be. It was the first and last time she'd ever felt free.

And perhaps that's why she'd decided to move her family to Seaside. She hadn't dissected it too closely, not that anybody at her former job had asked. Most of them hadn't even said goodbye.

John-John had been sad at first when she'd told him they were moving. He was only seven, but old enough to have a school he liked and friends he would miss. The fact that Wonderland was in Seaside had helped sweeten things. Every kid loved Wonderland, and her son was no exception.

Ava, on the other hand, was still not convinced. Teenage girls were difficult in the best of circumstances, and god knew these circumstances were less than ideal. At fourteen, Ava was old enough to understand why they had to leave Seattle, but she'd made it no secret that she resented Vanessa for moving them out of the city she loved. According to her daughter, going to high school at Seaside Academy in the fall was "tantamount to social suicide." The only saving grace was that she'd been hired to work at Wonderland for the summer, which would be her first real job other than babysitting.

The kids wouldn't be in Seaside until school let out in a few days, and in the meantime they were staying with their grandmother. The current living situation was another thing that displeased Ava. Her grandmother, she complained, cooked "weird, inedible things." Vanessa secretly agreed. Cecilia Castro—her late husband John's mother, not Vanessa's—had turned vegetarian at age sixty, and liked to feed the kids things like bean burgers and tofu pancakes.

Her cell phone rang, and the call display showed Cecilia's house. Vanessa smiled. It was too early for her mother-in-law to be calling, but not too early for John-John, who was always the first person awake.

She put him on speaker phone. "Good morning, sweetheart."

"How come you're already in the car?" he asked, sounding as if he'd been up for hours.

"I have an early work thing." Vanessa mentally cursed herself for having to lie. "What's going on, monkey?"

"I was thinking about Wonderland." John-John had no use for small talk. She could imagine him sitting in the living room, Cecilia's cordless phone pressed to his ear, wearing his Spider-Man pajamas. She missed him so much in that moment she almost couldn't breathe. "Apparently the Legion of Doom is the highest and fastest roller coaster in the world."

"In the world?" Vanessa said indulgently, knowing it wasn't. "Even taller and faster than Space Mountain at Disneyland?"

"Apparently," John-John said, because "apparently" was his new favorite word. "I should be big enough to go on it now. I wasn't last year, remember?"

Vanessa remembered. Wonderland had long been an annual summer getaway for the Castro family. They'd rent a beach house, and Frank Greenberg, John's old Army buddy who lived in Seaside, would be over for dinner almost every night. At the end of the week, they'd all go to Wonderland together, saying goodbye to Frank after Sunday brunch before heading home. Every August, every year, for nine years running.

But not this year. It was hard to believe how much had changed in six short months.

"If you're tall enough, then the Legion of Doom it is," Vanessa said. "Is your grandmother up?"

"Yes. She's making breakfast."

"What about your sister?"

"I tried to wake her but she threw a pillow at me and yelled at me to get out of her room. Apparently she was up late last night having a text fight with some boy. She said he's a douche. What's a douche?"

"It's, uh . . ." Vanessa scrambled to think of an appropriate way to explain it, realized she couldn't, then said, "It's a bad word. Don't say it again."

"Okay. Are you coming to pick us up tomorrow?"

"Not tomorrow, sweetheart. I'll see you on the weekend, remember? The house is almost unpacked and ready to go." *Except for your dad's things*, she thought, but didn't say. She pulled into her driveway.

"Okay." John-John was always so agreeable. "I have to go. Grandma says my omelet is ready." He lowered his voice. "It smells weird. She put vegan cheese in it."

Vanessa laughed. "Eat it anyway, it's good for you. I love you. I'll call you tonight."

She disconnected and let herself into the house. Dropping her keys onto the table, she headed straight for the kitchen, making a point not to look at the boxes in the living room still left to unpack. She'd left them for last, not quite sure what she was going to do with the contents inside. They were John's things, after all.

She turned on the coffeemaker and stared out the kitchen window. Wonderland was in the distance, and she could clearly see the looping roller coaster that was the Legion of Doom, that hopefully John-John was now big enough to ride. He'd be terribly disappointed if he wasn't, and Vanessa didn't think she could take seeing her kids any more disappointed than they already were. Beside the roller coaster was the giant Wonder Wheel, all twinkling lights and colorful chairs swaying slightly in the breeze.

The loneliness consumed her then. Taking a seat at the table, she cried for a good five minutes. Then she shook it off, as she'd been able to do every day over the past week, and went upstairs to take a hot shower. She needed to wash the scent of the man from the night before off her body. As she soaped, Vanessa prayed that she wouldn't see Oz—or whatever his real name was—again. There was no room in her life for anything complicated, even if she'd liked him a bit more than she was willing to admit.

An hour later, hair clean and dressed in fresh clothes, she walked through the glass doors into the Seaside Police Department, gun holstered at her hip. Though it was only her second time here, the officer staffing the reception desk recognized her the moment she entered.

"Good morning, Deputy Chief," he said. "Welcome to Seaside PD."

THREE

Oscar Trejo, vice president of operations for Wonderland Amusement Park, walked across the midway to the nearest trash can and neatly vomited his breakfast into it. He was dismayed to notice that the scrambled eggs he'd whipped up that morning, a couple hours after his date for the night had snuck out, looked almost the same coming up as it had going down.

The guy under the Wonder Wheel had been dead for a while, it seemed. Oscar had assumed he was sleeping, as they'd had incidents with homeless people sleeping inside the park before. But when he shook the man's shoulder, he'd rolled over, and that's when Oscar's stomach turned. The stench in the air wasn't because the guy was homeless. It was because he was dead, his face wholly unrecognizable because, well, he no longer had a face. Something—some kind of wild animal by the looks of it—had eaten most of it away, and what was left was a bloody stump Oscar had only seen in movies. Were it not for the stench of decay, he might have thought that someone from Elm Street had misplaced a prop.

He couldn't even begin to imagine how it had gotten here. It sure as hell hadn't been here the day before—a decomposing human body in the middle of the park would not have gone unnoticed.

The odor—a sickly sweet rot that seemed to permeate the air in a way no other smell ever had—hit Oscar again, and this time he heaved until his stomach was empty. The alcohol he'd consumed the night before wasn't helping matters. Fishing a tissue out of his pocket, he dabbed at his mouth, and then pulled out his phone to call Glenn Hovey. The security guard was still on duty for another half hour, and Oscar was aggravated that it hadn't been Hovey who'd discovered the body instead of him.

The security guard didn't answer. Cursing, Oscar left a message for Hovey to call him back, then tried the landline for the security office. Again, no answer. Either Hovey was in the bathroom watching something he shouldn't on his iPad, or the man hadn't shown up for his overnight shift. Again.

Chewing his bottom lip, Oscar called Bianca Bishop. It wasn't a call he wanted to make, but of course he had to. However, the CEO of Wonderland didn't answer, either. Where the fuck was everybody?

"It's too early in the morning for this bullshit," he said to himself, grimacing at the acidic taste of regurgitated eggs now present in his mouth. But really, was it ever convenient to find a dead body at work? It wasn't like finding a dead rabbit, or a dead rat, both of which turned up not infrequently, in which case he could just call someone in the maintenance department and have it removed. A dead human being was a whole different level of inconvenience, and while he felt bad thinking of it that way, it didn't make it any less true.

Grabbing a bottle of water from his golf cart, Oscar rinsed his mouth, trying to dilute the taste of the vomit. He mentally ran through his options.

Calling 9-1-1 was the obvious first course of action. But this was Wonderland. Things were done a certain way at the park, and if he broke protocol—which, in this scenario, meant calling 9-1-1 *before* getting Bianca Bishop on the phone—he was risking a clusterfuck. The fire department, the cops, and the paramedics would show up with their lights flashing, alerting the public that something terrible had just happened here. There'd be people everywhere, investigating, examining, scrutinizing, gathering whatever evidence they could find to explain the dead body and solve whatever crime had been committed. Reporters would appear and start asking questions. Wonderland would be the leading story on the news by noon. The publicity would be terrible, and Bianca Bishop's pretty young head would explode. And then she'd blame Oscar, even though it wasn't his fault.

But if he didn't call 9-1-1 and instead went to find his boss, he risked somebody *else* finding the body. The first wave of Wonder Workers were scheduled to show up in ten minutes, and there was no way they wouldn't find it, because it was currently rotting in the midway for everyone to see. One of the Wonder Workers would immediately call 9-1-1, which of course was the right thing do, which would result in the fire department, cops, paramedics, and flashing lights. Reporters would appear. The park would be on the news by noon. But in this scenario, pictures were bound to show up on social media. Because that's what the Wonder Workers did these days—they documented every aspect of their lives on Facebook and Twitter for the entire world to see. The pictures would go viral, Bianca's head would explode, and the whole thing would still be Oscar's fault.

He tried calling Bianca one last time. She did have an apartment right here in the park, on the top floor of the administrative building on the east corner, but he didn't know if she was there and he wasn't willing to go and knock. Last time he did that, she'd been in bed with someone. Though Oscar and the CEO weren't lovers anymore, he preferred not to know anything about her personal relationships if he could help it.

The call went to voice mail again, and he made his decision. He sent Bianca a brief text message describing what he'd found, and then with a big sigh, called 9-1-1.

After listening to his description of the scene and asking a few pointed questions for clarification, the emergency dispatcher assured Oscar that Seaside PD was on their way. As was protocol, the fire department and the paramedics would be coming as well. The dispatcher's voice sounded kind of familiar and he briefly wondered if it was someone he'd dated a few years back. But of course that would be inappropriate to ask while making an emergency call. All Oscar could do was hang up and wait for the fanfare to start. A dead body turning up anywhere in Seaside was always a big deal, but a dead body at *Wonderland* was something else altogether.

He trudged back to his purple golf cart. The park's front gates required an access card at this time of the morning; he'd have to drive back to the entrance to let everybody in.

As he gunned it through the park, Oscar thought, and not for the first time, how different his life might have been if he had never come back to Seaside. If he had stayed in the army instead of coming back to his hometown to work for his good friend Nick Bishop, who'd just bought the amusement park they'd both worked at as teenagers, and who'd had visions of turning it into a much different place. He had helped Nicky rebuild the park from the ground up, and it really should have been Oscar in charge of the park now, instead of Nicky's niece, Bianca.

No, he wasn't bitter, but he'd be lying if he said he wasn't disappointed.

The wail of sirens grew louder and Oscar stepped on the gas. Bianca would hit the roof when she got his message, that was as certain as the sun rising. All he could hope for was that she'd take her anger out on whichever teenage Wonder Worker she was currently fucking, instead of him.

FOUR

The Seaside Police Department's motto was "Protect, Respect and Serve." It was emblazoned in large letters at the bottom of the logo, which was everywhere—on the coffee mugs, on the business cards, on the wall of the main office, and on the T-shirts you could buy from the Seaside PD gift shop for twenty dollars plus tax.

Seaside's police force included thirty-five officers, six detectives, two sergeants, one deputy chief, and one chief of police. The wall in the main lobby featured every officer's photograph, and soon Vanessa's would join theirs. It was amazing to her that everyone's picture fit on one wall. The entire police department here wasn't even close to being as large as Seattle's West Precinct, from where Vanessa had transferred.

The officer who'd greeted her had passed her off to another officer, a blonde who couldn't be more than thirty, judging from the absence of wrinkles on her pert face. She'd introduced herself as Claire

Moran, and she'd made a point of telling Vanessa that she'd been "volunteered" to show her around. While her words were polite enough, her tone of voice and lack of warmth made it clear there were a thousand things she'd rather be doing.

During her quick tour of the department, Vanessa was halfheartedly introduced to a dozen or so officers and a handful of administrative personnel. The rest of the staff were either too busy to say hello, or simply not interested, and with each passing minute it was more and more obvious that she wasn't welcome here. Vanessa had no idea why she was being frozen out; this type of treatment was usually reserved for rookies, which she most certainly was not.

Sitting alone now in her new office, she unpacked the few small personal items she'd brought with her. A small framed photo of Ava and John-John was awarded the place of honor on her desk. Her black leather-bound notebook—no iPad mini for her, thank you—was placed beside the photo, along with her favorite mug from home. She was in one of six offices that lined the outer edge of the main area, and it had a glass wall that overlooked the department. Behind her, a small window showcased a view of—what else?—Wonderland.

There was a flurry of activity inside the department this morning, and whatever was going on, the officers seemed excited. Vanessa thought she heard someone say that a dead body had been found at the park, but snippets of disjointed conversation were all she could pick up.

Had someone died at Wonderland? It was ridiculous to have to ask. She was the deputy chief of the Seaside Police Department, for Christ's sake. And it was her first day, goddammit. What the hell kind of welcome was this? Mind you, the title of deputy chief in a police department this small, and in a town as small as Seaside, didn't mean what it would have in a larger city. While Vanessa outranked everybody here except police chief Earl Schultz, the brunt of her job was to head up the Investigative Unit, working major crimes cases hands-on. The rest of her time would involve assisting Earl in whatever administrative and political capacity he needed, which was the only aspect Vanessa wasn't thrilled about. She detested ass kissing in all its forms.

Her new badge, ID, and business cards were ready, but she didn't yet have a username to access her account. Officer Moran had showed her where the break room was and she'd poured herself her second coffee of the day. The coffee tasted like shit, but she sipped it anyway, in desperate need of caffeine thanks to all the alcohol she'd consumed the night before. Drumming her fingers on her desk, she couldn't help but think of the guy from the bar. Had he been disappointed to wake up this morning and find her gone? Would they run into each other again? Did she even want to?

She'd been at her new job for exactly twenty minutes and already she was thinking about a man. *Stop it*, she told herself. *Find something else to focus on.*

Opening the top drawer of her desk, she found a half dozen used ballpoint pens, a couple of business cards that said CARL WEISS, DEPUTY CHIEF on them (the man she'd been hired to replace), and a partially eaten Twinkie with the wrapper still attached. She tossed the Twinkie into the trash and sighed.

Happy first day, she thought. As her daughter would say, it sucked being new.

There was a light knock on her open door and she looked up to see a man standing there. Midtwenties, muscular and clean-cut, his hair buzzed short, he was dressed in civilian attire. His posture told her he was a cop; the gold badge clipped to his belt said he was a detective.

"Good morning." He had two coffee cups on a tray in one hand, and a stack of files in the other. The coffee was from the Green Bean café downtown, and the aroma was fantastic. "I was supposed to be the one to show you around on your first day, but I was running late this morning and the lineup at the Green Bean was long."

"Long, but worth it," Vanessa said, feeling absurdly grateful for his friendly demeanor. "Coffee cures all. Please say one of those is for me."

"I didn't know what you'd like, so one's an Americano and the other one's a vanilla latte." He held the tray up. "Your choice."

"Latte, please." She took the beverage and gave him a smile. "Way to suck up to your new boss."

He blinked. "I—"

"I'm kidding." She laughed. "I'll take suckage any day over the icy blonde who gave me the tour and made it clear I ruined her morning. Thank you for the coffee. Vanessa Castro." She offered him a hand, and they shook.

"Donnie Ambrose. Detective, Investigative Unit. It's nice to meet you. And you must be talking about Claire. She's never been a morning person."

"Have a seat." Vanessa gestured toward the chair across from her desk. "You look awfully young to be a detective, if you don't mind my saying."

"I'm twenty-six." He sat down, crossing his legs comfortably. "I was promoted about a month ago. But you'd think it happened yesterday; people here are still mad about it. Detective spots don't open up often, and competition is fierce. I've only been with PD for five years."

"You must have done good work as an officer, then."

He shrugged, a modest expression on his face. "I love the job, and I aced the detective's exam. I also graduated from PSSU with a dual degree in criminology and computer science, so that gave me a leg up."

"Impressive," Vanessa said with a smile. "I studied criminology at PSSU, too. What are you doing working for a small-town police department? The FBI loves guys like you."

"You think?" Donnie said with a surprised grin. "I'd love to work for the FBI, and god knows I'd love to get the hell out of Seaside. But it's not that easy to make the jump. I grew up here, and there's a lot of history. But, you know, maybe one day."

She nodded. History was a powerful thing. And she of all people understood how hard it was to start over someplace new.

"Those your kids?" he asked, glancing at the photo on her desk.

"Ava and John-John," Vanessa said. "Fourteen and seven, respectively."

"They look like you. You've got your hands full." Donnie placed the stack of files in front of her. "Anyway, Earl wanted me to make sure you were up to speed on all of IU's active cases. You up for it?"

"Of course. By the way, what happened at the park? I overheard some of them talking about a dead body?" She nodded toward the main room, which was still buzzing with activity. "Everybody seems so wound up."

"Nobody updated you? Call came in from Wonderland earlier this morning. One of the employees found a dead body near the Wonder Wheel. Deader than dead, actually." The young detective wrinkled his nose. "Apparently there's a stench."

"Really?" Vanessa was surprised. "If there's an odor, then that means he's been dead for at least a few days. Which means he couldn't have died in the park. Which means he died someplace else and somebody deliberately moved him." The wheels in her brain were turning, and despite her hangover, she was getting a little excited. She had expected things would be quiet in Seaside, but a decomposing body dumped in a public place was an interesting case, for any city. "The Wonder Wheel's right by the midway, isn't it?"

Donnie nodded. "The body was in plain view."

"Who caught the case? Maybe I should head over. Homicide's my specialty, assuming that's what this is."

"It's Earl's." The detective looked at her like she should have known that. "Because it's Wonderland."

"Seriously?" Vanessa was confused. In her experience, the chief of police's job was largely bureaucratic. She'd never heard of a police chief being a first responder to a crime scene.

"Earl handles all the Wonderland calls personally," Donnie said. "Things are done a specific way when it comes to the park."

Vanessa's desk phone rang before she could ask him to elaborate. Thinking it might be Earl, she answered it right away. "Detective Castro," she said, and across from her, Donnie grinned. "Oops. I mean Deputy Chief Castro."

"I'm looking for Carl Weiss." The man on the other line sounded cross.

"I'm sorry, he's retired," Vanessa said. "This is the new deputy chief. Is there something I can help you with, sir?"

"Yeah, I'm calling about my son for the three dozenth time. I want to know what you're doing to find him."

"I'm sorry, I didn't catch your name."

"It's not my name that matters, lady, it's my son's name. Aiden Cole." The man spelled it, making a point to overenunciate each syllable. Vanessa dutifully wrote it down in her black notebook. "He went missing three years ago and you guys aren't doing jack shit. He was only eighteen, still a kid. Did you say Carl Weiss is retired? I call that idiot every month for an update, and he didn't say anything about retiring the last time we talked."

Vanessa looked at Donnie and pointed to the files he'd brought with him, mouthing, "Aiden Cole?"

"Archives," Donnie mouthed back, shaking his head. "Basement."

She nodded. "Carl Weiss retired about a month ago, yes," she said into the phone.

"Well, hallelujah." The man snorted in Vanessa's ear. "He was absolutely useless, so I'll take that as good news. I rode that man's ass like a donkey about Aiden, calling him every month, because god knows he could never be bothered to call me. But then again, why would he? That would mean he had something new, and why would he have something new if he wasn't working the goddamn case?"

"I'm sorry, I don't have the file with me right now," Vanessa said. "I apologize, it's my first day. Is it all right if I call you back when I've had a chance to look it over?"

"Are you really going to call?"

"I give you my word. I'm a parent, too. I have a fourteen-year-old daughter, and I can't even imagine what you've been going through these last three years. I am so sorry." There was a long silence on the other line, and after a few seconds, Vanessa was beginning to wonder if they'd been disconnected. "Sir?"

"I'm here," he said. "Thank you for what you just said. You actually sound like you give a shit."

"I do," she said. "Now can I get your name and phone number?"

"David Cole." He sounded less harsh, and he gave her the numbers for his home, office, and cell. "I'm sorry I snapped at you. It's just, my dealings with Weiss were never productive."

"I'm sorry to hear that, Mr. Cole," Vanessa said. "Give me a day or two to look over the case, and then we can talk about your son more in depth. Does that work?"

"That's fine." His voice faltered. "Well, thank you. I look forward to hearing from you."

"We'll speak soon." Vanessa disconnected and

looked at Donnie, who'd been checking his text messages. "That was David Cole," she said.

"I gathered that." Donnie put his phone away. "He always calls every month at the same time. If he can't get ahold of Weiss, he'll shout at whoever's unfortunate enough to get stuck talking to him."

"Well, I don't blame him." Vanessa's sharp tone made the young detective sit up straighter. "If he calls every month, why is his son's case in the archives?"

"That's where they put all of Carl Weiss's unsolveds," Donnie said. "Aiden Cole was his case."

"What do you remember about it?"

"Not much," he said. "Because there wasn't much to remember. It was three years ago, I think. Aiden was supposed to catch the Greyhound bus to Seattle after the end-of-summer staff party at Wonderland, the one they do every year. And then he was supposed to catch the ferry to Bainbridge Island, where he lived. He never made it home. We don't even know if he got on the bus."

"And the party was the last place he was seen?"

"I believe so, unless Weiss found some new information at some point. Which would be in the file, which is archived in the basement, which is a disorganized mess. I can go dig it up, if you want," he said, looking unhappy. "Might take all day, though."

Vanessa thought for a moment. "What's Claire Moran's extension?"

"Three-five-five."

She punched it into her desk phone. "Officer Moran," she said when the woman picked up. "This is Deputy Chief Castro. I need you to retrieve a file for me in the archives."

"I . . . okay," Moran said on the other end, clearly caught off guard. "That's in the basement. I can ask someone—"

"I don't want someone, I want you," Vanessa said cheerfully. "You were so kind in showing me around this morning, I thought maybe you could use a change of scenery."

Donnie snorted and covered his mouth.

"Which file?" the officer asked.

"Aiden Cole."

"That's one of Weiss's files," Moran said, sounding mildly alarmed. "The archives aren't very organized . . . it might take awhile to find it."

"Great. Have it on my desk by the end of the day. Thank you." Vanessa hung up.

"Feel better?" Donnie asked.

"Much."

"Remind me not to get on your bad side."

"Always wise to remember that," Vanessa said with a smile. "So tell me, was Carl Weiss just stringing David Cole along because there was really nothing he could do to find his son, or was he just a really shitty—" She stopped, realizing she didn't actually know what Donnie's relationship was with the former deputy chief. She didn't want to stick her foot in her mouth.

Donnie laughed. "Don't censor yourself for me. Weiss was a terrible cop. Terrible. His strength was in schmoozing and ass covering and doing whatever Earl told him to do. He was a shitty investigator, which is probably why they brought you in." He leaned in. "Maybe I shouldn't tell you this, but most of the department wasn't too happy that Earl didn't promote from within. He didn't even do formal internal interviews. He just announced you were coming. *Via email*."

Vanessa sighed. "Well, that explains the not-so-warm welcome I received. I'm sorry."

Donnie lifted a hand. "You have nothing to be sorry for. It's not your fault. But folks around here tend to hold grudges, so try not to take it personally. The two sergeants who were in competition for your job hate each other, but they hate outsiders more." He paused, then said, "Rumor has it that Earl hired you because the new mayor asked him to. That true?"

Vanessa gave him her best Mona Lisa smile. "Which mayor?"

He laughed again. "All right, all right. None of my goddamned business, I get it." Donnie's phone buzzed in his pocket and he checked it quickly. "Speak of the devil, just got a text from Earl. You got your wish. He wants us at Wonderland. Everything else can wait."

Vanessa took a moment to down the last of her latte before following Donnie out of the office. "I guess dead bodies are pretty rare in Seaside. In Seattle, unless it was some kind of celebrity death or mass shooting, you wouldn't see both the chief of police and the deputy chief at a crime scene."

"It's going to be so much fun watching you get acquainted to our small-town ways." The detective grinned as they headed out of the building. He directed her to an unmarked Dodge and they both got in. "Mind if I speak bluntly about how things work at Seaside PD?"

"I would appreciate it, actually."

"When Wonderland calls—about anything, dead body, dead squirrel, anything—the chief goes running. Bianca Bishop, the park's CEO, is a real piece of work." Donnie made a face. "She has Earl's home number, and she never hesitates to use it whenever she needs PD for anything. Earl's at her beck and call."

"That seems like a huge waste of resources."

"Oh, I agree," Donnie said as they got into the car. "But Wonderland is the most important thing this town has. If anything goes wrong at the park, if the park doesn't do well, then Seaside doesn't do well. That's been proven before."

"Yeah, but we're the police. We don't work for the park."

"No, we work for the town, which can't survive

without the park." Donnie said this matter-of-factly as they pulled out of the lot. "It's how things have always been. As far as Earl is concerned, nothing that happens at Wonderland is ever a waste of time."

"But for the chief of police to—"

"It's *Wonderland*, Deputy." Donnie's tone was firm but kind. "I know it doesn't make sense to you, and trust me when I say that Wonderland is my biggest headache. I worked there as a teenager, and I know a lot of the management team, so when Earl can't be there personally, who do you think he sends? I know every nook and cranny of that place. It looks like fun and games from the outside, but trust me, that place is not what it seems."

Vanessa waited for the younger man to say more, but he seemed content to drive in silence. He was right, she didn't understand, but she was grateful for his advice. The last thing she needed was to get on Earl Schultz's bad side by saying something stupid. Especially since he hadn't wanted to hire her in the first place.

"My fourteen-year-old daughter's already got a job lined up at the park this summer," she said. "She starts next week. Are you telling me she shouldn't work there?"

"No. She'll be fine." Donnie's voice was flat. "Just tell her not to drink the Kool-Aid."

FIVE

Under the Clown Museum

Blake awoke with a start, and the first thing he was aware of was that his head was killing him. There was a dull pain throbbing from just behind his right ear, and reflexively, he tried to touch it.

But he couldn't, and the second thing he realized was that his arms were bound behind his back.

The third thing he knew was that he was horizontal. He was lying on his side on a damp cement floor, and wherever he was, it was crazy cold.

The fourth thing he became aware of was that there were eyes staring at him. Small, red, glowing eyes, watching him from across the cement floor. He wasn't sure if he was hallucinating, or if they were really there, because when he tried to focus on who or what the eyes belonged to, his brain would get fuzzy again.

None of this made any sense. The last thing he could remember was the Wonder Wheel. He had climbed that fucking thing, sure as shit, but whether that had been today or yesterday or a week ago, he couldn't say. He had climbed it, yes, because he could remember the wind in his hair and the warm morning sun on his face. But how had he gotten back down? And where was he now? That part was hazy.

The eyes were still staring at him, not blinking, not moving. An animal of some kind, had to be. He continued to stare back, mainly because it was too dark to see anything else, and then he heard a scuffling sound.

The eyes got closer. And then there was more scurrying, and the eyes got closer still.

Squinting, Blake tried to focus, and after a few seconds, he heard it. It was a grinding noise, the sound of teeth mashing against teeth. And then he saw it.

A rat. About five feet away from his face. It was looking right at him, whiskers twitching, its long tail pink and hairless and dragging behind it. Its eyes glowed, watching him, as if it was contemplating its next move. It seemed almost cartoonishly large, which made him wonder if it was really there, or if this was some figment of his cruel imagination.

Blake writhed where he lay, and discovered that it wasn't just his arms that were bound; his legs were, too. Panic kicked in, and all he knew was that he needed to get out of here. He needed to get away from the rat. He squirmed and wiggled, but even the slightest movement made the throbbing in his head worse.

And then there was music. It was impossible for him to tell which direction it was coming from, but the jangly tune was immediately recognizable.

> *Welcome to Wonderland!*
> *Or as we like to call it, Funderland!*
> *There's something here for everyone*
> *Whether you're three years old or eighty*
>   *years young!*
> *Stay, play, and have a great day*
> *That's the Wonderland way!*

What the *fuck*? Okay, that proved it, he was totally hallucinating. He must have hit his head on something climbing back down the wheel and knocked himself out, because now his brain was vomiting out random jingles. Every kid knew the words to the Wonderland song, and every kid could sing it by heart—the jingle hadn't changed in twenty years. This was all just a hallucination. Or maybe he was sleeping and having one of those lucid dreams he'd read about, and as soon as he woke up, the nightmare would begin to fade away. In a few minutes, he probably wouldn't even remember it.

Wake up, he told himself, wriggling again, trying to ignore the hammering in his head that felt totally real. *This is just a bad dream and none of this is really happening. You fell and you hit your head, and soon you'll wake up and realize how fucking stupid this all is. Too many horror movies, you asshole. You should never have marathoned the Saw movies on Netflix last week. Now look, all this creepy shit is in your head. So wake up. Wake up. Wake UP!*

The rat made the grinding sound again, and while it wasn't particularly loud, the sound cut into Blake's thoughts like a cleaver.

This was not a dream. As much as he wanted it to be, he knew it wasn't.

He watched, helpless, as the rat began moving purposefully toward him, claws scraping the cold cement, sharp little teeth gleaming under its whiskers.

Opening his mouth, Blake took the deepest breath he could manage, and screamed with all his might.

But no sound came out. All he could hear was the scurrying, growing closer, and then closer still.

SIX

Homeless Harry, as the dead body had been nicknamed by the good people of Twitter, had not yet been identified, and yet pictures of him were all over social media. It was Oscar's worst nightmare, the exact thing he had wanted to prevent from happening. The first picture showed up online at 9:05 a.m., posted by someone called @Chico_Roxxxx, who'd tweeted Dead body found at #Wonderland so fuckin gross his face is gone.

By 9:10 a.m., the picture had gone viral, and somewhere along the way, someone had dubbed the dead guy #HomelessHarry. Oscar could only guess that the nickname was based on the clothes of the deceased, which were ripped and tattered and soiled with dirt and god knew what else. He assumed the name Harry was selected because it made a nice alliteration. According to police chief Earl Schultz, they had no way of knowing right now what the dead guy's real name was. But whoever had tweeted the picture probably worked for the park, and when Oscar figured out who it was, heads would roll.

Bianca Bishop had just arrived at the scene. The CEO's vibrant red hair was still wet from a shower and pulled back in a ballerina bun, her face a mask of displeasure despite her carefully applied makeup. Oscar personally liked her better without the cosmetics, as the makeup and the bun made her seem older than her thirty-six years. He suspected it was why she never went barefaced in public. She'd taken some heat in the past for being such a young CEO.

The area at the bottom of the Wonder Wheel surrounding the dead body had been cordoned off with yellow crime scene tape. Bianca's eyes stayed fixed on it as she made her way through the throng of cops, first responders, crime scene techs, and park employees. The lights from the ambulances and fire trucks flashed blue and red on her crisp cream slacks. Oscar braced himself.

"You couldn't find me first?" the CEO hissed when she reached him. She stood so close, he could smell the toothpaste on her breath. "This is a fucking circus. How long have they all been here?"

"I called nine-one-one just before eight. You weren't answering your phone and I didn't know where you were. After I called, I went back to the admin building and buzzed your apartment, but you didn't answer." Oscar spoke calmly. She was already worked up; any defensiveness from him would only make it worse.

"You should have come up and banged on the door." She looked around in disbelief. "This is a fucking disaster. That crime scene tape might as well be a neon sign that says *dead body*. Is Earl here? This mess better be cleaned up as quickly as possible."

That mess is an actual person, Oscar thought, but of course didn't say out loud. He agreed that the yellow crime scene tape looked terrible, but so did the dead body. And so did the picture of it that was currently going viral. "I tried to get ahold of you—"

"You should have tried harder. The guy's already dead. Five minutes more wouldn't have made him any deader." Bianca's face was pink with anger underneath her makeup. "Obviously we can't open today. Not with cops crawling all over the goddamned place making it look like someone was murdered."

"Someone *was* murdered."

Her eyes cut to him. "How do you know that?"

"I heard them talking. He was hit on the back of the head. It's likely what he died from."

"And who is he?"

"Don't know. Probably a homeless guy, based on the way he was dressed. I overheard them say it looked like he was starving."

"Do you know how much we lose when we stay closed for even one fucking day?"

Of course Oscar knew. He knew down to the dollar what they could expect to gross today based on last year's same-day earnings. But it could have been worse. The guy could have died over the weekend, which would easily have lost them ten times more money.

"I told Earl we needed this wrapped up fast," Oscar said. "But it would be better coming from you."

A large man dressed in jeans and a plaid shirt was standing near the yellow tape, a few feet away from the tarp-covered body. He was engaged in deep conversation with the medical examiner, whom Oscar had also dated once upon a time. Bianca followed Oscar's gaze and her face relaxed slightly when she saw the chief of police. Earl Schultz's presence at the park was a sign of respect.

"I'm going to draft a written statement personally on behalf of Uncle Nick." Bianca didn't bother to look at Oscar as she spoke. "I'll release it as soon as Earl gives me the okay. Prepare yourself for the reporters—I want you to be the spokesperson for this, Oz. You and only you."

"No problem."

"And be goddamned careful with what you say. Make sure you get across that we're deeply concerned and sympathetic without accepting any responsibility.

And put a fucking sign outside the front gates to let people know we're closed for the day. Make a note on the website, too. And call all the Wonder Workers scheduled for today and tell them to stay home. They all get the day off. The last thing we need is more people walking around."

Instructions issued, she walked briskly toward Earl. Oscar used his cell phone to call the management office to delegate everything Bianca had just said. It occurred to him then that maybe he should have told her about the #HomelessHarry hashtag currently trending on Twitter, but he decided he didn't want to.

Across the midway, the chief of police greeted Bianca with a kiss on the cheek and a somewhat paternal smile. Earl Schultz had been the chief of police of Seaside PD for a long time, and he and the Bishops had often socialized together before Nick had taken off to travel the world. Oscar didn't doubt that Earl would see to it personally that everything was handled expeditiously. There wasn't much the department—or Seaside, for that matter—wouldn't do to keep the Bishops happy. Wonderland was by far the town's biggest source of revenue.

After a short conversation, Bianca was gone, speeding off in her purple golf cart the same way she'd arrived, with scarcely a glance back.

Earl approached him, hands in his pockets. "Sorry about all this, Oz," he said, as if it was somehow his fault that the park was in chaos. "I didn't want this to turn into a shit show, but a dead body is a big deal, and the more people we have here doing their jobs, the faster this goes. I know Bianca's anxious to get everything back to normal. We'll be out of here as soon as we can."

"High season starts this weekend, Earl. You know how stressed she gets this time of year."

The police chief nodded. He was a burly man, six two, with thick arms and a belly that stretched over his jeans. His eyes were large, droopy, and perpetually bloodshot due to years of smoking, making him look like a basset hound. "We'll get it sorted. The body's pretty rank. Whoever he is, he obviously wasn't killed here, so that gets us out of your hair a little quicker."

"How long do we have to stay closed?"

"I told Bianca that reopening tomorrow is unrealistic. Hopefully I can get you up and running by the weekend, but the Wonder Wheel is out of commission for at least a week since that's the area we're processing. What I'll do is run a temporary wall around the base, kind of like what you'd see at a construction site, and we can work inside it. I don't think we'll find much, though."

"I guess that's not so bad." The Wonder Wheel was a popular attraction, but it wasn't one of the newer rides like the Legion of Doom or the Beast. Park guests would demand a refund if one of those was unavailable. "So any initial thoughts on why the hell the body's in the midway?"

"My best guess right now is that whoever dragged the body out here wanted it to be found. But until we ID him, we can't even begin to know why he's dead or why he's here. Hopefully we'll get a hit on his prints. If not, we'll try dental records. If not, DNA, but it can take weeks for a match to come back, if there even is one." The police chief rubbed his face. "Who was at the park overnight? Anyone working?"

"It was supposed to be Glenn Hovey, but I'm not sure he showed up." Oscar had forgotten all about the man. "He wasn't in the security office when I called and he hasn't returned my messages."

"Okay, I'll have Donnie and the new deputy follow up on that. They're on their way over. Who else?"

"Nobody else," Oscar said. Clearly the police chief had no idea that Bianca had been in her apartment here all night, but if she hadn't made a point of telling Earl that little fact, then Oscar was sure as hell not going to say anything. "And what new deputy? You're not handling this your-self?"

"I'll stay on top of it, you know I will," Earl said. "But I have to delegate a little. I'm on the board of directors at Seaside Hospital and they put me in charge of the fund-raiser gala. I'm swamped, but I can't let it slide. There'll be a lot of important people there, and I need to take advantage of everyone being in one place so I can get the shopping plaza development deal locked. Speaking of which, any word from Nick? He still in Europe? I could really use his support on this. A push from Wonderland's owner would be huge."

Oscar hated fielding questions about Nick Bishop. "I haven't spoken to him. If you need him, it's best to email him. Anyway, Bianca's not going to be happy you've delegated this case to someone new."

"I'll keep an eye on it. And don't worry, the new deputy's an experienced detective from Seattle PD. You're in good hands." Earl clapped Oscar on the back before walking away.

The last thing Oscar wanted was to deal with a new deputy chief. Carl Weiss had been an idiot and a kiss ass, but at least he understood the chain of command with respect to Seaside and Wonderland. Carl knew which toes to step on, and which toes to avoid. He'd understood the importance of relationships and which ones needed to be prioritized. Someone from Seattle would have no way of knowing any of those things, and Oscar was surprised to learn that an outsider had replaced Carl Weiss.

Two figures were walking toward him from about two hundred feet away. One of them looked like Donnie Ambrose. The other one, he couldn't tell, but she had a distinctly feminine shape. Her curvy figure reminded him of the woman he'd been with the night before, the woman who was at least partly responsible for the hangover he was nursing today.

Not that it hadn't been worth it. The woman— likely a tourist, as he'd never seen her before at the Tango Tavern—had been nothing short of intriguing. Beautiful in an understated, girl-next-door way, she'd had an easy laugh and a love of sports and good beer. In other words, she couldn't have been anything less like Bianca if she'd tried.

He cursed himself. He had to stop comparing every woman he met to Bianca Bishop.

Jamie from the management office was calling his cell, and Oscar stepped into the shade of the Giant Octopus to take the call.

"Reporters are asking questions, Oz," Jamie said when he answered the phone. "Two so far, from the *Monthly* and the *Times*. Bianca told me to refer all calls to you, so you'll have messages in your voice mail when you get back to the office."

"That's the exact right thing," Oscar said. "Just keep funneling them to me. We're going to release a statement as soon PD gives the okay."

"Bianca's in a real tizzy." Jamie sounded muffled, as if she was speaking into the receiver with a hand over her mouth. "I'd stay out of her way today if I were you."

"Too late, already talked to her."

"By the way, don't know if you heard." The receptionist's voice was hushed. "Another picture's going viral."

"Christ, another picture of the dead body?"

"No, it's a picture of some kid on top of the Wonder Wheel," Jamie said. "He must have snuck in early this morning and climbed it. He took a selfie of himself giving the finger and uploaded it to Facebook, Twitter, and Instagram."

"What are you talking about?" Oscar couldn't believe what he was hearing. "Someone climbed the wheel? Who? When?"

"This morning. Apparently he's some kind of free climber," Jamie said. "I don't know the details, but I'm looking at the original tweet right now and it was posted at five thirty this morning. He's wearing the uniform, Oz."

"What's his name?"

"Blake Dozier. I looked him up, he's worked here for almost four summers. Do you think he had something to do with Homeless Harry?"

"Don't call him that." Oscar frowned, trying to make sense of it. "And I don't know what it means. I'm sure PD will find out once they talk to him."

"The thing is, Oz, I've seen this kid. The Wonder Wheel kid, I mean. He was, like, around a lot last summer. He seemed to be close with Bianca. Once, I forgot my phone at work and came back to get it, and they were in her office. Alone. They weren't doing anything, but . . . he had his hand on her leg."

Oscar was quiet for a moment as he processed this information. "You'll keep that to yourself, right? You know how Bianca is about people knowing her private business."

"I can't lie if someone asks me about it, Oz."

"I'm not asking you to lie," Oscar said quickly. "I just don't think it's necessary to volunteer that information unless someone specifically needs it. We don't know why the kid was in her office." Except that Oscar damn well knew why. *Goddamn you, Bianca.*

"Sure, Oz."

He disconnected the call. Feeling the presence of people behind him, he turned.

Their eyes met at exactly the same time, and it only took a second for Oscar to register who it was. Dressed in lightweight slacks and a smart white blouse, her gun holstered to her hip and her gold shield clipped to her pocket, she looked every bit like the deputy chief of Seaside PD that she was, and nothing like the woman who'd crept out of his bed buck naked only a few hours earlier. Minus the beers and dim lighting, she seemed more serious, less animated, and more intimidating. And yet no less attractive, despite her looking as tired as he felt.

She spoke first. Her voice, sweet and husky, was exactly as he remembered it.

"Well," she said. "This is awkward."

SEVEN

Bianca watched the commotion down below through the floor-to-ceiling window in her office. The flashing lights, the cops, the crime scene techs, the ambulance waiting to transport the dead body to the morgue—all of it was unacceptable. She could only hope that Earl Schultz was doing his job and making sure everyone was working as quickly as possible.

Wonderland being closed for a day or two wasn't the end of the world, but the bad PR very well could be. The worst thing that could happen to any amusement park was to be perceived as unsafe, and a dead, decomposing body on park grounds did not exactly paint a picture of wholesome family fun. Back in 2008, a teenager was decapitated by a roller coaster at Six Flags in Georgia, and the publicity had been terrible.

Bianca's office was on the fifth floor of the administrative building, which was on the very east side of Wonderland. The building had its own parking lot, which was convenient for the full-time staff who worked solely in the office. Close to two hundred employees worked in the admin building; it took a lot of people to run the park.

Most of Bianca's time was spent at Wonderland, though she rarely needed to be on park grounds, near the rides, or in the midway. *Please*. She had people for that. People who wore purple uniforms and who were grateful to have jobs. People she paid to create the illusion of fun, which was the whole point of an amusement park in the first place. Wonderland had lost its magic for Bianca a long time ago. That was the problem with peeking behind the magician's curtain— things were never as you thought they were. Uncle Nick had taught her that.

There was a knock on her open office door, and she turned, expecting to see the receptionist standing there. But it wasn't Jamie. It was a young man, maybe sixteen or seventeen—it was hard to tell their exact ages these days, as some of them matured so rapidly and others so slowly. Tall and lean, he had dark blond hair and the beginnings of a summer tan. Neatly pressed gray slacks complemented a sky blue button-down. Based on his age and the way he was dressed, it was easy to guess why he was here and what he was looking for.

"Sorry to bother you, but I think I'm lost." His voice was deeper than she was expecting. She mentally upped his age to eighteen. "I'm looking for Scottie Pile. I thought I found the right office on the second floor, but I was waiting for thirty minutes and nobody showed up. I would have asked the receptionist to direct me where to go, but there seems to be nobody here today. Maybe I got mixed up? I'm here for a job interview."

Scottie Pile was Wonderland's longtime games manager, the man in charge of all the game booths in the midway. There was an excellent chance that the kid did have the right day, and that Scottie didn't come in today because Oscar had said not to.

"Scottie might not be in." Bianca motioned him in. "But I can make a quick call to confirm that. Have a seat."

He entered her office cautiously, appearing a bit overwhelmed by its size and luxuriousness. Uncle Nick's office down the hall—unoccupied and unchanged since he'd stepped away from the day-to-day— was Spartan in comparison to the feminine plushness Bianca had opted for. Two cream-colored chairs sat across from her desk, and she pointed to one of them.

Her call to Scottie went to voice mail, where his recorded greeting informed Bianca that he was working from home.

"He's not here today." She hung up the phone. "He should be back tomorrow, though."

"Oh," the kid said, looking confused. He stood up. "I guess I did get the days mixed up. Sorry to bother you. Hopefully I can reschedule—"

"I'm sure you had the right day." Bianca took a seat across from him. His eyes were either green or hazel—she couldn't quite tell, and she suspected she'd have to be very close to him to know. The thought of getting close to him made her tingle, and she smiled. "We've had a . . . situation here today. The park's closed. You would have seen a sign if you had come in through the main gates, but you probably parked in the administrative lot as Scottie instructed you to, am I right?"

"Yes, ma'am." He looked relieved. "I'm glad it wasn't my mistake. I'll give Scottie a call and see if I can book another time."

"You didn't hear anything about what happened on the news?"

"No, ma'am," he said. "I drove in from Seattle, left the house super early this morning to get here on time. I was listening to the radio the entire way but nothing was said about Wonderland. If I'd heard something I'd have turned around, saved myself the three-hour drive."

Good. "It would be silly for you to reschedule," Bianca said. "You've driven all this way, and I'd be happy to do your interview. I've done one or two in my time." She reached across the desk with her hand extended. "Bianca Bishop, CEO."

"Xander Cameron. It's very nice to meet you, ma'am." Eyes wide as he shook her hand, he suddenly seemed a little intimidated. "I've seen your picture on the website, and I should have recognized you. If you don't mind my saying, you look a lot younger in person."

"I don't mind you saying," Bianca said. "I don't mind at all."

● ● ●

She already knew she was going to hire him. Why wouldn't she? He had the Wonderland look—young, clean-cut, enthusiastic. Looking the part was the first and most important step to getting hired at Wonderland; everything else could be taught.

The park did not hire sloppy kids, fat kids, kids who didn't speak perfect English, kids who looked too "alternative" (i.e., too many tattoos, piercings, or weird hairstyles), or kids who were "emo." Uncle Nick wanted his Wonder Workers to project an "all-American" image, and while they couldn't advertise that (the park was officially an equal opportunity employer), every kid needed to look like someone you could put in a TV commercial.

Xander Cameron was the poster child for the all-American boy. Sitting across from her with his easy grin and that long, lanky body, he was exactly the kind of kid she wanted representing Wonderland.

She asked him all the usual questions and he gave her all the usual answers, and she made sure to smile and nod at everything he said. She liked him. It was important that he like her.

He'd applied for a position on games crew, which almost all the boys his age wanted because it was the best opportunity for a Wonder Worker to make more money. Game runners were paid either their hourly rate, or a commission on their sales, whichever was higher. A good game runner could make upward of thirty dollars an hour on a Saturday in the summer— great money for an eighteen-year-old saving for college.

And college was definitely in the works. He'd already confirmed his place at the University of Miami in the fall, and would be leaving Seaside at the end of high season. Which gave Bianca two months. The perfect time frame.

"So you just graduated from West Seattle High?"

"Yes, ma'am. With honors."

She'd lost count of how many times he'd "ma'am'd" her so far, and it never failed to aggravate her. She was only thirty-six, for fuck's sake. Which was twice his age, but still.

"And what made you choose the University of Miami?"

"Oh, you know," he said, and a lopsided grin spread across his face. "I've been in Seattle all my life. I'm looking forward to the warm weather and sunshine."

And party girls and booze, which is the only reason anyone ever goes to college in Miami. "And why do you want to work at Wonderland?"

"I have several friends who work here, and they all say great things. I love the idea of working outside, and I love being part of a team."

It was the standard stock answer, but that was fine. Games crew didn't require a kid to be articulate, just friendly.

"And if you live in West Seattle, you'll require housing here in Seaside then?"

"Yes, ma'am," he said again, and she mentally slapped him. "I know I'm a late applicant, but my mom got sick back in March and I couldn't make it to the job fair. I was told there are still spaces in the dorms, though."

"I'm sure we can find a place for you."

Truthfully, Bianca had no idea. Wonderland leased dormitory housing at bargain rates from Seaside Technical College from May to September every year, a good deal for both the park and the college as STC didn't offer summer classes, anyway. It had been a brilliant move by Uncle Nick after he bought the park, allowing Wonderland to widen their applicant pool and attract better-quality employees. Seaside was too small a town to accommodate the housing needs of up to a thousand-plus summer staff, and staying in a dorm room had become part of the Wonder Worker experience. Dorm room assignments, however, were well beneath Bianca's pay grade.

"I don't know how much your friends have told you," she said, "but the hours here tend to be unusual. As you know, the park is open from ten to ten every day, but you'll often start earlier or finish later. And even if you're hired for games crew, you could be assigned at any time to another gig, depending on what we need. Are you flexible?"

"Yes, ma'am."

I bet you are. Bianca gave him another smile. "And I'm sure you also know that Wonderland does the most business on weekends. Rarely will you have a Saturday or Sunday off, or two days off in a row. This means we can't accommodate family vacations or weekend getaways with your girlfriend. Is that a problem?"

"It's just me and my mom, and we don't take vacations. And I don't have a girlfriend," Xander said, not realizing that questions about his girlfriend were inappropriate in a job interview.

Oh, you'll do just fine. "Tell me more about yourself," she said.

She watched his hands as he spoke enthusiastically about school (boring), his volunteer work at the Humane Society (also boring—Bianca had zero interest in animals), and his involvement in his church youth group (which on the surface might have seemed like a red flag, but she had learned over the years that good little church boys often made the most enthusiastic and creative lovers). He had strong hands, with long fingers and clean, clipped nails. She could imagine them touching her all over, and she licked her lips. His words blended together as he went on and on, but she perked up when he mentioned tennis.

"I played on the varsity team," Xander said. "I

was hoping to get a scholarship somewhere, but I wasn't quite good enough."

"I played tennis, too," Bianca said, feeling no need to go into detail about it. "Still do, but not as often as I like as I can't always find someone to play with who's as competitive as I am. I'm a member of the Seaside Racquet Club. If you'd ever like guest passes, let me know. I'm on the board of directors."

His face lit up. She saw then that his eyes were most definitely green. "That would be awesome. And if you ever need someone to hit with, I'm game."

"I'd like that. Just know that if you play with me, you're going to sweat."

He grinned. "Wouldn't have it any other way."

Another tingle went through her. This part—the opening cat-and-mouse dance, where she was sometimes the cat, and sometimes the mouse—was always her favorite.

"Well, I think that's everything." She stood up and offered him a hand.

He stood up, too, and grasped her hand tentatively, giving her a whiff of his cologne. He smelled like the beach and sea spray. She couldn't wait to taste him.

"Can I ask when you'll make a decision?"

"I already did. Welcome to Wonderland."

Xander's grip tightened and he pumped her arm several times, his grin widening to show pearly, even teeth. God, he was beautiful. Pure and untainted, full of hope and energy and that unshakable belief that life would work out perfectly for him simply because he wanted it to. It was the kind of optimism you could only feel at eighteen, when you were old enough to know what you wanted, but still young enough to believe you would get it.

Bianca loved them at this age.

He left a moment later, and Bianca forwarded her hiring decision to Human Resources. They would take the care of the rest.

She locked her office door, settling into her sofa by the window where she could once again watch the commotion down below. Reaching up, she pulled the pins out of her hair, freeing it from its tight bun. Her hair fell across her shoulders in deep red waves, all the way down to her waist. She massaged her scalp for a few moments, and the headache she'd had all morning finally began to subside. Then she undid the top button of her blouse and kicked off her shoes.

Unzipping her pants, Bianca pulled them all the way down, then reached inside her panties, feeling the wetness she already knew was there. Her hand moved rapidly, her fingers knowing exactly where to touch herself. Relief came a few minutes later, and when she climaxed, she whispered Xander Cameron's name.

EIGHT

Vanessa didn't know what to say, and neither, it seemed, did the man she'd had sex with last night.

Oblivious to the awkwardness between them, Donnie Ambrose went ahead and introduced them. "This is Oscar Trejo, VP of operations here at Wonderland. Oz, this is Vanessa Castro, Seaside PD's new deputy chief."

"Well," Oscar said. "This is a surprise. *Vanessa*, is it?"

"Have you two already met?" Donnie asked.

"Sort of. We met at—" Vanessa stopped, completely flustered. She didn't want to lie, but she sure as hell didn't want to tell Donnie the truth, either.

"The grocery store," Oscar said smoothly. "We were both there just before it closed, got into a bit of a heated discussion about the Seahawks, I'm afraid. I'm glad you didn't arrest me for the things I did last night."

Vanessa felt her face grow hot. Clearing her throat, she said stiffly, "We ran into the chief on the way out, and he brought us up to speed. You're the one who found the body?"

Oscar nodded, staring at her intently. "I can't even bring myself to look at it again. It'll be awhile before the image is out of my head. And I feel like the smell is in my clothes." He moved closer to her. "Do you smell anything on me?"

She took a step back. "I'm sure you're fine."

He gave her a small smile, then turned to Donnie. "If you spoke to Earl, then I'm sure there's no need to stress the importance of getting this all resolved as quickly as possible. High season starts this weekend."

Donnie gave Vanessa a look that said *I told you so.* "We'll do our best, but it takes as long as it takes, Oz. Anyway, I'm going to go talk to Gloria. She's the medical examiner. You coming?" he said to Vanessa.

"I'd like to talk to Oscar first, being that he's the one who found the body." She cleared her throat. "I'll catch up with you."

The young detective headed off toward the yellow-taped area where the body was still covered in tarp. It was standard protocol that it not be moved until the lead on the case had a chance to look at it, which Vanessa would do once she finished talking to Oscar—*Oz*—privately. There were way too many people here at the moment, some of whom were looking over at her curiously. They all knew she was new to Seaside, and suddenly she felt very exposed. Especially since Oscar was staring at her once again.

Had he been this handsome last night? Just over six feet tall, his black hair had just a touch of gray at the temples. His sleeves were rolled up, exposing his muscular arms and his strong hands. Hands that had touched her naked body. *Everywhere.*

"Why do I feel like this town just got smaller?" she said, more to herself than to him.

"Because it just did," Oscar said. "It gets worse. Everybody knows everybody. Why didn't you tell me you were the deputy chief?"

"Why didn't you tell me you were the VP of Wonderland?"

"Because—" He stopped. "There's no way to answer that question without sounding like an ass."

"Exactly." Vanessa took a breath. "Look, obviously last night happened. And at some point we might want to talk about it, but can we shelve it for now? It's my first day on the job."

"Certainly. But can I just say, it was totally un-cool of you to fake-name me." Oscar grinned. "There, it's out of my system. Now I can officially welcome you to Seaside. Oh, wait. Did that already last night. Twice."

She felt her face grow redder. Oscar was clearly having fun with this, but people were still watching, and she wanted to at least appear like she knew what she was doing. She forced herself to stay professional. "Can you tell me what happened when you found the body? What time was it?"

"Early. Seven thirty," he said. "Not long after you snuck out without leaving me your number. Or your real name, for that matter. You didn't have to do that, by the way. I would have made you breakfast."

"Oscar, *please*—"

"Okay, okay," he said. "In all seriousness, I usually get here by seven, and I'm almost always the first one. I like seeing the park in the morning when it's clean and quiet, before things get noisy and chaotic. I took a golf cart and did a round of the park like I usually do. It reminds me of what I do here. Sometimes, in the office, I forget what the point of this place is when all I'm doing is taking meetings and crunching numbers."

"And that's when you saw him?" It was hard to stay on point with him. He had such an easy manner of speaking, she found herself wanting to hear about his job.

"Yes." Oscar closed his eyes briefly. When he opened them again, there was no trace of humor left in his face. "You must see a lot of dead bodies in your line of work. I don't know how you sleep."

"Earl told me some kind of animal got to his face," Vanessa said. "That would be pretty traumatic to see, especially if you weren't expecting it."

"I touched him." He shuddered. "I know you're not supposed to do that, but I thought he was asleep. He rolled over, and that's when I saw that his face was gone, and I jumped back about three feet. I threw up," he added, looking ashamed. "In one of the trash cans. I hope I didn't ruin any potential evidence."

"That's a normal reaction, and besides, thousands of people come through this park every day. It's going to be impossible to isolate trace evidence, anyway." Vanessa resisted the urge to touch his arm. "Then what did you do?"

"I called nine-one-one." He stopped. "Wait, no. I called Glenn Hovey first, the security guard who was scheduled to work overnight. But I couldn't get ahold of him. I'm not even sure he showed up for work."

"Earl mentioned that," Vanessa said. "Any idea where he might be?"

"No, but his mother would probably know. You might want to start there."

"How long has he worked here?"

"Full time? Twenty years, same as me," Oscar said. "But we both worked here as kids, back when it was World of Wonder."

"And yet he's just a security guard and you're the VP of operations." Vanessa cocked her head. "That's interesting."

"Hovey's not stupid, but he's . . . different," Oscar said. "He was never going to be more than what he is. You'll see that when you meet him."

Vanessa looked up at the camera mounted to the lamppost closest to them. "You have security footage?"

"Earl asked me the same thing," Oscar said. "I'll tell him what I told you. The surveillance system was bought used back in 1995 when Nick—that's the owner—took over the park. It wasn't anywhere near state-of-the-art back then, and it's downright terrible now." He seemed embarrassed. "I can check to see if anything's there, but mainly the cameras are for show."

"You'd be surprised at how often that's the case," Vanessa said. "It's surprisingly effective. I'll need to see what you do have."

"I can get that going for you. The security office is on the first floor of the administrative building." He pointed east. "That brown building way down there. I'm assuming you need to spend some time here at the . . ."

"Crime scene," she said.

"Right. When you're done, give me a call." Oscar pulled out a business card and jotted a number down on the back. "That's my cell. So you don't have to talk to my receptionist."

Vanessa slipped the card into her pocket. "I'll see you soon."

"Looking forward to it." Oscar gave her another smile. "It's really good to see you again, by the way. If I didn't say it before."

He turned and headed for his golf cart before she could respond.

NINE

The body was in bad shape, but Vanessa had expected that going in. In her opinion, the smell was worse than its appearance. The man's face was almost completely eaten away, but the medical examiner was estimating he'd been dead for at least six to eight days, which accounted for the horrible stench. They'd know more once the body was examined in depth, but for now, the ME's best guesses were that the man was between the age of thirty and forty years old, he was probably homeless based on his muscle atrophy and the amount of dirt and grime on his skin and clothing, and he'd died of blunt-force trauma to the back of the head. As for which animal had eaten him, the ME suspected a large rodent—and it had happened postmortem, thank god. Somewhere in the park, or in the woods behind it, was a rat with a very full belly.

Why the dead body had been left in the middle of Wonderland for all to see was anyone's guess. Earl

Schultz had made the assumption that the killer wanted the body to be found, and that was usually true in cases like this. But Vanessa had worked more homicides than Earl ever had or would, and the positioning of the body—lying on its side, no posing or staging—suggested that the body being left in a public area might not have been planned after all.

Vanessa left the crime scene techs to finish doing their jobs. The body was being prepared for transport to the morgue. The next ten minutes were spent with Donnie, discussing the case and their observations. The young detective told her about the #HomelessHarry picture on Twitter, which pissed her off because it confirmed that the crime scene should have been secured better. There were too many people here, and she blamed Earl for that.

Donnie then told her that another picture had just surfaced on social media. An eighteen-year-old Wonder Worker, dressed in the signature purple uniform, had uploaded a picture of himself at the top of the Wonder Wheel earlier that morning.

"The time stamp says he posted the picture at five thirty," Donnie said. "Either he was the one who dragged Homeless Harry in, or the body hadn't been left here yet, because no way did he not see it or smell it when he started climbing the wheel. If it's the second one, that narrows down our window since we know Oz got here at seven thirty."

"What do we know about him?"

"Which one?" Donnie asked.

"The Wonder Wheel kid," she said.

"His name is Blake Dozier, and he calls himself an urban free climber." Donnie curled his fingers into air quotes. "Apparently he's done this kind of thing before. There's a picture of him on his Facebook at the top of a construction crane in downtown Seattle. I can't stand heights, so I don't get it."

"Free climbing? I've never heard of such a thing," Vanessa said. "Okay, see if you can track him down."

"Already on it. Once the park finds out about the picture, he's totally getting fired."

"If he had something to do with the body, losing his job will be the least of his worries." Vanessa wiped a bead of sweat from her eyebrow. It was nearing noon, and the midway was heating up. She fanned her face with her black notebook. "I need to check the security footage. Which one's the admin building again?"

Donnie pointed east. "Take one of the golf carts. You'll die of heat exhaustion before you get there."

"I'll walk, it's not that far. When you're done, text me, and we'll head back to the department together. You're my ride, don't forget."

She started heading toward the administrative building, and five minutes later was regretting her choice not to take a golf cart. The park was beginning to swelter, and by the time she reached her destination, she was drenched. Her hair was plastered to her forehead and she dared not lift her arms, for fear her blouse would reveal round sweat stains underneath her armpits.

Oscar was in the security office, talking with a paunchy bald man in his early fifties who was gnawing on a red licorice whip. The only difference between his purple uniform and that of a Wonder Worker's was that his shirt said SECURITY in large white letters. Both men turned when she walked in, and Vanessa self-consciously wiped her moist brow again with the back of her hand.

The security office wasn't much to look at. It was a small room with three computer monitors set up side by side, two hard drives, and a long desk filled with junk food wrappers. The monitors, at least, were flat screens. That seemed promising; the system couldn't be that old.

"Don't look so excited," Oscar said when he saw her expression. "The monitors are only five years old, but the rest of the system is ancient. Rudy, this is Seaside's new deputy chief, Vanessa Castro."

"Nice to meet'cha." Rudy gave her the once-over. Popping the last bit of licorice into his mouth, he cleared away the pile of food wrappers, depositing the entire mess into the wastebasket. "Sorry about the garbage. I quit smoking two weeks ago. Cold turkey. I'm doing good so far, but I want to eat

everything in sight. So much for my girlish figure."
He patted his stomach, which was bulging firmly
over his pants. He'd been eating everything in sight
for a lot longer than two weeks.

"It's hard to quit," Vanessa said. "Congratulations.
How'd you guys make out with the security footage?"

"There's hardly anything." Oscar sounded disappointed. "All we have is some spotty footage of
the kid climbing the Wonder Wheel—did you hear
about that? Apparently it's all over Twitter. Not that
I wanted to see a dead body being dragged down the
midway, but I was hoping we had that on tape,
knew you'd be pleased if we did. I'd hate for you
not to be pleased."

Vanessa gave him a look and moved away from him.

"I made you a copy." Rudy handed her a thumb
drive. "You can see the kid climbing from about a
third of the way up the wheel, all the way to the top,
and then taking the selfie. You see the pic? It's
actually pretty fantastic, though you'd need a death
wish to climb that high without a harness."

"I haven't seen it yet, no," Vanessa said. "And I
appreciate the copy, but I will need the actual hard
drive." Normally she'd need a warrant for something
like this, but she figured it couldn't hurt to ask. If the
VP of operations gave his consent, it would save a
lot of paperwork.

"Oz?" The security guard looked up with a
frown. "You want me to remove it?"

"Whatever she needs," Oscar said, not taking his eyes off her. "We want to cooperate in any way we can."

Looking dubious, Rudy dug a screwdriver out from the desk drawer and went to work.

"Any theories on how someone could enter the park without an access card?" Vanessa tried to pretend she didn't notice the way he was staring at her.

"Probably through the forest," Rudy said, though she'd posed the question to Oscar. "It's really not that hard, I been saying for years we should put up a fence back there. And Hovey's supposed to check the grounds every hour. That's part of the job when you work an overnight."

"You mean Glenn Hovey?" she asked Oscar. "The security guard who was scheduled last night?"

Oscar nodded, then with a quick glance down at the back of Rudy's head, he mouthed the word *yes*.

"You just have one person manning the security monitors?"

"That's all you really need at night," Rudy said, piping in again as he removed the back of the computer console. "Overnights are pretty boring; nobody wants them. During the day we have more security to keep things in order, but I mean, it's an amusement park, not a casino, and nothing really happens other than maybe the older kids getting into squabbles. Some car break-ins, but that's to be expected anywhere. And we've had a coupla incidents of vandalism at night, sometimes a homeless person sneaks in, but that's really it."

He got the hard drive out and handed it to her.

"Thanks," Vanessa said. "Either of you have a Facebook or Twitter account? Because I don't, and I'm curious about this Wonder Wheel picture. I'm wondering if Blake Dozier's camera inadvertently caught something going on down below."

"I don't have any social media other than LinkedIn," Oscar said. "Working here, the number of Wonder Workers I've employed over the years, I'd probably have ten thousand Facebook friends."

"You can't have ten thousand Facebook friends," Rudy said. "The limit's five thousand."

"You have an account?" Vanessa asked.

"Yes, ma'am, I have them all. Which one you want?"

"Whichever one has the picture."

Rudy typed into a different monitor and a moment later he had the Wonder Wheel kid's Facebook profile picture up on the screen. Vanessa almost gasped when she saw it.

The security guard hadn't been exaggerating when he'd said the photo was fantastic. Blake Dozier's arms were stretched outward, and it appeared as if he was floating, unanchored, in midair. His handsome face was perfectly lit by the early dawn sun, and his expression was one of exhilaration. Below him was Wonderland, and beyond Wonderland was the Pacific Ocean, glistening and never ending. He looked fearless and proud. The only thing marring the picture in any way was the middle finger shooting out from Blake's left hand.

A fuck-you to Wonderland? Why?

"Blake's worked here for a while, right?" Vanessa said. "Why the hostility? He made a point to wear his purple uniform shirt."

"He's been here three or four summers." Rudy looked up at Oscar. "You're gonna fire him, right, Oz?"

"Yup." Oscar's jaw was clenched.

"He obviously knew this picture would result in his dismissal," Vanessa said. "Why not just write a resignation letter?"

"The picture went viral," Rudy said. He reached for his bag of Twizzlers and offered them one. Vanessa and Oscar both declined. "The Facebook picture has over three thousand 'likes,' over a thousand 'shares,' and over five hundred comments already. On Twitter, it's been retweeted almost five thousand times. That's impressive. It's doing much better than the picture of Homeless Harry."

"I imagine that people would enjoy looking at this more than a dead guy," Vanessa said, still staring at the photo. "Did either of you know Blake?"

"Nope, but I do now. He's famous." Rudy pointed to the screen to show them the hashtag that read #WonderWheelKid. "You know you've made it when you're trending on Twitter."

"I didn't know him, either," Oscar said. "We have a thousand to twelve hundred Wonder Workers here during the summer. It's impossible to meet them all."

"Thanks again for your help, Rudy." Vanessa moved toward the door. "Oscar, can I speak to you outside for a moment?"

He followed her out of the security office and into the hallway.

"Tell me," she said, when they were alone. "Who has an access card to the park after hours?"

"Generally anyone whose position requires them to come in early," Oscar said. "Any administrative employee. Maintenance staff. Cleaning crew. Security, obviously."

"No Wonder Workers?"

"Rarely. But still, it's at least two hundred people."

"I'll need a list." Vanessa paused. "It's convenient that the camera stopped working just at the precise moment we might have seen who left the body."

"I know it seems that way, but the cameras cut out all the time," Oscar said.

"You said Glenn Hovey was scheduled to be here but you're not sure if he showed up for work. Do you track whose card gets swiped?"

"No, because they're not unique. The access cards

are generic." He saw the look on her face. "I know, our security is abysmal. But in fairness, there isn't much to protect. Everything's locked up at night, and as Rudy said, we're not a casino or Fort Knox. There's nothing to steal. Nobody's going to pick up a roller coaster and take it away somewhere."

"Other than Glenn Hovey, who else would have been at the park last night?"

He appeared to think about it for a moment, and then said, "Nobody." Moving closer to her, he touched her arm. "Are we done being professional now?"

Immediately Vanessa felt her face grow hot again. "Oscar—"

"Oz. And you're gorgeous when you blush."

"Oz. I think it's best we stay professional. I'm working a case that involves a suspicious death, and until I resolve it, it would be a conflict for you and me to be . . . involved." She felt a twinge of regret as she said the words.

"Why is it a conflict?" Oscar moved closer. "Obviously the guy wasn't killed at the park. And unless I'm a suspect, which I'm not because I was with you all night, I don't see the problem."

Everybody's a suspect, Vanessa thought. "It's not just that. My life is . . . complicated. At most, I'm not looking for anything more than a casual thing."

"I can be casual," Oscar said with a straight face. "I am amazing at casual."

"I can't." She took a step back. "I'm sorry. Last

night was great, but it was only ever meant to be one night. I hope you can understand that. And I do appreciate how cooperative you've been today."

"Maybe you'll change your mind." Oscar's tone was light. He took the hand she offered, assuming he was going to shake it, but he turned it over and kissed her palm gently instead. It felt more intimate than if he'd kissed her on the lips, and it took effort to withdraw her hand. "In the meantime, we'll be friends. I'll see you around, Vanessa. Call me if you need anything."

He disappeared down the hallway. When he was out of sight, Vanessa leaned against the wall, almost dropping the hard drive. Why did this have to happen to her now? He was single, she was single, and on the surface, there was no reason why they couldn't get to know each other better.

Except that she'd only ever loved two men in her entire life. One was dead because of her, and the other one was a criminal who'd used her to save himself. She seemed to be a magnet for toxic men, and if Oscar wanted her, then she could only assume that he must be toxic, too.

TEN

Just as Oscar Trejo had said, there was nothing much to see on Wonderland's security footage. Though there were several cameras placed in the midway, only one had been working at the time Homeless Harry would have been dumped, and that particular camera was not angled to show the pavement underneath the Wonder Wheel, nor did it show the path leading up to it. The footage showed only twenty minutes of Blake Dozier climbing up the last two-thirds of the Wonder Wheel, and that was all. There was nothing to show how he got down, what he might have seen, or when he'd left the park.

Vanessa decided that Donnie Ambrose was the perfect person to take a closer look. The young detective had a dual degree in criminology and computer science, which made him the closest thing Seaside PD had to a computer forensics expert. If Donnie couldn't find anything, they were probably out of luck, unless Earl Schultz was willing to hire an independent specialist.

She doubted he would be; the footage really wasn't much, and it wouldn't be worth the expense.

Leaving Donnie back at the department, Vanessa took the unmarked over to Blake Dozier's house, hoping to find the kid at home. But nobody answered the door, and his cell phone went straight to voice mail. Vanessa left a message, and then called Blake's father, who, as it turned out, was in China on business.

"Why are you calling me?" Derek Dozier asked, sounding half irritated and half sleepy. It was almost 5 a.m. in Beijing, and he wasn't pleased to be awake so early. "You want to talk to Blake, call Blake. Did you try him at Wonderland? They can page him if it's an emergency."

"He's definitely not at work, sir," Vanessa said. "And while it's not an emergency, your son is a person of interest in a case I'm working."

"Oh, Christ. What's he done now?"

"He broke into the park after hours and took a picture of himself at the top of the Wonder Wheel," Vanessa said. "And then he posted the photo online."

There was a pause, and then Derek Dozier said, "And?"

"I beg your pardon?"

"You're not seriously telling me that the deputy police chief of Seaside is calling me in China because my son climbed a Ferris wheel?" Dozier said. "Christ, you people really don't have anything better to do but say, 'How high?' when the park says, 'Jump!' My son's a free climber. It's what he does. He's not hurting anyone."

"It's not about the Wonder Wheel, sir, although I'm sure the park will take that up with Blake when they speak to him," Vanessa said. "Breaking and entering is still a serious offense, but that's not why I need to talk to him. Do you have any idea where he is?"

"You want to know where Blake is, you follow him on Facebook. That's how I keep tabs on him. He checks in everywhere." Dozier was starting to sound sleepy again. "And if he doesn't check in, it's because he doesn't need you to know. He's an independent kid, and I love that about him. He'll get back to you when he gets back to you. Works for me. Why are you special?"

At that, Derek Dozier had hung up.

Her next stop was Glenn Hovey's house. Donnie Ambrose offered to come with her for this one, as he knew Hovey vaguely from his own Wonderland days. She told the detective she was fine going by herself. Vanessa had always preferred working alone. Some cops were better when they partnered up, as they could feed off each other to get the job done. Vanessa hadn't had a partner in years, and she liked it that way.

She pulled up to the Hovey residence and double-checked the address she'd been given. Yes, this was the right house, but the 1960s-style rambler looked as if the Seattle Seahawks football team had thrown up all over it. For starters, it was painted in team colors. The siding was dark blue and the shutters were neon green, a color combination that looked great on a jersey, but terrible on a house. A six-foot-tall Seahawks "12" flag hung from the eaves trough above the garage, and pasted to the living room window was a Seahawks decal that covered the glass almost entirely. The hydrangea bushes in the garden were also blue, green, and white. The house had to be an eyesore for the neighbors, whose homes were all done in shades of beige and brown. Vanessa was a Hawks fan, but this was ridiculous.

She rang the doorbell, and a moment later a small woman in her late seventies was eyeing her suspiciously. She had a face like a road map, her hair silver with a purple tinge. Dressed head to toe in baggy Seahawks sweats, she was holding a Seahawks mug half filled with coffee. A lit cigarette dangled from the corner of her wrinkled lips, which were smeared with coral lipstick. The lipstick was the only thing that wasn't a team color.

Jesus, Vanessa thought. *Imagine if it was actually football season.*

"Whatever you're selling, I don't need it, don't want it, or can't afford it," the lady said. Her hand was shaking, an old-age palsy of some sort, and the coffee in her mug was dangerously close to spilling.

Vanessa held up her gold shield. "I'm Deputy

Chief Castro, ma'am, Seaside PD. I'm looking for Glenn Hovey. Is he home?"

The woman's eyes narrowed, wrinkling the already crinkled skin around her eyes even further. "What do you want with Glenny?"

"Is he home?" Vanessa repeated.

"I'm not telling you where he is until you tell me what this is about," she said.

Vanessa smiled. "I assume you're his mother?"

"I'm Sherry Hovey," the lady said. "Glenny didn't do nothing. He's a good boy."

According to Vanessa's quick background check, Glenn was fifty-three. Not exactly a boy. "I love your house." She made a show of looking around. "The colors are wonderful. I just bought my son a Russell Wilson jersey. He doesn't get it till his birthday, though."

The lady's demeanor instantly softened and the door opened a bit wider. "Well, I obviously had to repaint when the Hawks rebranded a few years back. Not all the neighbors are happy, but I think it adds color to the neighborhood." Her chin jutted out. "Our family's had season tickets dating back to 1976."

"Wow. I hope you got to go to the Super Bowl."

The old woman scoffed. "You'd think! We didn't get picked. Not the year before, neither. They do it by lottery, which is a load of bull crap considering we're the most loyal fans they got." The door opened wider. "I'd sooner sell this house than give up our Hawks tickets, that's how loyal I am."

"Hopefully next year." Vanessa clucked in sympathy, resisting the urge to wave away the cigarette smoke wafting into her face. "Do you think I could speak to Glenn, ma'am? You may have heard, a dead body was discovered at Wonderland."

The woman stiffened again. "Saw it on the news. Some homeless guy. Why would Glenny know anything about that? You trying to accuse him of something?"

"No, ma'am," Vanessa said. "I'm sure he didn't do anything. In fact, it doesn't even look like he was at the park when it happened. But he was scheduled to work that shift, and I do have a few questions for him."

"Damn that park, they're always accusin' him of stuff. Whatever happened ain't Glenny's fault. Wonderland thinks they're the sun that all of Seaside revolves around." The woman scowled and the door opened just a little bit more. "Mind you, Glenny can be a little flaky, you know. But that's why he needs to keep his job. He's got good medical and dental, and I got the Big C. Beat it twice so far, but it's back again. Without Glenny's insurance, I'd be on Medicaid." She shuddered, and the coffee came close to spilling again.

"I'm so sorry to hear that." Vanessa paused for exactly three beats, then said, "Do you know where I can find Glenn, Mrs. Hovey? He's not a suspect or anything, but I sure would like to cross him off my list and move on."

"Glenny's not here." Sherry Hovey hesitated. "I

don't exactly know where he is. He don't tell me where he goes. If he's not working, he likes to gamble—poker and blackjack mainly—so he's probably at some casino somewhere. He'll be back when he's back."

Vanessa made a mental note to put one of the officers on phone duty. All the casinos in the area needed to be called. "And when did you see Glenn last?"

"Let's see . . ." Sherry Hovey's face scrunched up. If a person could personify a prune, she was doing it. "Yesterday afternoon, I guess. I had a doctor's appointment, which he took me to, and then we went to Tres Hermanos for dinner with Margie from next door. Glenny don't much like Mexican, but Margie and I love it, and Glenny goes because he don't cook. And then he was supposed to go to work."

"And when did you last talk to him?"

"Not since then, neither. He don't have to check in with me, he's a big boy."

"Does he have a cell phone?"

The woman recited the number, and Vanessa jotted it into her notebook. "But he won't pick up if he don't know who's calling."

Vanessa handed her one of her freshly minted business cards. "Have your son call me as soon as possible, okay? He's not in any trouble. Just crossing my i's and dotting my t's, as the saying goes."

"Sure." The old woman held the card as far away from her face as possible and squinted at it. "I'll tell him."

"Go Hawks!" Vanessa said, pumping a fist.

The woman snorted. "Easy, sweetheart. It's not even football season yet."

The door slammed shut.

• • •

Vanessa sat in the unmarked Dodge with the window rolled down, trying to figure out her next move. She had a rookie officer named Nate Essex making calls to all the casinos within a hundred-mile radius—of which there were several—but she didn't expect to hear back from him for at least a couple of hours.

The woman who lived in the house next to Sherry and Glenn Hovey's was watering her tomato plants, and she had turned around several times to look at Vanessa inside the car. Their eyes met through the windshield, and finally the woman turned off her hose and motioned her over, looking around furtively as she did so.

Vanessa got out of her car. The woman wasn't quite as old as Sherry Hovey, but she had similar purple-tinged white hair.

"Good afternoon, ma'am," she said. "Did you need something?"

"I'm Margie Hamilton. Come inside." The woman led Vanessa through the garage and directly into a kitchen that smelled like beef stew and chocolate chip cookies. She promptly took a seat at the table and indicated that Vanessa should do the same. "I overheard you speaking to Sherry. Didn't want her to hear us talking. So you're the new deputy chief?" She pronounced deputy as *deppity*.

"Yes, ma'am, I am."

"Earl didn't mention he was hiring a woman."

"You know the chief?" Vanessa was surprised.

Margie Hamilton shrugged. "Oh sure. I used to live next door to him when he was married to his first wife. No, wait, Irene was his second wife." She thought for a moment, then waved a hand dismissively. "Anyway, we were neighbors about fifteen years ago, is what I'm saying. I downsized when Louie—that's my late husband—died. Had a massive heart attack on the way to work one morning, dropped dead in the driveway. The old house was too big for just me after Louie passed, especially once the girls were grown. Anyway, whenever I run into him at the grocery store, Earl always says hello."

"Mrs. Hamilton, did you know something about Glenn Hovey?" Vanessa asked.

"Oh sure, that's why I waved you in here. I didn't want Sherry hearing me, so what I'm telling you, you don't repeat to her, you know what I'm saying?"

"Got it."

"Okay, so Glenny, he's a little batty." Margie made a twirling motion with her finger near her temple. "He's not crazy or stupid or nothing, but he's kind of awkward, though some of that probably comes from living with Sherry for too long. She always says he got weird after what happened to him when he was fourteen. Or was he fifteen?" She paused again, then waved a hand. "He was still a boy when it happened, is what I'm saying."

"What happened to him?"

"The Clown Museum." Margie said this as if Vanessa was supposed to understand exactly what she was talking about. "It messed him up something awful. He was never quite right after that."

Vanessa bit back a sigh. It was important to be patient, and to not show frustration, even though she was tempted to shout at the woman to make her point already. "I asked Mrs. Hovey if she knew where Glenn was. She wasn't sure."

"Oh, she probably don't know. She don't *want* to know, you know what I'm saying? Sherry's protective of her boy, but she likes to pretend that his problem is gambling. His problem's not poker, no matter what she told you." Margie leaned in slightly, and did the twirly thing again with her finger. "His problem goes way deeper, know what I'm saying?"

Biting her lip, Vanessa said, "No, ma'am. No, I really don't."

"He's got other . . . addictions."

"Such as?"

"You know. Those blue movies."

"Blue movies?"

"Dirty movies. Sex movies." The older woman paused for dramatic effect. "*Porn*."

Vanessa tried not to laugh. "I see."

"He been caught two or three times watching porn at work. Can you imagine? That's not right. He's around all those kids, he got no business watching movies like that with kids around. But it's because of what happened to him when Glenny was a kid, you know what I'm saying? It's like he don't know that it's wrong."

This time, Vanessa did know what she was saying. "And how do you know he's been in trouble at work?"

"Because my grandson worked at Wonderland three summers in a row. He said all the kids know about Glenny." She lowered her voice to a whisper. "And it's not like the regular porn. It's really dirty stuff. It's not boy-girl stuff. It's boy-*boy* stuff."

"You're saying Glenn has been caught watching gay pornography while working at Wonderland?"

"You didn't hear it from me."

"But yet they never fired him."

Margie waved a hand. "They can't. On account of what happened to him."

"What happened to him?" Vanessa was beginning to feel like a parrot.

The old woman let out a sigh. "In the Clown Museum."

Vanessa forced a note of concern into her voice.

"Mrs. Hamilton, it would help me if you were specific. What exactly happened to Glenn in the Clown Museum?"

"He was . . . you know . . ." Margie Hamilton looked at her expectantly, waiting for Vanessa to catch on. "He was . . . molested. Back when he was a boy. By that Jack Shaw, the original owner. You know about Jack Shaw?"

"A little bit," Vanessa said. "I worked at the park for one summer, back when it was still called World of Wonder. They had just charged Shaw with the sexual abuse of several of the boys who'd worked for him."

"Well, Glenny was one of them boys. He was all prepared to testify at the trial, but then Shaw died, and there was no trial. And then a couple years later there was a new owner, and Nick Bishop didn't want Glenny talking about what happened in the Clown Museum anymore. Said it was bad for the park, that he wanted a fresh start. He changed the name, changed the logo, got everybody uniforms, and it was like nothing ever happened. Bishop promised Glenny a job for the rest of his life, so long as he promised to keep quiet about what happened to him. Sherry worries all the time that Glenny will lose his job, but she don't need to. They'll never fire him, is what I'm saying."

"I see." It was a lot to take in, and Vanessa thought hard before asking her next question. "Mrs. Hamilton, did you hear about what happened at Wonderland early this morning?"

"Of course. I saw it on the news. Homeless man was found dead."

It was Vanessa's turn to lean in. "Now, between you and me, and of course this will stay between us and I'll never breathe a word of what you tell me to his mother, but do you think Glenn might have had anything to do with that?"

"That's why I called you in here." Margie Hamilton stared at her like she was completely stupid. "I love Sherry, she's a good woman and she's been battling cancer for years now and she needs all the love and support she can get, but she is protecting her boy. As she should, she's his mother. Do I think Glenny had something to do with that man's death from this morning? I don't know. I wasn't there." Her voice lowered again to a whisper, even though they were still alone. "But here's what I do know. I know that over the years, even though me and Sherry are close and I invite her to come over when my family visits, I've never left Glenny alone with my grandsons. Or granddaughters. Never. Not once."

"I see," Vanessa said. Parental instinct—or in this case, grandparental instinct—was not to be taken lightly.

"And if he did do something to that homeless man," Margie Hamilton continued, "not that I'm saying he did, but *if* he did . . . it wouldn't surprise me. You know what I'm saying?"

Yes, Vanessa did. Completely.

Recipient(s): All Wonderland
Staff
Sender: Nick Bishop
Subject: Wear Your Uniform
             With Pride!

Dear Wonder Worker,

Do you remember your
first time at Wonderland? Do
you remember what a magical
experience it was to ride the
Giant Octopus, to have your
first (or hundredth) taste of
cotton candy, to win a prize in
our famous midway?

You are now part of re-creating
that magical experience for
someone else. The signature
purple uniform you wear tells
guests you're there to help
with whatever they need, which
I know you'll do with courtesy,
enthusiasm, and a smile!

As we begin our high season,
it is important that your uniform
always be clean, pressed, and
worn in accordance with the
guidelines in the Employee
Handbook. While wearing the
uniform, you should refrain from
engaging in any type of behavior
that might sully the reputation

of wholesome family fun that
Wonderland has worked so hard to
achieve. If you need to purchase
replacement items of clothing,
$10 will be deducted from your
next paycheck for each item you
require.

Wear the uniform with pride!
That's the Wonderland way!

Yours sincerely,
Nick Bishop
Owner, Wonderland Amusement
Park, Inc.

ELEVEN

Ava Castro's purple uniform shirt was ill fitting and about a size too big, which hid what little boobage she had. She wondered if she could shrink it by washing it in very hot water, because she wasn't crazy about the idea of spending ten bucks for a new one in a smaller size.

Assuming she was still allowed to work at Wonderland, that was. Her mother, annoying on a good day, had completely lost her marbles this morning, and it was all Ava could do to keep her cool. If she had any propensity toward violence and hadn't been taught the difference between right and wrong, she would be happily stabbing her mom with a pitchfork right now.

"But you were the one who told me to apply at Wonderland," she said to her mother, not even trying to keep the exasperation out of her voice. She knew she was crowding the already tiny space in her mom's en suite bathroom, but at least the woman *had* her own bathroom. Ava was forced to share hers with John-John, who couldn't aim for the toilet to save his life. "You were the one who got me all excited about it, and now you're telling me to quit? I haven't even started."

"I'm sure you can find something else." Her mother met her gaze in the bathroom mirror. She was blow-drying her hair, and the wind intermittently hit Ava in the face. "You're a great swimmer. Maybe the beach is hiring lifeguards. Or the YMCA."

"You have to be fifteen to be a lifeguard. And even if I was old enough, I wouldn't want to spend all summer at the YMCA. I want to work at Wonderland because there are a lot of opportunities there." Ava placed her hands on her hips and glared at her mother. How could her mom be the deputy chief of an entire police department, and yet be so dumb? "I don't get this. I told you I wanted to spend the summer with Grandma. Where my friends are. But no, you said I had to come to Seaside as soon as school was done, and that I should work at Wonderland. That's what you said."

"I know I did, but—"

"Is this because of that dead homeless guy?"

Her mom sighed and turned around. "Maybe."

"Mom." Ava took a breath and forced herself to speak calmly, even though her mother was a pro at driving her batshit. "Nothing is going to happen to me at Wonderland. There's, like, a thousand people that work there, and a ton more that visit, and I'm never going to be alone. Nobody's going to kill me and leave my body in the midway. And I'm also not the type to do something stupid like climb the Wonder Wheel and take a selfie with my arms up in the air."

"You saw that picture?"

"I saw both pics, but that's not the point. They've got me assigned to a hot dog cart in the midway. What bad thing could possibly happen from making hot dogs?"

"You could singe your eyebrows."

It was a joke, but Ava refused to laugh. "It's a good job. You should know, you worked there. It was, like, a century ago, but you did."

"Hey, now." Her mother yanked a brush through her hair and winced as she hit a snarl. She always brushed her hair too hard when she was rushing. "I'm just worried, okay? It's a strange case, and I'm hearing all kinds of weird things about the park."

"Like what?"

"Like there's a security guard who does inappropriate things."

"Then I'll make sure I stay away from the security guards."

"And what if that dead guy was killed by somebody at Wonderland?" Her mom turned to face her. "The killer could be working at the park right now."

"Then you'll figure out who it is and lock them up." Ava stepped forward and placed a hand on her mother's arm. "Because that's what you do. But anyplace I go will have its dangers. I could work at, like, Target, and have a boss who's a rapist. Or I start school in September and some messed-up kid in my class brings a gun to school and shoots everybody and we're all dead."

"Ava! Don't say that."

"But it could happen. You can't protect me from everything, or everyone. That's life, Mom. Remember what you said to me after Dad died?"

"No," her mom said, her face softening. "What did I say?"

"You said that life goes on." Ava attempted a smile she didn't totally feel, but she sensed she was winning this argument, not that there should have even been one in the first place. "You said that shitty things happen, and that it's nobody's fault."

"I guess I did say that," her mom said. "And don't say shitty."

"But you still carry a gun," Ava continued, pointing at the holster at her mom's hip. It was empty. Her mom kept her gun locked in the safe, and she never took it out until she was ready to leave for work. "Because it's your job, right? Well, Wonderland is my job now. And if we don't leave in the next three minutes, I'm going to be late for my first day. It's only an orientation session, but still."

"I guess we are." Her mother looked at her watch. "Okay, smarty-pants. You've made some valid points. Let's get moving. John-John!" she called out to Ava's seven-year-old brother, who was still in their bathroom.

Five minutes later, all three were in the car, with John-John in the backseat and Ava riding shotgun. Ava was getting dropped off at Wonderland first, and then her brother would be dropped off at day camp before her mom went off to work. It seemed like as good a time as any to bring up the thing she'd been thinking about for the past week.

"So, remember that concert I told you about last week?" Ava said.

"Which one?" Her mom sounded distracted as she made a left turn. A kid on a bike darted through the intersection at the last second and she braked hard, swearing under her breath.

"The one in Portland," Ava said. "The one Mc-Kenzie got tickets to. One Direction. Remember?"

"I thought I said no to that." Her mother glanced over at her. "Didn't I?"

"You said you'd think about it."

"Well, I thought about it and the answer is no."

"But it's just Portland," Ava said, trying not to sound exasperated. "You let me go to Whistler on a ski trip with McKenzie last year. And that was *Canada*."

"That was totally different. You went with

McKenzie's parents. I don't trust McKenzie's sister to drive you to Portland. It's way too far and she's only eighteen."

"It's three and a half hours. Three if Elana drives fast."

"And driving fast is supposed to convince me?"

Ava slumped in her seat. The only thing worse than not going to the concert would be seeing all the pictures McKenzie would be posting on Facebook and Instagram, none of which she'd be in. That was so not okay.

"Let Avie go, Mom," John-John said from the backseat, and Ava turned around and gave her little brother a smile. "Apparently it's very important to her."

"Why didn't you see the band when we were in Seattle?" her mother asked. "Didn't they play Key Arena? That would have been fifteen minutes from our house."

Was she being serious right now? Ava shot her mother a look. "I wanted to, remember? We had tickets."

"Then why didn't you go? I would have been okay with that."

"It was the weekend of Dad's funeral. I couldn't go, so McKenzie didn't, either."

Her mom sucked in a breath, as Ava knew she would. She felt a small stab of triumph.

Pulling up to a stoplight, her mother turned to her. "Ava, I'm sorry. I forgot." Her face suddenly brightened. "But hey, here's an idea. Why don't *I* take you girls? We'll make a weekend out of it. I'll even book us a hotel, wouldn't that be fun? Concert on Saturday, and then shopping on Sunday. No sales tax in Oregon. I'll ask Grandma to come down and stay with John-John. What do you say?"

Ava stared at her. This was unbelievable. The woman didn't understand her at all, nor did she even seem to want to. First, her mother practically forced her to get a job at Wonderland. Then, she tried to force her *not* to work there. Now her mother was telling her she wasn't allowed to go to a concert that she'd already been permitted to go to unless she came, too?

"I don't want to go with *you*. Don't you get that?" Ava's voice was loud in the small car, but she didn't care. "This concert's a big deal to me, and yet somehow it's always about you. We moved here because *you* wanted to come here. You think I want to live in this stupid little town?"

"Ava—"

"You think I like the fact that I have to start high school in September with a bunch of people I don't know? I've had the same friends since I was in kindergarten and now they're all going to the same high school without me. You think I like being pulled away from the house I grew up in, and all my friends, because *you* want to move, because *you* fucked up at *your* job and so *you* have to get out of Seattle?" Ava was in full shriek mode, and so angry she was spitting. "*You're* the reason Dad got drunk that night! *You're* the reason he's not with us anymore! *You're* the one who was having an affair—"

Her mother slapped her. Ava didn't see it coming, and the sound registered before the sting did. Immediately, she put a hand to her cheek, which burned. She stared at her mother, unable to speak. Did that really just happen? Did her mother just *hit* her?

Her mother had never slapped her before. Not ever. Not knowing what else to do, and more from shock and a bruised sense of self-righteousness than anything else, Ava burst into tears.

In the backseat, John-John started crying, too.

Her mother clapped a hand to her mouth, staring at her in disbelief. Behind them, a car honked. The light had changed. As if in a trance, her mother drove slowly through the intersection, then pulled into the parking lot of a Taco Time and cut the engine.

"Ava, I'm so sorry," her mother said with wide eyes. "I didn't mean to slap you, and I'm very sorry that I did. It's just . . . the things you said . . . you can't speak to me like that, Ava. No matter what, I am your mother, and you cannot speak to me that way, do you understand?"

Ava clutched her knapsack. "What I understand is that I hate you. And I'll walk to work if it means I don't have to spend another second with you."

She got out of the car and slammed the door as

hard as she could. She heard John-John shriek from inside the car, then heard him call, "Avie! Come back!"

She didn't care. She started walking toward Wonderland, which was easily visible and about a mile away. She forced herself not to look back.

• • •

A man drove up to the entrance of the park in a shiny purple Wonderland golf cart, stopping directly in front of the main entrance gates. Stepping out, he turned to the camera with a smile. Dressed neatly in a purple Wonderland golf shirt and pressed khaki slacks, he looked every inch the ideal Wonderland employee. The camera zoomed in on his face, where a row of perfect white teeth gleamed against his summer tan. Then the camera zoomed out, capturing the WELCOME TO WONDERLAND sign above his head. The sound crackled. They were watching this orientation video on VHS, not DVD, and the quality was terrible.

"Hi, there!" The man on the TV screen gave a cheerful wave as the camera zoomed in closer again. "I'm Nick Bishop, owner of Wonderland. If you're watching this video, it's because you've just joined our team of dedicated Wonder Workers. Welcome! I'm so happy you've decided to become part of the Wonderland family, and we're going to have a great summer together. If you're watching this with other

Wonder Workers, take a moment to say hello and introduce yourself. Don't be shy! Remember, your enthusiasm and friendliness are why we hired you."

The boy beside Ava stifled a laugh. They'd already been introduced by one of the supervisors earlier, and it was just the two of them now, sitting in a little room on the second floor of the administrative building. He was new, too, and so far Ava only knew two things about him—his name was Xander Cameron, and he was hot. Or OMG HAWT!!! as she'd texted McKenzie the minute the supervisor had left them alone. She was guessing he was at least seventeen. Maybe even eighteen. Which made him practically a man.

Xander was sitting on the chair a few feet away from hers, slouched down, his long legs stretched out in front of him. Ava wondered if she'd somehow be able to take a picture of him with her cell phone without him noticing so she could send it to McKenzie, but she'd have to wait until he was totally engrossed in the orientation video. Which, by his reaction, was likely not going to happen.

"This is so lame," he said, rolling his eyes.

"So lame," Ava agreed, though she likely would have agreed with anything he said.

"This video was probably made before I was born," he said. "As was this uniform."

Ava laughed, although secretly she thought he looked pretty damned good in purple. His shirt fit him perfectly. She'd been forced to tuck hers in quite a bit, which made it look even less flattering.

"We'll be here for about three hours," Ava said. "We have to watch all three videos."

"Oh god," Xander said, rolling his eyes again. "Are they going to test us on them? Because if not, I say we sneak out and go get some ice cream in the midway."

Was he kidding? She couldn't tell, and she panicked a little. If he was serious, what should she do? It would be totally lame to stay behind and watch the stupid videos by herself, and have Xander think she was being a baby for not sneaking out. But if she went with him to get ice cream, then for sure they'd get in trouble, and she definitely didn't want to get fired before she'd even started. Not after the fight she'd just had with her mom about it.

"I'm kidding," he said. "With our luck, we'd get nailed and end up on garbage duty. My friend Ryan worked here last summer and he was late three shifts in a row. They put him on garbage duty for two weeks. Like, all he did was push this massive cart up and down the park, filling it with trash from the bins."

"That's awful," Ava said, relieved that he'd just been joking.

"Yeah, that's a shit gig." He reached his arms over his head and stretched. The front of his shirt pulled up to reveal an inch of flat stomach, and Ava couldn't help but stare at it, her face growing hot. "Who did you interview with?"

"I did my interview back in March during the hiring fair." Ava tried to speak normally, though he made her nervous. "Via Skype, since I was living in Seattle then. It was with one of the managers, but I forget her name now."

"I was supposed to have my interview with Scottie Pile, the games manager. But he wasn't here the other day when I showed up, so the CEO herself interviewed me. She turned out to be pretty nice." Xander stifled a yawn. "So did you get the email about the uniform thing? I'm guessing the park is pissed that there's a picture going around of someone desecrating the sacred purple shirt by flipping the bird."

"I read it this morning." Ava was glad they had something to talk about. "And I actually thought the pic was pretty cool. But yeah, Wonderland probably wasn't thrilled. For sure he's fired."

"Yeah, and then they found that homeless guy? Too much bad press," Xander said. "Anyway, the Wonder Wheel Kid is a friend of my buddy's. I'll probably end up hanging out with him at some point this summer. I heard he's a good guy. Where did you get assigned?"

"Food services. Hot dog cart in the midway."

"Bum gig." Xander gave her a sympathetic look. "I got games. Hoop Shot."

"How'd you swing that?" Ava couldn't conceal her envy. "That's, like, the best games gig in the park."

He shrugged. "I said in my interview I was hoping to get games crew and it happened. Just lucky, I guess. I'm glad because I need to save up for college. University of Miami in the fall. You?"

"I . . ." Ava wanted so badly to lie to him and tell him she was older, but there was no point. "I'll be here. I start Seaside Academy in September."

"Is that a college?"

"No, it's a high school."

Xander frowned. "How old are you?"

"Fourteen. And a half," she added, as if that made a difference. "My birthday was in January."

"Shit, I thought you were older," he said with a grin, and she blushed. Of course he meant it as a compliment. "You could easily pass for sixteen."

"I get that a lot," she said, beaming. "I was hoping to get assigned to one of the Elm Street gigs since I'll be working here year-round, but they're hard to get into. I'd love to work on Elm Street for Halloween season and Fear Fest."

"I heard you have to be at least sixteen," Xander said. "Because the exhibits are scary and stuff."

"Hopefully in a couple years."

They turned their attention back to the video where Nick Bishop was now taking them on a tour of the midway. Ava's mind wandered back to the last time she'd been to that part of the park. Her dad had been alive then, because it was only last summer, and he'd died over the Christmas holidays, two weeks before Ava turned fourteen. The One Direction concert in Seattle was supposed to have been part of her birthday celebration, which obviously her mother had forgotten about.

It's funny how his death was the dividing line for everything. Ava could almost see it in her head; it was like there was this thick black line that separated everything that happened before December 24, and everything that came after. Before and after. Pre and post. Then and now. Old life and new life.

Her dad had been the strongest man she knew. Major John Castro, U.S. Army, retired. Three tours, one in Iraq, two in Afghanistan. The last one had changed him. He'd come back so . . . different. He'd come home, but his mind had stayed far away. Ava had only been twelve years old then, but she'd sensed the change even though she couldn't articulate it. Her mom described it as being "in a funk," something she assured her daughter would pass, but Ava knew now that the real term was *post-traumatic stress disorder*.

John Castro had always been a little "moody," according to her mother, but the proper word, as Ava had learned a couple of years ago, was *bipolar*. John Castro would spend weeks in a "low state"— another one of her mother's made-up terms—and when he was like that, when he was *severely depressed*, he wouldn't come out of the spare room for days on end. He "wasn't feeling well," he would mumble to Ava whenever she dared to ask, and eventually she learned not to ask because it seemed to upset him.

Mind you, it wasn't *that* weird, because his moods were all Ava had ever known. Not until she'd gotten older, and had started spending more time at her friends' houses, had she begun to suspect that her home life wasn't that typical, and that it wasn't normal for her dad to sleep all day and be awake all night watching old movies and smoking like a chimney, and not go to work. That it wasn't okay that her dad sometimes didn't shower for a week, or brush his teeth, or eat anything.

But when he was "up"—which was another word the in-denial Vanessa Castro liked to use—well, those were the good times. The house was a completely different place when her dad was *manic*. Because when John Castro was manic, it was exciting. He would shower every day and dress to the nines, his hair perfectly combed and his eyes bright. He would talk a mile a minute, filled with grandiose plans and spontaneous ideas, and he would make her mom laugh. He would work ten or twelve hours a day at the security consulting firm he'd started, and come home and still have a ton of energy. He'd take the family out on shopping sprees, buying Ava and John-John whatever they wanted, and everybody would accuse Vanessa Castro of being a "party pooper" because she'd make them return everything, because someone had to be *financially responsible*. Once, her dad had surprised her mom with a Lexus, which she'd demanded he take back to the dealership immediately. And another time, he'd surprised the entire family—her grandmother included—with a trip to Italy, to which her mom, after much protestation, had eventually acquiesced.

And that's how it went. Life revolved around John Castro's "moods." As awesome as it was when he was "up," there was always the inevitable crash, followed by weeks of darkness. Then he would come out of it and be just even, blissfully normal, for months, sometimes for as long as a year. And then something would trigger him, either up or down.

John Castro refused to admit that he had a problem. His family physician and two different psychiatrists had diagnosed him with bipolar disorder, but her dad refused to believe them. "They're paid to prescribe drugs," he would say. "It's all a conspiracy to sell me pills that make my mind dull and my body fat. I'm fine."

And then, in early December, after months of fighting with her mom about some old boyfriend of hers named Marcus Henry, John Castro crashed, for the last time. He fell back into his private hell, the place where everything was black and all he could do was sleep and sleep until it passed. And while it wasn't the first time Ava had seen him like this, it definitely seemed to be the worst. John Castro believed his wife was cheating on him.

"Your son is paranoid," Ava had overheard her mother say on more than one occasion to Cecilia Castro. "It's a symptom of the bipolar. He needs to be on medication."

"You don't think I've tried?" her grandmother would say. "He won't take them. The one time in his twenties he did, he complained they made him feel stupid."

Scared, Ava had finally tried to talk to her father herself. He had been in the spare room for almost two weeks, sleeping around the clock, and Christmas was coming. She was scared he would sleep right through the holidays. She had sat on the edge of the bed for an hour until he'd woken up, and then she'd forced her fear aside and had spoken from the heart.

"Daddy, you need help," she said. "You're bipolar, and it sucks, but it isn't your fault. You have, like, a chemical imbalance in your brain, but they can fix it. They make all kinds of medications that can help you. And if you don't like the first one, we can try a different one, as many as it takes until you feel normal." The tears had come then. "Daddy, please. You can't live like this. Mom can't live like this. We need you to get better."

He'd looked at her, his eyes bloodshot, his hair sticking up like a crazy man's, and for a split second Ava thought he might hit her. Not that he'd ever laid a hand on her, but she always thought that if he ever did, it would be when his mood was black.

"Don't you want to get better?" Ava said in a small voice. "Don't you want to feel . . . *even*?"

"No, I don't," he finally said. His voice was hoarse from underuse, and his lips were so chapped they looked like a cracked glazed doughnut. "Because as bad as this is, when the highs come, they're so good, honey. They're just so good."

"But it's not fair to us," Ava said. "Daddy, it's scary when you're like this, when you sleep for days and you don't talk to us. And it's scary when you're 'up,' too, because we never know what you're going to say or do, and Mom is always scared we're going to run out of money. I like it best when you're even. When you go to work like other dads, and then you come home and just have dinner with us and talk about normal things. I imagine that it's boring for you, but . . . it's what we need from you, Daddy. Please."

"I'll think about it, honey," John Castro said. "I promise."

"You'll see the doctor?"

"I said I'll think about it." Her father's voice had been firm. "Now leave me alone, please. I'm not feeling well and I need to sleep."

He died nine days later. Her mom had been the one to find his body.

The official cause of death was a gunshot wound, and her mother to this day was adamant that it was an accident. Her dad's gun-cleaning products had been laid out on his worktable in the garage where he'd died. Her theory was that he had forgotten to unload his weapon before he'd begun to clean it. The gun had gone off, killing him instantly.

The medical examiner's report, which Ava had found buried in her mother's underwear drawer, backed this up. The bullet had entered the skull just above the nose, an unlikely place if somebody was committing suicide which had been Ava's first thought—and the trajectory of the bullet, which was upward, also suggested an accidental but self-inflicted gunshot wound.

But Ava wasn't stupid. She knew her dad had been drinking that day; she'd smelled it on his breath when she'd come home briefly to get her stuff before heading over to McKenzie's house for a sleepover. She also knew that he'd had an old friend over, an old army buddy named Frank Greenberg. They'd served all three tours together, and her mom often called Frank when her dad was particularly low, as sometimes Frank was the only one who could reach her husband. And yet none of that was in the official report detailing John Castro's death. Frank Greenberg's name wasn't mentioned anywhere.

A few days after the funeral, Ava asked her mother about Frank. Vanessa Castro had looked her daughter in the eye and said, in a firmer tone than she'd ever heard before, "No, Ava. It's not Frank's fault that your father's dead. And don't you dare ask me that again. Frank and your father were best friends, and they loved each other, and his loss is almost as great as ours."

Ava would probably never know what really happened, but what she did know was that she blamed both her mother and her grandmother for her father's death. As far as she was concerned, neither of them had done enough to help him. But Ava was especially angry at her mother. Her mom was the one having the affair with Marcus Henry, which made her dad's sickness and paranoia worse, which was the reason her dad was drinking, and the reason he was dead. And her mother had supposedly done something to help Marcus Henry get acquitted of those drug charges, which was the reason Seattle PD had forced her out.

And now they all lived in Seaside, population who-gives-a-fuck. Where Frank Greenberg—good old Uncle Frank, of all people—had become mayor. Because Seaside was his hometown.

Wonderland was the only good thing Ava had right now. She had a lot of happy memories here, and she'd been thrilled to get the job, even though it was her mother's idea that she apply. Her plan was to work here year-round during high school, earning as much money as she could, and then she and Mc-Kenzie would apply to college together, someplace far away like New York or Boston. And she would never, ever come back.

A loud snore jolted her out of her reverie, and Ava turned to see Xander slumped in his chair, sleeping. Even with his eyes closed and his mouth hanging open, he was adorable. Those long legs, his lean-but-still-muscular arms, the perfectly mussed-up blond hair. Sure, he was four years older, but hey, he did say he thought she looked sixteen.

She quietly snapped a couple of pictures of him sleeping and texted them to McKenzie. Her friend texted back instantly with OMG SO GORG ur so lucky!!!! Are u feeling better now after the fight with ur mom???

Much better, Ava texted back. Smiling, she slipped her phone back into her pocket—employees seen texting during a shift would be reprimanded— and settled in to watch the rest of the cheesy orientation video. Beside her, Xander snored, and in that moment, everything was just fine.

TWELVE

Vanessa had never regretted anything faster or more intensely than that slap. She had never even come close to spanking or slapping either one of her children before, and she was painfully ashamed she had lost her temper with Ava. Her daughter was refusing to speak to her, and Vanessa didn't know how to fix the relationship that now seemed even more tenuous than before.

But she'd just wanted Ava to stop. Because everything her daughter had said to her was true. She *had* cheated on John, but it wasn't the long drawn-out affair that the press made it out to be. It was one time, with her old boyfriend Marcus Henry, after she and John had had a fight. And she had paid dearly for that mistake.

"You used me," she'd said to Marcus toward the end of his trial. She'd gone to visit him in prison, and he'd sat there, staring at her with a smug expression. She wanted to claw his eyes out. "You slept with me so it would taint your trial, and it's going to cost me my job, you sonofabitch. What happened to you?"

"I'm the same person I've always been," Marcus said with a shrug. "And so are you. We used each other. You were lonely in your marriage, and you needed me, so I was there. And when it came up that we slept together, I didn't lie about it."

"It didn't come up. Your lawyers brought it up."

"I did what I had to do," he said, his eyes meeting hers. She had told him things the night they were together, things about John that she probably shouldn't have admitted to anyone, ever. "Nobody should understand that better than you. We're survivors, you and me. We'll do whatever it takes, won't we?"

Marcus's lawyers suggested during the trial that Vanessa might have had access to drugs that had gone missing from the evidence locker. It didn't matter that the Office of Professional Accountability had cleared her a month later. It was enough for reasonable doubt, and Marcus Henry had walked. Right alongside any chance Vanessa had of maintaining her credibility at Seattle PD.

She had made mistakes, lots of them. She couldn't change the past. All she wanted was for her kids to be happy and healthy, and for the three of them to build a new life in Seaside.

Vanessa was wrapping up her first official meeting with Earl Schultz, and it was not going well. The chief of police was pushing hard for her to close the Homeless Harry case, but she couldn't move any faster than she was. Both Glenn Hovey and the Wonder Wheel Kid were still MIA, and no new leads had popped up.

"That picture of the dead guy that's all over the Web is killing the park, Castro." Earl's hound dog eyes were fixed intently on her face. "We need to reassure the public that everything's fine at Wonderland, that what happened is an isolated thing, and that there isn't some killer running around."

"All due respect, Chief, there *could* be some killer running around. How's the ID going?"

"Nothing yet. His prints aren't in the system, dental records should be back in a few days."

"What about the DNA?"

"Could be weeks. Maybe a month. Lab's backed up." The police chief cracked his knuckles. His hands were the size of Christmas hams. "Speaking of dental, did Gloria tell you that he's younger than we originally thought?"

Vanessa frowned. In her experience, a medical examiner's first impression was usually correct. "I thought she put him somewhere between thirty to forty."

"She thought so at first, because of the state of the body before he died," Earl said. "Emaciation, muscle atrophy, the condition of the hair and skin— all of it pointed to someone older. But now she's thinking he's closer to twenty. Give or take a year."

"That's a big difference. What changed her mind?"

"His wisdom teeth haven't come in yet."

"Oh," Vanessa said. And now they never would. "That'll do it. Did she confirm cause of death?"

"Blunt-force trauma to the back of the head. Something with a rounded edge. She thinks a baseball bat."

"And his face?"

"He was chewed up within the last couple days. Definitely by a rat." Earl shuddered slightly. "His clothes contained quite a bit of tree sap, suggesting he might have been dumped in the woods originally. Rat might have got him there. Anyway, you let me worry about the ID. What I need you to work on is who was at the park before the body was found."

"I'm doing my best, but without an ID, everybody who worked at Wonderland is a suspect," Vanessa said. "Hell, everybody who would know how to sneak into Wonderland is also a suspect. It's big pool, Chief."

"Then keep working on the security guard and the Wonder Wheel Kid. You gotta close this case quick, Castro, or at the very minimum give me something to reassure the public they're safe. You know why I don't mind them calling the dead guy Homeless Harry?" Earl didn't wait for her to respond. "Because nobody gives a shit whether a homeless guy's dead. Let's pray this guy doesn't turn out to be somebody important, because if he does, the bad publicity's only going to get worse."

"All due respect, Chief," Vanessa said again, "but everyone's life matters, whether he was homeless or somebody important. And why are we so concerned about Wonderland's bad publicity? We have enough to work on without having to worry about that."

"Because if Wonderland tanks, Seaside tanks. If you don't get this case moving, I'll be forced to find someone who can. But I'd rather it be you, so that people will stop assuming that Mayor Greenberg strong-armed me into hiring you. Which you and I both know he did, but nobody else has to know that." Earl looked at her sternly. "Put in whatever overtime you need to, pull whatever manpower you need to. I'd be more involved if I could, but I'm head of this charity gala next week and all of Seaside's finest are going to be there. They're all going to ask me about Homeless Harry if we don't have it locked up by then, so don't make a fool out of me, understand?"

Vanessa left her boss's office. Donnie looked up from his desk, and she motioned for him to come and talk to her.

"What's going on?" They went into her office and the young detective closed the door behind him.

She quickly got him up to speed with the information Earl had just given her. "I feel like I'm missing an integral piece of information, and it's bugging me. I can't accept that the Wonder Wheel

Kid isn't somehow tied to Homeless Harry, because it's just too goddamned coincidental that both showed up at the park the same morning. How are you making out with the surveillance footage?"

"I've watched it half a dozen times," Donnie said. "There's nothing useful on it."

"Earl gave me the go-ahead to do whatever it takes to solve this, so I might call a computer guy I worked with at Seattle PD. He freelances. Maybe he'll find something on it that can piece together what happened that morning."

He looked surprised. "I suppose it couldn't hurt."

"Okay, so we know Blake's a free climber. Climbing the wheel seems to be in keeping with his hobby, something he'd totally want to do." Vanessa was thinking hard. "But why wear the uniform? He has to know that a picture like that, with the middle finger and the purple shirt, would get him fired."

"Maybe he wanted to quit."

"Okay, but why? What happened? He's been with the park for years. There's nothing in his employee file to say that he's been a problem, or had any issues. If he wanted to quit, why not just quit? Why the need to go out with such a bang?"

"I guess we'll ask him that when we talk to him." Donnie rubbed his head for a good ten seconds, something she noticed he did whenever he was thinking. It reminded her of John-John, who did the same thing, only her son's hair would stick up in tufts afterward. Donnie's was too short.

"But that's the thing," Vanessa said. "He's nowhere to be found. You've been monitoring his social media account. Has he posted anything since the picture?"

"Nothing. No comments, no photos, nothing." Donnie paused. "Which, yeah, seems unusual for a kid who liked to post everything he was doing online. But you said his dad wasn't concerned?"

"Not even a little bit," Vanessa said. "I got the impression they weren't super close, and that Blake pretty much does his own thing."

"This would be so much easier if we could just figure out who Homeless Harry was," Donnie said. "It's shitty of Earl to push you so hard to close this when you have no idea who's even been killed."

"Well, we now know he's much younger than we thought." Vanessa tapped her pen on the desk. "That makes a big difference, actually, because if he's around twenty instead of being forty, then he probably worked at the park. I should call Wonderland and ask if there were any employees who've gone missing—" She stopped.

"What?"

Rifling through the papers on her desk, Vanessa pulled out a file and flipped it open. Aiden Cole's picture stared out at her. She'd asked that snotty Claire Moran to find his file in the archives the other day when the boy's father called, but then she'd forgotten all about it because of Homeless Harry.

"Aiden Cole. Remember him? David Cole called the other day and yelled at me? His son was eighteen when he was last seen three years ago." Vanessa read through the file quickly. It was woefully thin. "He'd be twenty-one now."

"The age fits, but that's still a stretch." Donnie looked skeptical. "Where's he been all this time? Homeless Harry only died within the last week."

"Maybe Aiden *was* homeless," Vanessa said. "Maybe he did leave on his own, and things didn't work out as he planned, and he ended up on the streets."

"The streets of Seaside?" The detective looked even more skeptical. "Deputy, that doesn't even make sense."

"The streets of Seattle. Or Portland. Or San Francisco." Vanessa waved a hand. "That part doesn't matter. It could be him." Logging into the Seaside PD database, she typed in Aiden's name. "Shit. No prints on file. I wonder if his dad has anything at home that might still have them."

"You really think it could be Aiden?"

"It's a lead." Vanessa's tone was grim, but determined. "I'm going to call David Cole, see if he's got anything I can use."

"Maybe you should tell Earl first. You did say he was the one working on the ID."

"Yeah, well, I'm not too concerned about Earl."

She flipped through her notebook, looking for the phone numbers she'd jotted down for David Cole. "I know what Earl's agenda is, and so do you. If he wants me to close this case, he's got to let me do my job. My way."

"Anything I can do?" Donnie asked. "Other than put on noise-canceling headphones for when the chief yells at you for keeping him out of the loop?"

"I'm not keeping him out of the loop." Vanessa gave him a dirty look. "I'm taking the initiative. You want to help, you can go assign Claire Moran to stake out Hovey's house. I want round-the-clock surveillance, and Earl said I could authorize all the overtime I wanted."

"You really do have it out for Claire." The young detective grinned.

"Well, I could ask Nate Essex, but I have him searching high and low for Glenn Hovey, the security guard. Plus, yes, I really do have it out for Claire." She finally found David Cole's contact information and picked up the phone. "Keep looking for the Wonder Wheel Kid. You're on all those social media sites, right? Start contacting Blake's friends, find out what they know. His dad might not be concerned about him, but I am. I swear to god, if one of these people we're looking for doesn't show up soon, I'm going to start thinking there's a bigger conspiracy going on."

Donnie's cell phone rang and he checked the ID. "It's Nate," he said, answering the call. "What's up?" He listened for a moment, then said, "Be right there."

"Did he find Hovey?" Vanessa asked, hopeful.

"Sorry, no. Pete Warwick got a call to the Devil's Dukes about an assault, didn't want to go alone, so Nate went with him. They need backup, a girl got hurt, and everyone's refusing to talk, including the victim."

"The Devil's Dukes? The biker club down on Clove Street?"

"The one and only. The guys, they don't respect cops, as Nate is quickly learning." He stood up. "They do slightly better with detectives, though, so I should go help him out."

"Can't someone else take it? I need you to work on finding Blake Dozier. You're better at the social media stuff than I am." Vanessa thought for a moment. "You know what, let me call David Cole really quick and then I'll go. It's about time I paid a visit to the Devil's Dukes anyway. I've always been curious about that place."

"You sure?" He raised an eyebrow. "It's kind of a harsh environment for a woman."

Vanessa smiled. "You just said the exact wrong thing. Text Nate, tell him I'm on my way. I can call David Cole from the car."

"I'd wish you luck, but I'm not sure you need it," Donnie said. "You've got bigger balls than most men."

"I've been told that before," Vanessa said. "And I've never been able to figure out whether it's an insult or a compliment."

THIRTEEN

Under the Clown Museum

Blake had no idea what day or time it was; all he knew was that he was starving, and if the rat ever came back to visit, he wasn't opposed to killing it with his bare hands and eating it raw.

Okay, maybe not. He had a squeamish stomach to begin with, but it was crazy the amount of fucked-up thoughts you could have when you were hungrier than you'd ever been in your entire life. A beetle had crawled by earlier and he'd missed it by one swipe. He used to think it was disgusting to eat bugs, like the contestants were forced to do on that old reality show *Survivor*, but now he understood that if you were starving, that beetle might have tasted like Chex Mix.

The only thing that outweighed his hunger was his fear that he was going to die down here. Slowly, painfully, alone, and in the dark, with only a trace of dim ambient light coming from somewhere in the tunnel. In this moment he truly couldn't think of a worse way to go. Drowning, fire, gunshot, bleeding to death—all of those things would be a faster death than what awaited him.

Blake was in a dungeon of some kind, that much he knew. Wonderland's midway was the last place he'd been, and the only positive thing about being on an involuntary fast was that it cleared the fogginess out of your brain, allowing you to start remembering things.

He could remember sneaking into the park and climbing the Wonder Wheel. He was certain he'd taken pictures once he reached the top, but whether he'd gotten a chance to upload them, he couldn't recall. That was where things started to get a bit hazy. He'd seen movement down below, someone in a golf cart, and then the wheel had begun to rotate. He'd lost his balance, almost slipping right off the goddamned wheel, but he'd managed to hang on long enough to get closer to the bottom.

And then he'd fallen. He estimated he'd dropped maybe ten feet, not enough to kill him, but enough to create massive bruises on both legs, a sprained shoulder, and what he suspected might be a mild concussion.

After that, everything had gone black, and at some point later on—much later on? a little later on?—he'd woken up on the floor here with his arms and legs bound. Then he'd passed out again, and when he woke up the second time, his arms and legs were free.

His best guess was that he was somewhere in the bowels of Wonderland. The crazy part was that he'd heard stories about this dungeon from his dad, but he'd always dismissed them as urban legend. He never thought it actually existed.

The joke was on him.

The space he was in could best be described as a jail cell. Concrete walls made up four sides of the ten-by-ten-foot space, and there were metal bars where there should have been a fourth wall, with a locked door in the middle. The key to the door hung on a metal hook outside the bars, about five feet out of arm's length, just close enough to torment him. He had a flush toilet, a sink with running water (which tasted clean, but you never knew), a small bed with a thin mattress and no pillow or sheets, and a thirteen-inch tube TV mounted to the upper rear corner of the cell, which didn't work. Whoever had built this had set it up to be a space someone could stay in for a long time, assuming you had food.

Which Blake did not. His stomach felt like it was grinding all the time, and when he wasn't thinking about how to get the hell out of here, he was thinking about food. He dreamed of food. He thought of all the food that was above him at the park right now being wasted: french fries carelessly falling out of paper cups, half-eaten hot dogs with ketchup and mustard being thrown into the trash, stale mini-doughnuts being tossed away and replaced with fresh ones.

He went over to the sink and splashed more water into his mouth. It didn't really help, though— if anything, the water made him more hungry. But he had to keep drinking, because he had to stay alive. Because it couldn't end like this. Whoever had brought him here was surely coming back.

Walking over to the bars, he put his hands around the cold metal and shook them as hard as he could. They rattled, which was a somewhat satisfying sound, but they weren't budging. The bars were probably a foot deep into the concrete that also made up the floor and ceiling.

"Help!" he shouted again. "Help! Anyone! Please!"

He continued to rattle the bars, but it was no use. Nobody could hear him. Nobody was coming. His hand went to his pocket, feeling for his phone, which of course wasn't there. He'd done this several times already; he was never without his phone, and he felt naked without it. But even if he could call someone, there'd be no cell service down here. And of course, the battery would be dead by now.

All Blake could hope for was that enough time had passed for people to actually be concerned about him. He was known for being the kind of guy who had no problem disappearing for a day or two, without feeling the need to tell anyone where he was going, or where he had been. Sometimes he went off on his own, and sometimes he went with friends. Derek Dozier had never been the type of father to worry about him, anyway.

Maybe this time, though, his dad would sense something was wrong. Maybe this time, he'd know his son was in real trouble and needed help. Blake could only hope.

He shook the bars some more, then broke down in tears, something he rarely did. A minute later, the crying had graduated to full-on sobs, the likes of which he hadn't suffered through since he was a kid. They heaved up from his chest in painful spasms to the point where it was hard to breathe.

And then he heard something. Footsteps.

They got louder as they got closer, and instinctively Blake backed up, moving away from the bars. A male figure appeared, dressed in all black, right down to the ski mask covering his face. In one hand he was carrying a cardboard box.

He stood in front of the cell, a few feet away from the bars, staring at Blake with eyes that appeared black in the very dim tunnel.

"Who are you?" Blake said.

No response.

"Who are you?" Blake screamed. "Let me out!" He rushed back toward the bars, his arms reaching through, clawing. "*Let me out let me out let me out!*"

It didn't faze the man in black, who reached into the box and began tossing food into the cell. It was all prepackaged stuff—candy bars, chips, cookies— but there were also a few bags of dried almonds, a few bananas and oranges, and a couple of plastic-wrapped sandwiches. The sticker on the sandwiches said SEASIDE MARKET, which was the grocery store on the south end of Main Street.

Blake went right for the sandwich, a limp turkey and Swiss on day-old rye bread. He almost forgot to rip off the plastic, and when he took his first bite, his stomach cramped with equal parts pain and pleasure. Nothing had ever tasted so good, and he had to stop himself from cramming the entire thing in his mouth.

Forcing himself to chew, he looked up. His captor was gone.

FOURTEEN

The Devil's Dukes Motorcycle Club shared a parking lot with Clove Street Auto Repair. Both were owned by a man named Tanner Wilkins, a longtime resident of Seaside who was a biker and an ex-outlaw. While the Devil's Dukes were described on their website as simply being "a place for Harley riders and cigar aficionados to meet and discuss shared interests," the long list of incident reports filed with Seaside PD, ranging from disturbing the peace to drug use to assault in all degrees, told a different story.

Two patrol cars were already parked outside, and a handful of Devil's Dukes members were standing around the front entrance, dressed in typical biker gear—jeans, shirts, and leather vests with the DD logo sewn onto the back. Officer Nate Essex, who'd been chatting amiably with the group, met Vanessa as she got out of her unmarked.

Vanessa liked Nate, a young redheaded rookie who'd joined Seaside PD a month earlier. The two had hit it off immediately; Nate was too new to be upset with her for unfairly securing her current position.

"So is this a club or a gang?" she asked him as they walked toward the clubhouse. "Any illicit business currently going on here? Drugs, guns, prostitution?"

The rookie shook his head. "I honestly don't know, Deputy, but I'm told Tanner Wilkins runs a pretty tight ship these days. About ten years ago, Double D was heavily into gang activity—drugs mainly, and some gun running. Supposedly they're clean now. At some point Wilkins decided to go legit, and other than a few old busts for marijuana possession and disorderly conduct, nothing much has happened here. Especially now that pot's legal in the state."

The dozen cars parked on the garage side of the lot were of various makes and models, but they all had one thing in common—they were all American made. "No Jap-crap," as Vanessa's father would have said, god rest his racist soul. There were three garage bays, doors open, and all contained cars being worked on by mechanics wearing coveralls.

A row of Harley-Davidson motorcycles were lined up neatly outside the clubhouse. Their owners scrutinized Vanessa from head to toe as she approached. She recognized Pete Warwick, Nate's partner, and gave him a nod. She introduced herself to the group.

Leather vests and boots aside, the club members

didn't seem like outlaws. Only two were sporting beards. The other two looked like they could be bankers on their day off.

"So why am I here?" Vanessa asked, addressing Nate and Pete.

"Jenna Wilkins took a beating," Pete Warwick said. "The witness says it was the boyfriend, Mike Bruin. He works as a mechanic on the other side of the lot."

Vanessa didn't recognize either name. She could only assume the victim was related to Tanner Wilkins in some way. "And where's Jenna now?"

"Inside," Nate said. "She refuses to speak to us, said she fell, but the witness assures us that's not what happened."

"Who's the witness?"

"Her friend Debbie. She's with Jenna inside."

"Did you see what happened?" Vanessa spoke to the bikers.

"No, ma'am," one of them responded. He had a long gray Vandyke, and the beard made him appear older, even though his eyes seemed young. "We didn't see anything."

"Injuries?" Vanessa asked.

"Lacerations on the face," Nate said. "Black eye. Goose egg on the temple. Bruises on the arms, and a gash on the leg from where she fell."

"And what's the story with the boyfriend?"

"Well, it's Mike Bruin," Pete said, in a tone that

implied the name should mean something to Vanessa. It didn't.

"And where is he now?"

"Enjoying his last few moments on earth," one of the younger bikers said under his breath, and his friend with the Vandyke jabbed him with an elbow.

"Bruin's in the second garage bay," Nate said. "Officers Kelly and Cisco are talking to him."

"Tanner's gonna kill him," the biker muttered again. "He won't care if Mike's stepdad—"

"Shut *up*, Ed," Vandyke said. To Vanessa, he said, "We didn't see nothing, we didn't hear nothing."

Nate was about to say something but was distracted by the shouting coming from one of the garage bays.

"I want to see Jenna!" a young man was yelling. He was trying to exit the garage, but two officers were holding his arms. "I want to see her! Let me go, you fuckers!"

"Why isn't he cuffed?" Vanessa was incredulous. "He should be cuffed and in the back of the squad car."

Nate and Pete exchanged a look. "Uh, well, that's why we called you," Nate said. "We weren't sure if that was the right move."

"Why wouldn't it be?" Other than the fact that this had happened at a biker club, this all seemed like your standard, run-of-the-mill assault-and-battery charge. "There's a victim. There's a witness. Protocol has it you arrest him and bring him in."

"Jennnnaaaaa!" the young man hollered from across the parking lot. "Jenna, I love youuuuu!"

"Christ," Vanessa said. "Go arrest him. I'll talk to Jenna." She looked at the bikers. "I'd appreciate it if you gentlemen stuck around. We might need your statements."

"We didn't see nothing, we didn't hear nothing," Vandyke repeated. The other three dropped their gazes to the asphalt.

Sighing, she entered the clubhouse, where the light changed immediately from bright sunshine to dim. The first thing she noticed was the smell. The room positively reeked of pot. It seemed to be everywhere, and the sickly sweet smell was so strong she almost gagged.

It took a few seconds for Vanessa's eyes to adjust, and when they did, she felt like she'd been transported to a different world.

Oak walls were stained a dark brown color. A narrow bar lined one side of the clubhouse, where an older man wearing a denim shirt sat hunched over on one of the stools, nursing a beer in one hand and a cigarette in the other. A few sofas and club chairs of different sizes were dotted throughout the space, and a sixty-inch flat-screen TV was mounted above the giant wood-burning fireplace. It would have been an entirely masculine room, except that the TV was showing *The Real Housewives of Beverly Hills*. Vanessa chuckled at the incongruence.

"If you're looking for Jenna, head to the back," the man at the bar said. He didn't turn around. "First bedroom."

"Did you see what happened?" She spoke to his back.

"Didn't see nothing, didn't hear nothing. I was sitting on this bar stool the whole time."

The line of the day, she thought. Following his instructions, she made her way across the clubhouse to where the bedrooms were. The first one's door was slightly ajar. She knocked before pushing it open all the way.

A young woman in her early twenties was sitting on top of the sparsely made bed, skinny legs splayed out in front of her. One hand held a Ziploc bag filled with ice cubes to her head, and her eyes were closed and puffy. Another woman, early thirties, sat beside her on a chair, leafing through a celebrity gossip magazine.

Neither woman heard her coming, and they both jumped when the door squeaked.

"Jenna?" Vanessa addressed the girl on the bed. "I'm Deputy Chief Castro. You okay?"

Jenna opened her eyes. She gave Vanessa the once-over, noting the badge clipped to her breast pocket. "I'm fine," she said, putting the icepack down. "It looks worse than it feels."

"Bullshit," the other woman snapped, closing the magazine. "Look what that fucking asshole did to her face. Fucking piece of scum. You arrest him yet?" she said to Vanessa.

"Shut *up*, Debbie." The young woman's voice sounded stuffy from crying. "I said I'm fine. I tripped and hit my head. I already told the other cop that I don't need to go to the hospital. You can go now."

"Actually, I can't." Vanessa stood near the edge of bed. "You've been assaulted, Jenna. I'm here to find out what happened, so I can help you."

"I *said*. I *fell*." Jenna put the ice pack back to her face. "I'm a klutz. What can I say."

Vanessa glanced over at her friend. Debbie's lips were pursed. She was clearly biting her tongue. "Can you give us a moment alone?"

"Just tell her," Debbie said to Jenna, standing up. She folded her magazine under one arm. "It's not the first time and it won't be the last. Enough's enough."

She left and Vanessa stood up, closing the door firmly behind her. Then she took the chair that Debbie had been occupying. "Let me see your face," she said gently.

After a few seconds, the younger woman turned toward her. The right half of her face was swollen and red. By tomorrow it would be full-out purple. There were three lacerations on her cheek, one on her lip, and one on her eyebrow. Despite the injuries, she was a very pretty girl. Strawberry blond hair, pert nose, bright blue eyes. Skin the color of porcelain. Dressed in a loose floral tank top and a white skirt, she looked like the girl next door, and not somebody Vanessa would expect to see hanging out in a biker clubhouse.

"You really should go to the hospital and have that looked at," Vanessa said. "You could have a concussion. That's serious."

"I hate hospitals."

"I do, too. But concussions are pretty serious, regardless of how they happened. Also, those cuts look pretty deep. You might need stitches. If they don't heal properly, you could have permanent scarring. Look." Vanessa turned her face away slightly and lifted up her chin, pointing to a pink scar just along her jawline. It was about an eighth of an inch thick and two inches long, and wrinkled. "See that? Fell into one of the weight bars at the gym last year. Got infected because I wouldn't get it looked at. Now I have this on my face forever." It was a complete lie—if only the injury had happened at the gym instead of at home, and by accident, instead of on purpose.

"What? Serious?" Jenna looked horrified. "Fine, I'll go."

"Good. Now we both know you didn't trip," Vanessa said. "Are you worried that your boyfriend will hurt you again? His name's Mike, right? Is Debbie right that this wasn't the first time?"

Jenna clenched her jaw, not answering. She

reached for the pillow beside her and clutched it to her chest. She looked very young and very vulnerable. "It's complicated," she finally said.

"You were arguing, I imagine. Maybe you lost your temper, moved toward him." Vanessa kept her voice soft. "Maybe he shoved you just to get you to go away. Maybe he didn't mean to shove so hard. You lost your balance." She pointed to Jenna's sandals, which were still strapped to her feet. "Three-inch wedges. I have a pair like that. Stepped on a pebble once, went sideways and hit the ground hard. Who knew wedges could be so dangerous?"

Jenna looked away, clutching the pillow tighter. "I wanted to hit him."

"How come?"

"I thought he was cheating on me." A tear spilled over onto the cheek that wasn't swollen. "I mean, he is. Everybody here knows it. I was the last to find out."

"That seems to be the way it always goes," Vanessa said with sympathy. "It's humiliating, isn't it?"

The girl looked up at her, and she was so forlorn it was all Vanessa could do not to hug her. "I was yelling at him. He was yelling back, telling me that I didn't know what I was talking about, even though I saw what she wrote to him on Facebook. He forgot to log out of his account, and I read all her messages to him, there were like a dozen of them, and I took screen shots, tried to show him I had proof. He wouldn't look at them, and instead he accused me of spying on him, saying that

I was crazy and paranoid." Jenna shook her head, looking genuinely puzzled. "Why do guys do that? Why do they always say you're crazy and paranoid when they're the ones cheating on you? I hate that."

"It's what they do to get you off their back," Vanessa said. "They make you feel like you're losing your mind, that you somehow made it all up."

"They must all take the same Douchebag 101 class," Jenna said, and Vanessa smiled. "Anyway, he called me a stupid, paranoid little bitch, and that's when I lost it. I lunged at him, and he punched me in the face. Twice. That's when I fell." Her face scrunched up and she began to cry, the sobs coming up painfully from her small chest.

"It's not okay that he hit you, Jenna. Has this happened before?"

The younger woman didn't respond. Her silence was more than enough. Then Jenna said in a tiny voice, "But it's my fault. It happens when I get in his face. I know it makes him mad, and that I shouldn't push him like that. I mean, it's . . . it's complicated."

Spoken like a true victim.

Vanessa nodded and patted the girl on the ankle. "It's not your fault, okay? It's never your fault. But thank you for telling me. I know that was hard." She plucked a tissue out of the Kleenex box on the night-stand. "When you're ready, we'll go to the hospital. Take some pictures, get you fixed up. It's going to be all right."

"Are you gonna charge him?" she said, blowing her nose. Vanessa handed her another tissue.

"If you don't, I'll kill him," a deep voice from the doorway said.

Both women looked up. A tall man was standing there, maybe six four with muscular arms and only a slight paunch. Tattoos ran down from under the sleeves of his T-shirt, all the way to his wrists, where two huge hands covered in silver rings were clenched into fists. Messy salt-and-pepper hair and a scruffy beard framed a face that was mottled with fury. His complexion matched the red tee he was wearing. Instinctively Vanessa's hand went under her jacket to her hip, where she wore her Glock, but he made no move to enter the bedroom.

"Can I help you?" Vanessa said, her voice crisp.

"Don't help me, help her." His voice was like thunder, and his eyes focused on Jenna. "Jesus fucking Christ. Look what that animal did to you."

"I'm okay," Jenna said, and then began to sob again.

"Did you not think I was going to hear about this?" His chest heaved and he pointed to Vanessa. "You gonna arrest that sonofabitch?"

"Sir, I just—"

"You arrest that no good piece of shit or I'll kill him, do you understand?"

Vanessa stood up, moving her jacket slightly away

from her body so he could see she was carrying. "I'm going to pretend I didn't just hear you threaten to kill someone. I'm sorry, who are you?"

"Tanner Wilkins. This is my club, my place of business, and that's my daughter," he said, his breathing hard and even. "Who the fuck are *you*?"

Vanessa was so startled by the hostility in his voice that it took her a second to respond. She continued to keep one hand on her gun. "I'm Deputy Chief Vanessa Castro. I'm trying to help your daughter."

"You must be new, *Deputy Chief*, so allow me to school you on how this is going to go." Tanner stepped in, fists still clenched. "First, you're going to arrest that no-good piece of scum Mike Bruin. Second, he's going to *stay* arrested—I don't give a flying fuck who his stepfather is. Third, he's going to jail. Where he's going to stay for a while. None of that anger management bullshit, none of that counseling bullshit, and none of that community service. He does time. Do you understand?"

"Most of that isn't up to me," Vanessa said. "I understand where you're coming from, sir, but I'm still talking to your daughter. If you wouldn't mind—"

"Of course I *mind*," Tanner said, his red face turning purple. "And you be sure to tell your boss that if Mike Bruin gets any special treatment, I will sue the department. And the town. You hear me? I am dead fucking serious. Your boss screwed my family over once. He's sure as shit not doing it again."

"My boss?" Vanessa was confused. "If you mean Earl Schultz, he—"

"You're goddamned right I mean Schultz," Tanner roared. He stepped all the way into the bedroom, and instantly the room felt smaller. He shook a sausage-sized finger in Vanessa's face, and Glock or no Glock, it was all she could do not to shrink back. "His precious weasel of a stepson isn't getting away with this, you hear me?"

Vanessa looked at Jenna. "Your boyfriend is the chief of police's *stepson*?"

"I told you it was complicated." The young woman burst into tears.

"You never listen to me," Tanner said to his daughter. "I told you that spoiled little rich kid was no good for you. And I talked to Debbie. She told me this isn't the first time. How could you not tell me? How could you keep seeing him? Have I not taught you better? How could you think you deserved this?" His voice cracked at the end, and he took a few deep breaths.

"I love him, Daddy." Jenna's voice was small, and then she burst into tears again.

What a goddamned mess, Vanessa thought. Earl Schultz's stepson had assaulted Jenna Wilkins. It explained why Mike Bruin hadn't been cuffed and in the police car when they'd arrived, and why she'd been called to the clubhouse to take care of what was basically your average, everyday domestic violence call. Nobody wanted to be the one who arrested the chief of police's stepson. It also explained why Mayor Frank Greenberg had agreed to recommend her for this job—an outsider was the only hope he had of achieving any balance inside Seaside PD. It all made sense.

Wilkins seemed torn between comforting his daughter and yelling at the girl some more. Changing his mind about doing either, he instead directed his fury back to Vanessa. "You listen to me, Deputy. I'm tired of how things are done in this fucking town. We finally voted in a new mayor because a lot of people—good, tax-paying people who were here even way back when the town was falling apart—feel the way I do, and want to see things change. This has got to stop, do you hear me? The department cannot continue to cherry pick the cases they decide to work. Schultz isn't going to make this go away, like he did with my son. Enough is enough."

"Your son?"

"Daddy, stop," Jenna said quietly. "Please."

"My son, Tyler." Tanner's jaw was clenched. "He went missing, eight years ago. Earl Schultz has done shit to find him, said Tyler probably ran away." He slumped, his shoulders rolling forward. "Do you know what it's like, year after year, not knowing where your son is? Not knowing whether he's dead or alive? And now my daughter's been assaulted? I don't give a flying fuck if Mike Bruin's mother is married to the chief of police. I want him arrested, charged, and convicted. I need justice for at least one of my kids. I don't think that's too much to ask."

Another missing boy? The timeline wasn't right for Tanner Wilkins's son to be Homeless Harry, but *two* missing boys, even if their disappearances were five years apart, felt like way too many. And if it turned out that Blake Dozier, the Wonder Wheel Kid, was missing, too, then *three* was bordering on ridiculous.

What the hell was going on in Seaside?

"First of all, you need to take a step back," Vanessa said to him. "I don't do well when I'm cornered, and I don't like being yelled at. Second, I'm new here. I don't give a rat's ass who Mike Bruin's stepfather is. Jenna told me what happened, and we're arresting him, don't you worry about that. And I can promise you he won't get any special treatment, not on my watch."

Wilkins eyed her, his posture relaxing slightly. He took a step back. "Fresh blood at Seaside PD." There was a grudging note of respect in his voice. "About damn time."

"And I care about both your kids," Vanessa said. "When all this is done, come talk to me about your son."

FIFTEEN

The good news was that Mike Bruin had been booked on charges of assault and battery. The bad news was that he'd spent exactly three hours in a holding cell before promptly being released on ten thousand dollars' bail.

"Not to be a downer, but don't be surprised if the charges disappear by the end of the week," Donnie said. The detective was leaning against the doorway to her office. "He used his one phone call on his mom, which is why he was only in holding for, like, a minute. His family's good friends with the judge. Earl plays golf with him every Saturday."

Vanessa motioned for him to come in. "Close the door," she said. "I'm sorry, but this is ridiculous. You didn't see Jenna Wilkins's face. She looks like she went three rounds with Joe Louis."

Donnie's face was blank, and Vanessa had to laugh. "Manny Pacquiao?" she said, trying again.

"Oh, right, boxing," he said. "I get it."

"God, you're a fetus."

"Sorry. I can't help that I'm twenty-six and only now entering the prime of my life." He grinned. "So you met Tanner, huh? I imagine that went . . . well."

"He was pretty scary, not going to lie. For one thing, he's huge, and for another, he was enraged. That's not a good combination. I pulled his file." She drummed her fingers on the desk. "Tanner has a colorful past. I counted seventeen arrests for drugs, weapons, and assault spanning a twenty-year period. But nothing in the last eight years."

"Word is that he straightened up after Tyler went missing."

"He mentioned Tyler," she said. "Do you realize that means two boys have gone missing from Seaside within five years? If it turns out Blake Dozier's missing, too, that makes three in the past eight years. That's crazy."

"Assuming the Wonder Wheel Kid's actually missing," Donnie said. "I'm still working on it. He might turn up. I've contacted some of his friends, and he's done this kind of thing before. He always comes back."

"Let's hope. So did you know Tanner's son?"

"Yeah. Tyler and I went to high school together. Worked at Wonderland at the same time, too, but we didn't run in the same social circles."

"I know it was a long time ago, but what do you think happened to him?"

"He just . . . disappeared." Donnie rubbed his

freshly clipped head. "I actually didn't think much of it at first. This is Seaside, you know? It's one thing to grow up here. That usually isn't a choice. But it's not uncommon for kids to bolt after high school. Most of my friends no longer live here. They went to college someplace else, and never came back."

"Yet you did."

The detective shrugged. "I had a girlfriend, fell in love, she wanted to stay here, that cemented it for me at the time. I went to PSSU, but I came home every summer. When I graduated, I applied to the police academy and got in. Eight weeks later, the department hired me. If that hadn't happened, I might have left, too. Not a lot of career opportunities in Seaside unless you work at Wonderland, really. I can't blame anyone for leaving. One day that might be me."

"What was your impression of Tyler? He strike you as the kind of kid who'd leave without saying goodbye?"

"Hard to say. I mainly knew who he was because of his dad. Back then, Tanner was a scary motherfucker. The Devil's Dukes was heavily into drugs and guns, and Tanner was a hard-core outlaw—"

Vanessa's intercom buzzed. "Deputy, Tanner Wilkins is here to see you." The officer calling her from the reception area sounded almost apologetic. "Should I send him back?"

Donnie raised an eyebrow. "Speak of the devil. Did we just summon him by talking about him?"

"Smartass." Vanessa pressed a button on the intercom. "Yes, I'll see him. Thanks."

"Brace yourself." Donnie pushed his chair out and stood up. "He probably heard that Mike Bruin is walking around, free. Tanner's going to let you have it."

"He already did earlier. How much worse could it be? Do me a favor," she said before the detective could leave. "Pull his son's file for me. I want to look it over."

"That's in the archives. I'll have to dig for it. Can't you ask Claire?" He grinned. "Kidding. I'll go get it, might take me awhile, though."

"I'll buy you a coffee. Thanks."

Donnie passed Tanner in the main area, and the two nodded politely to each other. A second later, the man was at her office door, looking even bigger and angrier than he had before at the clubhouse.

Vanessa stood up and extended a hand. "Mr. Wilkins. Please come in."

His enormous fingers squeezed her palm briefly before letting go. She didn't doubt he could break her hand if he wanted to without much effort. He took a seat opposite her and crossed one leg over the other, his massive motorcycle boot touching the edge of her desk.

"Mike Bruin's out on bail," Tanner said. "I've known you three hours and already you've lied to me, Deputy."

"I wasn't pleased, either." Vanessa stifled a sigh. "I would have preferred he sweat it out in the cell for at least one night. But the good news is that the judge ordered him not to go within a hundred feet of Jenna."

"And? That's it?"

"And there'll be a trial. He's charged with aggravated assault. It's not over."

"Are you fucking kidding me?" Tanner's face darkened. "Those charges are going to disappear faster than you can cry *nepotism*. They'll either be dropped, or they'll be reduced to a misdemeanor for which he'll do community service. Whichever way it goes, that weasel won't see the inside of a prison cell. I actually came here to talk to Earl, not you, but he's not here right now. Which means I get to yell at you, which is a lot less satisfying because you don't yell back. And, as you made a point to tell me earlier, you're too new to have had anything to do with it."

"I'm sorry anyway," Vanessa said. "I'm a parent. I have a teenage daughter. If something like this happened to her, I'd feel exactly the same way you do. How's Jenna?"

"She's been better."

A silence fell between them, not an awkward one, but it wasn't exactly pleasant, either. A few moments later he let out a long, slow breath.

"I fucking hate it here." Tanner's voice was soft. Looking down, he picked at a speck of dirt on his faded jeans. "Every year I keep thinking, this'll be the year I sell the shop and close the club, and I'll get on my Harley and ride the fuck out of Seaside and never look back."

"Why don't you?"

"Because Tyler might come home," he said, looking up at her. "And I don't want him to come home and I'm not here. I don't want him to come home and find the house he grew up in filled with some other family. I don't want him to come looking for me at the clubhouse only to find it's been turned into a fucking shopping plaza. His mother and I divorced six years ago. She left me for a guy named Steve who drives an Audi and sells vitamins for a living. They moved to San Francisco. Someone has to stay here and wait for Ty to come home." His voice choked on the last word, and he looked away.

Vanessa didn't feel the need to respond. There was nothing she could say that would make it better; nothing she could do would dilute his pain. His life had been on hold for eight years waiting for news—any kind of news—about his son, and while she could imagine what that felt like, she wasn't living through it, and with it, like he was.

She wondered if she should put him in touch with David Cole; maybe the two of them could support each other and talk about what they were going through. But then again, Tanner didn't look like the sharing circle type.

Donnie knocked on the door and entered her office with one of Seaside PD's signature navy blue file folders. He placed it on her desk and left without saying anything.

Tanner didn't even seem to notice. "Every year I hope Earl loses his job." His voice was still soft. "But every year, there he is, sitting on top of the throne like the proverbial eight-hundred-pound gorilla. I thought things might change when we voted Frank Greenberg in for mayor last fall. He and Earl don't like each other much. Are the rumors true? Are you and Greenberg friends?"

"Yes."

"Good friends?"

"Yes," Vanessa said, ignoring the implications. "What did Earl do exactly? To you? To Tyler?"

Tanner laughed, but there was not one speck of humor in it. "How much time you got?"

"Sum it up for me."

"Where do I begin?" He leaned back in his chair. "Let's see. First, he put that jackass Carl Weiss on the job. Weiss from the beginning didn't believe Tyler was missing. He did a half-assed investigation, and about a day later concluded that Tyler must have run away from home. When I pointed out that Ty was eighteen and didn't *have* to run away—if he wanted to leave, he could have left with my blessing—Weiss didn't care. He didn't care what I thought at all."

Vanessa nodded. She reached for Tyler Wilkins's folder and opened it, skimming through it quickly. "I'm listening," she said. "Please continue."

"So I went directly to Earl," Tanner said. "We've had our run-ins over the years. I've done some shit, and I get that maybe me and my club have been a pain in his ass for a long time, and that he thought I was an outlaw who didn't deserve to be helped. But it wasn't about me. It was about my son. All I wanted was for him to try and find my son. The operative word being *try*."

"And he didn't?"

"He sided with his deputy." Tanner's jaw was tight. "Backed that moron all the way. Said there was no evidence that Tyler hadn't left on his own, that there was no indication of any kind of foul play, and so the department couldn't waste hours or manpower looking for a kid who probably didn't want to be found. *Waste*," he repeated. "That was the actual fucking word our esteemed chief of police used."

Vanessa winced. She couldn't blame Tanner for being angry. Earl's poor word choice was about as insensitive as it got.

"First Earl screws over my son," Tanner said. "And now he's screwing over my daughter. It's a goddamned joke, and nobody does anything about it. Nothing's changed. Nobody has the balls to stand up to you people."

"I just moved here," Vanessa said. "Do I count as 'you people'?"

"Haven't decided." He met her gaze and held it.

For the first time, she noticed his eyes were a bright, vivid blue. Intense. Piercing. The salt-and-pepper scruff on his face made him look older than he was, and he was only forty-six, based on his file. The edge of one his tattoos was just visible above the neckline of his T-shirt, and Vanessa found herself wondering what the rest of it looked like.

"But you *are* a cop," he said. "You wear the badge. And now you live in Seaside. Give it a few months, Deputy. By Christmas, you'll be toeing the company line."

"Which is what?"

He leaned in, his eyes never leaving her face. "Wonderland and Seaside are pretty much married to each other. If you don't see that now, you will. And you know what they say—happy wife, happy life. You hear about the proposed shopping plaza they want to build on Clove Street?"

Vanessa nodded.

"These developers, with Earl's blessing and Wonderland's backing, keep wanting to buy me out so they can tear down my club and my shop, and put a fancy mall right in that spot. That's prime real estate, right off Main Street. Offered me top dollar, and then some. A deal like that would bring in a lot of money for Seaside, and there's even a nice spot a few blocks down on Clove where I could relocate that's a lot cheaper, too. Wouldn't hurt my business a bit. Know why I won't say yes?"

"Why?"

"Because fuck them. Fuck Earl, fuck Wonderland, fuck Seaside."

Vanessa looked at him for a moment, thinking. He continued to hold her gaze unwaveringly. Finally she said, "Why don't you tell me about your son?"

"I could, but why? You have the file right there, don't you?"

"I want to hear it from you." Vanessa reached for her notebook. "Because I give a shit. Let's start from the beginning."

Another silence fell between them. At first she thought he wouldn't say anything because he didn't trust her, and she couldn't say she blamed him. But then he began to speak.

"Eight years ago, Ty was a Wonder Worker. Surprise surprise. Everybody in Seaside was, at one time or another."

"I was." Vanessa smiled. "A long time ago, when it was still called World of Wonder."

That got a small chuckle out of Tanner. "You're older than I thought, then," he said. "But I never worked at the park. Didn't have time for a legit job like Wonderland. I was too busy outlawing and getting into trouble and building Double D. But I wanted it to be different for Ty. Because *he* was different. He was an artist. Does it say anything about that in the file?"

Vanessa shook her head.

"He'd always been good with painting, drawing, sculpting, that kind of thing. Wanted to go to art school, which didn't please his mother. She wanted him to get a business degree, or be a dentist, anything that would lead to a career. But I liked that Ty loved art. It made him more like me." Tanner lifted up his left arm, revealing a beautiful dragon tattoo. The colors had faded a little, but it had once been vivid, and beautiful. "These tats? Did them myself."

"They're awesome," Vanessa said. And she meant it.

"Anyway, Wonderland knew he was an artist, and so they had Ty do the mural at the side of the food court."

"The one that's a rendering of the midway?" Vanessa knew the mural, and was surprised to learn that it hadn't been painted by a professional. "It's beautiful."

"That was Tyler." The fatherly pride Tanner felt was obvious. "They didn't pay him extra or anything, but he was thrilled to do it. But he was only allowed to work on it at night, after the park was closed. Sometimes he wouldn't get home till three, four in the morning. And then one night, he never came home."

"Was he always alone in the park when he was painting?"

"Usually. Sometimes cleanup crew would be there, but otherwise it was just him and whoever was assigned to security."

Vanessa looked at the file. "Glenn Hovey. That's the security guard on schedule that night."

"Yep. He's a fucking weirdo if I ever met one."

You're not the first person to say that, Vanessa thought, recalling her conversation with Margie Hamilton, the Hoveys' next door neighbor. "In what way is he weird?"

"He just makes you feel uncomfortable," Tanner said. "Tyler said he stared a lot at the kids, the boys in particular. Hovey denied having anything to do with Ty's disappearance, said he wasn't even aware of when Ty left the park. Security footage from that night showed Ty leaving the park through the side gates, alone, so Weiss didn't press Hovey about it. And that's the last anyone saw of my son."

"When did you file the missing persons report?"

"Not till the end of the next day." Tanner heaved a sigh. "I was working late at the shop, and I didn't realize he was missing until very late the next night. My wife and I were separated at that time, and she'd moved to California with Jenna. Tyler stayed with me." He choked up on the last four words.

"It's not your fault." Vanessa rested her hand on his forearm for a second. "We can't be with our kids all time. Was anything missing from his room?"

"All I could confirm was that Tyler's bag was missing. It was this old smelly knapsack he'd gotten at an army surplus store when he was in Seattle once. He took it with him to work every day. I haven't seen it since."

"What about his clothes? Were of any them missing?"

"I don't know. Do I look like the kind of guy who notices people's clothes?"

No, he did not. She looked at the file again. "And his cell phone?"

"He had a BlackBerry Curve," Tanner said. "I know that because it was my old phone, which I gave to him. He must have had it with him. Part of me hopes . . ."

"Part of you hopes what?"

"Part of me hopes that Ty did run away, that he's out there somewhere, living his life, and happy." Tanner's voice was thick and his eyes moistened. "I'd be pissed that he didn't call, but I'd get over it in two seconds if I knew he'd been out there the whole time, and was okay. But my gut tells me that's not true. Ty was a good kid, a considerate kid. If he wanted to take off and do his own thing for a while, he would have told me and his mother. He would have said goodbye."

Vanessa's cell phone buzzed and she checked it, allowing Tanner the moment he needed to regroup. It was David Cole calling. She pressed decline, sending it to voice mail. Aiden Cole's father had promised to send her something with his son's fingerprints on them, but she hadn't received it yet, so the call could wait. Once she ran the prints against Homeless Harry's, they'd know immediately whether Harry was actually Aiden Cole. If it was, it would be terrible news for Mr. Cole. And what could that mean for Tyler, Tanner's son? Could he have suffered a similar fate?

"What is it?" Tanner said, interrupting her thoughts. "Your face is doing a thing."

"What thing?" Vanessa focused her attention back on him.

"You know, like you're thinking of something unpleasant."

"I'm working on something," she said, wanting to be honest with him as much as she could. "When I figure it out, I'll let you know. But I'll be honest with you, Tanner—" She stopped. She hadn't asked if it was okay to call him by his first name, but the man didn't even blink. "There's not a lot to go on."

"I know." The big man cracked his knuckles. "The private investigator I hired said the same thing. But unlike Seaside PD, at least he didn't keep insisting that my son ran away."

"You hired a PI?" Vanessa was surprised. A good private investigator was expensive. "Good for you."

"Nothing came of it, but I needed to feel like I had done everything I could," Tanner said. "He was a retired cop from Seattle PD."

"I came from Seattle PD. Who was it?"

"He's a lot older than you," Tanner said. "His name is Jerry Isaac. He was just starting his own PI firm back then. Know him?"

"Oh, do I." Vanessa couldn't help but grin. *PI firm* was probably overstating—Jerry Isaac was a one-man operation with a two-room office in an old building in Seattle's Fremont neighborhood. "I know him quite well. He was my training officer back in the day. You chose well; Jerry would have done everything he could. I'll give him a call, see if has anything else to add."

"I'd appreciate that." Tanner checked the time on his phone and stood up. "I should go check on Jenna. Thanks for your time, Deputy."

"No need to thank me," she said. "Just doing my job."

"No, I mean it," he said. "You've shown more interest in Tyler than anybody here did when he first went missing. It means a lot to be taken seriously."

"I don't know how much I can do, but I can promise I'll do my best." She offered him a smile. He didn't need platitudes or empty promises. No parent did.

"You ever need work on your car, come see me." He smiled back, and it made him look about ten years younger. "Or if I ever see you at the Monkey Bar—that's a local spot right near the clubhouse— beers are on me."

"That's not necessary," she said with a laugh. "But I appreciate it."

"Tell you what." Tanner's bright blue eyes were focused on her face. "You find my son, and I'll buy all your beers and work on your car—*all* your cars—for free, for as long as I live. How's that?"

"I'd be stupid not to take that deal." She offered him a hand.

"Yes." He squeezed her hand, holding it a little longer than necessary. "You would be."

SIXTEEN

The Wonder Wheel Kid's selfie was splashed all over the TV news. Blake Dozier's father, Derek, finally home from his business trip to China, had finally decided that it really *was* weird that his son wasn't returning anyone's calls or texts, and he'd filed an official missing person's report earlier that morning. Blake's smiling, handsome face at the top of the Wonder Wheel was the most current photo Seaside PD had, and it had made the jump from social media to mainstream media—with the middle finger blurred out, of course.

But believe it or not, that wasn't the top story.

The big news of the day was that Seaside PD had officially released the identity of Homeless Harry, and it turned out to be none other than Aiden Cole, the Wonder Worker who'd gone missing three years ago. The official cause of death was blunt-force trauma. Aiden had been murdered.

Wonderland was officially fucked.

Oscar continued to watch the press conference on TV, and police chief Earl Schultz was doing his best to downplay it all.

"Chief, is there any connection between Homeless Harry and the Wonder Wheel Kid?" a reporter called out.

"I think it's disrespectful to address them by their media-dubbed nicknames, Kurt, when we know what their legal names are," Earl said to the reporter. "And no, there is no connection at all between Aiden Cole and Blake Dozier. Aiden Cole was a cold missing persons case that is now a homicide, and Blake Dozier is a new case that will be investigated fully, and without bias."

"Is it true Blake Dozier was the only person at Wonderland at the time Aiden Cole's body was dumped there?" a female voice called out.

"We're still working on that, Sarah. We don't know who might have been at the park other than Blake at that time. As you know, Wonderland is a big place and it will take awhile to narrow down the list of people who might have been at the park at that time of the morning. Next question."

"Chief, do you have any working theories on who might have killed Aiden Cole?"

"He wasn't killed at the park, we know that for a fact, Jeff," Earl said, his tone firm. "There is no evidence to suggest any kind of foul play has taken place anywhere on Wonderland grounds. Wherever Aiden

Cole was killed, it wasn't at Wonderland, and I can't speculate about why his body was left at the park. As for Blake Dozier, we can't confirm that he even went missing from Wonderland. The picture that's circulating around is misleading. If Blake Dozier did meet with foul play, there's no evidence to suggest it happened on park premises."

Thank you, Earl. Oscar allowed himself a small smile in the privacy of his office. Bianca would be pleased. Earl had managed to protect Wonderland while at the same time being forthcoming about what he knew about the Wonder Wheel Kid and Homeless Harry. Not an easy feat. Genius, really. He made a mental note to thank Earl at the Seaside Hospital gala fund-raiser in a few days, assuming they didn't run into each other before then. Seaside was a small town, after all.

The comments on Blake Dozier's Facebook and Twitter page had climbed to well over a thousand. The commenters, who'd initially expressed admiration over Blake's Wonder Wheel selfie, had then turned sympathetic when the news broke that Blake was considered missing. A flurry of comments saying "Stay safe, Blake" and "Come back to us, Blake" filled up the middle portion of the comment thread.

But now, mere hours later, they were beginning to turn vicious.

Someone had suggested that Blake was not really

missing at all, that he had staged his own disappearance to draw attention to his picture. Another person, who'd apparently known him in high school, said that Blake had been an asshole who'd picked on him and so he wouldn't be surprised if Blake was lying dead in a ditch somewhere after having messed with the wrong person. And yet another kid, a fellow climber no less, said that Blake shouldn't even be calling himself an urban free climber because the Wonder Wheel was *only* 150 feet high.

One minute social media was your friend and saying kind things; the next minute social media was a self-righteous bitch telling you exactly what a fuck-up you were. Oscar wondered if Blake Dozier's father was reading these ugly comments.

He had gone to look at the Wonder Wheel earlier that morning, and the crime scene cleaning team that Earl had sent to the park the night before had done a stellar job. No traces of Homeless Harry, aka Aiden Cole, remained, though Oscar was sure if you held up one of those special blue lights to the dark asphalt, you would see traces of him still there. But that didn't matter. What mattered was what you could *see*, and everything appeared normal. The thick cardboard wall surrounding the base of the wheel had finally been removed. Even the stench was gone.

It was as if nothing had happened at all.

Oscar continued to watch KIRO-7 as Earl was peppered with a few more questions, to which he replied with vague, professional answers. In the background, standing slightly to the police chief's left, stood deputy chief Vanessa Castro. Oscar leaned forward to get a closer look.

Goddammit, she looked sexier than ever. It was a warm day and she wasn't wearing a jacket, so her gun was visible in its holster. Her silk blouse clung to the contours of her curvy but athletic body, and her midlength dark hair hung in shiny, loose waves around her face. Minimal makeup, but she didn't need any. Her eyes were large and expressive, and as Earl spoke, she scanned the audience, missing nothing.

Oscar was doing a little digging into her background, and with the press conference over, he turned his attention back to his computer. A quick Google search had turned up several articles linking Vanessa Castro to the Marcus Henry trial—they were the first six hits. Apparently Seaside's new deputy chief had been close friends with the drug kingpin, a friendship that dated back to when they were teenagers and Henry was still a resident of Seaside. It was brought up during the trial that Detective Vanessa Castro had been intimately involved with Henry before her husband died. After Henry's acquittal, she left Seattle PD and joined Seaside PD, which suggested she'd been pushed out of her old police department.

Further down the page of Google links was her late husband's obituary. Dated six months earlier, it said that Major John Castro of the U.S. Army, retired, had died three days before Christmas at the age of forty-one, leaving behind a wife and two children. In lieu of flowers, donations should be made to the Magnolia Foundation. Oscar had never heard of it before, and when he clicked on the website, he saw that the Magnolia Foundation was a not-for-profit organization that assisted military veterans in receiving treatment for a variety of mental health disorders, including depression, anxiety, and post-traumatic stress.

Interesting. Oscar had suspected that Vanessa had a colorful past—why else would someone choose to leave Seattle for Seaside, if not to get away from a colorful past?—but he hadn't expected a recently deceased husband and a questionable relationship with a high-level drug dealer. Vanessa had told him she was in no place for a relationship, and Oscar was beginning to understand why. In that sense, she and Bianca were alike.

He mentally cursed himself again. He had to stop comparing Vanessa—and every other woman he met—to his boss and former lover. With Bianca, it had always been just about sex, but with Vanessa, there was chemistry on all levels. Vanessa was smart and ambitious, but she also had a family. She seemed more centered, and softer in all the ways that mattered. She made Oscar want more. And he was ready for more.

After more than twenty years with the park, Oscar wanted out of Wonderland.

Having grown up in Seaside, he'd started working at the park as a part-timer when he was in high school. It was almost a rite of passage for the local kids that they'd work at the amusement park once they turned fourteen. Seaside's World of Wonder, as it was originally called, had been created and built by Jack Shaw.

Yes, *that* Jack Shaw, who'd built several of Seattle's tallest buildings. Jack Shaw, who was one of the Pacific Northwest's wealthiest men, according to *Forbes* magazine. Jack Shaw, who had a thing for young teenage boys, and who'd built World of Wonder just so he could have a legitimate reason to be around them. Jack Shaw, who'd eventually be accused of sexually assaulting more than half a dozen boys from the ages of fourteen to sixteen. Jack Shaw, who'd died horribly in a fire shortly after being formally charged with sexual abuse, and as a result had never been brought to justice.

At least not the legal form of justice, anyway.

Oscar was twenty-six and had just finished a five-year stint in the army when his mother told him the big news over dinner. She'd been thoroughly unimpressed with Nick Bishop's decision to buy the park, and was delighted that Oscar hadn't heard, because it meant she could drop the bomb herself while offering her opinions on the whole thing, of which there were many.

"You should see the dump that the park is now, Ozzie," Isabel Trejo had said to her son, lighting her third cigarette in a row. "Seaside's World of Wonder. *Christ*. What the hell is Nicky thinking? Hell, *I* still remember it from when I was a kid. It was tacky even then, though of course when you're a kid all you care about are the rides and the cotton candy. But it's a fucking dump. If anybody should know that, Nicky should. He said he got it for a bargain price, and he'd have had to, because who else would buy it?"

"It's been for sale for a while, hasn't it?" Oscar said, fanning the smoke away from his face. His mother didn't notice. They were only halfway through their meals, and she would go through at least two more cigarettes before they were finished. Oscar hated the way she looked when she smoked. The skin around Isabel's mouth was like paper, and it crinkled when she puckered to take a drag, instantly aging her twenty years.

"It was on the market for a couple of years. I didn't think Shaw's widow would be able to give it away. Obviously, she was desperate to get rid of it. Not for the money, of course; that bitch is loaded. But she'd want it out of her life, you know? She'd want it *away* from her. Not that I blame her."

"I can't believe Nicky would buy it. Are you absolutely sure?"

"Kiddo, it's all over town. Besides, I just talked to Betty at the bank." Isabel exhaled a long stream of smoke from her nostrils. "I stopped in to get some cash and she couldn't wait to tell me what he paid for it." She said the number, and it was lower than even Oscar could have imagined. "Your loco friend is now the proud owner of the world's ugliest amusement park. Christ, he's not even thirty. What the hell is he thinking?" she said again.

"Well, maybe he'll fix it up." Oscar's mind was racing. "Make it all shiny and new. I'm sure he has a plan."

"With what money? He just spent it all to buy the goddamned park. He finally gets his big payday and *this* is what he blows his cash on? Un-fucking-believable."

All Oscar knew about Nick's finances back then were the rumors he'd heard filtered through his mother. A couple of years after Oscar joined the army, Nick had been in a car accident, causing him to lose partial function of his leg, and he'd sued somebody and won. The full story, which he would learn from Nick himself later, was that an eighteen-wheeler had barreled through his car after it failed to stop at a red light. Nick had been rushed to the hospital with a leg that had been shattered in a hun-dred places (a likely exaggeration, but whatever),

along with a broken arm. At the hospital, he'd con-
tracted the infection that had caused permanent
nerve damage, forcing him to walk with a noticeable
limp even after his broken leg had healed. For two
years after, he'd been embroiled in a lawsuit against
both the trucking company (which had been aware
that the brakes for the truck were in need of servicing) and the hospital (which hadn't employed the
correct safety measures to prevent a staph infection).
And he'd won. How much, exactly, Nick had never
confirmed, but it had clearly been enough to buy the
park outright. The trucking company and the hospital both had deep pockets.

The money to renovate World of Wonder had ul-
timately come from the bank in town. The amusement park had long been an eyesore for Seaside, and
with Jack Shaw finally dead, nobody was more invested in seeing it cleaned up and thriving than the
town was. Though Nick Bishop had no credit to
speak of, his loan application had been pushed
through. And a year and a half later, Nicky reopened
the park, changing the name and rebranding it Wonderland. It was now bigger, with more rides, more
games, and more food. Wonderland had turned a
tidy profit ever since.

But some things remained the same. Nick hadn't
wanted to change everything. "Part of the appeal of
Wonderland is the memories," he'd said once, when
Oscar had suggested replacing some of the older

attractions with more modern ones. "Adults spend a lot of time here with their kids, because it was magic for them when *they* were kids. If we change too much, it ruins the magic."

Nick understood that part of the park's appeal was its retro vibe, therefore many of the attractions that had been part of the original World of Wonder were still here. The Tiny Tom Donuts hut, for instance. The sign looked exactly the same as it had back in 1985, with the neon cat dancing while holding a doughnut in its paw. Every other year the wires would short out and an electrician would be called in to repair it, but it was still here. The Hot Diggity hot dog stand, the Merry Go-Round, Adventure Mountain, the Puppet Theater, the House of Horrors, the Giant Octopus, the Clown Museum—these were all attractions that had been at the park since the beginning, since Oscar had been a fourteen-year-old Wonder Worker himself, since he'd survived Jack Shaw.

Nick could never really explain to Oscar why he had wanted to revive this place, though the two men had talked about it a couple of times. And Oscar could never really explain why he had agreed to work for his friend. But now, much older and wiser, it all made sense why the two of them had been drawn back to Seaside's World of Wonder.

Working here every day, the place where so many awful, terrible things had happened to him, allowed

Oscar to feel in control. It was, in a weird but effective way, a very empowering thing to be back at the place where as a teenager he'd felt so helpless. Working at the new Wonderland, for him and for Nick, and maybe even for Glenn Hovey, was like the ultimate fuck-you to Jack Shaw. A way of showing the dead pedophile—and the rest of the world—that he was just fine. *Fuck you, you couldn't break me. Fuck you, I'm not damaged. Fuck you, I'm second-in command of the Pacific Northwest's largest amusement park, and so how do you like that, you pathetic, disgusting sonofabitch?*

But now it was time to move on. He'd been thinking about it for a while now. Even Nick had gotten to a point where he'd wanted to leave. Now Oscar did, too, though he had no intention of leaving the park under the same circumstances Nick had. Bianca had been furious.

There was an old bar and grill on the beach that had been empty for a while. Owning his own business had always been Oscar's dream. As if on cue, his cell phone rang.

"Oz, it's Wendy Kerse from Seaside Credit Union," the woman on the other end said. "I just realized there's a couple of forms I forgot to have you sign when you were here a few days ago. Are you able to come in today?"

"I can come around noon, if that works," Oscar said. "Thanks, Wendy."

He hung up and exhaled. Buying the restaurant was the riskiest thing he'd ever done. It needed a complete renovation to get it where he wanted it to be, and he knew next to nothing about running a restaurant. But still, he could envision how it would be once it was all finished. Live music on the weekends. Cuban pulled-pork sandwiches. Mojitos. Fresh seafood. Tapas at happy hour. He already had a name for the place. He would call it El Mago. The Wizard. Because he was Oz, of course.

He was daring to imagine a different life, and it was scary as hell.

He already knew what Bianca would say when he told her. She would say, "Stay." She would say, "Don't leave me." She would say, "I can't run this place without you, Oz." Things she'd been saying to him for years already, and they had worked. He hadn't been able to walk away. Because he had loved her. He still loved her.

But he was beginning to realize that love was overrated. Love made you do stupid things. Awful things. Terrible things. Things you knew were very, very wrong. Even when the person you loved didn't love you back.

Fuck, *especially* when the person you loved didn't love you back.

SEVENTEEN

The television in the living room was a bit loud, but Vanessa wasn't about to tell Ava to turn it down. Things had been so tense between them lately, and all she wanted was to try and keep things peaceful as best she could. They had barely spoken since their big fight, and Vanessa had no idea how Ava was feeling these days. She didn't have a clue whether her daughter liked her job at Wonderland, whether she was making any friends, whether things were getting better for her in Seaside. Forcing Ava to talk was a bad idea. All Vanessa could do was hope her daughter would come to her when she was ready.

She had a lot to keep her busy in the meantime. With Blake Dozier officially declared a missing person, she now had three missing persons cases, and it was three too many, as far as she was concerned. Mind you, Aiden Cole's status was now technically a homicide. Her conversation with David Cole had gone as well as could be expected, but it was always difficult to hear a grown man cry.

"Thank you," he'd said, his voice thick. "I appreciate you letting me know."

"I really didn't do anything," Vanessa said, which was true. The body had just shown up. "But if there's anything you need, any questions I can answer for you, please call me anytime, day or night. It's still an active investigation, and I'll keep you updated as often as I can."

"Is it true . . ." There was a hitch in David Cole's voice. "Is it true that his face . . . his face was eaten . . ."

"Your son died quickly, Mr. Cole." Vanessa spoke as gently as she could. "When he was struck, it was with such great force that he was likely knocked unconscious immediately. He would not have felt or been aware of anything after that."

She cursed the Wonder Worker who'd posted the picture of #HomelessHarry on Twitter in the first place. They'd tracked him down and he'd been fired, according to Donnie, but the damage that he'd done to Aiden Cole's father could never be undone. David Cole had probably been following the Homeless Harry case with interest, as everyone else had, and to learn that the dead body was actually his missing son had to be a nightmare. She could only hope that he hadn't seen the actual photo.

"Why did they think he was homeless?" David

Cole asked. "Do you think Aiden spent the last three years starving on the streets of some city somewhere? Why didn't he just come home?"

"I don't have the answers to that, Mr. Cole," Vanessa said. "But I promise you, I will find out who did this. I am so incredibly sorry for your loss."

"Did you know that I've kept his room exactly the same? I don't drink orange juice, but Aiden likes it, and I still buy it every couple of weeks in case he comes home . . . and now I know he's not coming home . . ." David Cole broke down, sobbing, and a moment later, the phone disconnected.

Vanessa had lost a husband, but never a child, and the grief David Cole was feeling was unfathomable.

The case files for Aiden, Tyler, and Blake were spread out in front of her, and Vanessa stared at them all, trying to make sense of them. They'd all been Wonder Workers when they'd gone missing. They were all eighteen. They were all white. While on the surface it might seem like they had a lot in common, they didn't really, because most of the population of Seaside was Caucasian. And the overwhelming majority of Wonder Workers were under the age of twenty-one.

What was the goddamned *connection*?

Donnie Ambrose had offered to help her go over the cases, but she'd been taking up too much of his time lately, and there were other major crimes for the detective to work on. He'd made her promise to call him if she got stuck on something, and in the meantime, he'd continue to do what he could to find Blake Dozier, and also Glenn Hovey.

Vanessa had found herself irritated with Earl Schultz's press conference, in which he'd so cleverly exonerated Wonderland of any responsibility concerning both Aiden Cole and Blake Dozier. No evidence of foul play on park premises? Maybe that was technically true, but that didn't mean that Wonderland didn't have *everything* to do with what happened to them. Which Vanessa believed in her gut they did. She'd complained about it to Donnie over the phone earlier, who at this point was the only person she trusted.

"You're preaching to the choir, Deputy," the detective had said after she'd spent ten minutes ranting. "I get it. I've never liked the special treatment Wonderland gets, but it's not going to change. Not on Earl's watch, anyway. When he retires, maybe Seaside PD won't be so aligned with the park's agenda, but until then—"

"We toe the company line."

"Yeah." Donnie lowered his voice then. "Just watch who you bitch about it to, though, okay? You're all right with me, but remember, all ears lead back to Earl."

"Not an issue because nobody else really talks to me," Vanessa said dryly, but she knew he was right. "But thanks for the reminder."

Tanner Wilkins's son stared out at her from a picture that appeared to be his senior class photo from high school. He looked like a much younger, skinnier version of his dad. Dark blond hair, same bright blue eyes, and six four, according to the summary notes, which made him the same height as his father, minus forty or so pounds of muscle. He'd been eighteen at the time of his disappearance, three months shy of his nineteenth birthday. His file contained the usual: the official police report, brief statements from a half dozen Wonderland people including Oscar Trejo and the elusive security guard Glenn Hovey, and interviews with his parents, Tanner and Beth Wilkins. There was also a note that a copy of Tyler's file had been sent to retired Seattle police detective–turned–private investigator Jerry Isaac, whom Tanner had hired a few months after his son had gone missing. Tyler's file was as painfully thin as Aiden's was.

Vanessa checked the clock. It was only 8 p.m., not late at all. She reached for her cell phone and scrolled through it until she found the number she was looking for.

He answered on the second ring, his familiar voice deep and hoarse. "Well, I'll be damned," he said, and she could almost see his grin from two hundred miles away. "Miz Vanessa Castro. How the hell are you, honey?"

Vanessa smiled at the sound of his voice,

immediately conjuring an image of former Seattle PD detective Jerry Isaac in her mind. Tall and impossibly skinny, with dark brown skin, Jerry had an easy smile that went on for days. A few years back, Jerry's voice had no rasp, and it had instead been a rich baritone that could have gotten him hired as a movie announcer if he'd ever wanted to switch careers. A serial killer had slashed his throat, and his vocal cords had never been the same, though he sounded much better now than the last time they'd spoken.

"I'm doing well," she said warmly, happy just to be talking to him again. "You probably heard that I'm in Seaside. Traded in the big city for a small town."

"Seaside? You left SPD? No, I hadn't heard." Jerry's surprise was obvious. "Last I saw you was when?"

"John's funeral."

"Ah shit." There was a pause. "Of course. I'm sorry, sweetie. That was stupid of me. You doing okay?"

"Hanging in." It was her stock answer. Had they been face-to-face over lunch, she might have delved into more detail with Jerry, who would probably understand what she was going through more than most people. She didn't want to get distracted from why she'd called, though. "How are you?"

"Hanging in." The smile in Jerry's voice carried through the phone. "So you're in Seaside, huh?"

"You don't watch the news?" She found herself holding her breath.

"I didn't realize a job change was newsworthy," Jerry said with a laugh, but it was kind, and Vanessa found herself relaxing. "Not that it matters to me. I stopped watching the news a long time ago. There's never anything good in there. Too much horribly depressing shit going on in the world."

"That's funny, coming from a homicide detective."

"*Former* homicide detective. Been retired now for almost eight years."

"Miss it?"

"Not even a little bit." He cleared his throat. "But I'm assuming you didn't call to talk about that. What can I do for you, pretty lady?"

Ordinarily Vanessa hated being called pet names like "honey," "sweetie," or "pretty lady," but coming from Jerry, it never came across as condescending or offensive. Jerry Isaac had been one of her training officers when Vanessa started out, and though he'd had a reputation back then for being a ladies' man, he'd treated Vanessa more like a daughter than anything else.

"I'm looking at an old case in Seaside and your name came up," she said. "As a PI, not a police detective."

"Seaside case of mine?" Jerry paused. "Then you must be calling about Tanner Wilkins's boy, Tyler. Damn. That was a long time ago. One of my first cases when I went into business for myself. Spent a lot of time in Seaside. Don't tell me you found him."

"I wish," Vanessa said. "Unfortunately, he's still missing. I actually met Tanner regarding a different matter, and the subject of his son came up. I promised him I'd take another look."

Jerry let out a heavy sigh. "I don't know that you should have done that, honey. The case was dry back then. It would be dust by now."

"You're probably right, but here's the thing. A boy, same age as Tyler, also went missing three years ago. Aiden Cole. Also eighteen at the time of his disappearance, also worked for Wonderland, also went missing at the end of the summer. Well, he just turned up. A John Doe was discovered at Wonderland, and lo and behold, it's Aiden Cole."

"Shee-it. Aiden Cole is Homeless Harry?"

"I thought you just said you didn't watch the news."

"Saw the hashtag on Twitter," Jerry said. "How'd he die again?"

"Blunt-force trauma. ME thinks maybe a baseball bat. Dead for six days, maybe longer, before his body turned up at Wonderland."

Jerry emitted a low whistle. "Three years missing only to go out like that."

"Seaside is a small town, Jerry. Two missing boys felt like a lot to me. But now it's three. A kid named Blake Dozier's disappeared now, too."

"The Wonder Wheel Kid," Jerry said. "Saw that hashtag, too. What are your theories?"

"Don't have any." Vanessa sighed again. "What I do know is Ava's working at the park now, and I can't lie, working on this is making me more than a little concerned for her safety."

"Aw, I'm sure you have nothing to be concerned about," Jerry said. "Wonderland is a huge place. It has, what, something like a thousand employees during the summer?"

"Closer to twelve hundred, I think."

"The odds of anything happening to Miss Ava are no worse than if she worked anywhere else. But you're a mom, and a cop, so I get it. Three missing boys, and one turns up dead . . ." His voice trailed off.

"What is it?"

"Actually, make that *four* missing boys."

"*What?*" she said again.

Jerry's voice was grim. "Three years after Tyler went missing, I got a call from Tanner. A kid named . . . what was it again . . . Kyle something? Disappeared. His case was a bit strange. He worked for Wonderland, primary gig was in the Bandstand. He disappeared in the middle of a concert."

The Bandstand was the amphitheater inside Wonderland. Every summer they had a concert series, usually bands that hadn't made it to the big time yet, or bands that had made it to the big time, but twenty years ago.

"Go on."

"Some band was playing, can't remember who now. Something went faulty and there was an electrical fire backstage, and one of the band members was injured. He didn't die, suffered some burns and whatnot, but with all the chaos, the concert was shut down immediately. That was the last night Kyle was seen. Last anyone could remember was that he was backstage, working. And then just like that, gone."

"Did he cause what happened with the wiring?"

"No, I don't believe so. I don't think he had anything to do with getting the stage ready; he was more like a gopher to the bands that came through, getting them water and food and such. I only mentioned it because the last time Kyle was seen was just before the commotion erupted. Anyway, when a couple days went by and the kid didn't turn up, Tanner called me, even though we hadn't spoken in a few years. He thought it was too coincidental that Kyle went missing, too. He thought the park might be involved somehow."

"So did you look into it?"

"I couldn't," Jerry said. "I wasn't working for a while back then, if you remember."

"Oh, right." Vanessa immediately felt like a prize idiot. Now who was the one who was stupid? Five years ago, Jerry was fighting for his life in the hospital. "Shit."

"Oh, stop." Her friend's tone was dismissive. "Feels like a lifetime ago. Anyway, when I had the conversation with Tanner, I was home from the hospital, but not in a great place. At the time, I thought Tanner was reaching. Both his son and Kyle were eighteen, old enough to take off if they wanted to, and the idea of an amusement park causing their disappearances was just too big a theory to try and prove. But now there's two more, for a total of four. I don't know, maybe Tanner was on to something."

Vanessa thought for a moment. "When you investigated Tyler's disappearance, was there anything that didn't jibe?"

It was an open-ended question, the kind that only a seasoned cop could ask another seasoned cop. It had nothing to do with anything quantifiable; it more referred to gut instinct. Hunches. Things that didn't feel right, that weren't necessarily explainable. Jerry knew what she was getting at.

"When I took the job, I told Tanner I would investigate like a cop would, with no bias," Jerry said. "Which is exactly what I did. And in the end, it looked like everything the police initially said held up. I almost felt bad taking Tanner's money, though I'd spent a good couple of weeks asking questions and looking around. Witnesses saw Tyler at the park painting the mural and everything was fine. Then the security guard—I'd have to double-check this so don't take my word for it yet—said he saw Tyler a bit later on during his rounds of the park. But that was it. He never made it home."

"And Tanner said the security footage showed nothing," Vanessa said.

"Their surveillance system was a joke back then."

"They have the same surveillance system now."

Jerry snorted. "The only piece that didn't quite jibe was the security guard. Glenn something. I couldn't pin anything on him, there was nothing to point to him doing anything to Tyler, but I never liked him. He was weird."

"Glenn Hovey," Vanessa said. "You talked to him?"

"A couple of times. His answers were always vague. He said he must have been doing his rounds of the park when the kid left. He wasn't in front of the monitors and therefore didn't see anything."

"Glenn Hovey's name keeps coming up," Vanessa said. "He was the only person scheduled to be at the park the morning Blake Dozier disappeared, but he never showed up for work. We still haven't been able to locate him."

"Wait a minute. You mean the guy still works at Wonderland?"

"As far as I know, they haven't fired him."

"Shee-it." Jerry's tone was flat. "If that's the guy they keep on security, then maybe Miss Ava shouldn't be working there after all. I wouldn't want that guy watching my ass. Mind you, he's supposedly good friends with the owner of the park."

"I told her to watch out for security guards." Vanessa chewed on her bottom lip. "Maybe I should talk to her about it again. Glenn Hovey's close with Bianca Bishop?"

"More with her uncle, Nick Bishop."

"His niece runs the place now. I haven't met her yet. But maybe I should. I'd like to know what she thinks of three missing kids."

"I never spoke to her, but we did run into each other once as I was leaving the administrative building. She looked at me like I was a cockroach, asked me if I was lost. She had a lot of attitude for someone so young; she would have been in her late twenties when Tyler went missing." Jerry chuckled. "Her uncle was a lot nicer."

"Think she's racist?"

"More like elitist. She was up here and I was down there." Jerry paused. "But yeah, in hindsight, maybe she didn't like the color of my skin. If you talk to her, make sure you wear your badge and gun. I'm sure, to her, I was just an annoying civilian running around, asking intrusive questions. My feeling is she'll respect you more than she did me."

"I don't know about that," Vanessa said. "From what I've heard, Wonderland seems to think that Seaside PD works for them. An attitude like that comes from the top."

"True. Hey, you want my notes on Tyler? I can

FedEx them tomorrow. There might not be much more than what you already know, but it couldn't hurt to look them over. Something might jog."

"That would be great," Vanessa said. "But could you send it to me at home? I've kind of gone rogue on this—I'm not officially working on anything to do with Tanner's son. The Wonder Wheel Kid and Homeless Harry are my only active cases."

"Some things never change." Jerry chuckled and took down her address. "By the way, is Detective Carl Weiss still working there?"

"No, he retired about a month ago, as deputy chief. I replaced him. Why?"

"They made that guy deputy chief?" Jerry's rasp got worse. He sounded almost angry. "He was the most useless, unhelpful cop I'd ever met. His shoddy investigative work on Tyler's case is the reason I had no hope of finding him. There were so many people he didn't talk to, leads he didn't follow up on."

"Tanner said the same thing. As did Aiden Cole's father."

Jerry whistled. "Wow. How'd you get that job, anyway?"

"John's best friend, Frank Greenberg. He's the mayor here in Seaside now. Elected last year. He . . . did me a favor."

"Ah." There was a long pause. Jerry knew there was no point in asking; if Vanessa wanted him to know the details, she would have offered them.

"Well, who cares how you got it. Seaside needs you, clearly."

"I miss your face, Jerry. It's been way too long. I should come up and visit, once things settle down here."

"You do that, Miz Castro. It would be lovely to see you."

They said their goodbyes and hung up. In her notebook, Vanessa wrote down three names.

Glenn Hovey, security guard.

Carl Weiss, former Deputy Chief of Seaside.

Kyle ??

She drew circles around them all.

Recipient(s): All Wonderland
Staff
Sender: Nick Bishop
Subject: Your Career Path,
             the Wonderland
             Way!

Dear Wonder Worker,

I was only fourteen when I began my first job at Seaside's World of Wonder, around the same age a lot of you are. Now I'm the owner of Wonderland. How did I get from there to here? I worked hard, of course, and I followed my passions! And I encourage you all to do the same.

The job postings you see on our website aren't just for prospective Wonder Workers. They're also for you, the current Wonder Worker. If you ever see a job that excites you, apply! We want your experience at Wonderland to be as well rounded as you need it to be, and in alignment with whatever long-term goals you have, whether they're with the park or not.

No matter where I am in the world, I'm invested in the park, and I'm invested in you. If you need guidance about your career path, talk to your Team Leader today. He or she will help ensure that you find the best fit at Wonderland for YOU. That's the Wonderland way!

Yours sincerely,
Nick Bishop
Owner, Wonderland Amusement Park, Inc.

EIGHTEEN

Ava was grateful she'd been assigned to hot dogs. Not that she wanted to work at this hot dog cart forever, but it wasn't a bad first gig as far as food services went. You didn't get to choose your first gig at Wonderland, but you could always put in for a transfer down the road. Ava had her eye on Elm Street, but for now, hot dogs were fine.

Katya, her new friend, hadn't been so lucky. They'd met the other day while being force-fed a video on the importance of hygiene and food safety, and had bonded instantly over a love of One Direction, cupcakes, and dyeing their hair pink, which both of them wanted to do someday, but not right now. Katya had been assigned to Teriyaki Delight inside the food court. Both girls agreed that it was about as shitty a food gig as it got, as Katya would be required to wear a shiny kimono and cook with her face in the steam all day—indoors, no less. Compared to that, hot dogs were a breeze. They came precooked and all Ava had to do was grill them a bit and slap them in a bun. And the best part? Her cart was stationed right in the midway, allowing her to stare at Xander Cameron all day.

Xander was across from her in the midway now, doing his thing at Hoop Shot, which was considered to be the best game in the park. It cost the most tickets to play and was one of the most popular games (the grand prizes were regulation NBA jerseys from your favorite team), and since games crew was paid based on how many tickets they turned in at the end of their shifts, Hoop Shot was the most lucrative way to make money. Ava had overheard some of the Wonder Workers grumbling about what Xander, a newbie, must have done to score a gig so good. But it wasn't Xander's fault he'd had his interview with the CEO herself. Sometimes you got lucky.

"Ten tickets to play! You know you want to!" Xander called out to passersby on his megaphone. "You think you can shoot threes like Steph Curry? Come and show me, and I'll give you the jersey of your choice! Come on, big guy, you know you can do it, get on over here, and win your girl something she'll be proud of!"

He was totally perfect for the job, obviously completely comfortable talking to people. A group of girls about Ava's age stopped and stared at him, giggling. Despite Ava's jealousy, she couldn't blame them. He was gorgeous. End of story.

Their eyes met across the midway, and he grinned

and waved. Ava waved back, her face turning bright red as it always did, and she hoped he was far enough away that he couldn't see the goofy grin on her face.

"Garbage?" a voice said, interrupting her thoughts.

Ava turned to see a janitor in gray coveralls standing near her cart. He was short and stocky, with slicked back dark hair and a goatee. Behind him was a large garbage bin on wheels.

"Garbage?" he asked again, and she saw that he was holding a black Hefty bag full of trash he'd just removed from the large bin a few feet away. She'd been so busy staring at Xander she hadn't even noticed he'd done it.

"Right, sorry." Ava opened the metal door at the bottom of her golf cart where there was a small personal garbage container. She handed it over and he changed it quickly. "How's your day going?" she asked.

He looked up, surprised, as if he wasn't used to people talking to him. Which was probably because most of the Wonder Workers and guests *didn't* talk to him—he was a janitor, which unfortunately made him invisible to everyone. "I'm fine," he said. "Thank you."

"I'm Ava," she said, feeling chatty and buoyant. Working outside in the fresh air always made her feel this way. She noticed the tattoo on his neck, a red rose with black leaves. "I really like your tat. Wish I could get one, but my mom would kill me."

"Thanks," he said again. He looked thrilled that

she was speaking to him. "I got the tattoo after my mother died. Roses were her favorite flower."

He gave her a smile and a wave as he walked away, and while Ava wouldn't go so far as to say that she'd made his day, perhaps she had. And that was a good thing.

She resumed staring at Xander, who was encouraging a group of boys to try their hand at Hoop Shot. He'd be on break soon, and they'd been taking their breaks together a lot. Maybe it was because Ava snuck him free hot dogs, but she didn't think so. Unlike Katya, who didn't understand the appeal of Elm Street, Xander was supportive of her goal to work in one—or all—of the horror attractions. She'd told him about the weekend she'd spent at Fear Fest with her dad two years ago, when a demented clown had jumped out at them inside the Clown Museum and she'd screamed so hard the clown actually covered his ears. She had never seen her dad laugh to the point of tears, and the story had made Xander laugh, too.

For that, and for so many other reasons, she adored Xander.

Rumor had it that Bianca Bishop adored Xander, too. Normally Ava didn't put much stock in rumors—they were as ubiquitous as the stinky Axe body spray that all the boys wore—but this one bugged her. She didn't want to think about Xander hooking up with someone, let alone somebody that old.

He wouldn't hook up with the CEO, would he?

Speaking of the Dragon Lady, Bianca Bishop was making her way down the midway. Her vibrant red hair, though it was always pulled back into a bun, made her easy to spot from a distance, and Ava immediately straightened up. She and Katya agreed there was no way the red could be the CEO's natural color—the shade was too intense, and too pretty.

Bianca Bishop had been in the midway a lot lately, and she always said hello to Xander when she was. This only fueled the rumors, but clearly she remembered him, as she was the one who'd hired him. While Xander seemed to like her, the Dragon Lady made everyone else nervous. Even Ava, who had an alpha female for a mother, found herself more than a little self-conscious whenever the CEO was nearby. Because Bianca Bishop was always watching.

Just yesterday, for instance, Shane Cardiff had griped openly to his supervisor about working at the little kids' Merry-Go-Round for the third day in a row (mainly because there was no opportunity to meet girls his own age there). Bianca had been standing nearby when he was complaining, and she'd pulled him from the gig immediately. He was now cleaning the men's john inside the food court, which was the most used—and therefore the dirtiest—bathroom in the entire park. And not just for one day. Shane was scheduled there *all week*.

It was best to be invisible whenever Bianca Bishop was around. Being invisible meant doing your job with a smile and not doing anything that might catch her eye. Since she had no guests to serve at the moment— always *guests*, never *visitors*—Ava made a point of wiping down the sides of the grill. It wasn't dirty, but as her food services training video had proclaimed no less than five times: *time to lean, time to clean*. She figured the Dragon Lady would walk right by like she always did, but this time, the woman stopped.

"Hello," Ava said with a shy smile.

Bianca's eyes flickered down to the employee ID card clipped to Ava's purple shirt, which all the Wonder Workers were required to wear on park grounds. It had her name and photo on it. "Ava Castro. Hello. I'm Bianca Bishop."

"Yes, ma'am, I recognize you. It's nice to meet you." From across the way, Ava could see Xander staring at them. Their eyes met for a split second, and Xander deliberately made a goofy face to try and get her to laugh. She immediately redirected her gaze back to the CEO.

"Has it been busy?" Bianca asked.

"It's been steady," Ava said. You never, ever said you weren't busy. Managers and higher-ups didn't want to hear that it was slow. If it was slow, it was somehow your fault and suddenly you were on bathroom duty. "I had a lineup a little while ago and so I just refilled the condiments." The second part was true; the first part wasn't.

Bianca was scrutinizing her now, and on reflex

Ava stood up even straighter. Was her purple golf shirt clean and pressed and tucked in neatly? Check. Were her khaki shorts an acceptable length (no shorter than four inches above the knee)? Check. Was her long hair tied back from her face? Check. Were her fingernails clean and bare of polish (you weren't allowed to wear nail polish if you worked in food)? Check.

"Your mom is the new deputy chief of Seaside PD, isn't she?" Bianca said.

"Yes, ma'am."

The woman nodded. "That's what I thought. I haven't had a chance to meet her yet. When you talk to her next, tell her to come by my office the next time she's here at the park. I'd love to say hello and introduce myself. Wonderland has always maintained a close relationship with the Seaside Police Department."

"Yes, ma'am, I will." It didn't seem appropriate to mention that Ava was not exactly on speaking terms with her mother, nor did she plan to start speaking to her anytime soon. The only person who could hold a grudge longer than Vanessa Castro was Ava Castro. "She'll be here a lot this summer, I'm sure. My little brother loves it here, and he's been bugging her to take him."

"So what brought you all to Seaside?" The CEO's eyes were green, and they seemed to miss nothing. "Your mother was a detective in Seattle, wasn't she?"

"Well . . ." Ava wasn't sure how to answer. She'd been asked that question before by a few of the Wonder Workers she'd met so far, and would certainly be asked that question again when she started at Seaside Academy in the fall. She hadn't yet figured out her stock answer, so she decided to go with the truth. "My dad died six months ago, so my mom thought it would be good for us to get a fresh start."

"I see. Well, I'm sorry to hear that." Bianca's face didn't change. The words were right, but her tone was strangely wooden. "And how are you enjoying making hot dogs?"

"It's—" The change of subject seemed abrupt, almost harsh. "It's fine," Ava said. "I like it."

The CEO didn't blink. "Of course you like it. But if you had your choice, is there a particular gig you'd prefer?"

"Well . . ." Ava swallowed. "I mean, someday, it would be really great to snag an Elm Street gig. I was here for Fear Fest a couple years back and it was a lot of fun."

"You like that kind of thing." It should have been a question, but it came out a statement. "Which attraction in particular?"

"I . . ." Ava was caught off guard. "They're all great."

"But if you had to pick one."

"The Clown Museum, I guess," Ava said, since it was the first attraction that came to mind. "I think it's . . . really cool."

"Not too many Wonder Workers would choose the Clown Museum," Bianca said. "How interesting."

"I *love* the Clown Museum!" Normally she prided herself on not gushing, but the woman's lack of emotion made Ava want to be overly enthusiastic, as if to make up for it. "It would be awesome to help put the displays together, or to dress up like a crazy clown and scare people. But I know you have to be at least sixteen."

"Usually you do," Bianca said. "But what matters most is aptitude and maturity. You seem to possess both. And my uncle Nick firmly believes that it's important to place Wonder Workers in jobs they love."

"Yes, ma'am. I read his email this morning, and I do plan to apply for an Elm Street gig when I turn sixteen. I still have a year and a half to go."

"You've already thought that far ahead."

"Yes, ma'am." Ava smiled. "I'd love to stay at Wonderland until I go to college, assuming we stay here in Seaside."

"I see. Thank you for sharing. Have a good day, Ava."

The CEO continued on down the midway, pausing briefly to say hello to Xander like she always did. Around them, purple-shirted Wonder Workers whispered, and Ava found herself wishing that Xander wasn't so friendly with the woman. He was just giving everyone more reason to gossip.

When the Dragon Lady was completely out of

sight, Ava leaned against the side of her cart, trying to figure out what it was about the woman that was bothering her. It wasn't the rumors about her and Xander; they were just rumors. It wasn't the CEO's strong personality, either; Ava dealt with that every day at home. And it wasn't that she was mean, or strict, or a bitch, because those things weren't an issue as long as you didn't get on her bad side.

It was that Bianca Bishop was . . . fake.

She was speaking to you, but yet not really engaged. She said the right things, but the words didn't feel like they came from a genuine place. She seemed nice, but Ava had no doubt she'd throw you under the bus if you stood in the way of anything she wanted, and feel no guilt or remorse about it.

Sociopathic was a word Ava was familiar with, thanks to countless episodes of *Law & Order: SVU* and *Criminal Minds*. Not that Bianca Bishop was a criminal. Of course she wasn't. She was the CEO of Wonderland.

But if she *was* a criminal . . . if, say, she was a serial killer or something, it would make for a damn good episode of *Criminal Minds*, wouldn't it?

NINETEEN

Oscar had been tasked with expediting Ava Castro's transfer from food services to Elm Street, a process that normally took up to four weeks, provided that the Wonder Worker qualified for the new job. But Bianca Bishop had spoken. Ava was the daughter of Seaside PD's deputy chief, she reminded Oscar, and it was in the park's best interest to keep the girl happy.

Oscar was more concerned with making the girl's mother happy. He hadn't heard from Vanessa at all since the day Homeless Harry showed up in the midway, and he'd been thinking about her. A lot.

"Bianca thinks Ava will work out well," Oscar was saying to Anne-Marie Riker now. Anne-Marie was one of the Elm Street managers, a busy but friendly woman who always preferred to handpick her own Wonder Workers. "I'll send her over tomorrow at 10 a.m. I'd consider it a favor if you worked with her personally."

"But she's only fourteen, Oz." The displeasure in

Anne-Marie's voice was obvious. "I'm not sure I have anything appropriate."

"You'll find something."

The subtext was clear. This was not a request. Anne-Marie, five rungs down in the Wonderland food chain, knew damn well she had no choice in the matter. If the VP of operations asked you to do something, you did it, no questions asked.

With that taken care of, Oscar swiveled his chair to face the window, where the Avenue was bustling below. Soundproofed walls and windows prevented any sounds from penetrating into the administrative building, and it was as if the mute button had been pressed on *Wonderland: The Movie*. There was no comparison between the original World of Wonder and the park as it was today. Wonderland had evolved significantly over the past twenty years, and the new version was bigger, brighter, and busier. Back in the eighties, there had been no purple uniforms, no Human Resources Department, no employee handbook, no weekly pep talk emails to the Wonder Workers. There was certainly no Bandstand Amphitheater or summer concert series, and the midway back then had contained maybe fifteen games at most, all independently owned by whichever "carnie" had paid to set up shop in the park. Jack Shaw's vision for World of Wonder had been disjointed at best, but nobody had seemed to mind back then.

Little did the public know that he'd built World

of Wonder as *bait*. Because Jack Shaw had been a monster. And what better way to prey on boys of a certain age than to build an amusement park, which made *them* come to *him*?

The abuse hadn't happened right away. Oh, no. And it hadn't happened to every boy who'd worked for Shaw. Not at all. Jack Shaw was particular about the boys he chose, and he targeted only a certain kind of boy. The ones whose fathers weren't in the picture. The ones whose mothers were too busy to notice anything was wrong. The ones who wanted— *craved*—his attention, who wanted to feel special, who were missing a father figure and who would do anything to please Shaw and win his approval.

Boys like Oscar.

• • •

It had been Isabel Trejo's idea that her son apply to World of Wonder. Oz hadn't been interested at first. Who had the time or energy for a job? He was fourteen, and baseball was his life. Posters of Cal Ripken, Jr., wallpapered his room. He played in leagues year-round and was a rookie on his high school junior team, with dreams of making varsity the following year. It was likely to happen, his coach assured him, as long as he stayed focused.

So when the news hit that business tycoon Jack Shaw was returning to Seaside to build an amusement park, Oz merely thought it was a cool idea. World of

Wonder could be a good place for him and his friends to hang out, because there wasn't a whole lot to do in Seaside. And sometimes you needed a break from baseball, you know?

Isabel Trejo, of course, had a lot of opinions about the new amusement park.

"It's either gonna be the greatest thing Seaside has ever seen, or the ugliest thing Seaside has ever seen," she'd told her teenage son over breakfast. She turned her mouth to the side so she wouldn't blow a stream of smoke into his face while he was eating his eggs. "This town could use a pick-me-up, sure as shit. An amusement park will bring in the tourists, who'll need places to eat and sleep and party. Hell, maybe we'll finally get a shopping mall. Or a movie theater that shows more than two movies. But the whole thing could also flop."

"Why would it flop?" Oz asked, swallowing the last of his omelet.

"Because it's a risk, Ozzie Bear. This is Seaside. Pretty beach or no pretty beach, we're three hours south of Seattle, two hours west of Tacoma, and three and a half hours north of Portland. We're in the middle of bumfuck nowhere. Finish your eggs. I want you in line by eight thirty."

"Ma, I said I don't want to work there. I'm playing in two baseball leagues this summer."

She eyed him through a cloud of smoke. "You think I give a shit about baseball? Baseball doesn't pay the bills. You're fourteen and it's time you got a job. The house payment ain't getting any cheaper, and your dad ain't kicking in shit. Gas costs money. Clothes cost money. Baseball costs money. Food costs money, and god knows you eat more each week than a small village in Africa. Life costs money, Ozzie Bear."

And cigarettes cost money, Oz thought. *So does wine. What do you spend a week on booze and smokes, Ma?*

"You have zero work experience, and a job at the amusement park is your best bet for getting hired. I read in the paper they're looking to hire a hundred people minimum for the summer. No reason one of them can't be you." She took another drag on her cigarette. "Now finish your milk and I'll drive you over. Wear your raincoat. You could be in line for a while."

It was the first Monday of March break, and World of Wonder was conducting a hiring fair all week. You could fill out the job application while waiting in line, and be granted an interview on the spot. If they liked you, you were hired, it was as easy as that. Oz knew of at least five other boys his age who were planning to apply. The park would hire all week until the positions were filled, and the fair started at 9 a.m. He joined the line at 8:45. There were already sixty people ahead of him, most of them under the age of twenty-one.

By 11 a.m., Oz left the park with a couple of tax forms to fill out and a summer job lined up. Training was to begin a week before school let out in June, and they didn't mind that he played baseball.

"We wants kids like you," the hiring manager had said. "Kids who exude energy and fun. If you give your supervisor your baseball schedule, we'll work around it."

The first summer at the park was the greatest of his life. Oz hadn't expected to enjoy working so much, but every day was awesome. World of Wonder was small enough to feel intimate, but large enough to attract a ton of tourists from the surrounding areas. Every day brought new adventures, and he had opportunities to work in food, guest services, and once, when Colin Brace was out with the flu, his supervisor allowed him to operate the Wonder Wheel.

And Jack Shaw himself was around a lot. All the kids, boys *and* girls, loved him. When Jack Shaw stopped to talk to you, it was like you were the only person in the world who existed at that moment. He talked to you like you were a real person. He asked for your opinions. He laughed at your jokes. When one of the managers mentioned that Oz played baseball in a summer league, Shaw had showed up at the game, bringing popcorn for everybody. Oz had been floored, and then floored again when his coach told him that World of Wonder was now his team's official sponsor.

By the second summer, Seaside was a changed town. To handle the increase in summer tourism, several bed-and-breakfasts had opened up in Seaside, along with two new motels. Several new restaurants popped up, too. Isabel Trejo, a longtime housekeeper at the White Oaks Inn, had finally been promoted to head of housekeeping. A new housing complex just off the main strip was proposed, and there was talk that the mayor was meeting with developers to renovate the downtown area. There were rumors of a cineplex. Earl Schultz had just been promoted to deputy chief, and there was finally money to hire additional police officers. Crime rates went down. Life in Seaside was good.

And then it wasn't.

The rumors started to swirl. A fourteen-year-old kid named Danny Moskowitz had gotten wasted at a party near the end of summer and had drunkenly told his friends that Jack Shaw, Seaside's most important resident and the owner of World of Wonder, had sexually assaulted him inside a dungeon underneath the park.

Of course nobody believed him. The story was ludicrous. Danny was a known partier and drug user, a kid from a broken home who had been seen on more than one occasion following Jack Shaw around like a puppy. The idea that Jack Shaw would do such a thing was too ridiculous and insulting to even entertain. And a dungeon? Seriously? What was Danny smoking?

When his friends—all employees of the park, and all fiercely loyal to World of Wonder and Jack Shaw—accused him of lying, Danny recanted immediately. He claimed that he must have been drunk and high, that of course nothing had ever happened, and he admitted to having a substance abuse problem for which he needed serious help. A few days later, he left the park to enter rehab, though nobody knew which one.

But then a few weeks later, fifteen-year-old Peter Allred made similar accusations. He'd supposedly freaked out in the middle of having sex with his girlfriend. He, too, claimed that there was a tunnel under the Clown Museum that led to a dungeon where horrible things had happened to him. His girlfriend believed him. She told her older brother about it (minus the sex part, of course), who just happened to be a rookie police officer in the Seaside Police Department. Her brother brought it to the attention of his superiors. They'd laughed at him. Then the brother—Officer Carl Weiss, who would retire as deputy chief of Seaside PD some thirty years later— laughed, too. Because it *was* crazy, right?

Except that it wasn't. And Oz knew that it wasn't because he'd been down in the dungeon, too. Jack Shaw, his boss, his *friend*, had gotten him drunk, and then lured him into the dungeon under the guise of showing Oz the underground tunnel he'd built, that only a handful of people knew existed, telling him that it was a cool, secret place to hang out. He'd plied Oz with drugs, first offering him marijuana, and then giving him stronger stuff, all of which had rendered him useless, unable to fight off the man he thought of as a mentor and father figure. Unable to tell him no, that he didn't want it, to please stop.

Or *had* he wanted it? Had he asked for it? It was all so confusing. Oz loved Jack, after all. Everyone did. He'd trusted Jack, the man who told him every day how important he was to the park, how valued he was, and how he couldn't imagine the place without him. Oz would have done anything for Jack.

And so it was easy for Oz to tell himself it wasn't abuse. And when it happened again, it was easy to pretend he was sleeping. That he was completely un-aware he was being touched. That he didn't know he was being filmed. The alcohol and drugs made it all hazy, anyway. It was easier to tell himself that maybe he'd allowed it to happen, because the alternative was simply horrifying. Because when he'd asked Jack about it later, Shaw had expressed genuine sur-prise.

"I thought we were on the same page," he'd said to Oz. "I thought you liked it. I think you're amaz-ing. And don't worry, the tape is just for us. We can watch it whenever you want to. But think hard be-fore you tell anyone about us, okay? I would hate for people to misunderstand what happened. If they think you didn't want it to happen, that I somehow coerced you, which we both know isn't true, then they would absolutely want to see the tape. And you wouldn't want anyone else to watch it, would you?

The things that you did? After all, you're a star athlete, and nobody would want to know this side of you. But don't worry, I certainly won't tell anyone. It can stay our little secret."

No, Oz had no plans to tell anyone. He would rather have died before letting anyone else watch the tape. The embarrassment, the humiliation . . . it would all be too great. Jack was right, nobody would understand. Not his coworkers, not his high school friends, not his teammates.

So he'd never said anything. And for a while, he'd let it continue. The perks of being Jack's favorite were too great. He got paid more. He got all the best gigs. He could pick his own schedule. His baseball team got new uniforms, bats, and balls. The other kids deferred to Oz, and nobody ever wanted to piss him off, because he was important to Jack, and to the park.

So maybe certain things happened in the dungeon. Maybe it wasn't really okay. Who would believe him without proof? Who would believe that he didn't consent? Oz was fifteen when it started, old enough to know better, old enough to make it stop if he'd really wanted to.

And old enough not to want anybody to ever find out what was going on.

And hey, it wasn't like he was ever sober when it happened. He was drunk and high every single time, anyway. Most of the time, it felt like a bad dream.

Except it wasn't.

TWENTY

Glenn Hovey was officially MIA. Even his mother sounded a little worried.

"This isn't like Glenny," Sherry Hovey said when Vanessa stopped by the house again. "He missed one of my doctor's appointments so I had to ask Margie from next door to drive me. She's got terrible eyesight. She almost ran into a utility pole."

"Did you want to file a missing persons report?" Vanessa asked. "It's been a few days. I'm sure you're concerned."

Sherry Hovey hesitated. "Well, I don't think we need to get all in a tizzy about it. Glenny's always come back before."

The security guard, who was officially a person of interest in the Homeless Harry case, had never been away from work for this long. Donnie had put officers Nate Essex, Pete Warwick, and Claire Moran in rotation stakeout shifts outside the Hovey residence, but so far the man hadn't shown up. Vanessa liked Nate and

Pete well enough and felt kind of sorry for them that they'd gotten stuck with such a boring assignment, but Claire was still on her shit list for her attitude problem on Vanessa's first day.

It was clear to her now that there were very few people at Seaside PD who were unbiased. Everyone in the department seemed overly protective of Wonderland, and other than her conversations with Donnie Ambrose behind closed doors, she'd never heard a single person disparage the park in any way. That wasn't normal. Even now, with four missing boys, one of whom had turned up dead with his face eaten off, nobody seemed willing to say anything negative about Wonderland.

Even her daughter was beginning to drink the Kool-Aid, as Donnie had once put it. Ava was over the moon about her transfer to Elm Street, and as far as the fourteen-year-old was concerned, Wonderland was the next best thing to a One Direction concert.

"It happened just like that, Mom," her daughter said, snapping her fingers. "I got the email this morning. I must have made a good impression on Bianca Bishop. That's the CEO," she added, as if Vanessa didn't know. "I can't wait to tell Katya and McKenzie. And you want to know what the best part is?"

"What?"

"No more purple uniform." Ava's eyes were alight with triumph. "Elm Streeters wear all black, and the

T-shirts have a white clown face on the front. I mean, I would wear the T-shirt *anyway*. It's, like, a genuinely cool shirt."

"That's amazing, honey." Vanessa was delighted for her daughter, even though she suspected Oscar might have played a hand in this. But that was best kept to herself, because Ava was finally speaking to her again. "Who's Katya?"

"My friend from work." Ava was practically bouncing, high on excitement and teenage hormones. "She starts at Seaside Academy in September, too. She's sleeping over tonight, by the way. Her shift ends the same time as mine, so you can pick us both up. You'll like her. Her parents are Russian, and they're even stricter than you are. They only said she could sleep over because Katya told them you're the deputy chief." She paused. "Who would have thought your job would actually be a good thing for my social life?"

With everything at home much better, Vanessa decided it was best not to complicate her life further by adding a man to the mix. Oscar Trejo had called earlier, politely inquiring about Wonderland's security hard drive, which was still in Seaside PD's possession. Vanessa debated whether to email him or call him back. Email would be a lot less intimate, but a phone call seemed more professional.

Oscar answered on the first ring, and without preamble, she politely informed him that they needed to hang on to the hard drive as her detective was still combing through it. The security footage hadn't been helpful in the Homeless Harry case—which was why she'd originally asked for it—but she did need it for the Wonder Wheel Kid case. Blake Dozier was officially a missing person, and the park was the last place he was seen anywhere. Oscar said he understood and asked how the investigations were going. She replied that it was too soon to tell. Then the conversation changed.

"I want to see you again," Oscar blurted.

She closed her eyes. "We already discussed this—"

"Let's discuss it again," he said. "I want to see you. Have dinner with me. We'll eat, talk, not get drunk, get to know each other."

"I have a lot of baggage, Oz. More than you can handle."

"You need to let me decide what I can and can't handle," Oscar said. "You don't think I have baggage? Who doesn't?"

"The Wonder Wheel Kid is an active case. It would be . . . inappropriate of me to spend time with you. On a personal level, I mean."

"Am I suspect in his disappearance now?"

"Of course not," she said, caught off guard. "You were with me the night he climbed the wheel."

"Then why is it inappropriate?"

"Because . . ." Vanessa couldn't seem to come up with a good reason. "It just is."

"Vanessa—"

"I'm sorry, Oz." She hung up before she could change her mind.

The best way to get Oscar Trejo out of her head was to throw herself into her work. If she was using her job as an excuse not to get involved with him, then she'd damn well better *do* her job, even though it was her day off and she was at home. She turned her attention to Kyle Grimmie, the kid that her old friend Jerry had told her about on the phone the other night. Kyle had gone missing during a concert at Wonderland's Bandstand, three years after Tyler Wilkins, and two years before Blake Dozier.

According to the case file, a band called The Philosopher Kings had been playing that night, and the last time anyone could remember seeing Kyle was shortly before the commotion caused by the electrical fire backstage. His belongings, normally stored in a locker inside the staff lounge, were gone. This suggested—much like Aiden and Tyler—that Kyle had left town of his own accord. Carl Weiss had conducted a few short interviews with the people who'd worked with Kyle that night, but no leads had surfaced.

Was that because there were no leads? Or because former deputy chief Carl Weiss had done yet another piss-poor job investigating this boy's disappearance? She had thought about speaking to him before, but had always gotten sidetracked. She couldn't put it off any longer. This was getting ridiculous.

Vanessa was working all four cases simultaneously, and had spent most of the last day making calls to Wonder Workers who'd known Blake, Aiden, Kyle, and Tyler. So far nothing had panned out. It was hard enough tracking down employees who'd left Seaside long ago, and when she was able to get one on the phone, they either couldn't seem to remember much, or there was simply not much to remember.

For obvious reasons, retired police officers didn't have publicly listed phone numbers, but Carl Weiss's contact information was easy enough to access once Vanessa logged into Seaside PD's system from her home laptop. A few seconds later, the phone was ringing, and she prepared herself to finally hear the voice of the man whose name was on three of the four cases she was currently looking into.

To her disappointment, the former deputy chief of Seaside wasn't home. But his wife was, and she cheerfully informed Vanessa that her husband was in Cabo San Lucas with two of his fishing buddies. It was their annual boys' trip, and he wouldn't be home for another few days.

"Would you care to leave a message?" Mrs. Weiss asked. "I assume this has something to do with Homeless Harry? That was Carl's case, you know. Aiden Cole's father called Carl all the time about the slow progress. But there just wasn't any information—it was like he upped and vanished. Poof. Gone. Then all of a sudden he turns up at the park and he's all *mauled*? By some animal? I can't even imagine. How did his father take the news? I'm sure he was—"

"Thank you, ma'am. I won't keep you. I'll try calling your husband again in few days."

"We should have lunch sometime," Mrs. Weiss said. "Are you a member of the Seaside Racquet Club? I play tennis there twice a week, and the café makes wonderful lettuce wraps if you're doing the low-carb thing. You're new in Seaside, aren't you? It's important you get acquainted with the right people. Did you receive a welcome package when you moved in?"

"I did not, ma'am, no," Vanessa said.

"Now, see, that's exactly why I stepped down as the head of the welcoming committee, because no one seems committed to doing their job." On the other end, Mrs. Weiss clucked. "I also have a weekly mah-jongg group if you're into—"

"Oh, my other phone is ringing," Vanessa said, which of course it wasn't. "It was wonderful talking to you, Mrs. Weiss. I'm sure we'll speak again." She disconnected quickly.

She needed a break. Maybe it wouldn't be the worst thing to put the files away for a bit and actually use her day off as a day off. For the first time in a long time, she had nowhere to go and nowhere to be. John-John was at day camp. Ava was working her first shift somewhere on Elm Street. It might be nice to go out and do something normal. Go shopping. Grab coffee. Get a pedicure. Or call Oscar Trejo back, tell him she'd changed her mind, and that she was up for a little afternoon delight if he was.

The doorbell rang, and her crazy thought evaporated. "Saved by the bell," she said to herself with a small laugh.

She padded to the door to see who it was. This time of the afternoon, it was probably a delivery. Maybe Jerry's file had finally arrived. She pulled back the sheer curtain to peer out the window, and let out a squeal of delight.

The man standing on her porch was skinny, six four, with a short, neatly trimmed Afro. His arm was raised as if he'd been about to ring the doorbell again. Their eyes met, and a grin spread over his face, white teeth bright against his brown skin. She flung open the door and threw herself at him.

"Didn't think you were going to answer the door," Jerry Isaac said in his hoarse baritone, laughing. "My next stop was the beach."

Vanessa pulled back to look at her friend. She hadn't seen him in six months, and the former Seattle PD detective looked really good. For the first time in years, he wasn't wearing a turtleneck. The scar at his throat, exposed by the loose T-shirt he was wearing, was still visible, but it had faded to a flat, slightly pink line.

"Am I dreaming?" She was unable to keep the excitement out of her voice. "What are you doing here?"

"I said I'd FedEx Tyler Wilkins's file to you." He lifted up an old file folder. "Consider me FedEx, pretty lady."

She hugged him again. "God, am I glad you're here," she said. "I was about to do something really stupid, and you just saved me."

"I'm not even going to ask."

"Come in," she said. "I've got food, I've got drinks, we can sit and talk and catch up—"

"Slow down," he said, laughing. "I'm here all week, honey. Decided I deserved a little beach time and so I've got me a room at the White Oaks Inn. They had a last-minute cancellation and I called at exactly the right time."

"White Oaks Inn?" She gave Jerry her best dirty look. "What, my house isn't good enough for you? Cancel it. You can take John-John's room and he can bunk in the living room. He likes doing that, anyway."

"I do that, people will say we're in love." Jerry grinned at her. "Hell, even I know how fast rumors spread in Seaside and I don't even live here. Honey, I'm fine with the inn. It's walking distance to the beach, and from what I remember, they do a mean sausage and waffles in the morning." He patted his nonexistent stomach. "That should help fatten me up."

"Well, at least come in and let me make you some lunch."

"I was thinking we could go out. I thought I'd stop by the Devil's Dukes, say hello to Tanner. Why don't you come with? I'm sure he'd love to see you." There was a gleam in Jerry's eye.

"Love to see me?" Vanessa reached for her purse. "Are you being sarcastic? Both times I've seen that man, he's yelled at me."

"I think that means he likes you."

"Oh, stop," Vanessa said.

"Too soon?" Jerry suddenly looked embarrassed. "Shee-it. I'm not here five minutes and already my foot's lodged in my mouth. It hasn't been that long since John—"

"Don't be silly," Vanessa said with a smile. She followed Jerry out to the driveway. "That's not what I meant. I'm a cop. He's a biker and an ex-outlaw. Not exactly a match made in heaven."

"Whatever you say."

"I'll drive." She unlocked the unmarked. "You're really here for a week?"

"Yes, ma'am," Jerry said. "Talking to you got me all riled up about Tyler again, and I feel bad that I never looked into Kyle Grimmie when Tanner asked me to. Maybe I could have prevented the next two boys from disappearing. Or maybe not, I don't know. But what I do know is I'm not going home until I figure out what happened to Tyler Wilkins, once and for all."

TWENTY-ONE

In his office at Wonderland, Oscar looked down at the number he'd scrawled on the scratch pad in front of him. Wendy Kerse, the loan officer from the bank in Seaside, had left a voice mail on his cell phone asking him to call her back. It was, of course, regarding the loan he'd applied for to buy the restaurant by the beach. But he couldn't determine from her tone whether the news would be good or bad, and he was afraid to find out.

Taking a breath, he called her anyway.

"Oz, great news. You've been approved," Wendy Kerse said. "I'm sorry it took so long, but I got you an interest rate at a point lower than I originally quoted."

"That's . . . fantastic." Oscar couldn't speak for a few seconds as he processed this news. "Thank you. Thank you so much."

"I'll have the paperwork ready for you in an hour or so, so come in anytime and we'll get everything signed. It should be a quick escrow so you'll have the keys in thirty days. Congratulations."

"Thank you, Wendy."

"Anytime." There was a slight pause, and when she spoke again, her voice sounded a little softer. "Listen, if you're here around noon, we could do the paperwork over lunch. The café right next door does a great tuna melt."

"I . . ." Oscar was thrown. Was she suggesting a date? Wendy Kerse was a few years younger than he was, and quite attractive, and ordinarily he would have been interested. But his thoughts were still with Vanessa, and he had a feeling that if he was spotted out with the bank officer—something that was bound to happen—it would kill any chance of anything happening with the deputy chief.

"I'm sorry, I actually have a lunch meeting. But I can come near the end of the day, if that works." He purposefully did not suggest having lunch at another time.

She got the hint. "Of course." She spoke a little too quickly. "See you then."

He hung up, and a moment later, a silly grin spread across his face.

Goddammit, he was about to own his own restaurant. Cuban and Spanish food, live music, an expanded patio for breezy summer dinners, maybe even a small dance floor—he could see it all in his head. El Mago would be the start of a new life.

He swiveled his chair to face the window, looking down at the park below. Was he finally ready to leave this place? He'd be walking away from a good salary, generous benefits, and a job he knew so well he could do it in his sleep. But that was the problem, wasn't it? Could he spend the next twenty years of his life at a job he could do without thinking?

His intercom buzzed.

"Good, you're there," Bianca said when he answered. Instantly, Oscar's happy buzz faded. "I need to talk to you in my office. Now."

"Can it wait?" he said. "I'm right about to—" There was no point in finishing his sentence. She'd hung up already.

Cursing, he stepped out of his office and into the main waiting area, where Jamie was seated at the reception desk. She looked up, her thick black-framed glasses perched at the tip of her nose.

"When did Bianca get in?" He kept his voice low.

"Just now."

"What kind of mood is she in?"

Jamie rolled her eyes and pushed her glasses farther up her face. "The same mood she's always in. Hurried and bossy, with a side of mildly annoyed."

Oscar stifled a sigh. "Thanks for the heads up."

"Why does she want to see you?"

"I was going to ask you that."

"Why would I know? She doesn't tell me anything." Jamie frowned. "Quit standing there and skedaddle. Or do you want to add 'pissed off' to the menu?"

She had a point. A few seconds later, Oscar was down the hall and at Bianca's door.

The CEO was sitting on the small sofa near the far window, legs crossed primly, the view of Wonderland unobstructed behind her. Of course her office had the best view of the park, second only to her apartment on the top floor.

Not that he'd been inside her apartment for a while.

"Close the door, Oz."

He did as he was told. "Everything okay?" he asked.

She directed him to sit, and he took a seat on the opposite end of the sofa, as far away from her as possible. She always made him just a little bit nervous, although he supposed that was part of the attraction. But all that was in the past. Now there was someone new he couldn't stop thinking about.

"I just called Earl Schultz and got an update on the Homeless Harry case," she said. "They're still investigating, Oz."

"Of course they are," Oscar said. "It's a homicide now."

"And the Wonder Wheel Kid?" Bianca stared at him, her face unreadable. "They're still investigating him, too. Earl's been doing the best he can to deflect attention away from the park, but that's getting harder to do considering their pictures are splashed all over the Internet."

"Give it time." He did his best to sound reassuring. "It'll die down."

"Once something's on the Internet, it's there forever." The CEO's eyes narrowed slightly. "Earl told me the new deputy chief's been working on both cases. What's your take on her?"

"I don't know anything about her." Oscar shifted slightly. Bianca knew nothing about his night with Vanessa, and he intended to keep it that way for as long as possible. "Why would I?"

"You talked to her for a while the other day, didn't you? When she was here at the park. What was your impression of her?"

"She's . . ." Oscar thought hard, not wanting to say the wrong thing. "She's very professional. She seems to know what she's doing."

"But the surveillance footage didn't show anything, right?"

"I watched it before I handed it over. It just showed the Wonder Wheel kid climbing, that's all."

She exhaled. "I hate that PD has our hard drive. It makes me feel very . . . exposed."

Only Bianca Bishop could take something like that personally.

"I had to give it to her," Oscar said. "It's best to cooperate, and she would have gotten a warrant, anyway."

"I looked her up," Bianca said. "She's very attractive. Recently widowed. Two kids. New in town. I imagine she's lonely. It wouldn't be the worst thing in the world if you . . . befriended her. I'm sure you were your usual charming self when you met her, but why not invite her to lunch? Or dinner? You're both single. Nothing wrong with that."

Oscar frowned. "You trying to pimp me out?"

"Jesus Christ." Bianca gave him a dirty look. "Don't be so goddamned sensitive. I'm not saying you should fuck her. I'm saying, get closer to her. She probably doesn't know many people here. She might appreciate the friendship, and we'd be able to keep tabs on how the Homeless Harry and the Wonder Wheel Kid investigations are progressing."

"I thought Earl was keeping you informed."

She pursed her lips. "Good old Earl seems to have taken a step back. He's been slow returning my calls, and when we spoke earlier, he actually encouraged me to contact the new deputy chief directly. I understand he's busy with all that city council revitalization bullshit, but I hate that I can't rely on him to give me updates in real time right now. I have to wonder if he's on his way out of the department. Did you know that the reason he hired Vanessa Castro is because she's friends with Frank Greenberg?"

"No, I didn't know that."

"Apparently our mayor and her late husband were in the army together. Mayor Greenberg made it very clear to Earl that if he didn't hire her, his job was in jeopardy. Talk about calling in a favor, since it seems like she left Seattle PD under some controversy. Apparently one of her old boyfriends is a drug dealer. And her husband might have killed himself, though the official report says he shot himself by accident. Which I suppose I understand; she does have kids. The stigma of suicide would be terrible."

"Everyone has a past, B." Oscar met Bianca's gaze with a steady one of his own. "Even you."

"I'm just saying. Get a little closer. It couldn't hurt."

Oscar sighed. He didn't know why he was even bothering to argue; Bianca would push and push until she got him to agree. He could always save himself the trouble and just tell her that he already had a relationship—of sorts—with Vanessa, but for some reason, he was feeling extremely protective of whatever it was he had with the new deputy chief. And he didn't want to tell Bianca about it because he didn't want his former lover to belittle or diminish it, something she was likely to do.

Ironically, the last woman he'd felt this protective over was Bianca herself.

"I'll see what I can do," he finally said.

"Does she know I was here at the park that night?" Bianca asked.

Oscar shook his head. "I never mentioned it. To anyone."

"Good, let's keep it that way." The CEO smiled. "Anyway, that's not the only reason I wanted to speak to you. Here," she said, handing him a letter-sized envelope. It must have been in her hand the whole time, but he hadn't noticed it. "Surprise. You've earned it."

Not understanding, Oscar took the sealed envelope and tore it open. Inside was a certified check made out to him, and the amount had four zeros attached. Nick Bishop's signature scrawl was in the bottom right corner. He stared at it, completely confused. It was a signature he hadn't seen in years. Everybody at Wonderland was paid electronically; they employed a team of accountants for that.

He looked up. "How is this—" he said, but Bianca cut him off.

"It's a bonus," she said. "I know our profits are a bit down, but that's not your fault. Cash it, you've earned it. I know we could have done this electronically, but there's such an air of ceremony in cashing a check, don't you think? Besides, when you go to the bank and deposit your bonus in person, people will know the park is doing well, and we need for people to believe that. We've taken such a beating in the media lately."

Oscar stared at her. Had she lost her mind? "I don't understand," he said.

"Come on, Oz." Bianca tilted her head slightly. "Don't play dumb with me. I was at the bank this morning. I know about the restaurant. Your loan was approved, wasn't it?"

Fuck. Was nothing confidential in Seaside? Oscar sat up straighter. "Yes, but I haven't made any final decisions. I just thought it was worth exploring. I didn't say I was actually going to do it. And if I did, it doesn't mean I'd leave the park. It would be, you know, a side thing."

As soon as he said the words, he knew it was a lie. He wanted out. He had never wanted out more than this moment.

He was so, so done.

"Oz, nobody understands more than I do what it's like to have worked here for so long." Bianca turned and looked at the view of Wonderland. "Over twenty years for you, nineteen for me. I was only seventeen when I started here. It was supposed to be a summer job. You think I thought I'd still be here almost two decades later, running this place? Sometimes I think the best thing to do would be to sell it."

"Then sell it."

Her gaze reverted back to him. "It's always a possibility, Oz. Six Flags calls every year to see if we're interested in making a deal, and I got word that Cedar Fair might be interested, too. I feel like any year could be our last year here at the park . . . at least the park as we know it. If a big corporation takes over, they won't keep us. They'll clean house and appoint a new management team. And then what would I do?"

She was unbelievable. Everything, as always, was all about her. "I'm sure you could work out a deal so that you, at least, could stay. If not, you'd move on to something else. As would I."

"Doing what? I never went to college. The park is all I know." Bianca's voice was matter-of-fact. "You're buying a restaurant, for god's sake. That's a full-time job, Oz. I went through this with Uncle Nick. I know an exit strategy when I see one."

Oscar said nothing, because there was nothing he could say to that.

"But I'm not ready to leave yet," she said. "Maybe one day, but not yet. And while I'm here, I want you to be here, with me. With Uncle Nick gone, I can't do this by myself. You know how hard it is for me to admit that."

Oscar again didn't know what to say. Nothing he was thinking at the moment was anything he could share with her.

He had his secrets, she had hers.

They sat in silence for a moment. Looking out the window again, she reached up and unfastened her signature bun from its tight coil, allowing her auburn hair to spill over her shoulders in waves. Instantly it made her look years younger, not that she was old to begin with. At thirty-six, she was twelve years younger than Oscar, and very beautiful. People often didn't notice how attractive she was because of her strict demeanor and the buttoned-up way she dressed and wore her hair.

Running her fingers through the strands, she massaged her scalp, the tension gradually easing out of her face. Her hair was almost waist length, something most people didn't realize. She rarely allowed herself to be seen wearing it loose.

With the late-morning sun on her face, she looked vulnerable. And sad. He still felt affection when he looked at her, this hellion of a girl who'd agreed to work at the park only because her uncle talked her into it. He'd watched her grow up and mature, until that one crazy night when they'd discovered each other in a physically intimate way that had changed him forever.

But he didn't love her anymore. Not that way. Finally, blessedly, it was over.

"B . . ." His voice was quiet. "I won't lie, okay? I do want the restaurant. I've been here a long time, and I need something . . . more. I'm not getting any younger, and if I don't take the risk now, I never will." He put the check back into the envelope and held it out to her.

"I'll double it," she said. She didn't take it.

"What?"

"Your bonus. I'll double it. And I'll add another ten percent to your salary."

"B, that's—"

"Okay, fifteen percent. And profit sharing. We talked about that before. You deserve a piece of this place. I'm CEO, I can make that happen." She mistook his silence for hesitation. "Okay then, twenty percent. Do the math, Oz. Twenty percent more than what you make now. Where else could you possibly make that kind of money?"

"Nowhere. But it's not about the money, goddammit." Frustrated, Oscar stood up and started pacing. "I don't need this anymore. More importantly, I don't *want* this anymore."

"What about me?" She looked directly at him. Her green eyes were sad. "You would really leave me?"

"I should have left a long time ago."

If it were anyone else, those words might have been

hurtful, but it was Bianca Bishop. She didn't feel things like other people. Because she wasn't like other people.

"I've been thinking a lot about us." She attempted a smile, but it seemed desperate and not at all sincere. "I know when we talked last year you said you wanted more from me, and I couldn't give you what you wanted. But I think I can now. I think you and I could be—"

"I've met someone."

"Oh." She was quiet for a few seconds, and then her sadness morphed into anger. "I see. So that's what this is really about. You've met someone and now all of a sudden you want a whole new life. After everything Uncle Nick's done for you. After everything *I've* done for you."

"And what exactly is that?" Now Oscar was getting angry, too. "Everything you've done for me, everything Nicky's done for me, I've paid back. And then some. I've been nothing but loyal to both of you, and to this park—"

"You'd be nothing without us." Bianca's eyes narrowed into slits. "Nothing."

"Don't do that. Don't say things you'll regret. Don't make it ugly." He tossed the check onto the table. "Keep your money. I'll stay till we find someone to replace me."

"I thought you loved me, Oz." She reached for his hand.

He stopped in his tracks. "I did love you. But you never loved me back, I see that now. Everything I've done, I did for the wrong reasons. And you've never been grateful. You were too busy fucking your little Wonder Worker boy toys."

"*What?*"

"You think I don't know about that?" He extracted his hand from hers. "I know you were involved with Blake Dozier. You were upstairs, in your apartment, all night that night. Were you with him before he disappeared?"

"I—" Bianca seemed completely flustered. "No, of course not. I would never . . . I mean, we did . . . I had nothing to do with his disappearance."

"I didn't ask if you did. But thanks for confirming that you were sleeping with him."

She turned red. "It's none of your business."

"Holy shit," Oscar said. He took a step back, the realization dawning on him. "That's why Blake climbed the Wonder Wheel. That's why he did it wearing his uniform. He knew a stunt like that would get him fired, but he didn't care. *You're* the one he was giving the finger to. It was his way of telling you to fuck off. Are you the reason he's missing?" He stopped, then held up a hand. "You know what, don't answer that. I really don't want to know."

"You're so angry with me." Bianca's smile was sad. "Oz, please. Let's try again. Give me another chance."

Oscar gave her a sad smile of his own. "I've given you enough," he said. "I'm done."

TWENTY-TWO

Vanessa sat impatiently inside her office at the department, waiting for the chief of police to finish up his phone call. Earl Schultz had scheduled a status meeting with her but he was running fifteen minutes behind, which ordinarily wouldn't be a big deal, but she had plans to meet Jerry for an early dinner. They were heading over to Wonderland to surprise Ava, who still hadn't seen Jerry yet, and then the three of them would pick up John-John from day camp.

Her head was throbbing slightly from the day before. She and Jerry had spent her afternoon off with Tanner Wilkins, first at the Devil's Dukes, and then at the Monkey Bar for a late lunch, a local spot Vanessa had never heard of that served the best burger she'd ever tasted. If Tanner liked Vanessa in the way that Jerry had suggested, she definitely didn't see it. The man was certainly nicer to her than he'd been at the beginning, but the conversation had focused on his son. The three of them had gone over Jerry's notes and Tyler's police file, dissecting every detail surrounding the boy's disappearance, trying to find something—anything—that might have been missed. They hadn't come up with any new theories, and it was disheartening.

There was a knock on her office door. "I got something, Deputy," Donnie said.

Vanessa perked up. "You found Glenn Hovey?"

"No, sorry, nothing new there." Stepping in, the young detective closed the door behind him. "You got a minute?"

"Earl's going to summon me at some point, but he's already running late, so yes, I do." She smiled at him. "What's up?"

"I know you'd mentioned sending the Wonderland surveillance footage to an outside forensics expert, but you don't need to now. I watched the footage a dozen times and was about to give up on it, but something kept gnawing at me, so I went over all of it again." Donnie placed a thumb drive on her desk. "Did Oscar Trejo explain to you how their security system works?"

"Not really." Vanessa reached for her coffee and took a sip. "All I know is it's old and pathetic, and he didn't disagree."

"It's definitely both those things." Donnie sat down. "The cameras are a hot mess. Some of them work, but not all of the time. Some don't work at all. The picture quality, as you know, is shit. The computers are supposed to be recording everything from every camera all the time, but the system is buggy, so it only records some of the time. The system is also set to erase every twenty-four hours—"

"Twenty-four?" Vanessa almost choked on her coffee. "Then what's the point of recording at all?"

"Twenty-four," Donnie repeated. "Which means if you hadn't grabbed the hard drive when you did, we might have lost everything that happened the morning Blake Dozier took his infamous selfie."

"But it wasn't helpful anyway." Vanessa frowned. "We couldn't see anything. And the video cut out."

"I don't think it did cut out, actually. I think someone stopped the recording. On purpose."

She stared at him. "Don't tease me."

"I don't know how much you know about computers—"

"Very little. You need to explain it to me like I'm a five-year-old, and not get technical, because I won't understand it anyway."

"Fair enough." The detective leaned forward, rubbing the back of his head like he always did when he was thinking, a sure sign his brain was firing on all cylinders. "Okay, so when something's deleted on a hard drive, that doesn't necessarily mean it's gone. A lot of stuff is retrievable if you know where to find it. When I went back and looked at the footage, and I mean really looked, like a techie would, I discovered three things. One, the camera in the midway that was pointed toward the wheel didn't actually cut out. Otherwise it would have continued recording static, or showed nothing. I think someone stopped it from recording, on purpose. Which tells us that someone with access to the security office was in the park that night."

"Glenn Hovey."

"He'd make the most sense, but really it could be anyone with access to the admin building. Two," Donnie said, getting ramped up, "the system didn't cooperate when that person pressed stop. The recording glitched, kind of like a hiccup, and then it just continued recording. And it recorded for approximately one more hour."

Vanessa was beginning to get excited. "Please oh please, tell me you were able to retrieve that hour."

"Unfortunately, no."

"Shit."

"Whoever it was came back to the security office and checked it to be on the safe side—which was smart—and then erased that extra portion. And then for good measure, wiped it again."

"I knew it was too good to be true."

"All but two and half minutes, that is."

"*What?*" Vanessa said.

"I was able to retrieve two and a half extra minutes." Donnie was triumphant. "Because of that stupid glitchy hiccup, whoever tried to wipe that portion of the drive missed that part. Which means that the shitty security system—for all its dated and archaic ridiculousness—is the reason we have those two and a half minutes. They were deleted, but not wiped, and so I was able to get them back."

"Nice work, Detective." Vanessa grinned. "So? Don't keep me in suspense. What did you see?"

"Stick this into your hard drive." Donnie came around to her side of the desk. She inserted the thumb drive into her computer and the video began to play. "I copied just this portion of it so you can see it real quick."

They both watched her monitor. The video started with a repeat of Blake Dozier reaching the top of the wheel, and then taking selfies. His arms were extended while he used his cell phone to snap several pics.

"I never fail to get vertigo watching this," Donnie said. "I'm sorry, but this kid is nuts."

"Agreed."

The video then glitched slightly, just as the detective said, and then after a couple of seconds, it continued. "Okay, we're in overtime. Watch closely."

Vanessa did. At first it was more of the same. Blake appeared to be typing into his phone, both hands now. Two minutes passed.

"Based on the timestamp, this is probably when he was uploading the photos to Twitter and Facebook," Donnie said. "Okay, right now. Watch. Wait for it . . . wait for it . . . there."

The video went black.

"Did you see it?" Donnie said.

"That he lost his balance?" Vanessa was confused.

"Because that's what it looked like to me. It almost looked like he was about to slip."

"Yeah, but did you see *why* he lost his balance? Let's watch it again." The detective rewound it back about twenty seconds. "Watch closely. Don't look at Blake. Watch the spokes of the wheel. Makes it easier to spot what's happening."

Vanessa focused on the spokes as Donnie instructed, and a few seconds later, she saw it. "Holy shit. Did the wheel *move?*"

"At least a foot, by my guess." Donnie paused the video. "At that height, that could have been enough to cause him to slip. The bars between the spokes he was standing on are thin, and slanted. It would have been hard enough to keep his balance with the wheel moving."

"But he didn't fall." Vanessa stared at the screen. "If he had, his body would have splattered all over the midway. And if that had happened, no way could anyone have cleaned it up that fast. We would have found traces of it when we processed Homeless Harry."

"Right. If Blake's dead, he's dead some other way. But this footage does prove that someone turned on the Wonder Wheel while he was on it." He went back around the desk and sat down again. "When I worked at the park way back when, you needed a key to turn on the Wonder Wheel's motor. Whoever killed Blake had access to that key, which, from what I remember, was kept in a box in the maintenance building."

"Which is just off the midway, right? Gray brick structure?"

"That's the one. Whoever's in charge of ride maintenance each day has to inspect the Wonder Wheel first. If it checks out okay, the key is signed out to whichever operator is working the first shift."

"And does the key stay in all day?"

"Usually. Whoever worked the last shift then checks the key back into maintenance."

"So what you're saying," Vanessa said, thinking hard, "is that for the wheel to move, someone had to *make* it move, and to do that, they'd have to know where to get the key. Blake's weight couldn't have caused it to rotate?"

"No way. That wheel weighs, like, two hundred and fifty thousand pounds." Seeing the look on Vanessa's face, the detective shrugged sheepishly. "I looked it up."

"Good work. This is a break in the case, for sure. It looks like someone was trying to kill Blake." Vanessa drummed her fingers on the desk. "It had to be Glenn Hovey. He was the only person scheduled to be there that night. He has complete access to the park after hours, and obviously the security office, and he'd know exactly which cameras worked and which ones didn't. He'd also know how to delete footage off the hard drives. He probably knows how to operate the rides. Not to mention, he watches porn during his shifts and his neighbor thinks he's a creep. And lastly—and this is the big one—*where the hell is he*? It all fits. At the very least, I can charge him with the murder of Aiden Cole."

"Congratulations Hovey, wherever you are," Donnie said. "You've just graduated from a person of interest to an official suspect."

Vanessa's intercom buzzed, and Earl's voice blared through the speaker on her phone. "Ready for you."

She gave Donnie a look. "Well, this should be fun. And here I was worried I didn't have anything new to report."

"The chief isn't going to like that someone murdered the Wonder Wheel Kid at his precious park." Donnie rubbed his head. "Don't envy you having to be the one to tell him that."

"I'm not going to be the one." Vanessa gave him a sweet smile. "Come on, techie. Get your ass up. I'll let you take all the credit."

TWENTY-THREE

Under the Clown Museum

Blake had been out of food for a while now. How long, exactly, he couldn't say, but he knew that every part of his body was hurting. He was doing his best to stay hydrated, drinking as much water as he could every chance he got, but it wasn't enough. The candy bars, cookies, and wrapped sandwiches hadn't lasted more than a couple of days, and he was in agony once again.

Food and escape were all he thought about, all day long. He could see why solitary confinement was an effective punishment. Deprived of everything but the basics, you could drive yourself mad just sitting alone all day, being forced to think your thoughts. There was nothing to distract you, nothing to keep you from mentally dying, and the time dragged so slowly it felt as if the world had stopped spinning on its axis.

But at least guys in prison got an hour a day

outside in the fresh air, where there was sunshine. At least guys in prison could read books to pass the time. At least guys in prison—murderers, child molesters, drug dealers—had three square meals a day, clean clothes, showers, and warm blankets. They were not subjected to endless hours in the dark, where there was no concept of day or night, and you had only the stench of your own body to keep you company.

Blake was wracked with another spasm. He clutched his stomach and moaned. Holy fuck, the hunger was terrible. It was almost as if his entire body was eating itself to stay alive, and no amount of water would make the spasms stop. He cried out again as the pain overtook him, then started to sob into the bare mattress.

Anything was better than this. Anything.

A small sound caught his attention, a rustle of some kind. Blake forced himself to calm down so he could hear it. The only light in the tunnel was coming from the corridor to the right of his cell, and he'd assumed it was a slowly dying lightbulb based on the way it flickered. Sometimes he heard sounds coming from that direction, too, like the Wonderland jingle that had played when he first woke up here. But since he'd never heard it again, he thought maybe he'd imagined it.

But the rustling sound right now was real. Trying to ignore the cramps in his legs, Blake got out of bed and walked toward the metal bars. On the cement floor, a one-liter Camelbak thermos was rolling toward him, coming from the same direction where the lightbulb occasionally flickered. The thermos was not unlike the one Blake kept in his backpack at all times. Made of transparent blue plastic, he saw right away that it wasn't filled with water. Nor did it appear empty.

Crouching down, he reached between the bars of the cell and picked it up. Several mini candy bars were stuffed inside, the same ones that had been tossed to him by his captor the other day. He twisted off the lid and shook them out. There were five—three Twix and two Three Musketeers. Tearing the wrapper off of one of the Twix bars, he ate it quickly, and then ate another.

Forcing himself to stop, he looked out into the tunnel, where it was dark.

"Hello?" Blake called out, not feeling it was necessary to shout. He kept the volume of his voice moderate; wherever the candy bars had come from, it couldn't have been too far away. Nevertheless, his voice echoed slightly throughout the tunnel. "Hello? Is anyone there?"

No answer.

"Hello?" He didn't dare speak any louder, for fear that whoever had brought him here would come back and take away the food that quite possibly he wasn't allowed to have. "If you're out there, please say something. Hello?"

Still no answer. He emptied the bottle, putting the candy bars into his pocket. He screwed the lid of the thermos back on and placed it on the floor outside the bars. It hadn't rolled very fast when it had appeared in front of his cell, so when he rolled it back, he did his best to approximate the same speed.

"My name's Blake," he said. "Thank you for the candy bars. Whoever you are, I'd really like to talk to you."

Another moment of silence passed, and then softly, music began to play. It was coming from the same direction as the candy bars had, and that's when Blake realized that the dim flickering light he'd seen was not from an aging lightbulb. It was from a TV.

It hit him then, and he felt like smacking himself for not realizing it sooner. There was *another* cell beside his, and whoever was in it, their TV worked. There was a comedy on, judging from the faint sounds of canned laughter. Instantly Blake was jealous. A working TV would make all the difference down here. Just to be sure, he reached up and pushed the button on his own TV again, but it still didn't turn on.

Another hunger cramp seized him, and Blake unwrapped his third candy bar. The other two he needed to try and save, because who knew when he'd be fed again. Whoever was in the next cell probably had his own ration, and Blake would have to do better the next time his captor arrived with food.

His pressed his face against the cold metal bars, wishing his head fit through so that he could get a glimpse of who was beside him . . . or at least get a glimpse of their TV. The light continued to flicker, dimly illuminating the section of the corridor to the right of him that was normally always dark.

The flickering light caught something in the corridor. Curious, Blake strained to make out what it was. He squinted. Lost it. Squinted again. Saw it. Then felt the horror rise up inside him, threatening to gag him, threatening to unleash the little bit of food he'd just consumed, which he couldn't afford to vomit up.

A dead body lay about ten feet away.

Its clothes were in tatters, an emaciated grimace carved into its decaying face, and the hollow spaces where its eyes once were stared directly at Blake, seeing nothing.

He screamed.

TWENTY-FOUR

The pizza box was in Ava's hands as Vanessa came down the stairs, and she felt her daughter's scrutiny.

"Hot date?" Ava's voice was dry.

"Does that mean I look nice?" Vanessa asked, hopeful.

Her daughter shrugged. "You look all right. Those sandals new?"

Vanessa looked down at her feet. She was wearing black strappy sandals with three-inch heels, black leggings, and a loose gray tunic top. "I bought them a year ago, I think. Haven't worn them till now. You approve?"

"They're okay." Then, grudgingly, "What size are they?"

"Eight," Vanessa said. "You could wear them. You walk better in heels than I do, anyway."

"Can Katya sleep over?"

"Again?" Vanessa frowned. "Why don't you just hang out with John-John tonight? He was looking forward to it."

"Katya's an only child," Ava said. "She'd probably love to hang out with John-John, too."

"Nice try," Vanessa said. "You two have been doing a lot of sleepovers. Take the night off and spend some quality time with your little brother. Please."

"Fine." Ava took the pizza into the kitchen without a word. Vanessa allowed herself a small smile as she reached for her purse to touch up her lipstick. You never knew which way it was going to go with teenage girls.

Little boys, on the other hand, were so much easier. John-John came bounding out of the kitchen, a slice of pepperoni pizza in his hand. He'd picked off all the mushrooms, because some kid at day camp had told him mushrooms were a fungus, and that a fungus was like a disease.

His face lit up when he saw her. "You look nice! Where you going?"

"I told you already. Jerry's still in town. We're going to have dinner and talk about work stuff."

"Can I come? I like Jerry."

"He likes you, too, but not this time, buddy. You're going to stay home with your sister and eat pizza and watch movies. You be good and do what she says, okay?"

He frowned and rubbed his head with his free hand, and his little face was so cute she had to refrain from kissing him. He was starting to squirm away from her kisses, which broke her heart. He was growing up way too fast.

"Can we watch *Batman*? It's on Netflix."

"Ask your sister. If it's okay with her, it's okay with me."

"Avie, can we watch *Batman*?" he hollered.

"Yeah," she said from the other room. "But you're not allowed to talk during the movie. That's the rule."

"Okay." Turning back to Vanessa, he whispered, "She's bossy."

"Yes, she is." She laughed. "Bed by nine, okay?"

"Why?" Her seven-year-old's voice instantly took on a whiny tone. "Jaden gets to stay up till ten."

"That's why Jaden has a hard time waking up for day camp," Vanessa reminded him. "Remember how his mommy couldn't wake him and he missed swim time the other morning?"

"I guess. How come Avie doesn't have to go to day camp?"

"Because Ava's a big girl and she has a job," Vanessa said. "When you're older, you'll have a summer job, too."

"I wish I could be at Wonderland all day. I'm going to work there when I'm fourteen." John-John said this like it was news to her. "I think it's the greatest place in the world. But not in the Clown Museum like Avie. Too scary. I want to make the roller coasters go zoom. Jaden says his big brother is a roller coaster op'rator and he gets to push the button that makes it go and apparently it's so much fun."

"The Clown Museum's fun," Ava called from the kitchen. "I get to dress up in a costume and scare people all day. It's way better than wearing that fugly purple uniform like everyone else."

"What's fugly?" Vanessa asked her son.

"It means ugly," John-John said. "But with an *f*."

"Oh." Vanessa didn't understand. It came to her a few seconds later, and she sighed. *Fugly* was teenage speak for *fucking ugly*. She bent down and gave John-John a kiss on the forehead. He managed to stay still while she did it, but just barely, and not without making a face. "That's not a nice word. I don't want you to use that word."

He squirmed away and went back to eating his pizza.

"I'm locking the door behind me. I should be home around ten. Did you hear that, Ava?" she called.

Her daughter had moved to the living room, where her voice could barely be heard over the sounds of the TV. "Yeah."

"I have my phone with me. Text or call if anything happens."

"We're fine, Mother," Ava said. "Nothing bad is going to happen."

"You know what I'm talking about, Ava." Vanessa's tone was stern. They'd had another discussion earlier that day about her daughter staying safe at the park. "You know what I'm working on right now. Do not answer the door, and if someone calls, do not say that I'm not home."

"I *know*!"

Vanessa took one last look at herself in the full-length mirror and fingered the bouquet of pink roses she'd placed earlier on the hallway table. Then she left, locking the door behind her and tugging at it to make sure it was really secure. She used to do the same thing when they lived in Seattle, and not in a million years would she have thought she'd have the same concerns in Seaside, the smallest, prettiest town in southwestern Washington.

• • •

The lights inside the Tango Tavern were low. Vanessa stood near the front entrance for a moment and scanned the room. It was maybe two-thirds full, and she didn't see anyone she knew. All tourists, all people passing through. Which was why she'd chosen this place the first time.

She had lied to her kids. She wasn't meeting Jerry for dinner; her old friend had other stuff to do.

Taking a seat at the bar, she ordered a Ninkasi IPA, always her beer of choice when it was available. She was halfway through it when the doors opened and Oscar Trejo walked in. Her heart skipped a beat, then began thumping painfully to make up for it.

He was alone as he said he'd be, dressed in a pair of dark blue jeans and a button-down with the sleeves rolled up. He walked right up to her, ignoring the admiring glances that several of the female patrons were giving him. He looked good, and smelled even better.

"Thanks for meeting me," Oscar said. "I wasn't sure you'd show up."

"Well, you're persistent, I'll give you that." Vanessa gave him a small smile. "Three voice mails, six texts, and a dozen pink roses. I should have held out for the singing telegram."

"That would have been tomorrow, had you said no to tonight." He grinned, sliding onto the bar stool beside hers. The bartender approached. "What she's having."

A moment later they were clinking bottles. "To us," he said.

"I wasn't aware there was an us," Vanessa said. "Oz, I barely know you. You barely know me. We had a fun time here the other night, and that's all it was ever supposed to be."

"Ouch." Oscar pretended she had just stabbed him in the heart. "You are not the woman I remember from that night. She was a lot more easygoing than you are."

"She was also 'Lynn,' remember?" Vanessa played with her beer bottle. "Lynn, who didn't talk about anything personal. Lynn, who wasn't the deputy chief of police of Seaside. All I wanted that night was some company. As did you."

"I like you." Oscar swiveled in his stool so he was facing her directly. "I don't care what your name is. I don't care what you do for a living. I like *you*. I know we just met. But so what? When I woke up the next morning and you were gone, I was disappointed, and I'm never disappointed. Usually all I feel is relief. And then when I saw you again, even though the circumstances were terrible, I can't explain it . . . I was just so happy to see you."

He touched her arm. She flinched slightly, and he removed it.

"I'm coming on really strong, I know that," Oscar said. "But I have a feeling that if I don't, you won't take me seriously. And life's short. I've wasted a lot of time doing things that don't make me happy, and I don't want to do that anymore. I want to do things that feel right. I want to trust my gut. And my gut tells me that if I don't go all out trying to convince you to give me a shot, I'll regret it. And I don't know about you, but I can't afford to have any more regrets."

Vanessa met his gaze. Every word he was saying rang true. She knew exactly what he was talking about. She was filled with so much regret, things she wished she could change, things she'd do over in a heartbeat if she could.

But she couldn't. In life, there were no do-overs. There was just right here. Right now.

"Okay," she said. "I'm going to lay it all out, and I want you to listen, okay?"

He winced. "That bad, huh?"

"That's up to you to decide," Vanessa said. "I really have no business getting involved with anybody right now. My husband died six months ago, suddenly and tragically. We did not have a good marriage, not for a long time, and then he died, and it's been hard on my kids, and hard on me. I left my last job on the verge of being fired because a boy I loved when I was a teenager grew up to be the Pacific Northwest's largest drug dealer and he used our relationship to manipulate his trial, which was great for him because he got acquitted, and terrible for me because it tainted my reputation. I had to call in a favor to get this job, which involved a lot of begging and pleading, neither of which I enjoy or am particularly good at. I moved my kids out of a house and city they loved because there were too many bad memories there, because we needed a fresh start, otherwise we weren't going to make it. I've had more one-night stands than I can count; one was during my marriage, and there've been a whole bunch since. The former makes me an adulteress and the latter makes me a slut, neither of which should be appealing to someone like you, who seems to be looking for something more profound than I'm able to give you. I don't trust anybody, and in general, I think people are liars and cheaters, because I am, and it's not fair to hold anyone else to a higher standard than I hold myself. I am about the worst person you could ever be with outside of a one-night stand, and if you were smart, you'd get off that bar stool and run."

A silence fell between them.

"You done?" Oscar finally said. "Because that was a really great monologue and I wish I was as articulate as you, but I'm not. You think I don't have baggage? You think you can scare me off? I wasn't looking for your autobiography. I don't give a shit about your past. We all have one. All I care about, all that matters, is how you feel. About me. Right now. Assuming you feel anything at all."

"I don't know how I feel," Vanessa said. "Mainly because I've spent a lot of years trying not to feel things, because feelings suck. But what I know is that I haven't been able to stop thinking about you since that night. That's never happened to me, either. And all I want to do right now is stop talking, go back to your house, and get naked with you. That's what I know."

He paused for a heartbeat, then said, "Don't bother to finish your beer, I have beer at home."

He slapped a twenty-dollar bill on the counter, took her by the hand, and led her out the door.

• • •

"I can't stay the night," Vanessa said to him ten minutes later. They were back at his place, standing face-to-face in his bedroom, both fully clothed. Unlike the last time, they were both sober, and the lights were on. "I have to get home early this time."

"Okay," Oscar said.

He stared at her a moment longer, then pulled her close and kissed her deeply, his tongue entering her mouth. The kiss wasn't rough, but it wasn't exactly gentle, either; it was passionate, and urgent. Instantly, she was aroused. This didn't feel anything like it had the first time. Even though they were still very new to each other, they were no longer strangers.

His hands moved down the length of her waist to her buttocks, where he squeezed. Her hands found their way under his shirt, and she moved her palms across the small of his back to the little tuft of hair just above his ass that was pleasingly fuzzy. Their kissing grew more urgent, and she grinded herself against him.

Suddenly he pulled back. "No," he said. "I don't want us to rush. We might not have all night, but there's enough time for us to go slow. You said you wanted to be naked with me." He took a step back. "So get naked. I want to see you."

Smiling, Vanessa pulled her tunic top over her head. In the soft light of the bedroom, his eyes feasted on her. She unstrapped her sandals, then hooked her thumbs on either side of the waistband of her leggings. Slowly, she inched them down. And then she simply stood there, dressed only in her bra and panties, allowing him to see everything he wanted to see.

"God, you're beautiful," he said.

She reached behind her back and unhooked her bra, letting her breasts fall slightly to their natural drop. Her nipples were pink and erect, and he licked his lips when he saw them. Then slowly, she slid her panties down, allowing him to see all of her. She gazed back at him unself-consciously as his eyes roamed her naked body, pausing on breasts, then her navel, and then the part between her legs, freshly shaved in the shower an hour earlier.

When he spoke, his voice was thick. "Lie on the bed."

She did as he told her, lying back on the mattress with her head propped up on his pillow and her knees slightly parted. He never took his eyes off her as he undressed, first unbuttoning half his shirt, then impatiently yanking it over his head. He slid off his jeans, and then his boxer briefs. He was fully hard, and she stared at him with longing.

But before getting on top of her, he grabbed her ankles and pulled her down toward the end of the bed until her ass was resting on the edge. Spreading her legs, he dropped to his knees, and her back arched with pleasure as his tongue found her.

She climaxed after only a couple of minutes, and then he stood back up and entered her. His climax wasn't far behind. Breathing hard, he collapsed on top of her.

"I wanted that to last longer," he said, burying his face in her neck.

"It was long enough." She kissed his head. "It was amazing."

"Please tell me there'll be a next time. I need to see you again."

"We have to be careful." Vanessa stroked his hair. "I'm still working on the Blake Dozier missing persons case and the Aiden Cole homicide. Until it's closed, I can't be seen acting friendly with you. People will talk, and Seaside is a painfully small town, as I'm learning."

"What we just did was more than friendly."

"I could lose my job."

"I understand." He paused for a moment. "So how close are you to finding Blake?"

"Not as close as I'd like," she said. "But there's a good chance he's dead. We're working it like it's a homicide, because that seems to be where the evidence is pointing."

"What evidence?"

"I shouldn't be talking about it with you," she said. "I shouldn't be discussing active cases, especially now that there's a chance he was killed on park grounds. You're the VP of operations. It complicates things."

"Not for long." Oscar said. "I'm moving on soon. Bought a restaurant, going to fix it up."

"Wow." Vanessa was impressed. "You weren't kidding when you said you were moving in a different direction. I'm sure the park will be sorry to lose you."

"Maybe. But there are big changes happening over there, too. Bianca's thinking it might be time to sell the park. But keep that to yourself, okay? Can't let any rumors get out." He touched a finger to her lips.

"Mum's the word. But can Bianca make that decision? I thought it was her uncle who owned the park."

"He does. But at this point, it's in name only. He's nothing more than a signature. Bianca makes all the decisions." Oscar's face clouded over, and then it cleared and he kissed her again. "So is there anything I can do to help you find the Wonder Wheel Kid? Or anything you need to know about Aiden Cole?"

"There's an arrest warrant out for Glenn Hovey," Vanessa said. "And we're getting a search warrant for his house tomorrow morning. But keep that to yourself, okay? Can't let any rumors get out."

"Mum's the word," Oscar said, and she smiled. "I've known Hovey a long time. We both worked together under Jack Shaw. Nicky, too. We've all had our issues because of it. Hovey especially, so I guess I'm not that surprised you're arresting him."

"Did Jack Shaw . . ." Vanessa didn't know how to ask, but he was the one who'd brought it up. "Were you one of his . . ."

"We all were."

"God, I'm sorry," she said. "And yet you went back to the park?"

"We all have our way of dealing with our demons. Some people choose to run away, but we chose to face them."

"Shaw died before it could go to trial, right?"

"In a fire. House burned down. Ruled an accident, but I don't think it was," Oscar said. "Jack Shaw hurt a lot of people. A lot of people would have wanted to hurt him back."

"And I don't suppose you know who might have done it."

He raised an eyebrow. "If I did, I wouldn't tell the deputy police chief. The bastard had it coming. Everybody was relieved to see Jack Shaw dead."

"Karma."

He shook his head. "Justice."

"So is that why you've never fired Glenn Hovey?" Vanessa asked. "All that history you share?"

"Nicky believed wholeheartedly in loyalty," Oscar said. "Mind you, I don't know what he'd think about it now. Hovey's definitely gotten weirder over the past few years, especially since Nicky's been gone. Nicky was always the strong one, the rock. Bianca tries, but she's nothing like her uncle. She has her own demons. She's the one who keeps Hovey on."

"You think Hovey could be a murderer?"

"Couldn't anybody?" Oscar said.

Just like that, an image of her late husband's bloody head flashed through Vanessa's mind. The gun, hot and smoking, in her hand. The weight of John's raging threats still hanging in the air, her terror of him hurting her giving way to an even deeper fear as she realized what she'd just done. The screams inside her chest building quickly, trying to claw their way out, but she couldn't make a sound, not even a peep, because John-John was sleeping in his room on the third floor of the house. Frank Greenberg, John's best friend, coming into the garage at that exact moment, understanding immediately what had happened, and understanding that Vanessa hadn't had a choice, and that her going to jail was the last thing her kids needed after everything they'd already been through. Frank helping her position the scene to look like John had accidentally shot himself, which officially made him an accessory. Her kids believing that their dad had been careless while cleaning his gun, while everybody else secretly thought it was a suicide. Which, considering the way John had been behaving, it might as well have been.

But technically, legally, it wasn't. It was a cover-up of a cover-up, a lie on top of a lie. Vanessa knew all about demons, oh yes, she did.

"Hey. Where'd you go just now?" Oscar said.

Rather than answer the question, she reached up and pulled his head down toward hers. Their lips met, and a few minutes later, they were both breathing hard once again.

"How much time do you have?" He was panting in her ear, his hands busy under the sheets.

She glanced at the clock. "No more than a half hour."

"I won't need that long."

A few moments later he was inside her again, though Vanessa's mind was elsewhere. John was never far from her thoughts, and she imagined him looking down on her now from wherever he was, blaming her for everything, deeply disappointed because she hadn't been a better wife or a better mother, and because she hadn't been able to fix him, even though she'd tried.

She'd tried.

Recipient(s): All Wonderland
Staff
Sender: Nick Bishop
Subject: Friendships and
             Relationships, the
             Wonderland Way!

Dear Wonder Worker,

Part of the Wonderland
experience is the camaraderie
you build with your fellow
Wonder Workers. Nothing compares
to spending an entire summer
alongside hardworking, fun-loving
individuals, and it's natural to
want to socialize with your friends
after hours.

However, friendships that extend
beyond platonic are both tricky and
risky. While there's no set rule
in the Employee Handbook regarding
fraternization between coworkers of
equal levels (i.e., Wonder Worker
to Wonder Worker), a romantic
relationship can be awkward for
your fellow coworkers. Should you
choose to pursue a relationship,
please refrain from demonstrating
physical affection while working,
and please save all conversations
of a personal nature for after
hours.

Romantic relationships of any
kind between employees of differing
levels (i.e., Wonder Worker to Team
Leader) are considered a violation,
and may result in your dismissal.
Wonderland believes in providing
a safe, fair working environment
for everyone. That's the Wonderland
way!

Yours sincerely,
Nick Bishop
Owner, Wonderland Amusement
Park, Inc.

TWENTY-FIVE

Things were better between Ava and her mom. Not perfect—she couldn't imagine they'd ever be perfect—but they were better and that was good for now. That being said, if her mother had any idea where she was right now, it would pretty much destroy any goodwill they'd managed to rebuild over the past little while.

Ava had gotten off work early, but had texted her mom to say that she'd been asked to stay late, and that one of the Wonder Workers would drive her home. Her mom didn't question it—she was totally wrapped up in her job these days, and seemed distracted all the time, not that it was any different from how things had been in Seattle. In any case, there'd been no reason for Ava to say no when Xander Cameron invited her back to his dorm room to hang out.

Because it was *Xander*. Who was *eighteen*. The

boy with the blond hair and golden tan, whose eyes crinkled when he laughed, had actually invited her back to his dorm room. She had texted both Katya and McKenzie a little while ago to tell them, and both had squealed appropriately (as much as a person can using emojis and exclamation marks, anyway).

Ava was sitting sideways on Xander's small bed, and he was beside her, his long legs stretched out and resting on the floor. He hadn't been assigned a room-mate, so they had the entire room to themselves. An open bag of Cheetos sat between them, and they were drinking root beer and watching *Candyman* on his laptop, a horror movie from 1992 that had scared the bejeezus out of Ava when she'd watched it with her dad a couple of years ago.

"This movie's so old," Xander said. "Look at their hair and their clothes. This is from, like, before I was born."

"It's a classic," Ava said. "I dare you to say Candyman five times."

"No fucking way."

"Come on, do it," she said, poking him. The premise of the movie was that if you said Candyman five times in front of a mirror, it would summon a man from the depths of hell who'd died a terrible death as a slave. Who would then, of course, kill you in another terrible way. "Come on, chicken."

"Candyman, Candyman, Candyman, Candyman—" Xander stopped, dissolving into laughter. "I can't do it. Protect me. I'm scared." He pulled her closer to him.

Ava happily snuggled into him, every fiber in her body tingling. Part of her couldn't believe she was actually here, in Xander's room, alone. Yes, they were friends, and yes, they talked and hung out on breaks together at work, but he was four years older than she was. What she felt for him went a lot deeper than friendship. What he felt for her was . . . well, the truth was, she didn't know. Sometimes he treated her like a buddy. Other times he treated her like a little sister. And right now, with their bodies touching and his arms wrapped around her, it felt like something else entirely.

She looked up at him, and he looked down at her and grinned. She returned the smile, her heart thumping wildly in her chest. He held her gaze for a moment, and then his eyes flickered down.

"You have a cute nose," he said.

"You think so? I was actually thinking of getting it pierced. My mom would freak, but I wouldn't do a big piercing. Just a tiny one, for a bit of sparkle."

"You should. That would look good on you." Xander continued to hug her, his gaze moving down a little more. "You also have really nice lips. Anyone ever tell you that?"

"I always thought they were too small."

"They're not." His voice was husky. "They're just right."

He moved his head closer to hers, and she braced herself.

Oh my god it's really going to happen he's really going to kiss me Xander Cameron's going to be my first kiss oh my god I'm going to die I can't believe this is happening . . .

And then his lips met hers, and she felt like she was melting. He kissed her gently at first, and then a little harder, her insides turning to mush.

It was better, so much better, than Ava could have ever imagined. Xander's kisses tasted sweet from the root beer, and his face smelled like soap and water. She parted her lips slightly, feeling his tongue slip in, warm and soft and gentle. Yes, she liked this. She liked this a lot. Opening her mouth a little more, she met his tongue with hers, feeling every inch of her body go from warm to hot in a matter of seconds.

Then Xander's hands moved slowly up from her waist to her breasts. She almost didn't notice it until she felt his hand cup her boob. Despite herself— despite how good it felt—Ava stiffened immediately. Xander sensed the change and stopped right away, pulling back to look at her.

"Sorry," she said, a little out of breath. "Sorry, I just . . . I wasn't expecting that."

"Too fast?"

"Um . . . maybe a little. Sorry," she said again, feeling like a complete and total idiot.

"No, I'm sorry." Xander moved away from her completely. The laptop slid off the bed and he caught it just before it hit the floor. "Sometimes I forget how young you are."

"I'm not that young." Ava mentally cursed herself. "It's just, you know—"

He smiled at her. "It's okay, you don't need to explain. I don't know what I was thinking, anyway. We're just friends."

"Right . . . of course." She was quiet for a few seconds, not knowing what else to say. Just because things had moved a little quicker than she expected didn't mean she didn't want things to move at all. The kissing had been good. Scratch that, the kissing had been *great*.

You idiot! she screamed at herself silently. *You're ruining it. Fix it! Fix it now.*

She cleared her throat. "It's just . . . what if we were more than friends? I mean, I'd be okay with that."

Xander smiled again and reached for his root beer. "You're cute. But it's better that we stay friends, you know? I would hate for things to get complicated."

"I guess." Ava slumped a little. She couldn't remember the last time she'd felt so high one moment, then so defeated the next. "I mean, obviously I care about our friendship."

"Me, too." He patted her leg, and just like that, they were big brother/little sister again. "Besides, and I probably shouldn't tell you this, but . . . I'm sort of involved with someone."

He might as well have slapped her in the face. For god's sake, his tongue had been touching hers less than a minute ago, and she could still taste his root beer in her mouth. "Oh?" she said, struggling to keep her composure. "With who?"

"Can you keep a secret?"

"Sure."

"It's Bianca Bishop."

Ava thought she'd misheard him. "What?"

"Bianca Bishop," he said with a grin. "I know, it's crazy. But . . . I like her. And she likes me."

"*What?*" Ava said again, staring at him. "You're having a thing with Bianca Bishop? But she's like . . . old. And she's . . . the boss. Of, like . . . the whole park. I don't understand." She couldn't seem to process what he'd just told her. "How is this possible? I mean, are you messing with me? Are you just saying this to make me feel bad?"

"Of course not," he said. "She and I are, you know, together. I mean, it's a real thing. We're really into each other."

"I can't believe you." Furious, Ava got off the bed, looking around wildly for her knapsack. She spotted it in the corner and tossed it over her shoulder.

"See, this is why she told me not to say anything." Xander looked like he wanted to kick himself. "She told me people wouldn't understand, and she was right. But I thought that maybe you would. I thought you were mature enough to handle it, and I really needed to tell someone."

"Handle it?" Ava repeated, staring at him. Now she understood what her girlfriends meant when they said boys could be total assholes. "Seriously, is this really happening right now? Did you just stick your tongue in my mouth and then tell me that you're involved with *Bianca Bishop*?"

"I'm sorry." He looked up at her from the bed, where he was still sitting. "I'm not trying to hurt you. I think you're a cool girl, I do, it's just, I got carried away for a second."

"With her or with me?" Ava said. When he didn't respond right away, she made a sound of disgust. "You know what, don't bother to answer that. So what kind of relationship is it, anyway? With the Dragon Lady?"

"Don't call her that." Xander's tone was sharp. "She hates that. We're . . . I don't know. We're close."

"You've kissed?"

"Yeah."

"Did you hook up?"

He paused then said, "Yeah."

"More than once?"

"A few times."

"Oh my god, that's disgusting," Ava said. "She's, like, my mom's age."

"It's not this ugly thing like you're trying to make it sound." Xander got up off the bed, and he was starting to look angry. "The Bianca you know is nothing like the person she really is. When we're alone, she's totally different. I don't know how to explain it. We care about each other."

"And how long's it been going on?"

"For a while." Xander averted his gaze. "Since I started at the park."

"Oh, wow." Ava wasn't sure if she should laugh or cry. "So the rumors are true."

"What rumors?"

"People said you guys always look really cozy," Ava said. "She always says hello to you in the midway, when she doesn't talk to anyone else, ever, unless she's reaming them out for something. You know what people are saying about you? People are saying you're her boy toy, that the only reason you got the Hoop Shot gig is because the Dragon Lady's hot for you. And now it turns out you're hot for her, too." Shaking her head, Ava moved toward the door. "I gotta get out of here."

"Just stay, please," Xander said. "I thought you told your mom you weren't going to be home till later. Let's at least finish the movie. Candyman, Candyman, Candyman, Candyman, Candyman," he added with a hopeful smile.

Ava refused to laugh. "Why aren't you hanging out with your girlfriend?"

"She's busy tonight."

"So I'm your backup."

He threw his arms up over his head in frustration. "It's not like that. I care about you. I thought we were friends."

"I'm not your consolation prize." Ava had heard that line in a movie once, but she couldn't remember which one now. Nevertheless, it felt good to say it. "I'll see you at work, I guess."

"Please don't tell anyone about me and Bianca," Xander said. "She'll kill me."

Ava walked out of his dorm room, slamming the door shut behind her. That, too, felt good.

TWENTY-SIX

The warrant had come through to search Glenn Hovey's house, and Sherry Hovey wasn't exactly being cooperative.

"You people can't come here and traipse through my house and my private property." She was following Vanessa around with a cigarette in one shaking hand and a coffee in the other. There was something more than just coffee in the mug, based on the smell. "I have valuable things in here. Collector's items dating back to when the Hawks were founded. You break something, it can't be replaced. This is my house, and I do not give you my permission to search it."

"We don't need your permission, Mrs. Hovey," Vanessa said, "but I understand your concerns. We'll be careful with your things, I promise."

She nodded to Officers Nate Essex and Pete Warwick, who were starting on the main-floor bedrooms. Donnie and Vanessa would take the basement, where

Glenn Hovey slept. She had sent the young detective on ahead.

This was the first time Vanessa had set foot inside the Hovey residence, and it was just as ridiculous as the outside. Everything was Seahawks. The sofa blankets had the Seahawks logo. The throw pillows—which looked homemade—were made of old Seahawks jerseys, with the players' numbers right in the center. There were three, no, four Seahawks posters framed on the walls of the living and dining rooms. A recent picture of a beaming Sherry Hovey standing beside the current Seahawks quarterback Russell Wilson was framed above the fireplace mantel, right next to a football signed by the old quarterback, Matt Hasselbeck.

"I don't understand what you're even looking for," Sherry Hovey said. "You think Glenny killed that Homeless Harry guy? Glenny wasn't even in town."

"It's all on the search warrant, ma'am. I'm authorized to look for everything and anything pertaining to both Aiden Cole and Blake Dozier."

"Who?"

Vanessa suppressed a sigh. "Homeless Harry and the Wonder Wheel Kid."

"Why would Glenny know anything about them? I told you last time, my Glenny's a good boy. Just because he's missed a few days at work, it don't make him a murderer." Sherry Hovey looked up into

Vanessa's face. She was tiny, and her teeth were bared, reminding Vanessa of an angry Chihuahua. "Did Margie from next door tell you something about Glenny? I thought I saw you go into her house the first time you were here. She denies it, but I know what I saw."

"I can't comment on that, Mrs. Hovey," Vanessa said. "But the sooner you let me do my job, the sooner we'll all be out of here and you can resume your . . . whatever you were doing."

"Damn that Margie." The tremors in Sherry Hovey's hands caused her coffee to finally spill over. It landed on the front of her hooded sweatshirt, which was pink this time, but still emblazoned with the Seahawks logo. "That nosy woman needs to keep her damn mouth shut. She's never liked my Glenny. She keeps him away from her grandkids, but yet it's okay if Glenny drives us to the mall or comes with us to the movies."

Vanessa's cell phone pinged. Donnie Ambrose was texting her from downstairs. Found something.

"Excuse me, Mrs. Hovey." She pulled a pair of latex-free rubber gloves out of her pocket. "I need to go check on my detective."

"Don't you be touching nothing down there!" the woman hollered as Vanessa proceeded down the stairs to the basement. "Glenny don't like it when his stuff is moved around!"

Blissfully, Vanessa couldn't hear her once she got

all the way down the stairs. The basement was finished, but it looked straight out of the seventies, down to the green shag carpeting. The wood-paneled walls absorbed whatever natural light there was, which wasn't much, as the lone window tucked in the highest part of the wall was blocked by one of Sherry Hovey's blue hydrangea bushes. Though dated, the basement was clean and the furnishings sparse, a far cry from the Seahawks extravaganza on the main floor.

"Deputy?" Donnie's voice wafted from the back bedroom. The door was open, and Vanessa could see the wood chips from where the detective had kicked it in. "I had to break the door down, Hovey kept it locked. I was going to ask his mother if she had a key, but then realized if she did, Hovey wouldn't have needed to lock it."

"That's fine, the warrant covers it." Vanessa entered the bedroom. "What did you find?"

Like the outer area of the basement, Glenn Hovey's bedroom contained minimal furniture. A double bed was centered on the back wall, flanked by a nightstand on one side and a small dresser on the other. A closet with no door revealed that Hovey didn't have much of a wardrobe. Half his clothes were his Wonderland uniform—several purple golf shirts, several pairs of khaki pants and shorts, a fleece Wonderland vest, and a couple of hoodies with the Wonderland logo—and the other half was a dreary mix of sloppy-looking T-shirts, button-downs, cardigans, and jeans, all in bland colors.

Donnie had a box on the bed. It was metal, with a lock. "I found this behind the nightstand," he said. "I might have missed it because it was hidden in the wall, but a picture fell over. When I went behind the nightstand to pick it up, I noticed one of the wood panels looked off. This was tucked inside."

The picture Donnie had knocked over was a four-by-six framed photo of Glenn Hovey in better days. Compared to his current employee ID photo, this Glenn Hovey was about thirty years younger, thirty pounds lighter, and he had a full head of hair. He was standing at the front entrance of the park beside two other boys, and the big colorful sign above them said WORLD OF WONDER. Upon closer inspection, Vanessa realized that the boy on the right was a young Oscar Trejo. Oz hadn't changed much; the only real difference was that his hair was longer and shaggier, and parted in the middle à la Chachi of *Happy Days* fame.

"Any idea who the third guy is?" she asked Donnie, who glanced over at the photo.

"That's Nick Bishop," he said. "If you ever go up to the fifth floor of the admin building where the management offices are, you'll see old pictures like this framed on the wall of the reception area. Haven't seen this one, though."

"They really do go way back." Vanessa had never

seen a picture of Wonderland's owner before. He was clean-cut and handsome, with a sardonic smile that suggested he was a bit of a wise-ass. She turned her attention back to Donnie. "Okay, so what's in the box?"

"I had to pry this one open, too." Donnie flipped up the lid where the latch was now busted. "Glenn Hovey liked to keep things locked, clearly."

Vanessa looked down. "I can see why." The box was filled with a bunch of Wonderland ID cards. One by one, she picked them up, examining each card carefully. There were twenty-four in total, all belonging to teenage boys. "Hot damn."

Of the two dozen cards, five were names she recognized; the rest were unfamiliar. A tingle went down her spine. The five she knew belonged Tyler Wilkins, Kyle Grimmie, Aiden Cole, Blake Dozier, and Jack Shaw.

"Bingo," she said under her breath. "Got you, motherfucker."

She picked up Jack Shaw's ID card. The others were made of white plastic with the Wonder Worker's photo right on it and a magnetic strip running down the back. Shaw's was simply a business card with his name and picture. The date underneath his photo said May 24, 1985, which was probably the date it was issued.

"If this is in here with the others," she said, holding up Shaw's card, "and assuming these are Glenn

Hovey's souvenirs, then I think we might know who burned Jack Shaw's house down."

"That's a lot of victims," Donnie said. "Almost enough to fill a school bus. Do you think he killed all of them?"

She looked through the ID cards again, lining them up on the bed side by side, according to the dates of issue shown underneath the photos. The oldest one dated back to 1995, the year the park reopened as Wonderland. The newest one was Blake Dozier's.

"He's been doing this a long time. And they're all blond. How did I not notice that before?" Vanessa frowned. "I wonder if the rest of these boys are missing, too. Or did they turn up dead somewhere outside of Seaside?"

"That's easy enough to check into, I'll get Nate Essex on it." Donnie paused. "If they are, how much you want to bet that Carl Weiss worked some of their cases? Or maybe all?"

"Shit, you're right." Vanessa stared at the detective. "It's not just Hovey, Weiss is also a common thread in all of this. I almost forgot about him. He's in Cabo. I wonder if he's back by now."

"Did Weiss work at World of Wonder back in the day? Under Shaw?"

"Maybe," Vanessa said. "A lot of the old-timers here in Seaside did. But he's older. Oscar Trejo, Glenn Hovey, and Nick Bishop are all in their late forties now. Carl Weiss is probably in his early sixties. But that doesn't mean he doesn't know Hovey personally."

"You think they're together on this? Serial killers working in tandem?"

Vanessa thought hard for a moment, then shook her head. "I hate to make that leap. Whatever the connection, it's not coming to me yet. It will, though. My gut tells me Weiss knows more than what's in those files."

Their cell phones pinged at the same time. Checking, they both looked up at each other.

"Did you get the same message I just did?" Vanessa said.

"Only if it's the one that says Glenn Hovey's in custody in Las Vegas." Donnie grinned. "The fucker's been out of state this whole time."

"U.S. Marshals are escorting Hovey back on the first flight, and he'll be here in a few hours." Vanessa checked the time. "You okay finishing up here? I want to go to talk to Weiss, find out what he knows, once and for all. Assuming he's home."

"Yeah, I got this," Donnie said. "By the way, you'll want to stop at the store and pick up a bottle of whiskey. It'll help."

"I don't drink whiskey."

"Not for you, for Weiss." The detective chuckled. "He's more likely to talk if you get him liquored up, and he loves his whiskey. Don't let his wife see it, though. He's not allowed to drink when she's home."

"Okay, I'll pick up a bottle of . . ." She frowned. "What's a good brand?"

"A good brand is Macallan," Donnie said. "But don't waste your money on that. Jim Beam, twenty bucks, do just fine."

"Thanks for the tip." Vanessa headed for the stairs. "Owe you one."

"You can pay me back by letting me sit in when Glenn Hovey gets here," he said. "And Deputy, be careful when you talk to Weiss. Remember what I always say."

"All ears lead back to Earl," Vanessa said over her shoulder. "Got it."

TWENTY-SEVEN

On the way to Carl Weiss's house, Vanessa's cell phone rang. She picked up through the unmarked's Bluetooth, and a bunch of static blared through the speakers. "Castro."

"Uh, hi . . . this is Jacob Wei? I received a message that you called?" The voice on the other end was young, polite, and uncertain. "I'm sorry I couldn't get back to you sooner. I wasn't able to get a cell signal to check my voice mail until now."

It took Vanessa a moment to place the name. Oh, right. Jacob Wei was Aiden Cole's roommate, and she'd tried calling him twice the other day. She pulled over onto the side of the road. She was halfway to Weiss's house, but she didn't want to drive and talk at the same time. Reaching for her purse, she pulled out her notepad and pen. "Hi, Jacob. Thanks for calling me back."

"No problem. I'm working on a fishing boat, and so I don't get cell phone reception until we're back in Alaska. Uh . . . your voice mails said you were calling about Aiden? Did you find him?"

"We did," Vanessa said. "I'm so sorry, Jacob, but Aiden is dead."

There was a long silence on the other line. When Jacob spoke again, his voice sounded as if he was crying. "I thought . . . I mean, obviously I knew that could be the outcome, but when you called, your message said he was still missing."

"He technically was still missing at that time. I'm so sorry."

"Shit," Jacob said. "I gotta call his dad. What happened?"

"It's an ongoing investigation, so I don't have all the details yet, but his body was found at Wonderland."

"Aiden is Homeless Harry?" Jacob sounded horrified. "Are you shitting me?"

"You heard?"

"The boat has Wi-Fi. It's spotty but it popped up in my Twitter newsfeed. It's seriously Aiden? What happened to him?"

"We're working on that, I promise. When did you last see Aiden?"

"At the closing party," Jacob said. "He wasn't there long. He wanted to get back to Seattle that night to hang out with a friend before going back to Bainbridge the next day."

"Do you know the name of the friend?"

"Only her first name. Caitlin."

Vanessa blinked. She wasn't expecting him to say a name at all, let alone a girl's name. In the file, Carl Weiss had noted Aiden's plan to stay in Seattle before catching the ferry home to Bainbridge Island, but the friend's name was unknown. Vanessa assumed it was because Weiss had asked around, and nobody knew. This was way beyond shoddy police work. This was someone not even trying a little bit . . . or someone who was deliberately trying *not* to get to the truth. Her opinion of the former deputy chief, whom she hadn't even met yet, plummeted even further.

"Did Aiden say who Caitlin was?" she asked. "Last name? How did they know each other?"

"No idea about the last name. But they liked each other. In, like, more than a friend way. That's why he was going to see her. He was pretty excited about it."

"Were they in a relationship?"

"It was going that way," Jacob said. "But she lived in Seattle, and he was working in Seaside, so they didn't see each other much. And they kept things on the down low."

"When did they meet?"

"Sometime in mid-August, maybe a couple weeks before the season ended."

"They met at Wonderland?"

"Yeah, she was down for the weekend with her family. Turns out they knew each other in grade school. He hung out with her at the beach after work that day, and the rest, as they say, is history."

Vanessa jotted the information into her notepad. "And why was it on the down low?"

"Uh . . . Aiden was sort of already seeing someone," Jacob said. "I mean, not to make him sound like a douche, but he kind of had to keep Caitlin under wraps. But he was planning to end it. With the other one, I mean. He was really into Caitlin. He wasn't an ass. He was, what's the word . . . conflicted."

"He told you all that?"

"Yeah. Aiden was my roommate and one of my best friends. I told the other detective all this."

"You told Carl Weiss that Aiden was involved with two girls?" *Christ, Weiss*, she thought, feeling a stab of anger. *Did you do any work at all, you old, useless bastard?* "What else did you talk about with Deputy Chief Weiss?"

"Pretty much the same stuff you're asking me now. Did I think he was the type to run away, did I know of anyplace he might be. Between you and me though, it felt like he was just going through the motions. I don't think he really gave a shit about Aiden. I felt like he could have done more, you know? I know Mr. Cole thought so."

"I'm sorry you felt that way," Vanessa said. "Tell me about the other relationship Aiden was in. Who was she?"

"Uh . . . it's not in the file?"

"Confirm it for me."

"Well, it was the Dragon Lady herself," Jacob said. There was a pause, as if he was waiting for a reaction from Vanessa. When he didn't get one, he said again, "The Dragon Lady? As in, Bianca Bishop?"

"What?" Vanessa wasn't sure she heard him correctly. "Are you talking about the CEO of Wonderland?"

"It started at the beginning of that summer," Jacob said. "At first when Aiden told me, I was, like, whoa, because she's ancient, you know? She's like, in her *thirties*. But Aiden told me she pursued him pretty hard. She wanted him bad. I told him it wasn't a good idea to go there, but he didn't listen, hopped right on the train to Cougarville. It wasn't just the age difference, you know? I mean, she's the CEO. Can you imagine if it was the other way around? Like, a middle-aged male CEO and a teenage female Wonder Worker? People would freak."

Midthirties was hardly middle-aged, but Vanessa wasn't about to correct him. "So then Aiden and Bianca Bishop were having sex?"

Jacob barked out a short laugh. "It was more like, what kind of sex *weren't* they having? He spent almost every night at her apartment inside the park. He was, like, never in our room. Which was fine with me, because those dorm rooms are tiny, but it was seriously four or five nights a week, every week. I was, like, dude, how are you getting any sleep? But it turned out not to be a problem, because she pretty much let him set his own hours. I mean, that was part of the reason he was with her. She let him do whatever he wanted at the park."

"Back up. There's an apartment *inside* Wonderland?" Like everything else, this was news to Vanessa. An apartment inside an amusement park was an unusual thing—why had no one mentioned that to her? Why hadn't Oscar? Her head was beginning to hurt.

"Yeah, on, like, the top floor of the admin building. It's pretty swanky from what Aiden told me. Dragon Lady stays there during high season. Made it real easy for Aiden and her to hook up. I mean, they'd fu—" Jacob cleared his throat. "They'd have sex during his lunch break. He'd just pop over to the admin building for a quickie."

"Did anybody know they were involved, other than you?"

"I doubt it. He wasn't even supposed to tell me. Dragon Lady was, like, super paranoid about anybody knowing her personal business. Once, Aiden tried to take a picture of the two of them, just so he had something to look at, you know? She found out and went crazy. Deleted it and then broke his phone, then had to buy him a new one. I think that's when things started to change for Aiden. It's like he realized that maybe all the hot sex wasn't worth it." A sigh wafted from the other end. "Why are the crazy chicks always the ones who are good in bed? Anyway, you want me to send you the picture?"

Vanessa almost dropped her pen. "You have it?"

"He texted it to me right before she went ballistic. It's nothing that racy." Jacob sounded almost disappointed. "From what I remember, you couldn't see a lot, but it's clear they were involved. Pretty sure it's still in my phone somewhere. This is a new phone, but everything should have transferred over. I don't delete anything."

"Send it to me right away, please. Do not get back on your boat until I have it, okay?" She thought hard. "So how did the relationship end?"

"Uh . . . Dragon Lady ended it," Jacob said. "I didn't get the details, but Aiden told me she broke it off before he could. He was kind of upset, even though it's what he wanted anyway. I guess nobody likes being dumped. The way he described it, it's like Bianca had gotten what she wanted from him and had decided she was done. He felt kind of . . . used. They argued, she said stuff, he said stuff, and at one point he threatened to go to Human Resources and file a sexual harassment complaint." A foghorn in the background blared. "He would never have done it, but he was pissed, you know? I told all this to Weiss."

Yeah, well, he didn't write it down. Vanessa jabbed her pen angrily into the paper as she made notes.

"Listen, I only have a couple more minutes, but are you planning to talk to Aiden's dad again?" Jacob asked.

"I will at some point. Aiden's case is now a

homicide, so I'll be updating him when I can. Why?"

"When you do, please don't tell him about Aiden seeing Bianca Bishop. I never told Mr. Cole about it. I couldn't, because it would have been a direct violation of bro code, you know? Aiden would never have wanted his pops to know he was messing with some older lady, and the CEO of Wonderland, no less. It would have, like, embarrassed him."

"I can keep that to myself for now," Vanessa said. "But I can't promise I won't tell him ever, Jacob, do you think Bianca Bishop could have been involved in Aiden's disappearance, or even murder? Did he ever talk about her being violent? Or making threats?"

"Other than breaking his phone, you mean?" A bitter laugh. "Nah, there was nothing like that. He would have told me. And I mean, she was the one who ended it, so why would she hurt him?"

"People have all kinds of reasons to hurt other people," Vanessa said. "Whether they make sense to us or not."

"I guess," Jacob said. "Anyway, I should go. I need to give Aiden's dad a call. He can be a little intense, but he's actually a really nice guy. I meant to touch base with him so many times, but I got busy—" He got choked up again.

"It's okay. You were a good friend to Aiden, you know that, right?" The mothering instinct in Vanessa took over as she did her best to sound reassuring. "You had his back. That's obvious."

They said their goodbyes and Vanessa disconnected, seething with anger. If it turned out that Weiss had deliberately screwed up Aiden's, Tyler's, and Kyle's cases, she would have no problem being their families' star witness when they sued the bastard and the police department for gross negligence.

Her phone pinged. Jacob Wei had come through; he'd sent her the picture of Aiden with Bianca Bishop. She clicked on it so it filled the entire screen of her phone.

The photo, clear and unfiltered, showed Bianca lying on her side, fully naked. Aiden Cole was also naked, and he was spooning her from behind. The shot was clearly taken postcoitus, as both their bodies were glistening with sweat. The CEO's hair, a vibrant red, was spread out on the pillowcase, and her eyes were closed. Aiden was grinning into the camera, a smile on his young face.

As Jacob had said, it wasn't exactly racy, but boy, was it ever intimate. She saved the photo to her phone, and then emailed it to herself to be on the safe side. Then she called Donnie Ambrose.

"That was fast." He sounded surprised. "Done with Weiss already?"

"Haven't even gotten to his house yet. Listen, if things are under control at Hovey's, I need you to go to Wonderland and talk to Bianca Bishop."

There was a slight pause on the other end. "The Dragon Lady? I'm afraid to ask why."

"I just spoke to Aiden Cole's roommate from three years ago," Vanessa said. "And he told me Aiden was sleeping with Bianca. He even sent me a naked photo of the two of them that Aiden texted him, which I'll forward to you. I want you to talk to her, find out what she knew about his disappearance. Hey, did you know she has an apartment right inside Wonderland? She was probably there the night Blake Dozier climbed the wheel."

"I don't know if I want to see the picture." Donnie sounded disgusted. "You know how I feel about Wonderland."

"I also know you're an excellent detective who'll be able to keep his bias in check," Vanessa said. "Ask her if she was involved with Aiden, see what she says. My guess is she'll lie about it, but we have proof."

"You really don't want to do this yourself?"

"I can't be in two places at once, and right now I'm so pissed at Carl Weiss I can't see straight. His work on Aiden's case—all their cases—was shoddy, and that's putting it nicely." When the detective didn't say anything, Vanessa said, "Come on, it'll be fun. Here's your chance to stick it to the Dragon Lady herself. That, and it's a direct order."

"Pulling rank, huh?" Donnie sighed. "Fine. I'm on it."

TWENTY-EIGHT

Former deputy chief of police Carl Weiss lived on the outskirts of Seaside, away from the beach and the bustle of downtown and Wonderland, in an older neighborhood on Lakeshore Drive. Vanessa had heard of the neighborhood, known for its mini mansions and affluent residents, but this was her first time visiting.

Lakeshore Drive wrapped around Belle Lake, a small but pretty oval-shaped lake that sparkled like crazy when the sun was out. Earl Schultz, Frank Greenberg, and Nick Bishop all had addresses here, too, and while Vanessa could understand how the last three could afford it, she couldn't imagine how Carl Weiss managed a house in this neighborhood on a small-town deputy chief's salary.

The Weiss residence was set on a third acre of perfectly manicured lawn. It was a sprawling, older Craftsman, with mature trees and a flourishing garden. As she pulled her unmarked into the generous driveway, a Filipino gardener who was trimming hedges near the garage glanced over at her curiously. Vanessa parked beside a silver Mercedes and gave him a small wave as she stepped out, throwing her bag over her shoulder as she headed for the front door. She pushed the doorbell and waited.

A Filipino housekeeper answered.

"Can I help you?" Her voice was soft, with only a trace of accent. She was young, maybe late twenties, with a pretty face. She was wearing jeans and a T-shirt and had a small flowered apron tied around her waist.

"Is former deputy chief Carl Weiss home?" Vanessa held up her credentials.

"Who may I say is asking?"

"Vanessa Castro. The *current* deputy chief."

The woman's eyes widened slightly. Before she could answer, a woman's voice called out from a different room somewhere behind her.

"Jade, who's at the door?"

A woman, whom Vanessa could only presume was Mrs. Carl Weiss, appeared in the hallway. Even from a distance, Vanessa could tell she was well maintained, and suddenly the house made more sense. Salon-highlighted blond hair framed a tanned, tight face, and she was wearing coral-patterned Lululemon yoga attire from head to toe. She headed toward Vanessa carrying a small dog with curly fur in one arm, and a yoga mat under the other.

"Who's this?" Her voice was bright. Her pink lip gloss matched her freshly pedicured feet. Thanks to the Botox and fillers, it was impossible to tell how old she was, and Vanessa's best guess was that she was somewhere between forty and sixty.

"It's the deputy chief from Seaside PD, ma'am Melanie." Jade stepped aside.

"Well, hello." Gray eyes took Vanessa in all at once, darting from face to badge to gun holster and back to her face again. "How wonderful of you of stop by. We spoke on the phone the other day, didn't we? I'm Melanie Stratton-Weiss. What can I do for you?"

"Hello, Mrs. Weiss," Vanessa said. "I'm Vanessa Castro, the new deputy chief of Seaside PD. I was hoping to speak to your husband. Is he available?"

"It's *Stratton*-Weiss." The woman's smile never left her face. "But please call me Melanie."

"My apologies, ma'am," Vanessa said. "Is your husband home?"

"Well, yes he is, he arrived late last night, but he's pretty tired today and is taking a nap. But I can tell him you stopped—"

"Mr. Carl is awake now, ma'am Melanie," the housekeeper said. She was standing back from the front door, behind her boss. "He woke up fifteen minutes ago. I was preparing a snack for him." She gave Vanessa a small, knowing smile.

"Well, thank you, Jade." The older woman's smile

hardened slightly. "But he's not expecting visitors today, so I think it's best that he—"

"Who's at the door, Mel?" A man's voice boomed from somewhere on the second floor. "There's an unmarked Dodge in the driveway. Who's here?"

"Deputy Chief Castro, sir," Vanessa called out before his wife could answer. "I was hoping to talk to you about one of your old cases."

Pursing her lips, Melanie Stratton-Weiss stepped aside. "I'm late for yoga class," she said. "Otherwise I'd stay. I'm studying for my certification. Do you practice yoga? There's a wonderful studio—"

"Mel, for god's sake, invite her inside." Carl Weiss came down the stairs. He was dressed in baggy sweatpants and a faded Wisconsin Badgers T-shirt, his hair still wet from a shower.

Frowning, his wife slipped past Vanessa and headed for the Mercedes.

"Deputy Chief," Weiss said with a grin. "Isn't this a nice surprise."

• • •

He looked pretty much the same as his wall portrait at Seaside PD, which nobody had bothered to take down, only he was deeply tanned, grayer, and sporting a beard that looked about two weeks old. He showed her into the den, where they took seats opposite each other. Jade brought in a tray with two sandwiches, a pitcher of iced tea, and two glasses.

Weiss looked at the pitcher and frowned, then grabbed one of the sandwiches and took a bite.

"I'm sorry to bother you at home, Deputy," Vanessa said. "I tried calling you last week, but your wife said you were away."'

"Call me Carl." He took another bite of the sandwich. Crumbs fell onto his shirt and he absently brushed them onto the carpet, something only a person with a housekeeper who did all the cleaning would ever do. "Deputy is your title now."

"It's Vanessa, please."

"So how it's going over there?" Weiss said. "You guys still working on the Homeless Harry thing? Heard about it this morning when I got back. Christ, that's an icky situation. How long was the kid dead?"

"A few days, based on the stage of decomp," Vanessa said. "He died six, maybe eight days before his body turned up. Are you aware that Homeless Harry was Aiden Cole? He was one of your cases. Disappeared three years ago."

Weiss nodded. "Yeah, I read that part, too. Not the way you want a missing persons case to resolve, that's for damn sure. How'd David Cole take the news?"

"Not terribly well."

Another bite of the sandwich, another frown at the iced tea, and a big sigh. "Well, thanks for coming to tell me. Closure is closure, even if it's not the outcome I was hoping for. David Cole called almost every month. He never let me forget that his son was out there."

Vanessa reached into her bag and pulled out the bottle of Jim Beam she'd picked up on the way over. "I could use a drink. You?"

She could almost see his mouth watering. "Mel know you brought that in?"

"I kept it in my bag."

He put the sandwich down and reached for the glasses. "Open it. We have at least two hours. She always gets a latte after class with her yogis. Let's drink."

She poured the whiskey and they clinked glasses. Vanessa's sip was tiny; Weiss's was not. Wiping his mouth with the back of his hand, he leaned back and smiled at her. While he wasn't a wholly unattractive man, he seemed a little uncouth for the likes of Melanie Stratton-Weiss, and Vanessa wondered what drew the woman to him.

"So what else can you tell me about the Cole case?" he said. "I'm assuming that's why you're here?"

"We don't have a lot so far. The suspect was taken into custody in a different state and is being transported here as we speak."

"You're not gonna tell me who it is? Someone from Seaside?"

"It's Glenn Hovey."

"Christ," Weiss said. "That weirdo again."

"Again?"

He took another sip of his whiskey. "His name came up on a couple other things involving the park."

"Kyle Grimmie and Tyler Wilkins," Vanessa said.

The older man raised an eyebrow. "So you're working that angle, then. I don't blame you, I guess."

"What angle is that?"

"That there's a connection between them."

"All due respect, Carl, I don't think that's an angle. I think at this point, that's a given." Vanessa braced herself. "David Cole wasn't too happy with the way his son's case was handled. Neither was Tanner Wilkins. Both parents believed more could have been done."

"You've seen the case files for them?" Weiss poured himself another whiskey. "You saw how little there was to go on."

"Yes, and our job is to dig. And when we find something, or if something falls in our lap, we take it and run with it."

"All due respect, Vanessa, I don't need a lecture on how to be a cop." Weiss threw back another shot. "I was in law enforcement when you were still in pigtails."

"Then why didn't you question Bianca Bishop about her sexual relationship with Aiden?"

"Who says I didn't?"

She blinked. That wasn't what she was expecting him to say. "It wasn't in the file."

"A lot of things weren't in the file," Weiss said. "But I knew. Of course I knew. And I questioned her. Of course I did."

"What am I missing?" Vanessa was completely lost. She set her drink down on the table. "If you followed through, why are there no notes in Aiden's file? Why wouldn't you write that down?"

"Because I couldn't," Weiss said. "You're too new to Seaside to understand how things work here. And I'm too old and too tired to explain it to you in detail. What I can tell you is that the Bishops—both Bianca and her uncle, Nick—revived this town from near-death. They carry a lot of weight in Seaside, and deservedly so. I didn't put what I knew about Bianca and Aiden in the file because those case files can be accessed by anyone at Seaside PD, at any time. I didn't want to take the chance that rumors might start, so I kept it all up here." He tapped the side of his head. "Had there been anything to show Bianca Bishop had anything to do with Aiden's disappearance, I'd have been all over it. But there wasn't. They had a fling, end of story."

"Did Earl Schultz know?"

"Who do you think told me not to write it down?"

Vanessa let out a long breath. The level of ass-covering in Seaside just kept going deeper and deeper. "What else should I know? Who else was she sleeping with?"

"Tyler Wilkins," Weiss said. Vanessa almost fell off her chair. "When I was searching the kid's room after Tanner reported him missing, I found a drawing. A sketch, done in colored pencils. Folded up under his bed. Tyler was an artist, did you know that?"

"Yes, but it wasn't in his file." She was unable to resist the jab.

"He was good, too," Weiss said, ignoring it. "The sketch was of Bianca, sleeping, naked from the waist up. Unmistakably her, down to the long red hair. I took it with me, confronted her about it, and all this was before Aiden, obviously. She denied anything happened between them, said Tyler used to follow her around, that he seemed to have a crush on her, and that the sketch was just an expression of his imagination. I didn't believe her." He poured himself another drink. His words were beginning to slur. "Earl told me to keep it quiet, that unless I knew for a fact she'd done something to Tyler, Bianca sleeping with her Wonder Workers wasn't enough to accuse her of a crime. Tyler and Aiden were both eighteen, after all."

"Do you still have that sketch?"

"Earl took it. He obviously didn't want it in the file."

"And Kyle Grimmie?"

"I could never verify whether she had a relationship with him, but you know how these things go." He reached for the bottle of Jim Beam again. Vanessa had lost count of how much he'd drunk. "If she slept with two, she's probably slept with twenty."

"Cop to cop, you think she's capable of murder?"

Weiss heaved a long sigh. "I hate that question. I'm sure you do, too, though you have to ask it. You already know the answer."

"Which is?"

"Everyone's capable of murder," he said. "Everyone. In the right circumstances, in the right place and time, anyone could kill anyone. Any cop worth his salt knows that."

He was absolutely right, of course.

"What else can you tell me?" she asked. "I've got four missing boys, Carl. One turned up dead. The other three are likely dead. Nineteen more potential victims. All teenagers, all blond, all worked for the park. Their Wonderland ID cards were in Glenn Hovey's possession, and I'll be questioning him later today. But should I be looking at Bianca Bishop, too? Because unlike you, I don't give a shit who she is, or what she's done for this town. I'm too new to feel any sense of loyalty. I just want these cases solved."

Carl Weiss stood up and walked to the window, staggering a little bit. The blinds were down, and he reached for the cord and tugged. Sunlight spilled into the room, and the view from his den was beautiful. Belle Lake sparkled.

"If it were up to me, I'd move." The former deputy chief spoke slowly. His words were fuzzy. "But my wife loves it here. This is her house, you see. Her first husband was a plastic surgeon, made a ton of money until he dropped dead from a heart attack on the golf course. Do you know why she married me?"

"I have no idea." Vanessa remained seated on the chair. She was speaking to the back of his head, and she had no idea what Carl Weiss's marriage had to do with the fact that Bianca Bishop might have teamed up with Glenn Hovey to kill her teenage lovers.

"Because even though I'm sloppy and old and not that bright, I had some clout in this town as deputy chief. We've had dinner at the mayor's house—not Frank Greenberg, the one before him—and also at Nick Bishop's, whose house is on the other side of the lake. She liked that I was in a position of authority; she already had a ton of money, so what she wanted was status. I knew all the right people. But if it were up to me, I'd leave. I'd buy myself a little condo in Cabo, get a little fishing boat, and spend my days out on the water."

"So why don't you?"

"Because it's Seaside. It's like Hotel California. Every time I try to leave, I keep getting sucked back in. And truth be told, it's all I know." He turned back to her. "Is it true that you got hired because of Greenberg?"

"Yes."

"He owed you a favor?"

"He didn't owe me anything. He owed my late husband. They went way back."

"So now you owe him a favor?"

Vanessa didn't answer. She hadn't even seen Frank since she'd moved here, and she had no plans to. What they'd done with John that night could destroy them both, and it simply made sense to stay away. "I think he and I are even," she said.

"Good. Keep it that way. You don't want to owe anyone in Seaside anything. It's too high a price to pay when they call in their favors. That's the only piece of advice I could ever give you." Carl Weiss turned back to the window. "You can show yourself out, Deputy. Leave the Jim Beam."

She did as he asked. On the drive back to the department, she called Jerry at the White Oaks Inn. Without preamble, she told him that Tyler Wilkins had been sleeping with the Dragon Lady of Wonderland, and that Carl Weiss had deliberately omitted that fact from the case file. Then she listened through the car's speakers as the easygoing private detective let loose a string of obscenities that would have made a sailor blush.

TWENTY-NINE

Bianca Bishop knew what the Wonder Workers called her behind her back: Dragon Lady. Blake Dozier, also known as the Wonder Wheel Kid, had told her about it once while they were in bed together. He'd thought it was funny, and had laughed when he said it. She, on the other, had not laughed, though she supposed there were worse nicknames.

Blake had thought a lot of stupid things were funny. He had snapped pictures of them once while they were lying in bed together, postsex, sheets tangled, bodies naked. She'd flown into a rage when she'd woken up a bit later and he'd showed her the photos, which he'd already uploaded to Instagram. Why did teenage boys always do this? It didn't matter that in this one, her face wasn't in the pictures. You could still see her signature red hair and part of her breast, and the idea that she was out there, exposed in any way, was abhorrent to her. The only saving grace was that he'd Instagrammed the pictures in the middle of the night, and so hardly anyone had seen them. She demanded he delete them immediately, and then threatened to break his iPhone if he didn't delete them from there as well.

She should have known better than to trust someone with her privacy who prided himself on documenting every single thing he did on social media. Blake had begged for her forgiveness, and she'd given it, but his phone was never to be seen in her presence again after that night. When Aiden had tried taking pictures of her three years earlier, she'd smashed his phone to pieces. Which had been no easy feat, considering smartphones were built to withstand blunt force.

Her affair with Blake had lasted longer than most, which is probably why he took it so hard when she'd said it was over. He'd followed her around like a hungry puppy for weeks, arranging to bump into her at places he knew she'd be, trying to talk to her about their relationship. It had gotten annoying. And discretion was important. It was bad enough that Oscar knew she had slept with Blake, but she wasn't concerned about her VP telling anyone. She had her secrets, he had his, and if she went down, so would he.

It was all Patrick's fault.

Even thinking about him now, she still felt that familiar tingle. Patrick Voss had been her first love, an eighteen-year-old golden boy with hair the color of beach sand and eyes like the sky just before twilight. She'd fallen deeply in love with Patrick when she was only seventeen. They'd worked together at the park, and they'd had big plans for their lives. Even though Uncle Nick disapproved of her having such a serious relationship at that age, she hadn't cared. Patrick had promised to take her away from Seaside. Patrick had promised her a new life.

But Patrick had broken that promise. And then he'd broken her heart. And then he'd done the worst thing of all: he'd tried to leave Wonderland. He'd tried to leave Seaside. *Without* her.

It was nineteen years later, and the thought still made her want to smash something. Because she still wasn't over it. Because she still couldn't let him go.

• • •

When Uncle Nick had first bought Wonderland, Bianca hadn't been the least bit interested in working there. It was a stupid amusement park, and she had more important things to keep herself busy. She was midway through her senior year of high school and had just received her early acceptance letter to Stanford in the fall. Not only was she going to her first-choice school—*of course* she was going to her first-choice school—she also had a scholarship. It wasn't an academic scholarship, because realistically, she was smart, but not brilliant. It was for athletics, but it was exactly what she'd been working for her whole life.

Bianca had been a competitive tennis player.

She had dreams of winning a grand slam one day, but realistically knew it might never happen. She was a very good player—competitive, determined, and utterly focused—but as her coaches liked to remind her, she lacked that X factor, that extra amount of god-given talent that separated the good players from the great ones. You were born with it or you weren't, and Bianca knew there was no point in deluding herself that any amount of hard work or dedication—both of which she had in spades—would make up for it. She'd never win Wimbledon or the U.S. Open. She'd never be a Steffi Graf or a Martina Navratilova.

But that was okay. She was good enough to get a scholarship to Stanford, and good enough to maybe spend a few years on the ATP tour after she graduated, playing tournaments and traveling the world. The Olympics were a given. And when she was done with tennis, she'd go to graduate school. For law. Or business. She had it all planned out.

Tennis was Bianca's ticket out of Seaside.

But then she'd gotten injured over spring break of her senior year of high school. Bianca had gone horseback riding at a ranch in Raymond, something she'd done a hundred times, and the horse—the same horse she'd ridden a hundred times—was startled by a low-flying plane. He bucked her off. She'd hit the ground badly, at an awkward angle, and had felt something in her back break.

Lying on the ground as she waited for someone to come help her, she felt true terror for the first time in her life. Her fear, in that moment, outweighed the pain.

Three surgeries followed. After the third one, due to her age and her exceptional physical health, her doctors were confident she would walk normally again. Her tennis career, however, was over. Her back would not be able to withstand the rigors of six-hour practice sessions and two hours of strength and cardio training every day. So it was goodbye, Stanford. Hello, Puget Sound State University.

And hello, Wonderland.

Uncle Nick had always looked out for Bianca. He was the one she'd first played tennis with when she was little, the one who'd encouraged her to follow her dreams. When her father left Bianca and her mother, it was Uncle Nick who'd stepped into the father role. Uncle Nick was who she called when her mom was too drunk to drive her to tennis practice. Uncle Nick took over her guardianship when her mom died of cirrhosis after Bianca's sixteenth birthday. Uncle Nick was always there.

So when he suggested she come work at the park for the summer to get her mind off tennis, she agreed. Bianca had never been into amusement parks, but she knew she needed something to keep her busy while she worked on accepting that her dreams would never materialize, and that her life would never be the same.

"It's going to be fun," Uncle Nick had said to her, just after her high school graduation. "You're my niece, so you can set your own hours, choose your own gigs. You can basically write your own ticket at the park until school starts. It'll be good for you, B. I promise."

And he'd been right. It was good for her. It was exactly what she needed.

Her first summer at Wonderland had been the first time Bianca had ever felt like a regular teenager. For the first time since she was a little kid, she didn't have a grueling schedule. No more 6 a.m. tennis practices, no more strict diet, no more having to choose between homework and sleep. No more high pressure from tournaments. No more coaches yelling at her.

She could just . . . be.

And then she met Patrick—tall, blond, and impossibly handsome. They'd taken one look at each other and had fallen in love the way only two teenagers could. It was movie love, all angst and passion and arguing and laughter and whispers in his dorm room in the afternoons when his roommate was working at the park. Before Patrick, she'd never even kissed a guy, but a week after they met, he'd already taken her virginity. It had been the greatest night of her life—she didn't think it was possible to feel so close, so connected, to another human being. They couldn't get enough of each other.

Together, they made plans. Patrick was also attending PSSU in the fall. They would both live on campus during freshman year, and then in their sophomore year, they would move in together, get a little apartment in Seattle's University District. Patrick would study hard and write songs and play guitar and perform in coffeehouses. Bianca would study hard and teach tennis and prepare for law school. They made plans. All kinds of Big Plans.

Stanford had never seemed so blessedly far away.

But toward the end of the summer, Patrick started pulling away. At first she didn't think anything of it. Sure, he'd canceled a couple of dates, and there had been a couple of times when Bianca had stopped by his dorm after her shift and he hadn't been there. But then he stopped returning her calls, and his roommate would always be vague about where he was. When they did speak, their conversations were shorter, more rushed. When she saw him, he was distant. Preoccupied. Distracted.

Still, she wasn't overly concerned. Why would she be? They were in love. So when he finally broke up with her in August, two weeks before college was supposed to start, she honestly hadn't seen it coming.

"Have you met someone else?" she'd asked him, struggling not to cry. They were standing outside the Tiny Tom Donuts hut in the center of the Avenue. It was the end of the night and the park had just closed, and whatever doughnuts weren't sold, the Wonder Workers could eat for free. There was always a bit of a crowd, and Bianca pulled him aside so nobody could eavesdrop. "Is there another girl?"

"It's nothing like that," he answered, staring at his feet. "It's just . . . it all feels so serious, B. You and me, I mean. And we're starting college in a couple of weeks. You don't really want to go to college being in a serious relationship, do you? Don't you want to meet other guys?"

"Other guys?" What the hell was he talking about? "No, of course not. There's nobody else for me but you. I love you, Patrick. You mean everything to me. And you love me, too."

"I care about you a lot." His smile didn't quite touch his eyes. "You're a cool girl, and I hope we stay friends. But I just want to go to school and have fun, you know? I want to pledge a fraternity. See if I can put a band together. College will be hard enough without throwing a relationship into the mix, too. You understand, right? I think it's better this way, for both of us."

She didn't understand. She didn't understand at all.

And he'd been lying when he said it had nothing to do with other girls. Two weeks later, after the end-of-summer Hawaiian luau party where he'd avoided her and had kept himself surrounded by all his friends, she'd waited for him outside his dormitory.

She needed to talk to him alone, about something very, very important. When the employee shuttle pulled up, she took a deep breath and stepped forward. But he hadn't gotten off the shuttle by himself. He'd gotten off the shuttle with a *girl*.

Bianca only knew her by reputation. Her name was Connie Shepherd, and she was a year older. She had deep red hair that looked vibrant even in the dark, which made girls like Bianca—whose natural hair color fell somewhere between light brown and dark blond depending on the season—feel plain. She was gorgeous, confident, and not the least bit socially awkward like Bianca often was. Connie was a natural flirt, and all the boys liked being around her, though Bianca didn't think Patrick had ever paid much attention to her before.

Well, he was noticing Connie now. After they stepped off the shuttle together, he took the redhead by the hand and kissed her. Then he pulled her into his dorm building, laughing. And while Bianca couldn't see what happened next, she could picture it, their naked bodies pressed against each other, rubbing and writhing. Patrick kissing Connie all over, doing things with his tongue that he'd done to Bianca, things that made her feel special, things you would only do to someone you really loved. And he was probably telling Connie that he loved her, that she was the only one he loved, and they were probably going to lay in bed all night, making Big Plans.

Bianca had never been one to fly off the handle. Her coaches had always praised her ability to stay focused and calm in tough situations, which had won her a lot of match points, and was probably her biggest strength as a tennis player. Rarely did she lose because of nerves. Anger—when she felt it, which wasn't often—always began as a slow burn. First there was a little spark, and then there'd be a flame, and if the flame burned long enough, there would be rage.

Pure, white-hot, unfiltered, unapologetic rage.

Bianca had missed a menstrual period and had just taken a pregnancy test that morning after a stealth trip to a pharmacy in a neighboring town; she didn't want anyone she knew to see her. The test came out positive, and the baby was Patrick's. Of course it was. She'd never been with anyone else.

Her plan had been to go to Patrick's dorm and tell him the news in person. She had no idea how he'd feel about it—*she* didn't know yet how *she* felt about—but she'd been certain Patrick would take her in his arms and tell her that they were in it together, and that everything was going to be all right. He would hold her and stroke her hair and assure her that she wasn't alone, that he loved her, and that he would always love her.

But that was before she'd found out about that slut Connie Shepherd. Oh, how Bianca hated her.

Two mornings later, Connie Shepherd, age eighteen,

was found dead in the woods two miles east of Wonderland. There was a trail near the Falls River where Connie liked to run in the mornings before work. Her body had been spotted by a fellow jogger later that morning, right where the river washed into the bay. After a brief investigation and citing lack of evidence, Earl Schultz, the deputy chief of Seaside PD, concluded that Connie had likely tripped on the trail and had fallen down the bank into the river and drowned. There was a huge gash just above her knee and another one on her temple, both consistent with a fall, but whatever evidence there might have been to suggest foul play had been washed away by the water. Connie Shepherd's death was ruled an accident.

A week after the funeral, Uncle Nick arranged for Bianca's abortion. He knew the father was Patrick, and he knew that Patrick had left her for Connie, and that Connie was now dead. But he never asked Bianca about any of it. He simply accompanied her to the appointment, paid the bill, and brought her back to the park, where she recuperated in his apartment inside the administrative building.

In the fall, Bianca opted to stay at Wonderland, the place where she felt the most safe. She never attended Puget Sound State University, or any college, for that matter.

And neither had Patrick.

• • •

Bianca poured herself a glass of red wine and waited for the knock on her apartment door she knew would come. The thought of Patrick, even after all these years, filled her with a mix of emotions that was still confusing, emotions that only quieted down when she was with someone new. She had never loved anybody like she loved Patrick, and it was easy to pretend it was him she was making love to here in the apartment, with Wonderland just down below. The other boys, all carefully chosen, helped fill the empty space Patrick had left, and for the short time those relationships lasted, she felt almost whole again.

As she did right now, with Xander Cameron. It hadn't taken long to seduce him. It never did. Eighteen-year-olds had their drawbacks, but a voracious appetite for sex was not one of them.

It was sunset, and Wonderland was alive, the lights glittering like fallen stars. The windows of the admin building were soundproofed, so Bianca couldn't hear the carnival music blaring or the happy screams of little children or the whooshing and whirring of the roller coasters. Looking out the window was like watching a movie with the sound off. Even with no lights on inside the apartment, it was bright, the glow from Wonderland casting moving colors and shapes on the white walls. The spectacular lights could be seen easily from the freeway, and they worked better than any billboard, their bright gleam promising passersby fun and excitement and joy. The Wonder Wheel at the very north end of the midway rotated slowly, and she watched it thoughtfully.

Bianca was no stranger to thoughts of suicide; she'd seriously considered killing herself twice before. The first time was after she was told her tennis career was over. The second was after she'd aborted her baby—and to this day, she still couldn't decide which experience was more painful. If she ever contemplated suicide a third time, she knew exactly how she'd do it.

She'd take a ride on the Wonder Wheel until her chair reached the top, and then take a big swan dive. It was 150 feet from the highest point of the wheel to the concrete, and death would certainly be quick. Bianca wondered if she would actually hear herself smack the pavement in the few milliseconds before she died, and believed that if she did, the sound would be quite satisfying.

A light knock behind her ended that thought, and she turned away from the window. She licked her lips in anticipation of everything that would happen once she opened her apartment door, and she took one last sip of wine in preparation.

She greeted her guest with a welcoming smile. It wasn't Xander, her current lover. But that was all right; she hadn't been expecting him.

"Come on in, Oz," she said.

THIRTY

Donnie Ambrose was waiting when Vanessa arrived back at the department. She had a lot to tell the young detective, but for now, it could wait.

"They're in interview room three," Donnie said.

"They?"

"Glenn Hovey and his mother. She insisted on being with him." He made a face. "I already want to strangle her. She's like a little yappy dog you just want to kick, but can't."

"Do your best to restrain yourself." Vanessa's tone was dry. "I'm surprised he hasn't hired a lawyer. Let's hope he doesn't ask for one. How did Nate make out with the ID cards we found?"

"He ran the nineteen names we didn't recognize through the Missing Persons Database; nothing came up. He checked for death certificates; nothing there, either. Obviously, this doesn't prove they're all alive and well—he'd have to look into each one more thoroughly to verify they're okay—but so far it looks like just the five are dead, including Jack Shaw." Donnie looked disappointed. "I was so sure we had him."

"We still do," Vanessa said. "Five of the twenty-four are dead, and Hovey was in possession of their cards. Maybe the others were intended victims; I can work with that. Now, don't keep me in suspense. How'd it go at Wonderland?"

"Bianca Bishop wasn't at the park." Donnie followed her down the hallway. "Receptionist said she was out, didn't know where, but I got the feeling that even if she knew, she wouldn't tell me. I went to Bianca's house, she wasn't home. I obviously didn't have a warrant so I couldn't search."

"What about the apartment that's right in the admin building?" Vanessa gave him a look. "You should have told me about that, by the way."

"I assumed you knew." Donnie looked surprised. "It's not a secret, it's sort of common knowledge."

"For who? People who've spent their whole lives in Seaside and who've worked at the park for years?"

"Point taken."

"Well, don't feel bad. Oscar Trejo didn't mention it to me, either," Vanessa said. "I asked him point blank if there was anyone else at the park the morning the Wonder Wheel Kid climbed it, and he said no."

"He could have been telling the truth. Just because the Dragon Lady has an apartment there doesn't mean she was there that night."

"You knew what her nickname is, too?"

Donnie grinned and ducked, pretending as if she was about to hit him. "Sorry. Again, common knowledge for everybody but you."

She rolled her eyes.

"By the way, Earl called, looking for you. Wants an update on everything, says he feels like he's being kept out of the loop. I told him you'd call him when you could."

Vanessa sighed. That's because Earl *was* being kept out of the loop; it wasn't an accident. "What was his mood?"

"Distracted. Stressing over the development deal, apparently he got into it with Tanner Wilkins at the city council meeting earlier because Tanner won't sell his property on Clove. Plus the gala thing is tonight."

"Wow, such a busy bee, our chief of police," Vanessa muttered. "Doing everything *but* his job."

They had reached interview room three, but before she could open the door, her phone pinged. Checking it quickly, she saw it was a text from Ava.

Working late again tonite. Ok if I sleep over at Katya's?

Vanessa frowned. She didn't like Ava working late, not while there was a potential serial killer running around loose at Wonderland, and this was the third time in the past week that Ava would be sleeping over at her friend's house. "Hang on," she said to Donnie. "It's my kid. Go on in, but don't start without me."

He disappeared into the room, and she remained

in the hallway and texted Ava back. Who else is with you tonight? I don't want you leaving work alone.

Her daughter's reply was quick. Supervisor works till close. Katya's dad is picking us up. Will be lots of people around, don't worry.

Vanessa supposed that was okay. Jerry, still in town for another couple of days, had volunteered to hang out with John-John until she got home, and he'd picked up the seven-year-old from day camp already. Based on the looks of things, it was going to be a long night with Glenn Hovey. Having Ava over at her friend's house, where there was parental supervision, was better than leaving her at home by herself. She texted back. Ok, that's fine. Let me know when you get to Katya's. You guys have fun. Love you.

Love u 2.

Vanessa put her phone away and pushed the door open to the interview room. Donnie was seated across from Sherry and Glenn Hovey.

"Mr. Hovey, it's nice to see you finally. We've been looking for you," she said. "Mrs. Hovey, it's good to see you, too."

"Can I smoke?" Sherry Hovey didn't bother to say hello. In her pruned hands was a pack of Marlboros and a pink plastic lighter. She shot Donnie a dirty look. "This numbnut here says I can't smoke."

"I'm sorry, ma'am, you can't," Vanessa said. "But there are designated areas outside. In fact, you don't even need to be here. It would be better if we could talk to your son alone."

"I'm not going nowhere. Anything you say to him, you can say in front of me, otherwise we're calling a lawyer." She turned back to Donnie. "Can I at least get some coffee?"

"Sorry, we're fresh out," the detective said with a smile.

Glenn Hovey looked nothing like the old picture Vanessa had seen in his room earlier that day, nor did he resemble his employee picture, which must have been at least five years old. The Glenn Hovey sitting in front of her was a man of medium height, maybe five nine, with about sixty extra pounds on him, most of which were around his middle. His hair was thinning and his pink scalp was visible beneath the few light brown wisps that remained. He was wearing a beige golf shirt that was too short and too tight, and there was a stain on it right where his belly began to protrude. In the quiet of the interview room, Vanessa could hear a faint wheeze, and thought the man probably had asthma.

Sherry Hovey drummed her nails on the table. "I told Glenny you were here to talk about the Wonder Wheel Kid and Homeless Harry. But he doesn't know nothing about either."

Vanessa ignored her. "Where've you been the last little while?" she said to Glenn.

"For Christ's sake, he was in Vegas," Sherry

Hovey said. "That's where he was arrested. His car is still there. How are we supposed to get it home, by the way? And who's going to pay for it?"

"Mrs. Hovey, if you want to stay in the room, you will have to be quiet," Vanessa said firmly. "This is a police investigation and if you interrupt again, I will ask this fine young detective here to call you a taxi."

The woman opened her mouth to say something again, but her son gave her a look, and she shut it.

"What were you doing in Las Vegas, Mr. Hovey?" Vanessa asked again.

"Playing poker." Glenn picked a loose thread off his shirt. "Big tournament just off the strip. It's how I supplement my income."

"How'd you do this time?"

"Pretty good." A smiled lifted the man's chubby cheeks. "Eight thousand."

"Eight thousand!" Sherry Hovey smacked her son in the stomach, which jiggled, almost comically. "You didn't tell me that. We can finally buy a new stove." She extracted a cigarette from her pack. Across from her, Donnie shook his head, and cursing, she put it back.

"I spent some of it." Glenn shifted away from his mother slightly. "Not sure how much is left."

"Did you go to Vegas with friends?" Vanessa asked. "Or did you go alone?"

"I went alone. But I hung out with friends." Glenn's eyes darted to his mother's face. "Why?"

"What friends?" Mrs. Hovey said. "You got no friends. And how much money is left?"

"I have friends." Glenn's face turned red. "I have lots of friends, Ma. Just because you don't know them all—"

"I'll need their first and last names." Vanessa pulled out her black notebook. "I need to give them a call to verify where you were."

"How much money is left?" The old woman reached for her cigarettes again, remembered, and pushed the pack away again. "You ran through eight grand in a week?"

"Also, I'll need addresses," Vanessa said. "What hotel did you stay at? Did anyone stay with you?"

"I—" Glenn paused, his head turning from his mother to the deputy chief, clearly unsure whom he was supposed to be talking to. He finally settled on Vanessa. "Are their names really necessary?"

"Oh, just tell her." Sherry Hovey tapped her lighter impatiently on the table. She was trembling all over, clearly fighting off a nicotine craving. "Tell her so she'll stop asking you questions about the Wonder Wheel Kid. You're looking for his alibi, right?" she said to Vanessa.

Glenn's wheezing was a bit louder. "I wasn't even at the park that night."

"Yeah, and that's why you're gonna get in trouble," his mother said. "How many shifts have you missed? You know we need you to keep that job."

"My job's not in danger, okay, Ma?" Glenn looked back at Vanessa. "I wasn't at the park when the kid's body showed up. And I wasn't there when the other kid climbed the Wonder Wheel."

"It's a very long drive to Las Vegas," Vanessa said. "You must have known you'd be gone awhile. Why didn't you notify anyone at the park?"

"I got my schedule mixed up." He scratched his head. "I didn't know I was working that night."

"And which hotel did you say you stayed at?" It felt like Vanessa was asking the same questions all over again. "Do you have an invoice, anything to verify you were there? What about food or gas receipts?"

"I didn't stay at a hotel, I stayed with friends. I didn't keep any receipts. I didn't think I needed to."

"Did you give these people your money?" Sherry Hovey's prune face darkened. "You don't need to pay people to be your friends, Glenny—"

"Mrs. Hovey, *please*," Vanessa said in frustration. She looked over at Donnie, who seemed both amused and fascinated by the two of them. "I'll need names. Then we can move on."

"You better not have spent all the money you won," the old woman said. "You know we need that new stove. Three out of the four burners don't work. How am I supposed to cook?"

"You don't cook. Macaroni and cheese from the box isn't cooking," Glenn snapped.

"It's the only thing I can taste," his mother snapped back. "The chemo killed my taste buds."

"It's not the chemo, it's the cigarettes."

"You buy them for me!"

"You nag if I don't!"

Giving up, Vanessa sat back and crossed her arms. There was no point in interfering. Sherry Hovey was too amped up, and despite the warning Vanessa had given earlier, she couldn't take the chance that the woman might call her son a lawyer if asked to leave.

"You know we need money for the stove, and instead you're spending your money on people who are just using you," Mrs. Hovey said to her son.

"It's my money and I can spend it how I want." Glenn's voice had gotten loud. "You have your disability and dad's pension, which is more than enough to cover the house."

"Yeah, *my* house, and I can decide who lives there." Sherry Hovey's voice was equally loud.

"You don't want me to live there? I don't have to live there!" Glenn's voice had gone full hysteria. "I'd be happy to leave, Ma! Then you can have the neighbors drive you to all your appointments—"

"Excuse me," Vanessa said, but neither Hovey heard her.

"You're lucky I let you live with me," Sherry Hovey shrieked.

"Let me? *Let me?* You couldn't survive there without me! I pay all the bills!"

"You do *not*! You pay the cable bill so you can watch your sex movies on Cinemax!"

"I also pay for the Internet—"

"Yeah, so you can watch more sex movies! I don't use the Internet! I don't even have email!"

"Well, you should have email! What person in this day and age doesn't have email?"

"*Excuse me!*" Vanessa banged her fist onto the table several times. She wondered if anyone else in the department could hear the screaming match, and then wondered how they possibly couldn't. "Mr. Hovey, we need to stay on topic. I need to know who you were with in Las Vegas—"

"His name is Sergio, okay?" Glenn was addressing Vanessa but still glaring at his mother. "I don't know his last name."

Sherry Hovey's mouth dropped open again. "Sergio?" she said. "Who is this Sergio?"

"Do you have his phone number?" Vanessa said.

"We correspond mainly by email through his website," Glenn said. "But I do have his number if you want it. And his address. He's the one I've been staying with."

Sherry Hovey inhaled sharply and smacked him on the stomach again, sending ripples all through his midsection. "Who is this Sergio? Is this man conning you out of your money? I told you a thousand times, Glenny, you're too trusting—"

"He's a hustler, Ma," Glenn said, and Vanessa

watched as a look of horror spread across Sherry Hovey's face. "He's a prostitute, and I pay him, okay? You happy now?"

"You pay a *man* for *sex*?" The old woman placed a hand over her heart, her eyes twice the size they'd been a moment ago. "Oh, Glenny . . . are you *gay*?"

"Yes." There was no denying the note of satisfaction in Glenn's voice. "I've told you that before, Ma, but you never listen because you don't want to hear it." He looked at Vanessa and Donnie. "I was with Sergio the whole time. You're welcome to call him. Anything else?"

"Yes, there's one more thing." Vanessa went in for the kill. "Why do you have twenty-four Wonderland ID cards in your bedroom, in the basement, in a locked box, inside the wall?"

"I . . ." Completely caught off guard, Glenn looked from Vanessa to his mother, to Donnie, to his mother, and back to Vanessa again. For once, his mother was quiet. She hadn't been expecting the question, either. "I . . . you found those? I . . . I collect them."

"You collect them?" Vanessa leaned forward, pushing her notebook aside to give the illusion that there were no barriers between them. "Meaning, you keep them as souvenirs? Are they your victims, Mr. Hovey? Is Aiden Cole one of your victims? Because his ID card was in there, too. Along with Blake Dozier's. Why do you have Homeless Harry and the Wonder Wheel Kid's cards? Did you kill them? Did you kill Blake Dozier before you left for Las Vegas?"

"It's not . . . it's not like that . . ." Hovey looked around again wildly, but even his mother seemed not to know what to say. "I found the ID cards at the park. They're just lost cards. Of boys I knew. Of boys I . . . liked."

"Liked?"

"You know," he said. "Boys I saw around, and had crushes on."

"They all looked the same," Vanessa said. "All the boys are blond, and quite handsome. You have a type?"

"I . . . I call it the 'Wonderland look.'" Glenn Hovey was wheezing louder now. "Boys that look like that always get hired at the park. They're eye candy for the teenage girls who hang out at the park all summer. I like looking at them, is all."

"Oh, Glenny," his mother said in dismay.

"So what you're saying," Vanessa said, "is that every single one of those boys just happened to drop their Wonderland ID card somewhere, and you just happened to come along and pick it up? Including the one we know is dead, and the one we know is missing?"

"Well, they . . . they didn't all lose them. Some of them . . . some of them I might have taken."

"Because you killed them and wanted a souvenir?"

"No!" Glenn was starting to sweat. His body odor was detectable. Even his mother was wrinkling her nose. "I didn't kill them. I just . . . wanted something of theirs. If they're cute, I take their cards. They leave them everywhere, and it's no big deal, they can get new ones made up, takes five minutes. I don't even look at their names. If I took Blake's, it must have been last summer, because I haven't taken any cards since . . ." He glanced over at his mother. "Since I met Sergio."

"Come on." Vanessa let her disgust show. "That's really your explanation? Do I look stupid to you?"

"It's the truth." Glenn's wheezing was alarming now, and he was fumbling in his pocket. Pulling out an inhaler, he stuck it in his mouth and pulled the trigger. "I see a card, the boy's cute, I take it."

"You realize that's about the lamest, saddest excuse I've ever heard, right?" She rolled her eyes. She stood up, and Donnie followed suit. "We have what we need for now. But you're not going anywhere. We have a lot of calls to make to verify what you're telling us. Settle in. You'll be here for a while."

Glenn and his mother were both quiet as Vanessa and Donnie let themselves out. But as soon as the door shut behind them, the screaming started up again.

"For the love of all that's holy, what the fuck was *that*?" Donnie said, his eyes wide.

"That, my friend, is what happens when you live with your mother too long." Vanessa sighed. "I love my son, but god help me if he's still at home when he reaches middle age."

The screaming match grew louder, and then there was the sound of a chair falling over.

"Should we go back in? Make sure they're okay?"

"Just wait a moment." Vanessa cocked her head toward the door. A minute later, the screaming subsided. She waved a hand. "They're fine. They probably do that every day."

"Do you believe him? Glenn Hovey, savior of lost Wonderland employee ID cards?"

"I don't know what to think," she said. "His excuse for having them is so pathetic I almost believe him."

Vanessa checked her phone as she headed back down the hallway to her office. No text yet from Ava, which made sense, as her daughter would still be at work for a couple of hours before going to Katya's house. But there were no messages from Oscar, either, and she found herself disappointed.

She wondered where he was.

Opening a new message window, she sent Oz a text.

I miss you.

THIRTY-ONE

Bianca's skill, Uncle Nick liked to say, was that she was exceptionally good at getting people to do what she wanted them to do. She enjoyed the look on Oscar Trejo's face as her VP of operations took in the sight of her, dressed only in her red silk robe.

"Are you coming in?" she said with a smile.

He hesitated at the door, holding the reports she'd asked him to pull together. His gaze was feasting on all the parts of her that weren't covered by the robe. It had been awhile since he'd seen her in it—well over a year, in fact—but his gaze told her that he remembered exactly what the red silk robe signified, and that she never, ever wore anything at all underneath it.

Bianca knew she looked beautiful. Her long red hair, normally in a bun during the day, hung to the small of her back. Very few people ever got to see her with her hair down—it was a privilege she reserved only for the special ones. Her feet were bare, her toenails painted a fresh coat of red. They matched the silk robe she was wearing.

"I thought you wanted to discuss business." The hitch in Oscar's breath was unmistakable.

"We will," she said. "But I've missed you. Things have been so distant between us this past year. It's time we reconnected."

"B, I thought I made it clear—"

"I know," she said. "You're seeing someone. Well, so am I. That's never mattered before. Right here, in this moment, it's just and you me. Nobody else exists."

"Bianca . . ." The words caught in his throat as she loosened her robe. His eyes went straight to the sliver of skin between her breasts, now exposed.

"Remember the first time we made love?" She stepped back so he could take her all in. "It was the night of my twenty-eighth birthday. I came to you because I was sad and scared and alone, and you did everything you could to make me feel better. You've always taken care of me, Oz."

"That's not my job anymore."

"You've always made me feel safe," she said. "That's why I always come back to you."

Her robe fell open all the way, revealing her nakedness. She allowed the slippery silk to fall off her shoulders. One of her hands went to her breast, and she fondled her nipple, already hard. The other hand slipped between her thighs, where she touched herself lightly.

"I've missed you so much, Oz. There are things you do to me that no one else has ever done. You're the only real man in my life now. You know that, don't you? You're the only one who counts." She brought her fingers to her lips.

That was all it took. Men were so predictable.

"Oh, Jesus Christ." He dropped the reports where he stood and grabbed her roughly, his end-of-day stubble scratching her as he kissed her face, her neck, her collarbone, his hands everywhere all at once.

A few moments later, in the living room up against the window, he was inside her. Below them, the lights of Wonderland glistened. There were still people at the park, but it didn't matter. At night, the windows of the admin building had a golden glow, and nobody would be able to see anything from the outside. And even if they could, it didn't matter.

"You're going to be the death of me, Bianca." Oscar grunted in her ear as he thrusted. He was going deep and hard, but she'd been anticipating this all day and was ready for him. Her back moved up and down the window, which was cold on her skin, but well lubricated from their sweat. It had been awhile since she'd been fucked like this. She was teaching Xander a lot, just like she'd taught all the boys, but none of them would ever come close to matching Oscar's strength, stamina, and natural aggression. "Every time I try to walk away, you suck me back in. You're killing me, do you understand that? I hate you. And I hate what I've done for you, you fucking bitch."

"Good," she said, raising her hips to meet his, her fingernails clawing his back. "Harder. Fuck me like you hate me. The more you hate me, the rougher it gets, and you know that's how I like it."

• • •

She didn't enjoy talking about anything personal, but men needed it occasionally, and so she forced herself to go along with it.

"Why am I here?" Oscar asked her.

Bianca lay unself-consciously on the carpet, a sofa pillow propping up the back of her head, a throw blanket around her thighs. The rest of her was exposed. She knew he liked to look at her. Looking at her naked made it very difficult for him to deny her anything.

"Because I've been wrong," she said. "All these years, Oz, I've been wrong. I want to be with you."

"You're only saying that because you don't want me to leave the park."

She turned her body toward his. "Let's pretend, for one moment, that you believe me. What would your answer be?"

Sighing deeply, he reached over and curled a finger around a lock of her hair. "I'm involved with someone, and I want to see where it goes. She's . . . it's . . . different this time."

"You don't want me?"

He put his face in his hands, lying back on the carpet. "No." His voice was muffled. "I don't. Not anymore. I can't do this anymore."

Bianca stared at him. Surely he was just testing her. Surely he didn't really mean that. Because what would she do without Oscar? She'd never allowed herself to contemplate being at Wonderland without him, and now he was leaving her. Just as Patrick had. Just as Uncle Nick had. Ungrateful and selfish, all of them.

She stayed calm and reasonable as she spoke. "Fine. I understand. I guess it took you meeting someone new, and deciding to leave, to finally make me realize how much I've always loved you."

"Don't do that." Oscar sat up and looked around for his clothes. His pants were on the sofa, his shirt was on the floor. "I need to go. This should never have happened. I'll leave the reports with you, and if you still want to, we can discuss the sale of the park tomorrow."

"Don't go." She put a hand on his thigh. "Please. We don't have to make love again, but everything's about to change, and I'm scared, Oz. The park is all I know. Can I just have this one last night with you? I won't be able to sleep otherwise. Please? Stay?"

"You've never asked me to stay over before." He looked at her, his brow furrowing. "Usually you're kicking me out. This is strange for me."

Bianca stood up, took him by the hand, and led him into the bedroom. She lay down beside him, tucking her head into the pillow beside his. "Just get some sleep. In the morning, we'll simply be two old friends who've worked together a long time. But for now, for tonight, just be here with me. Okay?"

His face looked tired, and he opened his mouth to argue, but then changed his mind. "Okay." He closed his eyes.

She listened as he fell asleep, watching the light from the midway below cast interesting patterns on the walls and ceiling, and across the signed Seattle Mariners baseball bat that was encased in glass and mounted on the wall opposite the bed. Bianca was not a baseball fan, but the bat had belonged to Uncle Nick, and she liked it where it was. The bat was the first thing she saw every morning, and the last thing she saw at night, and it reminded her of her uncle.

She didn't want Oscar to leave her, and deep down, she knew he would. They all did, eventually. By summer's end, Xander would leave her for college, but their relationship would be well over by then. Bianca always ended things well before they did. That way, it could never hurt.

She wasn't good with people leaving.

It had been a terrible conversation all those years ago when Uncle Nick had announced his plans to take off, telling her that he wanted to see Africa, Australia, Europe . . . and that he was seriously considering selling the park.

"It's time, B," he'd told her, and she'd known

exactly what those three words meant without having to ask. "There are so many things I want to do, and I want to do them while I'm still young enough to enjoy it."

It was midnight, and the park was closed. Another high season was officially behind them and the celebrations were over. They were the only two people still on the premises, and they had just finished off the last piece of Bianca's birthday cake. Her birthday always fell close to Labor Day weekend, and it wasn't usually a happy time, as there was never anything to look forward to except a long winter and a quiet park. Wonder Workers would begin leaving in mass exodus, and only a small full-time staff would remain until the following summer.

"Where will you go?" Bianca could feel the panic rising from her gut. Her stomach churned, and her mouth tasted sour despite the sweet cake. "When will you be back?"

"I don't know." Uncle Nick shrugged, looking more tired than she'd ever seen him. The fatigue ran from his eyes to his toes. He was swinging his baseball bat from side to side. It had signatures on it from a dozen Seattle Mariners baseball players, and was his prize possession. "All I know is I'm burned out. I need a break. I'm making you CEO."

Bianca should have been thrilled. CEO before the age of thirty? But instead, she felt herself panic even more.

"You can't leave," she said. "I can't run this place alone."

"You won't be alone." He smiled at her, and it was his indulgent, *oh-you-silly-girl-you'll-be-fine* smile. The bat twirled in his hands. "You have Oscar, you have Scottie, you have the entire management team to help you. I didn't run this place by myself, and you don't have to, either. Besides, you already know how to do my job. You have full access to all the accounts, and you're the one who sends out those peppy emails every week from me anyway. Hell, you even sign my name better than I do. You're practically running this place already. I won't sell the park until the right offer comes along. But it will, and when it does, I'm letting it go."

"And when that happens, what am I supposed to do?" Bianca asked. "Where will I go?"

"Anywhere you want." Uncle Nick's nonchalance, and the ease with which he was able to have this seriously important conversation, was infuriating. He tapped the floor with the bat, and the sound began to irritate her. Bianca reached forward and took it from him.

"But we've worked so hard . . ." The bat was sweaty in her hands, and she stared at it, because it was too hard to look at her uncle right now.

"Yes we have, and this is as good as it will ever be." He turned to look at the park down below. Sparkling. Always sparkling. "I raised this place from the dead to become the largest amusement park in the Northwest.

I've turned Seaside into the most profitable small town south of Seattle. I've made money, a lot of money. And most importantly, I've made my peace with the past. Jack Shaw didn't get the better of me." He turned and looked back at his niece. "Just like Patrick didn't get the better of you. Neither did your injury. Look at you now, the success you've become. Look at us. We don't *need* this anymore, B. And I know I don't want it anymore."

"Then give it to me." The words were out of Bianca's mouth before she thought them through, but as soon as she said them, she knew they felt exactly right. "Give me the park. Or I'll . . . I'll buy it from you."

He smiled his indulgent smile again. "What, CEO isn't enough for you?"

"Not if you're going to sell it and put me out of a job." She almost said *put me out of a home*, but she caught herself in time. "There's no point in being CEO of nothing."

"I wish I could." He smiled. "But I deserve top price for this place, and no bank would finance you at that number. Don't worry, you'll figure your life out. This was only ever supposed to be a pit stop for you anyway."

"What if I go with you?" she said. "We'll sell the park and travel together. We always said we wanted to go to Italy and Paris. So let's do it."

Uncle Nick shook his head. "This next phase of

my life is something I need to do alone, B. It's my journey, my adventure. You'll find your own. Just give it time. When you're ready, you'll—"

That's as far as he got before Bianca hit him with the baseball bat. It cracked the side of his cheek with a surprisingly crisp blow. The blood began to gush immediately from where it had cut his cheekbone. He looked at her, dazed and in shock, and opened his mouth to say something. But he wasn't able to speak another word, because Bianca hit him again.

And again.

And again.

His blood splattered the sofa, the ceiling, the walls, the lamps. She continued to hit him until he stopped moving.

And then she made a call, to someone who loved her, and Uncle Nick's body had been quietly and efficiently taken care of.

The furniture and the carpet were replaced. The walls and ceiling were repainted. It looked as if nothing bad had ever happened here, and that's all that mattered. Life since then had gone on, with nobody the wiser that the beloved owner of Wonderland was dead.

She owed him so much. Maybe it was time to let him go. Maybe it was time to let them all go.

Beside her in bed, Oscar stirred, and Bianca touched his cheek gently. His face, though weathered from hard work and the sun, was handsome, his hair thick and dark with only traces of gray at the temples. For forty-eight, he was in excellent shape, not an ounce of fat, his muscles still hard and defined. Fine matted hair covered his arms and torso. He smiled slightly in his sleep, but he didn't wake up.

She traced a finger down his chest to where the bed sheet covered his hips, then pulled it back to expose him. She stared at him like this for a few seconds, and then leaned forward. Her hair fell over his stomach as she slipped him into her mouth, arousing him again.

He awakened with a moan and said her name.

Climbing on top of him, she guided him inside her, looking down at him as he gazed into her eyes. His expression was a blend of lust, wonder, and self-loathing. She knew the power she had over him, and she was going to exploit it one last time, before he was gone forever.

"Say my name again," she said, tracing his mouth with her finger.

Oscar did as she requested, repeating it over and over.

As she rocked her hips, Bianca thought, and not for the first time, how much easier everything would be if she could just love him.

THIRTY-TWO

The worst part about working in the Clown Museum? The creepy janitor who was always staring at her. The best part? Everything else.

Ava shifted her weight slightly on the wooden pedestal she was standing on, glad the room was kept cool. If it wasn't, she'd be sweating in her costume, and that would not be okay, as it had taken her a good hour to apply her makeup at the start of her shift. The YouTube videos she'd watched the other evening had helped her get the look just right.

She'd started by whiting out her face with theatrical foundation, and then she'd shaded and contoured with three different flesh tones. Bright pink blush spots highlighted the apples of her cheeks, and she'd glued huge, fluttery false eyelashes over her own lashes, which by far had been the most difficult part. Her lips were a deep red, painted in a generous cupid's bow.

On her head was a wig full of brown ringlets, with

yellow bows resting two inches above her ears on either side. The wig was itchy and it took a lot of effort not to scratch her head and dislodge it. The nineteenth century–style yellow dress she was wearing, with stiff puffed sleeves and a petticoat, also itched, but it fit her perfectly. A gold-plated necklace with a massive fake yellow sapphire pendant completed the ensemble, and it was so heavy it felt like it weighed five pounds around her neck.

But it was worth it. When her supervisor had seen her for the first time, she'd actually gasped. Ava looked exactly like a life-sized porcelain doll, which was, of course, the whole point.

"You look amazing." Anne-Marie had clapped her hands together in delight. "How'd you get the makeup so perfect?"

"YouTube," Ava said with a grin. "I'll get faster as I keep doing it. Hope you don't mind if I change up the look for next time. I have all kinds of ideas."

"As long as you look like a doll, I don't care what you do. Get as creative as you want," Anne-Marie said. "Okay, now remember to watch for the light. We always make sure to space out everyone as best we can, but unless the light is red, assume that you need to be 'on.' But when it is red, take advantage of the free time and move around, get the blood flowing in your legs. Standing still is so much harder than it looks. Ready?"

"Good to go."

"You know, I had my doubts about hiring you. I

thought you were too young." Anne-Marie gave her a smile. "I'm glad I was wrong."

It was so much fun, Ava could hardly believe she got paid to do this. Her mom might be concerned about a potential serial killer stalking Wonderland, but it was her mother's job to worry about stuff like that. All Ava knew was that she loved it here; everything about Elm Street and the Clown Museum felt exactly right. Now if only the janitor would stop creeping around, staring at her.

She knew his name was Carlos Jones, because like all Wonderland employees (with the exception of performers, as Ava was at the moment), he was required to wear his ID at all times. They had met before when she'd been assigned to the hot dog cart in the midway, and she'd made the unfortunate mistake of introducing herself to him after he'd emptied her garbage bin. She'd asked how his day was going, and had even complimented his neck tattoo, a red rose with black leaves. Carlos Jones had seemed shocked that anyone had even noticed him, and from that day on, he'd made a point to be nearby wherever Ava was working. How he even knew her schedule, she didn't know, but she felt like she was being punished for being nice. She'd complained to Anne-Marie about him, who assured her he was harmless.

"Nobody's ever complained about him before that I'm aware of, but then again, nobody ever really talks to him," Anne-Marie said. "He's usually extremely quiet. Just ignore him like everyone else does. If it becomes a serious problem, I'll talk to his supervisor."

What qualified as a serious problem? Ava wondered. She didn't know, but she was determined to follow Anne-Marie's advice of simply pretending the janitor wasn't there. It wasn't easy, though. Carlos Jones wasn't much taller than she was, but he was built like a heavyweight boxer, and whenever he was around, the room instantly felt smaller.

Ava was assigned to the Dollhouse all week, which was a room inside the Clown Museum dedicated to nothing but dolls. Anne-Marie had explained to her that the park had once been owned by a man named Jack Shaw, whose elderly mother had been an avid porcelain doll collector. When she died, she'd left her entire collection to her son, who'd thought the perfect place to display it was inside the Clown Museum.

Over time, Shaw had added to the collection. Dolls ranging from the size of Barbies to the size of Ava, in all kinds of dresses and hairstyles, were displayed inside the dimly lit room, their glassy eyes staring into nothing. The smaller and more valuable ones were encased in glass, but the majority were set in displays designed to make it look like they were inside a room from an actual dollhouse. Several signs that read LOOK BUT DON'T TOUCH were placed everywhere.

There was a small lightbulb in the upper corner of the room above the door where guests entered, which Ava had to keep an eye on. When the light was red, it meant she had at least three minutes before guests would enter the Dollhouse. The red light was Ava's opportunity to walk around, stretch, and have a sip of water from the bottle she was hiding behind her pedestal. When the light turned yellow, she had thirty seconds until someone entered the room. When the light was green, it was show time.

As she looked up, the light in the corner went from red to yellow. Adjusting her position on the pedestal, Ava took a breath and stood completely still, relaxing her face into one devoid of expression. A few seconds later, the light turned green, and a boy of about seventeen or so entered, followed by his girlfriend. As they walked in, tinkly carnival music began to play.

"This is so creepy." The girlfriend spoke in a hushed whisper. "I don't think I like this. These dolls are even scarier than the clowns."

"Why would anybody collect these things?" The boyfriend sounded equally freaked out. "They look like dead little girls."

"Right?" the girlfriend said. "It's so wrong. Let's get out of here."

"We have to pass through here anyway. Might as well take a couple pictures."

They perused the dolls slowly, taking their time. They read some of the plaques at random, snapping pictures here and there.

"This one is from the eighteenth century," the

girlfriend said. "It was owned by a French duchess. That's pretty cool."

"The life-size ones are just *sick*." The boyfriend stooped to read the plaque on the doll right beside Ava. She was standing between two actual dolls, and she dared not move. Every muscle in her body was still. "This one's name is Genevieve, and it was custom made in France for Evelyn Shaw, the mother of the founder of the park. It cost twenty-five thousand dollars. That's a lot of money for a doll. Bree, come look. She's as big as you."

His girlfriend stood beside him. "Totally sick," she said with a nod. "I can't believe somebody actually makes these for a living. What kind of person would do that?"

"Probably the same person who mounts animal heads on the wall. People are all kinds of freaky." The boyfriend reached over and squeezed her ass. "But you know, you would look cute in that doll dress. I wonder what she's wearing underneath."

"Pervert." The girlfriend giggled. She pulled her boyfriend close and they kissed. Ava couldn't see whether there was tongue involved, as she wasn't able to look directly at them, but she imagined there was as she could hear them slurping.

They finished kissing and moved in front of Ava.

"God." The girlfriend visibly shuddered. "Sean, this one looks almost real. I swear it's breathing."

"That's because that's what your brain expects

you to see. It's like when you're on a broken escalator. It's not moving, but you feel like it is because you know it should be." The boyfriend leaned closer to Ava. His breath smelled like he'd just eaten a caramel apple, which he probably had. "See, I could have sworn she just blinked. But it's all in my head. Man, that's freaky."

"'*Custom made especially for Wonderland,*'" the girlfriend recited, reading off the plaque that was mounted close to Ava's elbow. "Her name is Ava. Sean, listen to this. '*Look into her pendant, dear. See your face so clean and clear. Make a wish and do not fear, for what you ask is very near.*' It says seventeen wishes have been granted by people who've looked into the pendant."

Both of them leaned in, staring into the fake yellow jewel. Their faces were an inch away from Ava's neck.

"Hello," Ava said in a pleasant voice, timing it perfectly.

The boy sprang back about four feet, and the girlfriend screamed so loud Ava thought the glass displays might break.

"Holy shit!" the boyfriend hollered. "It is real! Oh my god, I think I just shit my pants."

The girlfriend's hand was across her mouth, her face a mask of horror even though the sound she was making suggested laughter. "Oh my god oh my god oh my god!"

"I knew that could happen, I read about it online," the boyfriend said, cracking up. "But still, that was fucking *sick*."

"Please exit through the doors on the right," Ava said in her pleasant voice, still standing on her pedestal. She raised her arm and pointed, then let it drop back to her side. "And allow the guests behind you to enjoy the same surprise you just did. Thank you for visiting the Dollhouse. Enjoy the rest of your evening."

The two left giggling, and when they were gone, Ava relaxed her posture. The light in the corner turned red, and Ava stepped down, stretching her arms over her head. She never would have thought standing completely still would be so much work, but it was like a workout in itself. Ava was working the pedestal for the next half hour, and then her coworker Kristie, who was also dressed as a doll and who was greeting guests as they entered the museum, would relieve her. The two would trade off every thirty minutes until the end of the night.

Oh, how she loved this job. This beat making hot dogs any day of the week.

When Ava had told her best friend McKenzie in Seattle about her transfer to Elm Street, McKenzie had been really excited for her. Both agreed that working at Wonderland was one of only two perks to living in Seaside, the second one being the beach. But when Ava had told Katya about the transfer, her new work friend had seemed a little jealous. After all, Katya was still stuck at Teriyaki Delight, wearing the thick kimono and cooking with the steam in her face. Ava got to dress up in costume and scare the crap out of people. There was no comparison.

"Not sure why you'd want that job, anyway," Katya said when Ava had told her the news. "That place scares the shit out of me. And I've heard things about the Clown Museum."

"Like what?"

"Like, people have died there," Katya said. "There's some monster that lives under the museum and he'll come out and snatch you."

"You've been reading way too much Stephen King," Ava said, drawing a blank stare from her friend. She sighed. "Never mind."

"Well, you're a braver person than me, I guess." Katya's expression was dubious. "I'll keep an eye on Xander for you. I see him in the food court every day. Now that you're not speaking to him, he's always asking me for free teriyaki."

"Do you give it to him?"

"Duh. Of course."

Ava was still upset about what happened between her and Xander in his dorm room, and she had to admit, she missed him. He'd always been supportive of Ava and her love of all things horror, and if he could see her now in her doll costume, he'd think it was cool. She was thinking she might want to be friends with him again—once she had a little time to heal her wounded ego, that was. But she'd never understand or condone his relationship with Bianca Bishop. Ever.

"Hey there," a voice said from the corner, and Ava jumped. She turned to see Carlos Jones standing there, a broom in one hand. She hadn't even heard him enter the room. He'd come in through the door marked EMPLOYEES ONLY, which was painted black to match the walls. And now he was approaching her, his eyes never leaving her face.

"I'm working." Ava spoke sharply. "If you talk to me and we're seen, it will ruin the surprise."

Right on cue, the light in corner of the room changed from red to yellow. Flooded with relief, Ava pointed to it, and Carlos Jones shrugged and walked back through the door from where he'd appeared.

Ava stepped back onto her pedestal, making a mental note to tell her mother about him. Maybe her mom could run his name or something. Not that the man had actually done anything, mind you, but there might very well be some kind of psychopath stalking the park. There was no reason why it couldn't be creepy Carlos Jones.

As the light turned from yellow to red, Ava couldn't help but think how cool it was that her mom was the deputy chief of police of Seaside. If anything bad ever happened to her, her mom would never stop looking, and she'd bring the entire police force with her.

The thought was comforting.

THIRTY-THREE

Under the Clown Museum

If Blake had a pen and piece of paper, he would write notes to the person inside the cell next to his. He had so many questions for his dungeon-mate. What was their name? Were they a girl or a boy? How long had they been here? Had their captor ever said anything about letting them go at any point? And last—and this one was kind of important—how'd they get their goddamned television to work? Blake had called out these questions several times, with no answer, and could only assume that the other person wasn't able to talk.

Clearly his captor didn't kill everybody, or at least didn't kill them right away. Blake wanted to know what to expect. His dungeon-mate, whether the person realized it or not, was keeping him alive. Not so much because of the food sharing—Blake was much better at rationing his supplies now—and obviously not because they were able to make conversation to pass the time, which obviously they weren't. It was the simple knowledge that someone was *there*. Someone was *close*. Sometimes Blake talked for an hour at a time, and though his dungeon-mate never responded, he might hear an occasional tapping sound, as if the person was saying, "I'm listening." It made all the difference in the world.

Once, Blake had rolled over a mini Snickers bar inside the Camelbak thermos. He didn't particularly like Snickers bars anyway, and thought it would be a gesture of goodwill, considering the person had given him five candy bars when Blake was in the throes of hunger spams. Awhile later, the thermos had come back to him with a Twix bar inside it. They had done that a few times now, trading Snickers bars for Twix, and he supposed that in itself was a form of communication.

His captor had been back to replenish their supplies twice. Blake had still not heard the man's voice. He was always dressed in shapeless black clothing, always wearing a ski mask, and in the dark of the dungeon, it was impossible to distinguish any physical characteristics. The only thing Blake was certain of was that he was a man. Once, Blake had thought his eyes looked blue, but it could just have been the way the light from the TV in the next cell was reflecting.

Footsteps approached once more and Blake sat up

in the dark. He was probably sleeping sixteen hours a day at this point, maybe more. There was nothing else to do; there was no daylight to regulate his sleep cycle. He rubbed his eyes, and a moment later, his captor appeared with a box. Blake's stomach growled at the sight of it. Candy bars were okay, but he was craving the turkey and Swiss sandwich he hoped would be inside.

"Dressed in the usual attire, I see." Blake made a halfhearted attempt to sound like his old self. "You really should consider wearing something other than black. I think blue is the hot color this season. If you let me out, we can go shopping, and I'll help you pick some stuff out."

No answer.

"I do like the mask, though. Are masks back in style now? I was thinking of getting one to cover my zit. Or do you think that's overkill?"

Again, no answer. Blake gave up. It wasn't worth the energy.

"Look, man," he said. "I don't know who you are, but everyone's looking for me by now. You can't keep me here forever. Eventually, they'll find me. I have no idea what you look like, so why not just let me go?"

No response. Instead, his captor started tossing in food, all the same stuff as last time and the time before, and soon there was a variety of junk food and sandwiches scattered across the floor.

Blake walked slowly toward the bars and placed his hands on the cold metal. "There has to be something we can do to negotiate. Whatever you want, just ask me. Is it money? My dad's got lots. He works all the time and he does pretty well. If you tell him what you want, he'll find a way to pay it."

Again, nothing.

"Or maybe it's something you want from me, specifically." Blake's voice grew desperate. "If you tell me, maybe I . . . maybe I can give it to you." He regretted the words as soon as they were out of his mouth. Who knew what sick things this psycho might make him do?

A short laugh emanated from the man in black, catching Blake off guard. Lifting an arm, he pointed to the decaying body in the corner.

"You know why he's over there?" his captor said. His voice was so low Blake had to strain to hear him. It sounded like a normal voice, and just like the rest of him, nothing was distinguishing about it, either. "Because he talked too much. So keep talking. I know they train you to do that. All you Wonderland boys, you think you have so much to offer the world. You think you're so young and so beautiful, that you're special. It never occurs to you that things won't work out as planned, and that you won't get the things you want. Well, I have news for you. You're not special, and there are a hundred other boys right above you, right now, who have exactly the same things to offer as you. So keep talking. Keep talking, and piss me off. See how that works out for you." He pointed again to the dead body. "Ask Tyler how well that worked out for him."

He disappeared from Blake's view, and a few seconds later, Blake could hear food being tossed into the next cell. And then his captor was gone.

As he bent down to gather his food off the floor, he started to cry again. It was really fucking hopeless; he was never getting out. Not anytime soon. He didn't know who Tyler was, but Tyler was dead, and eventually Blake would be dead, too. Nobody was coming for him, because nobody believed this dungeon really existed.

The TV in the next cell went to commercial, and once again, for what felt like the hundredth time since he'd been here, the Wonderland jingle began to play. *Welcome to Wonderland! Or as we like to call it, Funderland! There's something here for everyone* . . .

Walking to the bars, Blake spoke to his dungeonmate. "Turn it off." His voice was thick from crying.

The music kept playing. The lights from the TV kept flickering.

"*Fucking turn it off!*" Blake screamed as loudly as he could, and a second later, the TV shut off.

The silence, for the first time, was a relief.

THIRTY-FOUR

Vanessa thought it best not to tell Tanner Wilkins that his missing son had been sleeping with Wonderland's CEO, not until they knew definitively whether Bianca Bishop had been involved in Tyler's disappearance. Jerry agreed.

"Tanner's mellowed out over the years, but he still goes from zero to sixty in three seconds whenever it has anything to do with his kids," Jerry said to Vanessa that morning. She noticed he was rubbing the back of his neck, and guessed he had a knot in it because he'd slept on her sofa the night before while babysitting John-John. Vanessa hadn't made it home until well after midnight. "If she turns out to be the doer, we'll tell Tanner everything. If it was just a fling and nothing more, we say nothing, because if the kid had wanted his dad to know, he would have told Tanner himself. Damn, my neck hurts."

"It's the sofa, it's old," Vanessa said. "I'm sorry

you got stuck playing nanny to my kid, Jerry. Can I at least pay you for last night?"

"Girl, please." Jerry looked about as offended as she'd ever seen him. "Your kid is the coolest kid I know. We watched the Avengers movie, ordered pizza, and made popcorn. Best night I've had in a while. If you need me to watch him again, let me know."

"He'll be okay, he's got a sleepover tonight with his friend from day camp." Vanessa still felt bad. "But this isn't why you came here. You came to Seaside to help me solve Tyler Wilkins."

"Yeah, and that's exactly what I'm doing, isn't it?" The private detective grinned. "I'm helping you with what *you* need, so you can work your ass off solving this thing. In the end, it's all the same. Besides, the progress you've made since I've been here shows I've taught you well, Grasshopper. So go succeed where I couldn't. If I leave here knowing Tanner finally has his closure, I'll have peace of mind."

"Thanks, Jerry." Her guilt alleviated somewhat, she managed a smile.

"By the way, I ran a background check on the name you gave me, the creepy janitor Miss Ava complained about. Carlos Jones."

"And?"

"Nothing. Clean. No arrests, not even a parking ticket. I managed to sweet-talk someone at Wonderland HR to look into his employee file, and he's been a janitor for two years at the park, never late, works overtime when asked, never even takes a sick day. He's gotten merit raises both years. Some people are just weird. But she was right to check if she didn't feel right about it."

"That's good to know. I'll tell Ava."

Vanessa had also tried apologizing to Oscar for being so busy, but that was hard to do when the man wasn't responding to any of her messages. She was starting to feel like she'd been dumped. It didn't take a relationship expert to tell her, "He's just not that into you."

She didn't know what she did or didn't do, and suspected it wasn't anything in particular, other than allowing herself to be caught. Men loved to chase. They loved the hunt, they loved the sex, and when they were certain they had you, they left. She'd sent him three texts, two more than she was comfortable with, and all had gone unanswered.

Okay, then. Fuck it. That's what she got for letting him in.

Of course, it was always possible that he'd just used her to get details on the cases involving the park. Even though Oscar was leaving Wonderland— assuming that was even true—he was surely still loyal to it, and would want to tell his CEO as much as he could about Seaside PD's investigations. Vanessa tried not to think about the fact that his office was right down the hall from Bianca Bishop's, whose plush space she was sitting in right now.

Donnie Ambrose hadn't been able to track the

woman down the day before, and in hindsight, it was probably for the best. It was really Vanessa's job to put Bianca Bishop on the spot, because once Earl Schultz found out about today, heads would certainly roll. Earl had been wrapped up in city council meetings and gala planning all week, which Vanessa had taken advantage of, as having her boss distracted allowed her to do her job without feeling micromanaged.

Bianca sat primly across from her, hair in a bun, blouse buttoned up to the chin, appraising her with green eyes that revealed nothing. During Vanessa's time at Seattle PD, she'd interviewed prostitutes, gang bangers' girlfriends, abusive mothers, and a woman who'd drowned her newborn baby on purpose. And yet she'd never met anyone like Bianca Bishop.

She'd read an interesting book a couple of years back called *The Psychopath Test*, in which the author, Jon Ronson, suggested that as much as 4 percent of all CEOs could be classified as psychopaths. Psychopathic traits included narcissism and a lack of empathy for others. In that regard, Bianca Bishop appeared to fit that definition fairly well. Wonderland's CEO seemed completely self-absorbed and emotionally distant. And charming, when she had to be.

"I'm really glad you've come by," Bianca said. "I've been looking forward to meeting Earl's new deputy chief, and I must tell you, I was pleased he hired a woman. We don't have nearly enough women in positions of authority here in Seaside."

"Thank you," Vanessa said. "I didn't expect to be so busy right off the bat, was hoping to settle in a little bit more, but dead bodies are notoriously inconsiderate of a cop's personal needs." She waited a beat for the laugh—or at least smile—the joke should have generated, but the CEO's face remained blank. "Anyway, my son is a huge fan of Wonderland, and I've been promising to bring him here since we moved. Haven't been able to make it happen yet."

"How old is your son?"

"Seven. He's hoping he's big enough to ride the Legion of Doom."

Bianca crossed her legs. "If you're interested, I'd love to offer him a special tour of Wonderland. If he can be here early one morning before the park opens, I can have one of the ride mechanics show him how the Legion of Doom is maintained. He'll be allowed to operate the control panels to make the roller coaster move."

"He would go nuts for that."

"Call me directly and I'll arrange it." Bianca's words were polite, but her face continued to remain largely expressionless. "I met your daughter the other day. How's she enjoying Elm Street? I hear she's doing very well."

Ah, that explained the sudden transfer. "You make it a point to check on your new Wonder Workers?" Vanessa smiled. "I wouldn't think you'd have time for that."

"I don't normally," Bianca said. "But she struck me as enthusiastic, mature, and ambitious. That's a rare combination in girls her age. I wanted to ensure she was in the right job to make the most of those qualities. But you're right, I'm normally much too busy to have personal contact with the Wonder Workers."

"So then I suppose you don't consider sex to be personal contact."

Bianca blinked. "Excuse me?"

"You were having sex with Aiden Cole, is that right?" Vanessa didn't miss a beat. "Also known as Homeless Harry?"

"*What?*"

"Aiden Cole," Vanessa said patiently. "You were sleeping with him three years ago just before he went missing. You just said you don't have much personal contact with the Wonder Workers, so I assume that means you don't consider sex to be personal contact. Or perhaps the Wonder Workers you're sleeping with are the exceptions to that rule. Which is it?"

Bianca's face reddened. "I can assure you, I've never had a sexual relationship with any of my Wonder Workers. How dare you come into my office and accuse me—"

She stopped. Vanessa was holding up the naked picture of Bianca and Aiden Cole, the one Jacob Wei had texted her. "Normally I'd ask if this was you, but considering I can clearly see your face in the photo, I don't think it's necessary. You have gorgeous hair, by the way. You should really wear it down more."

Bianca let out a breath and leaned back in her chair. Her demeanor—which had been polite but strangely distant to begin with—shifted to hard and cold. "Where did you get that?"

"I can't say," Vanessa said. "And I apologize for showing it to you, but I wanted to spare you the trouble of lying to me."

"Why are you here, Deputy?" Bianca stared at her. "Is it to embarrass me? Because if that's the case, I should tell you that you've made a huge mistake. The chief of police is a very good friend of mine, and once I tell him how you've treated me, he will be very disappointed."

"And the mayor is a very good friend of mine," Vanessa said. "And when he hears of Earl's disappointment in me, well . . ." She held out her hands, palms up. They were empty. "These are all the fucks he'll give."

The CEO fell silent. A few seconds later, having regained her composure, she said, "Are you always this aggressive and rude?"

"Only when someone lies to me." Vanessa put her phone away. "I have no patience for liars. If you're straight with me, this will go much faster. I personally don't care whether you had with sex with Aiden Cole, because he was eighteen and it was legal. It's obviously inappropriate given the fact that you're the boss of, well, everything, but that's not for me to judge. And he looked pretty happy in that picture."

"Do I need a lawyer?"

"Why, did you kill him?"

"Of course not!" Bianca said hotly.

"Then why would you need a lawyer? Aiden is dead. It's not like he can file a sexual harassment suit against you, which he threatened to do, didn't he?"

Bianca's jaw tightened. She seemed not to know what to say to that.

"How long were you sexually involved with Aiden?" Vanessa asked.

"Six weeks. Seven. I can't remember, exactly."

"And why did it end?"

"It ran its course," Bianca said. "As relationships do. He wasn't surprised. He'd already moved on, anyway. But he did get upset, and some unkind things were said. I didn't take them personally."

"Was Tyler Wilkins upset when you ended it with him, too?"

Bianca sat up straighter. "Tyler Wilkins? What are you talking about?"

"You were sleeping with him, too," Vanessa said. "I have pictorial proof of that, as well. Do you need to see it, or can we skip that part and just go straight to the truth?"

Bianca stared at her, trying to gauge whether Vanessa was bluffing. Vanessa didn't have the sketch of Bianca nude that Carl Weiss had found under Tyler's bed, but she had no doubt it had existed.

"It was also a brief fling," Bianca finally said. "What have I done that's so wrong? I'm here at the park all the time. I live in Seaside, for Christ's sake. Do you know how difficult it is to meet men here? They're all married or they're teenagers. Haven't you ever slept with anybody you worked with?"

"How many Wonder Workers altogether?" Vanessa asked.

"There have been , , , several."

"Kyle Grimmie?"

"Yes."

"Blake Dozier?"

A full five seconds passed, and then the CEO slumped in her chair a little. "Yes."

"Did you kill them?"

Bianca's head snapped up. "They're dead?"

"We think so." Vanessa was surprised by Bianca's reaction. The woman seemed genuinely shocked. "We haven't found them yet, but there's evidence to suggest that Blake, Tyler, and Kyle are all dead, yes."

The CEO slumped deeper into her seat and let out a long, slow breath. "I didn't kill them."

"Assuming I believe you," Vanessa said, "I have to ask you the next obvious question. You were sleeping with these boys—sorry, young men. They've all gone missing. You weren't concerned about that?"

"I . . ." Bianca looked around, helpless. It seemed to be the first genuine emotion, other than shock, that the woman had registered since Vanessa had begun speaking to her. "Of course I was concerned. But you have to understand boys at that age. They don't stick around. The ones who are local, who grew up in Seaside, they want out. The first chance they get, they go off to college, or they join the military. They leave. The ones who are in Seaside for the summer to work at Wonderland can't wait to go back to where they came from once the season's over. They leave, too." Her expression grew distant. "Some go off and do great things. Some are never heard from again. I don't track where they go. When they're gone, they're gone."

There was an element of truth to what Bianca Bishop was saying, but of course Vanessa couldn't let her off the hook that easy.

"Okay, back to Blake," she said. "Did you see him before he died?"

Bianca shook her head. "No. I was actually trying to avoid running into him. He didn't take the breakup well. He wanted to get back together."

"Were you in your apartment here the night he died?"

"Yes."

"You didn't see or hear anything unusual?"

"The walls are soundproofed. I wouldn't have heard a thing."

"So you were alone."

"Yes."

"That's a terrible alibi," Vanessa said. "Why didn't you tell anyone you were here?"

"Nobody asked."

Sadly, Vanessa could believe that. She herself hadn't been aware that there was a private apartment inside Wonderland, because Oscar hadn't mentioned it, and neither had Earl. Neither had Carl Weiss, for that matter. She'd had to hear it from Donnie, who'd told her as an afterthought.

"Tell me about your relationship with Glenn Hovey."

Again, Bianca looked surprised. "Well, he's worked here a long time. Since the beginning, actually."

"When the park was still World of Wonder."

"Yes. He and my uncle Nick were friends. They'd both been through a lot." Bianca paused. "With Jack Shaw."

"Are you aware Glenn's been arrested and is in our custody?" Vanessa asked.

"Jesus Christ," Bianca said. "No, I didn't know that. Earl didn't tell me."

"It's not Earl's job to tell you." Vanessa leaned forward. "Glenn Hovey had several items belonging to Blake, Aiden, Kyle, and Tyler hidden in his home."

Bianca stared at her. "He killed them?"

"We're still piecing it together," Vanessa said. "Do you yourself have a personal relationship with Glenn Hovey?"

"I . . . oh, Christ." Bianca squinted, as if a headache had just come on, and she removed the pins and elastic holding her bun in place. Her hair was longer than Vanessa expected, and a vibrant shade of red that couldn't be natural. But it was gorgeous nonetheless, and as she massaged the tension out of her scalp, Vanessa could finally see the appeal she might have on a young male Wonder Worker.

"I used to torment him a long time ago," Bianca said. "I was nineteen, and I'd been at the park for maybe two years, and I was a very angry person. Back then, Hovey was in his thirties, and he was very socially awkward. The only reason my uncle kept him around was because Uncle Nick had an extreme sense of loyalty to those he'd felt helped him. I didn't know the whole Jack Shaw story back then, and suffice to say, I wasn't the kindest person. I teased Hovey a lot about his shyness around girls, not realizing he was quite sexually confused at that point. One night, just for fun, I came on to him. We didn't actually have sex. He had . . . performance issues. Which I made him feel ashamed of."

"How did Glenn Hovey help your uncle Nick?"

Bianca closed her eyes, continuing to massage her scalp in circular motions. "Uncle Nick told me that Hovey killed Jack Shaw," she finally said. "He went to his house when Shaw's wife was away. Dumped gasoline over him while he slept. Lit a match."

"Are you kidding me?" Vanessa's mind flew back to the conversation she'd had with Oscar while they were in bed, when she'd asked him if he knew who killed Jack Shaw. Oscar had said that if he knew, he wouldn't tell her.

"I don't know if it's true," Bianca said. "I didn't ask questions. After Shaw's house burned down, I know that Uncle Nick had a lot of intense conversations with Carl Weiss, whose little brother was one of Shaw's victims. Carl spoke to the fire chief, and the fire was declared an accident—just your run-of-the-mill natural gas explosion. But nobody was sad Jack Shaw was dead. Nobody wanted to know how it happened. They were just glad it did."

Vanessa felt her own headache coming on as she worked to process this. If Nick Bishop and Carl Weiss both knew the truth, then obviously Oscar did, too. They'd all covered it up.

"You can't possibly understand it, but Shaw's death was a good thing for everyone," Bianca said. "I understand if you're going to arrest Hovey for Aiden Cole and the other Wonder Workers, but for Jack Shaw? Even if he did it, no jury within two hundred miles of Seaside would convict him for that one."

"And then your uncle bought the park a few years later," Vanessa said. "Turned the place around. Turned Seaside around."

"Along with the assistance of the banks here in town, the support of Seaside PD, and the old mayor, yes. Everybody wanted Uncle Nick to succeed with Wonderland."

"So who all knows the truth about Shaw's death?" Vanessa wondered just how deep the conspiracy went.

"You mean, who was aware of what Hovey told Uncle Nick?" Bianca was choosing her words carefully. "Just Earl, the fire chief, me . . . and Oscar Trejo."

Vanessa did her best not to react.

"There's nothing Oscar doesn't know," Bianca said. "And there's nothing he wouldn't do to support Uncle Nick, or the park, or me personally, for that matter. We're extremely close, he and I."

Vanessa's heart skipped a beat. "In what way?"

"We've known each other a long time." Bianca finally offered a small smile. "First we were friends, and then it turned into something more. We've had our ups and downs, and we've been with other people during that time, but I think we're on the right track now."

"Romantically, you mean?" Vanessa found herself holding her breath.

"Yes," the CEO said. "We've been spending a lot of time together. Yesterday, we both canceled everything and just spent time together alone, reconnecting. I've spent a lot of years pushing him away, but that's all done now. He's my equal, and that's what I need. No more Wonder Workers. I want a stable, normal relationship with someone who knows me and loves me, despite my flaws."

Doesn't every woman? Vanessa had to refrain

from expressing the thought out loud. Well, that explained why Oscar hadn't bothered to return any of her texts. She was surprised by how she was feeling right now. She was sadder in this moment than she expected to be, and more jealous than she'd ever been in her entire life. With great effort, she forced to herself to put her feelings aside and focus on why she was here: to solve a series of murders.

"If you were here at the park when Blake Dozier climbed the Wonder Wheel and when Aiden Cole's body showed up, how is it possible you didn't see anything?" Vanessa pointed at the window. "Look at this view. You have a clear shot right to the midway. I don't understand how you couldn't have noticed someone climbing the wheel, or someone dropping off a dead and partially decomposed human body."

Bianca winced. "I didn't see anything. I was sleeping."

"You didn't see Glenn Hovey? He was scheduled to work that night."

"I was sleeping," Bianca said again. "If I saw him, I'd have said something."

"As I said before, that's not much of an alibi." Vanessa stood up. "I think we should finish this conversation at the police department."

"What? Why?" Bianca stood up, too. "I was here all night. And do you really think I'm strong enough to drag a dead body across the park? If anyone killed Aiden, it was Hovey."

"And we've arrested Hovey because he's our main suspect," Vanessa said. "Especially in light of the evidence we found, and what you just told me about him killing Jack Shaw. But it's not the whole story, and I think you know more than you're telling."

"What reason would I have to lie?" Bianca said. "You don't think I want whoever's murdering these boys to get caught? Of course I do. It's terrible publicity for the park—" She stopped, realizing what she'd just said. "Obviously it's a tragedy. But I had nothing to do with it. Hovey's always been obsessed with boys he can't have, and I'm probably partly to blame for why."

The CEO had already confessed to sleeping with each of the missing boys, which alone was enough for probable cause. She was hiding something more, though, and Vanessa could feel it.

"Until I can clear you, you're a suspect," she said. "Maybe you helped Hovey. Maybe you were upset that your boy toys were leaving you, and you had him do your dirty work. You have no alibi for where you were—"

"Okay, fine. You want a better alibi? I was trying to protect him, but—" Bianca took a breath. "I wasn't alone that night, okay? I was with someone, and he'll vouch that I was nowhere near the midway when Blake Dozier climbed the wheel, and when Aiden Cole's body was dumped."

"I'll need a name."

"Oscar Trejo."

Vanessa blinked. "Excuse me?"

"I was with Oscar that night," Bianca said. "All night long. You can ask him yourself. I didn't want to say before because I didn't want Oscar to be involved. He's already thinking of leaving the park, and something like this—I wanted to keep him out of it. But that's who I was with, and it's easily verifiable."

Of course it was. It was easily verifiable because Bianca Bishop was *so certain* that Oscar Trejo would cover for her. Even if it was a barefaced lie. Oscar hadn't been with Bianca that night—he couldn't have been; he was with Vanessa. But the CEO obviously didn't know that. Whatever she said, she was certain her VP of operations would cover for her.

Because he probably always had. And if they were back together, then he probably always would.

What else had Oscar done for Bianca Bishop?

"Come with me," Vanessa said. "I'd rather not walk you out in handcuffs, but I will if you're resistant."

"You're arresting me? For what?"

"Obstruction of justice. Making false statements. Conspiracy. Take your pick."

"Talk to Oscar! He's right down the hall." The panic was beginning to show on Bianca's face. "Earl won't stand for this."

Vanessa pulled out her handcuffs. "Bianca Bishop,

you have the right to remain silent. Anything you say can be used against you in a court of a law. You have the right to an attorney . . ."

She walked Wonderland's CEO out the door of the administrative building and down to her unmarked amid a flurry of whispers and stares. Once she had Bianca secured in the backseat, she called Donnie Ambrose on her cell phone.

"I've arrested Bianca Bishop," she said. "And I'm on my way back to the department with her right now."

"Holy shit." The detective almost choked on whatever he was eating. "Are you out of your mind? Does Earl know?"

"Haven't talked to him. Listen, I need you to come to Wonderland immediately and bring someone else in."

"Who?"

"Oscar Trejo," Vanessa said. "I'd have done it myself, but I only have one pair of handcuffs."

Recipient(s): All Wonderland
Staff
Sender: Nick Bishop
Subject: Reminder About
              Sexual Harassment
              Policy

Dear Wonder Worker,

The concept of sexual
harassment is a tricky one, and
while all of you were required
during your orientation to watch
a video on the subject, here is
how the U.S. Equal Employment
Opportunity Commission defines
it:

Sexual harassment includes
unwelcome sexual advances,
requests for sexual favors,
and other verbal or physical
harassment of a sexual nature.

We at Wonderland have taken
it one step further. As defined
in the Employee Handbook,
sexual harassment is any type
of behavior that makes another
person feel uncomfortable. This
includes sexual jokes or innuendo,
unwanted flattery, comments made
about one's physical appearance
(whether positive or negative),
and touching of any kind for

which the other person has not
given consent.

If any of the above has
happened to you, please
report it to your supervisor
immediately. We're always
striving for a happy, healthy,
professional work environment.
That's the Wonderland Way!

Yours sincerely,
Nick Bishop
Owner, Wonderland Amusement
Park, Inc.

THIRTY-FIVE

The creepy janitor was hovering just outside Ava's dressing room door inside the Clown Museum. She felt trapped, and she couldn't call anyone to come rescue her. The park's Wi-Fi didn't work inside the museum, and the cell signal, even on a good day, was nonexistent. Maybe when Xander showed up later, he could give Carlos Jones the evil eye, and the janitor would stop staring at her once and for all.

Yes, Ava had finally decided to forgive Xander. Earlier that morning, she'd received a long, heartfelt text from him about how sorry he was for how things went down. Because of their age difference, it wasn't right for them to be more than friends, but their friendship was important to him, and he missed her. Things with the "other person" had cooled, and while he was disappointed, it was probably for the best.

She had texted him back immediately, and a few texts later, they had made up. She didn't ask what had happened with Bianca Bishop; she wasn't sure she wanted to know. What she did know was that she was looking forward to seeing her friend again. Xander had invited her to a bonfire party at the beach that started at 8 p.m., and Anne-Marie had agreed to let her off early.

Ava hadn't told her mom she was going. No way would her mom be cool with her hanging out at the beach with an eighteen-year-old—at night, no less— so she'd said she was working till close and sleeping at Katya's afterward. She didn't feel good about the lie, but it was no different than what Ava had been doing most of the week anyway. Her mom was so wrapped up with work she seemed almost grateful her daughter wasn't at home alone. John-John would once again be spending the night at his friend Jaden's house, whose parents were aware that Vanessa Castro was Seaside's deputy chief, and who were happy to help out.

Vanessa Castro, Mom of the Year, queen of passing her kids off to other people. When she was younger, Ava had hated it. She'd hated being stuck at people's houses when her dad was deployed and her mom was working, but now that she was fourteen, it kind of worked in her favor.

A creak outside her dressing room door caused her to freeze, and she cocked her ear toward the hallway once again. The door opened and Ava jumped, but it was only Anne-Marie.

"Kristie's sick," her manager said. "She picked up a bug and went home with massive diarrhea."

"Um, TMI." Gross though it was, Ava's heart sank. She already knew where this was going.

"I'm going to need you to work your full shift after all." Anne-Marie gave her a sympathetic look. "Sorry. But the bonfire goes till midnight, right? If you get out of here right at ten, you'll make it with plenty of time for s'mores."

"It's okay," Ava said. "I'll stay. Is that janitor still out there? He was hovering outside the door when I first got here."

"I didn't see him. He's still bothering you?"

Ava raised an eyebrow. "I actually asked my mom to run his name through the police database. So yes, it's safe to say he creeps me out."

"What did she find?"

"Nothing came up. But it doesn't make him any less creepy."

"Just keep ignoring him," Anne-Marie said. "By the way, I'm splitting right at nine thirty to pick up my mother-in-law from the airport, so you're on your own for closing. I'll check with the ticket booth before I leave, though. If there are no more guests coming through, you can head out."

"So I'll be alone after nine thirty?" Ava frowned, thinking about Carlos Jones.

"Absolutely not. The girls at the front will know you're back here. They won't leave without you."

"My friend Xander was supposed to meet me here at eight to go to the bonfire," Ava said. "If you see him, can you tell him to come back right at nine thirty for me?"

"Ooh, that tall drink of water?" Anne-Marie winked. "You got it."

Ava finished applying her makeup at the small vanity table, and then removed her clothes quickly, keeping an eye out for any sign of Carlos Jones lingering outside the door. The dressing room, just an unused supply closet, was small but functional enough. A row of costumes hung from pegs along one wall, and an extrawide full-length mirror was bolted to the other. She grabbed the yellow doll dress labeled "Ava" and slipped it on. Though it fit snugly and was always itchy, she rather liked the way she looked in it—bosomy and ultrafeminine—neither of which she felt when she wore her regular clothes.

She stood in front of the mirror and adjusted the dress until it fit exactly right. She then pulled her wig on, fluffing the ringlets so they hung in perfect spirals. The low-heel shoes—yellow satin to match the dress—were a size too big, but that was better than being a size too small, and at least she didn't have to walk much in them.

Stepping back, she was pleased with her appearance. She had tried something new with her makeup, and her porcelain doll face appeared as if it had old cracks in it. The effect, when combined with the wig and dress, was eerie and perfect.

She left the dressing room and closed the door firmly behind her. Making her way down the darkened hallway—everything in the Clown Museum was dark or dim, which was part of the ambience—she entered the black room of the Dollhouse and assumed her place on the pedestal.

"You look very pretty," a voice said from across the room.

Again, she jumped. Carlos Jones was staring at her, and just like the last time, she hadn't heard him come in. Why was nobody ever around when the janitor was here? His eyes looked like two shiny black holes in the middle of his face, and though he was short, the width of his broad shoulders spanned the doorway.

"I wasn't going for pretty," Ava said in a sharp voice. "I was going for strange and disturbing. But thanks, I guess."

"You're welcome." The janitor appeared oblivious to her sarcasm. The yellow lightbulb over his head made his face look sallow and shiny. "So how do you like working here?"

"I like it fine," Ava said. He was walking closer to her. She was standing on her pedestal, with nowhere to go. "The light's going to turn on any minute. You should go."

"Usually they hire sixteen-year-olds for Elm

Street gigs," Carlos Jones said, stroking his goatee. It was the most words he'd ever said to her at once. "But you look a little younger than that. You've got that little girl look about you still."

"Maybe that's because I'm dressed up like a porcelain doll," Ava said. "Now please go away so I can work."

"I heard your supervisor say she's leaving early. I'll make sure to keep an eye on you."

Ava fought back a shudder. "That's not necessary. My boyfriend *and* my mother are coming to pick me up after my shift. You might have heard, my mom is the deputy chief of police of Seaside." She said this last part as loudly and clearly as she dared.

"My mom is dead, remember?" Carlos Jones stretched out his neck and pointed to his rose tattoo. "I keep this here to remind me of her always."

The light above his head turned yellow. Ava made a point to look up at it.

"I guess I'll let get you to work," he said. He was out the door just in time for the next guests to pass through.

Since she couldn't make any physical movements, Ava's sigh of relief was all in her head.

•   •   •

At 9:30 p.m., one of the ticket booth girls came back to tell her there were no more guests coming through for the night. They would be locking up the Clown Museum early. That sounded good to Ava, and she bolted back to the dressing room to change.

She was pulling off her doll wig when the door to the dressing room suddenly slammed shut. Startled, Ava turned around, but she was still alone.

"What the hell?" she said out loud, and it was then that she heard the door to the old supply closet being locked. And it was being locked the only way a supply closet door could be.

From the *outside*.

THIRTY-SIX

Mother's guilt was a very real thing. Ava had asked to sleep over again at Katya's house, and Vanessa had said yes automatically without even thinking about it. John-John was sleeping over at a friend's house again, too, officially making her the worst parent in the world. When this was all over, she was switching to day shifts, turning her phone off in the evenings, and spending some serious time with her kids, doing whatever *they* wanted to do.

But until then, it was back to work.

Earl Schultz was currently attending the gala fund-raiser for Seaside Hospital he'd been stressing about for the past while, where he was no doubt rubbing elbows with Mayor Greenberg, the entire city council, Carl Weiss and Melanie Stratton-Weiss, three retired Seahawks players, and the rest of Seaside's elite. Bianca Bishop and Oscar Trejo had probably intended to go as well, but with both of them in separate interview rooms at Seaside PD, neither were going anywhere anytime soon. Vanessa's invitation must have gotten lost in the mail, though she wouldn't have attended even if she had been invited. Tickets were five hundred a plate.

Bianca Bishop had called for an attorney, but her lawyer was currently attending the gala as well and could not be reached. Oscar had also called a lawyer, who, according to Donnie, was the only criminal defense attorney within fifty miles of Seaside available on such short notice. Apparently Oscar had been reluctant to hire her, but felt he had no choice.

"Oz was pretty upset you didn't talk to him first, Deputy," Donnie said as they stood outside the interview rooms. "He seemed to take it personally that you didn't give him the heads up, acted like you guys had become friends."

"We're not friends."

"Listen, do you want me to sit in on the interrogations?" Donnie asked. "Because I'd be happy to if you need someone to play good cop/bad cop with. But Bianca's not going to talk until her lawyer gets here, and I get the feeling Oz might open up to you more if I wasn't there. But obviously, it's your call. I'll do whatever you tell me."

Vanessa glanced at the young detective, and for the first time noticed how tired he looked. Despite his upbeat demeanor, he had circles under his eyes and three days' worth of stubble on his face. Christ, she'd been working him to the bone since she arrived in Seaside, and he'd never once complained. She knew she got tunnel vision when she was working, but this was bordering on ridiculous. Everybody fell victim to Vanessa when she was on a mission—first her kids, then Jerry, and now Donnie, the only real friend she had in Seaside.

"Go home," she said. "Get some sleep. You're right, Oscar might talk more if it's just me. And Bianca's not going anywhere."

"You sure?"

"That's an order. Glenn Hovey all squared away for the night?"

"He's in county, yeah. Bail hearing's tomorrow."

"Good. Tomorrow we get to charge him with the murder of Jack Shaw as well." She updated him quickly. "The bodies just keep piling up, don't they? Now get out of here."

He left with a tired smile, saying to call him if there was anything she needed.

As she headed toward the first interview room, she sent Ava a text. Just a reminder to let me know when you get to Katya's. You know the drill. Love you.

She waited. Nothing. And then the text message—normally encased in a blue-colored bubble signifying the text had gone through—turned green. This meant that either Ava's phone was off—and it was never allowed to be off when Ava wasn't with her mom, a condition of having a phone in the first place—or she was somewhere with no cell signal or Wi-Fi.

Vanessa frowned. If she didn't hear back from Ava after she finished questioning Oscar, maybe she'd have one of the officers drive by Katya's house to make sure the girls were all right.

Oscar and his lawyer were waiting in the interview room when she entered. She'd seen the lawyer's name on the sign-in sheet, but she wasn't quite prepared for Jane Cartwright.

Tall, six three in ballet flats, Oscar's lawyer had the height and build of a champion swimmer. Somewhere in her forties, she was sheathed in a long cream-colored summer dress, a pink cardigan draped over her well-defined shoulders. Pale blond hair framed a square-jawed face softened by expertly applied makeup. Jane Cartwright stretched out a hand, and glossy pink lips parted into a smile as they shook hands. Her long fingers squeezed Vanessa's palm gently.

"Jane Cartwright," the lawyer said in a husky voice. "Nice to meet you, Deputy Chief Castro."

"Nice to meet you, too," Vanessa said, looking up. She glanced over at Oscar, but he refused to make eye contact with her.

"I would have thought Seaside's new deputy would have been at the gala tonight," Jane said. "Everyone else seems to be."

"I wasn't invited," Vanessa said.

"Neither was I."

They exchanged a smile.

"So what are the charges, Deputy?" The lawyer

folded her hands on the table. "My client wasn't clear on that."

"He isn't being charged with anything," Vanessa said. "I have some questions, is all."

"So it's a fact-finding mission," Jane said. "Regarding what, exactly?"

"Homeless Harry and the Wonder Wheel Kid."

The lawyer let out a laugh that sounded like a bark. Her hands flew to her mouth. "I'm sorry," she said. "It's just . . . that sounded like a movie title. You know, like *Butch Cassidy and the Sundance Kid*? Homeless Harry and the Wonder Wheel Kid, where the moral of the story is, 'Be nice to everyone, kids, even if they're different than you.' Sorry, it's not funny, but . . ." She covered another laugh. "Sorry, I can't help it."

Vanessa laughed, too. She couldn't help it, either. Jane Cartwright's giggles were infectious.

Oscar, however, failed to see the humor and glared at his lawyer. "Really? I'm paying you two hundred dollars an hour so you can joke around with the jilted lover who arrested me?"

"I didn't arrest you," Vanessa said. *And ouch*, she thought. *Jilted lover?*

Jane Cartwright finally got her giggles under control. "You two have a personal relationship? You didn't mention that," she said to Oscar.

"*Had*," he said. "As in past tense. As in, it tends to kill the mood when the girl you like sends her detective flunky to your workplace to haul you in for questioning."

"Yes, but that has nothing to do with why we're here," Vanessa said. She found herself wishing she'd had Donnie stay. It might have balanced things out in the end. "I have questions, is all."

"Go ahead and ask them," Jane said. "But Mr. Trejo doesn't have to answer if he doesn't feel comfortable, or if I instruct him not to."

"For Christ's sake, call me Oz," Oscar snapped at his lawyer. "Last I saw you, your name was James."

"All righty," Vanessa said, giving Oscar a stern look. "Let's get started, shall we?"

He sat up straighter and crossed his arms.

"I have reason to believe that Glenn Hovey, a longtime employee at Wonderland, killed at least four teenage Wonder Workers." Vanessa never took her eyes off Oscar's face. "Blake Dozier, Aiden Cole, Kyle Grimmie, and Tyler Wilkins. There may be nineteen more potential victims, but we're still working on verifying that." She said this last part with a perfectly straight face; Nate Essex's preliminary check had showed they were all alive.

"Nineteen?" Oscar blinked. "Are you joking?"

"Am I laughing?" Vanessa said.

"And Oz can help with this how?" Jane asked.

"We also have reason to believe that Bianca Bishop, Wonderland's CEO, conspired with Glenn

Hovey to kill those boys," Vanessa said. "If not conspired, then she told him to kill them, or perhaps implied that he should, or, at the very least, she was completely aware he was doing it and said nothing."

"That's a lot of possibilities, Deputy. You're clearly fishing." Jane turned to her client. "Don't say anything until I tell you to." She turned back to Vanessa. "What evidence do you have against Bianca Bishop? And why would Oz know anything about it?"

"Because she was sleeping with them." Oscar's voice was dull. "And I was sleeping with her."

"Oz, for god's sake, keep your mouth shut." Jane's exasperation was obvious.

"It doesn't matter." Oscar's gaze fixed on Vanessa. "That's what this is about, isn't it? You found out about me and Bianca, and you're doing this to get back at me."

Vanessa had to laugh. "You overestimate yourself, Oz. I'm investigating a confirmed homicide and a whole slew of missing persons cases, and your name came up. That's the only reason you're here."

"I don't love her," Oscar said. "Despite what she told you, I don't love her, and we're not together. We were never together, not in any real way. I didn't call you back because I knew I fucked up with her, and I was ashamed of that, but I don't want her. I want you."

"I'm confused," Jane said. "I feel like everybody is sleeping with everybody, except me."

"Oh, shut up, James," Oscar snapped. "This isn't

about you. If anyone else had been available, trust me, I would have called them."

"It's Jane, and stop being a dick," the lawyer said. "I'm a top-notch lawyer you're getting for half the price I used to charge, so consider yourself lucky. I'm here to protect you and make sure you don't say anything to incriminate yourself."

"Do *you* two know each other personally?" Vanessa asked, looking between the two of them.

"We played baseball together, that's all," Oscar said. "Back in high school."

"Actually, we were friends up until my transition," Jane said.

"You're wearing makeup, for Christ's sake," Oscar said. "How is that not weird for me?"

"Pretty sure it's not about you, Oz," Vanessa said, giving Jane a small smile. "Now can we please focus? You said you were aware Bianca was sleeping with her Wonder Workers."

"Aiden and Blake, yes. Tyler and Kyle, I suspected, but I never confronted her. There were others, too." Oscar rubbed his face. "Though I would never have guessed the number was nineteen."

"Do you have any knowledge of who murdered them? Did you ever suspect Bianca?"

Oscar looked at his attorney, who shrugged.

"How the heck would I know what you're planning to say?" Jane said. "Whisper it in my ear first, if you want."

Oscar made a face. "I want immunity."

"Can't promise that until I hear what you have to say," Vanessa said.

Hesitating, Oscar leaned closer to Jane and whispered in her ear. Jane's eyes widened, and she whispered something back. It went on for another minute.

"Okay," Jane finally said. "Here's the thing. We need you to promise immunity, right now. Oz has firsthand knowledge of a crime having been committed that involves Wonderland, but before he says a word, I need a guarantee that he won't be charged with withholding the information, even though he had nothing to do with committing the crime itself."

"If that's true, then fine." Vanessa already suspected where this was going. Oscar had known all along that Glenn Hovey had murdered Jack Shaw, and he was about to confess that he'd been part of the conspiracy to cover it up.

"I don't know anything about Bianca killing those Wonder Workers. I don't know if she put Hovey up to it; I have zero knowledge of that. But Bianca *is* a murderer. I know that for a fact." Oscar put his head in his hands. "God, I can't believe I just said that."

Vanessa blinked and sat back in her chair. That was not at all what she'd expected him to say. "Who did she murder?"

He looked up, his eyes misty. "Nick Bishop. Her uncle."

Vanessa stared at him, then looked over at Jane Cartwright, whose face was serious. This was not a joke and she couldn't conceal her shock. "Nick Bishop? As in the owner of Wonderland? He's *dead*?"

"For eight years now."

"I don't understand," Vanessa said. "How is that possible? My daughter still gets emails from him every week."

"Bianca writes those," Oscar said. "She always has. From the beginning, Nicky gave her as much responsibility as she wanted. Eventually, as he started stepping back from the day-to-day, she took over his duties. She has access to everything—his email, his online banking, the payroll, she can even sign his name. The signature's a near-perfect match."

"So what motive would she have to kill him?" Vanessa asked.

"He wanted out." Oscar sighed heavily. "Nicky had been fielding offers from Cedar Fair, Paramount, Six Flags, even Disney was sniffing around for a while. He didn't want to be at the park anymore. His joy came from transforming the park into something new. Once he'd done that, the passion was gone. He was getting restless. I know the feeling."

"So she killed him." Vanessa leaned forward. This

was a bombshell of epic proportions. Even Jane Cartwright seemed enthralled.

"He told her he wanted to travel," Oscar said. "He wanted to spend some time figuring out what to do with the rest of his life. He and I had talked about it before, but I wasn't sure if he was serious. Bianca was upset. She didn't want him to go. He was the only family she had, and up till this point, he'd done everything for her. She asked him to leave the park to her, but he wanted to sell it, and he wanted top dollar. He offered to hold off on the sale for a year or two, and in the meantime he'd make her CEO. It wasn't good enough. They argued, and she got angry and lost control. She slugged him with a baseball bat. It wouldn't entirely surprise me if it was the same one that killed Homeless Harry." He frowned. "Sorry, I mean Aiden Cole."

Vanessa was trying to process it all. "And you found out about this when?"

"She called me right after it happened." Oscar's voice grew distant as he remembered. "She was in Nicky's apartment inside the park, and she called me, said he was badly hurt, and I rushed over. All I remember is seeing the blood. It was everywhere. She didn't just hit him once."

"And what did she expect you to do?"

"She wanted me to help her get rid of the body. She was so calm, I assumed she was in shock. She told me no one could ever know what she had done, that the park wouldn't survive the bad publicity if they knew the owner's niece had killed him."

"And you helped her move the body?"

"I bent down." Oscar's eyes began to water. "There was blood all over his face. He looked . . . smaller somehow, and I almost couldn't bring myself to touch him at first. I couldn't believe what Bianca had done. Nicky was her only family. He was my friend. I wanted to call nine-one-one, but we both knew if I did, we'd lose the park, and she'd go to prison. I wrapped him in a blanket and got a wheelbarrow from the maintenance shed. I moved him."

"Where did you put the body?"

"In the underground tunnel. In the dungeon. Under the Clown Museum."

Vanessa heard a gasp, and realized it had come from Jane.

"I thought that was an urban myth," the lawyer said. "Danny Moskowitz, Pete Allred . . . what they said all those years ago about Jack Shaw, it was actually true?"

Oscar nodded. He wiped his eyes with the back of his hand, and Jane handed him a tissue she'd pulled from her purse. Looking at Oz now, Vanessa could only feel sorry for him. All these years, keeping a secret like that.

The body count at Wonderland was continuing to pile up, and it made Vanessa's head spin to think of all the victims. Jack Shaw, Nick Bishop, and Aiden

Cole, that they knew of. Tyler Wilkins, Kyle Grimmie, and Blake Dozier, who were likely dead as well. Would their bodies be in the dungeon, too, alongside Nick Bishop's? It would not be the ending the boys' families had prayed for, but it would be closure.

Who had killed them? Was it Glenn Hovey? Was it Bianca? Was it Oscar? All three? At this point, Vanessa didn't trust Oscar at all. Whatever spark had been between them was gone.

"I'll send out a search team first thing in the morning," Vanessa said softly. "Oz . . . I have to ask, why didn't you tell anybody eight years ago? How could you have kept the secret for so long? And how could you ever have been involved with Bianca after that, knowing what she'd done?"

A sob escaped from his chest. When Jane Cartwright put an arm around her old friend to comfort him, he didn't pull away.

"I loved her." Oscar's voice was broken. "We were all we had after Nicky died, and god help me, I loved her."

THIRTY-SEVEN

The door would not budge. Not even a little bit.

"If this is a prank, it isn't funny," Ava called through the door for the dozenth time. "Let me out right now, or I'll report you."

Not that she could report anyone, since she was locked in, and her phone had no signal. The door was heavy, and she wasn't sure anyone could hear her pounding. She wasn't even sure anyone was out there.

Who had locked her in? No way was it an accident, because the door had never been locked before, not to Ava's knowledge, anyway. Was it Carlos Jones? Was it because she'd been bitchy to him? Was he trying to teach her a lesson? He was a janitor; he'd have the key to every door in the place.

Her useless cell phone confirmed that it was 9:45 p.m. Hopefully Xander was still coming to meet her, assuming that Anne-Marie had passed along her message. At the very least, the ticket booth girls had to know she was still back here, and when Ava didn't come out in the next ten minutes, one of them would come looking for her. All she had to do was be patient and keep banging on the door until they did.

She pounded on the door with all her might, yelling at the top of her lungs. After two minutes, she gave it a rest, her hands red and sore. Then two minutes later, she banged again. Then yelled. Then banged. Then yelled.

Looking around the small dressing room, Ava sighed. It would be a long night if she got stuck in here, especially since she'd told her mother she was sleeping over at Katya's, and Katya thought she was hanging out with Xander. If this was karma for lying, Ava had no intention of doing it ever again. The dressing room was cold, and there were no pillows, no blankets, and nowhere to sit or lie down except for the hard concrete floor. All she could do was pile a bunch of old costumes together into a makeshift bed.

Checking the time again, she saw that it was now 10 p.m. All over the park, attractions were shutting down, guests were being ushered out, and Wonder Workers were beginning cleanup duties. By ten thirty, the park would be empty, save for a security guard or two, and maybe someone from the maintenance crew.

Like Carlos Jones, for instance. If he'd locked her in here on purpose, then he was probably intending to come back for her. Maybe he was Wonderland's serial killer after all. Just because he didn't have a police record didn't mean he didn't get away with crimes all the time. Ava had seen on *Criminal Minds* that there were as many as one hundred active serial killers in the United States at any given point. Assuming this was true, and that four or five of them were operating in Washington—which seemed to be the hotbed state for serial murderers—there was no reason to believe that Carlos Jones wasn't one of them.

A dead body had already turned up at Wonderland, after all. Another boy had gone missing. Or was it three missing boys? Ava had overheard her mom talking about it with Jerry the other day, and wished she had paid closer attention.

Oh my god, she thought. *I'm going to die.*

Then again, she didn't fit the victim profile. They were all male. Eighteen. Blond.

Holy shit. Xander.

What if Xander was out there right now, and Carlos Jones was about to kill him? Ava couldn't believe she hadn't put that together before now.

With renewed vigor, she banged on the door with both fists, yelling as loud as she could. Maybe the reason she was locked in here was because Carlos Jones had seen her with Xander before, and he had locked Ava in the supply closet as a way to lure Xander into the museum. If that was the case, her friend was as good as dead, and so was Ava. . . .

"Stop it." She spoke to herself out loud, mimicking the tone her mother would have used, had she been here. "You stop it right now, Ava. You're inventing stories in your head. You stop it right now."

She needed to calm the hell down. She was getting herself all worked up about things she didn't even know would happen, and she needed to chill out before she gave herself an anxiety attack.

Karma was a bitch, there was no doubt about that. This is what she got for watching too many horror movies and being addicted to those crime shows. And this is what she got for lying to her mom. Her smart, capable, deputy police chief mom who'd have dropped everything in a heartbeat if she suspected Ava was trapped somewhere for even five minutes.

Yup. Karma.

She pounded on the door again, yelling some more, but her hands were throbbing and her voice was getting hoarse. Taking a break, she went and stood in front of the full-length mirror where she'd applied her makeup earlier. Other than the wig, which she'd removed as soon as she'd walked in, she was still in full costume. With the yellow dress, her hair all askew, and her cracked white porcelain doll face, Ava had to admit this was exactly the look she'd been going for. She looked just like an old, discarded doll.

Pulling out her phone, she snapped a selfie in the mirror. She would upload it to Instagram tomorrow, because surely by tomorrow, this would be hilarious.

The dress was still itchy, but she didn't want to take it off because she was only wearing shorts and a tank top underneath. It had been hot when she'd arrived at the park earlier that day, and all she had in her backpack was a light hoodie. She pulled it on over her doll dress. Now she looked extra ridiculous She snapped another selfie.

She went back and pounded on the door for as long as her hands could take it, then finally stopped. There was no point. It was after 11 p.m. now. Nobody was coming.

Slumping against the full-length mirror, Ava couldn't help but feel sorry for herself. How could Xander not come looking for her? How could the ticket booth girls not have realized she was still back here?

The mirror seemed very cold on the back of her head, and as she sat against it for a minute, she soon realized why. A cold draft of air was coming from somewhere behind it. Which didn't make any sense, as none of the walls inside the supply closet were part of the Clown Museum's exterior.

Before she had a chance to investigate, she heard the door unlock. In a flash, she was on her feet again. Wildly, she looked around for some kind of weapon, in case it was Carlos Jones coming to kill her. But all that was within reach was an old aerosol can of L'Oréal Elnett hairspray sitting on the vanity table. It wouldn't do much damage, though she supposed she could always spray it into the janitor's eyes. The stuff did smell disgusting.

The door opened, and as she feared, it was Carlos Jones. Ava planted her feet and held up the hairspray, bracing herself for whatever was about to happen next.

"What are you doing?" The janitor seemed genuinely surprised to see her. "Park's been closed for an hour. Everybody's gone home. You're not supposed to be here after hours without permission."

Ava let out a sigh of relief. So he wasn't going to kill her after all, and it had all been some kind of unfortunate accident. Feeling stupid for being so paranoid, she lowered the can of hairspray. "I got locked in. Thank god you're here. I've been pounding on the door and nobody heard me."

"I was next door, cleaning the House of Horrors. It must have been me who locked you in. I assumed you left early with the other girls. I'm so sorry about that. Hope you weren't too scared." He was staring at her intently, but Ava was beginning to realize that it was just his way. Like Anne-Marie said, he was harmless.

"I'm fine now," Ava said. "I'm glad you came back. I really should get going."

She checked her phone, and it was now eleven

thirty. It was too late for the bonfire, but she could still potentially meet up with Xander at the beach. They could hang out for a bit, and then maybe he could drive her to Katya's, where her friend would let her in through her back bedroom window whenever she got there. She reached for her backpack.

"By the way, your friend was here earlier," the janitor said. "The tall one. He came by at eight o'clock looking for you."

"He did?" Ava was confused. "Then why didn't he come back?"

"Because I told him you went home."

"Why would you do—" She stopped.

And then Ava knew. It was the light in his eyes, which had just changed from dull to sharp. It was the line of his posture, which had straightened, making him seem taller, somehow. And it was the way he was moving ever so slowly toward her in the tiny dressing room, when there was already nowhere to go.

"You know why," Carlos Jones said. Even his voice sounded different than it had a moment ago. It was richer, smoother, more confident. "I know you like me. I see the way you watch me when I'm working. That's good. I like you, too. I like you a lot."

Instinctively, Ava backed up. "My mom's waiting to pick me up," she said, her tone firm. "She just got off work, and she's waiting for me outside the main entrance, and she's probably freaking out—"

"Your mom's not here," the janitor said. "Because you lied to her, didn't you? You didn't tell her about the bonfire, or your plans to hang out with your boyfriend. She thinks you're somewhere else. Somewhere safe." He smiled. "She's not coming for you. Nobody is." He took another step toward her.

"You stay away from me." She backed up as far as she could. She was still holding the can of hairspray, and she held it up again.

"You're very pretty, you know," Carlos Jones said. His grin widened. "I don't even mind the cracks in your face. You look like a dead little girl, and it's kind of exciting, actually." His hand went to his crotch, and he began massaging his penis through his coveralls. "Come on, take off that hoodie so I can see your tits. Then I want you to pull down your panties and spread your legs with your dress still on. I want you to lie still. Very still. Pretend like you're dead." His breath was coming faster, and his hand was moving in a solid rhythm, his erection clearly visible through the thick cloth. "Oh yeah. Oh yeah, this is turning me on. This is going to be fun."

Opening her mouth, Ava screamed louder and longer than she ever had in her life. He reached for her, and she aimed the hairspray can and pressed the nozzle as hard as she could. But nothing happened. The nozzle was clogged and wouldn't depress.

Carlos Jones grabbed her by the arm and they wrestled. The screams coming out of Ava were a new sound—on some level she was aware that she was the one screaming, but at the same time, it didn't sound like her at all. She managed to yank her arm away, but he bumped up against her roughly, pinning her against the full-length mirror. She dropped the can of hairspray and it clattered onto the concrete floor.

"Why are you wriggling so much, baby girl?" His hot breath was in her ear. "You're supposed to be playing dead, remember?"

"No." It was all she could think to say. "No."

"Shhhh." The length of his body was pressed against her, and she couldn't move. He wasn't tall, but he was thick and muscular, and his body felt like a rock. He had both her wrists in one hand, and they were pinned above her head. "It's better if you relax. It hurts more if you fight it. If you ask me nice, I'll be gentle. This is your first time, isn't it? Or do you let your boyfriend touch you wherever he wants, you dirty little girl?"

Ava had never felt so small or so helpless. She continued to writhe, but the more she did, the more he seemed to like it. His erection was right in the middle of her stomach, hard and terrible. "No," she said in a smaller voice. "No."

"Shhhh now." He ran a long, wet tongue up the side of her neck to her earlobe, and then she felt it exploring the inside of her ear. "Just relax. It'll feel so good if you relax."

She screamed again, right into his ear, as loud as she could.

"Argh!" He pulled back, clapping one hand over the side of his head. "You fucking bitch!"

She tried to move past him, but he slammed her against the mirror, and it cracked against the back of her head. The world spun out, her vision narrowing into a small hole, and then her legs went out from under her. She slumped forward, the mirror crashing down around her. The wood frame came loose from the screws and it dropped to the floor behind her with a thud. She sat on the floor, dazed.

Carlos Jones was rubbing his ear. "You stupid little slut. Now you've made me angry. You like it rough, little girl? I can be rough. Oh, I can be very rough."

She blindly grabbed for a shard of glass, her fingers closing around a jagged edge. It cut her thumb, but she barely felt it. "Don't come near me," she gasped, holding the shard out. "I'll cut you, I swear I'll cut you." She made a wild slashing motion.

He looked down at her in contempt. "You'd cut your hand even worse than you'd cut me," he said, but he stayed back.

He was probably right about that, but it was a chance she might just take. The hairspray can was in reach and she grabbed it again with her other hand, getting to her feet again. "You get out of my way. You get out of my way right now."

A breeze hit her from behind, and she almost didn't notice it, except it was very, very cold. It ruffled the bottom of her doll dress, and she chanced a quick look around. There was a door behind her. What the hell? The mirror had been covering a door this whole time? From the cold draft that was coming out of it—which explained why the dressing room was always so chilly—there had to be something behind it.

A way out of this nightmare, maybe.

"Put down the glass, little girl." Carlos Jones stepped toward her. "You don't want to cut me. I know you don't. You're already bleeding. Let me help you."

He was right. She didn't want to cut him if she didn't have to. She lifted the hairspray again and pressed hard. Finally, it dispensed, and a stream of thick, strongly perfumed mist hit Carlos Jones right in the eyes.

"Argh! You fucking bitch!" His eyes squeezed shut and he rubbed at them frantically.

He lunged for her, but missed, because she had flung open the door and was tumbling down a flight of stairs into darkness.

THIRTY-EIGHT

Vanessa could have kept Oscar in county lockup for the night along with Glenn Hovey if she'd wanted to, but frankly, she was likely to learn more about him by letting him go. She wanted to know if there was anything else Oscar wasn't telling her, so for now, he was being charged with accessory to murder after the fact. The district attorney, currently attending the gala for Seaside Hospital along with everybody else in town, would draft his immunity agreement in the morning. In the meantime, Oscar's bail had been set at $250,000, which he'd been able to post quickly thanks to Jane Cartwright's cousin being a bail bondsman. He was free to go. On his way out, he touched her arm.

"I'm sorry," he said.

"I know," she said.

When they were gone, Vanessa tasked officers Nate Essex and Pete Warwick with watching him at all times. She wanted to know every move Wonderland's VP of operations made; where he went, who he talked to, how his moods seemed.

"You're on him like white on rice, you understand?" she said to the young officers. "He might know something about Aiden Cole and the rest of the missing Wonder Workers. Who knows what else Bianca Bishop might have asked him to do. Never let him out of your sight."

"Got it, Deputy Chief."

Wonderland's CEO, on the other hand, was a different story. She and Glenn Hovey were the prime suspects for the murder of Aiden Cole, and the possible murders of Blake Dozier, Kyle Grimmie, and Tyler Wilkins. And of course, Nick Bishop. She screamed bloody murder as Vanessa escorted her down to the jail, twisting and writhing in her handcuffs, long red hair tangled and flying.

"You cannot do this! Do you know who I am? I want my lawyer!"

"You called her and she didn't call back," Vanessa said patiently. "I assume she's at the gala with the rest of Seaside's power elite. But I'd be more than happy to wake up a public defender, if you want. You know, someone who's fresh out of law school and who wasn't smart enough to get a job in a private firm, someone who won't know how to argue for bail, or will get you stuck with a million-dollar bail or more. You're being arrested for two murders, after all."

"I have an *alibi*!" Bianca screamed. Spittle hit

Vanessa in the face, and she made a show of wiping it off. "I told you I was with Oscar Trejo all night! He'll tell you. Did you even ask him?"

"I didn't have to," Vanessa said. "Because he was with me all that night."

The look on Bianca Bishop's face was priceless—Instagram-worthy, as Ava would have said.

"Sure you don't want a public defender?" Vanessa asked again. "Or can you hang out here all night till your lawyer calls you back?"

"Go to hell, you whore," Bianca spat. "You probably fucked Frank Greenberg to get this job, didn't you?"

"Even if I did, it's still better than you murdering your uncle to get *his* job. Let's not throw stones, shall we?" Vanessa paused. "And for the record, I've never slept with Frank. He's a good man. Not that it matters to you."

With Bianca squared away, Vanessa called Earl Schultz, who picked up on the fourth ring sounding drunk and giddy. It only took about thirty seconds for his buzz to fade once Vanessa filled him in on what was going on.

"Christ, Castro," Earl said in her ear. "Are you sure? Bianca Bishop killed Nick Bishop?"

"Oscar moved the body to the tunnel," she said. "It's after midnight now, so I was going to put together a search party first thing tomorrow morning. We're running a skeleton crew here."

"I suppose if Nick's been in the tunnel all this time, he's not going anywhere, so a few more hours won't matter," Earl said. "Christ, I was wondering why Bianca and Oscar didn't show up tonight. Why didn't you call me before?"

"You know why."

There was a slight pause. "I guess there's something to be said for objectivity. I'll meet you at the park at 6 a.m. We'll keep the search team small; you know how rumors work in this town. You, me, Donnie, and another two officers max, whoever's around and discreet. Who's watching Oscar?"

"Essex and Warwick."

"Good." Big sigh. "Nice job, Castro. Get the search warrant prepared as quickly as you can. We need to do everything by the book here."

Vanessa sat in her office, exhausted, but there was still work to be done. She began putting together the warrant, and then it occurred to her that Ava still hadn't texted or called to let her know she'd arrived at Katya's. Looking at the time, she chanced it and called Jerry. He answered on the first ring.

"Did I wake you?"

"Nah, I'm watching TV. Just got home from the pub a little while ago. Had a couple beers with Tanner. His daughter's abusive boyfriend got off with community service and probation. But don't worry, he doesn't blame you. Now I'm watching *The Bone Collector*, Denzel Washington and Angelina

Jolie. If someone ever makes a movie about my life, I want Denzel to play me."

"Of course you do, but let's talk about your Hollywood fantasies tomorrow," Vanessa said. "I need a favor. Can you drive by Ava's friend Katya's house? She was supposed to text me once she got to Katya's, but I haven't heard from her, and my messages aren't going through properly. Katya's parents don't have a house line, just cell phones, and I don't want to wake them if I don't have to. I'm stuck here working on a search warrant we need for the crack of dawn, which is a challenge because I think the night court judge went home."

"I'm sure Ava just fell asleep and her phone's dead," Jerry said. "But sure, I can drive by. What's the address?"

She gave it to him. "Thanks, Jerry."

"Investigation panning out?"

"Another dead body at the amusement park," she said. "Wholesome family fun at its finest. I'll fill you in after you tell me Ava's sleeping and I'm free to kill her when she wakes up."

Fifteen minutes later, Jerry called back.

"Katya's there, but I didn't see Miss Ava," Jerry said. "I peeked in Katya's bedroom and I can clearly see her sleeping. Kinda felt like a pervert looking through the window; thank god nobody saw me or I probably would have been shot. I checked the other bedroom, but it's just her parents in there. What do you want me to do?"

"Shit." Vanessa's heart sank. She looked at the clock on her wall, then back down at the warrant. Fuck it, everything else would have to wait. "Something tells me they might not answer the door if they see a tall, skinny black man standing on their porch at 1 a.m. If anyone's going to scare the Melniks, it should be me. I'll be right there. Wait for me."

"What about your warrant?"

"I still got time. It can wait."

Vanessa arrived at Katya's house about ten minutes later. Jerry was sitting in his car, and he got out when she pulled up.

She knocked on the door, quietly at first, and then louder when nobody answered. Finally, with no other option short of banging on a bedroom window, she rang the doorbell. A few seconds later all the lights in the small house went on.

Peter and Karolina Melnik looked alarmed when they opened the door, dressed in pajamas and a nightgown, respectively. When Vanessa explained, they called for Katya immediately. The young girl came to the door, rubbing her eyes.

"She was supposed to sleep over tonight." Katya stretched her arms out over her head and yawned. She was wearing sweatpants that had been cut into shorts and an old Seahawks T-shirt that had probably belonged to her dad.

"That's news to me." Karolina Melnik frowned at her daughter before looking back at Vanessa. "I didn't know that. They didn't tell me."

"What was the plan?" Vanessa asked the girl.

"There wasn't really one," Katya said. "She asked if she could crash here tonight, and I said sure. She said it wouldn't be till late, like around midnight or even later, and I told her I'd leave my window open so she could climb in."

"That's not safe!" Karolina Melnik was horrified. "Your window is supposed to stay closed at night, that's why we got air-conditioning." A string of words in Russian followed.

"Have you done that before?" her father asked.

Katya shrugged, which in teenage speak meant, *Hell yeah, all the time.*

Vanessa forced herself to stay calm. Sensing her distress, Jerry squeezed her arm. "Katya, where did Ava say she'd be between 10 p.m. and midnight?"

The girl's eyes darted between Vanessa's face and her parents' faces, and then to Jerry's, who was the only adult who didn't appear upset. He simply smiled at her. "She had plans to meet a friend at the beach."

"What friend?"

"I don't—"

"Katya." Her mother's voice was one note shy of a shriek. "You tell the deputy chief what she wants to know right now, so she can find her daughter and we can all go back to sleep. Right now, Katya." Another long string of Russian words. It didn't take a translator to understand that the woman wasn't happy.

"His name is Xander Cameron," Katya finally said, shuffling her feet. "There was a bonfire party at the beach, and she really wanted to go. He's eighteen, which is probably why she didn't tell you about it."

"Eighteen!" Vanessa said, but again Jerry put a hand on her arm.

"He works with us at the park and they did their orientation together."

"Are they . . . are they involved?"

"No, they're just friends," Katya said, and Vanessa breathed a small sigh of relief. "She just has a thing for him, is all. But he was involved with someone else, and they got into this big fight and . . ." She lowered her voice. "Xander was having a thing with the Dragon Lady. Ava told me about it the other night."

"Xander and the Dragon Lady? As in Bianca Bishop?" Vanessa exchanged a look with Jerry.

Katya nodded, clearly eager to tell what she knew. Teenagers often made more helpful witnesses than adults. "He told Ava, and then she told me, but not until a few days after he told her. I was kinda mad she didn't tell me, like, *immediately*, but I get that she was all butt-hurt about it and that she needed some time to get over it before she could talk about it."

"Don't say 'butt-hurt,' Katya," her mother said. A permanent frown seemed to be etched into her face. "That's distasteful."

Katya sighed.

"So where is she?" Vanessa asked.

"She's probably still with Xander," Katya said. "But the bonfire only goes till midnight, and then beach patrol shuts it down. So they're either hiding somewhere at the beach, or they're back at his dorm, or they're heading here."

Her father said something in rapid Russian, and then her mother said something, too. Sighing, Katya said, "I'm sorry, Mrs. Castro. I shouldn't have agreed to help her lie to you, but she's my friend, you know?"

"Well, I appreciate your honesty now," Vanessa said. "Can you keep your phone on tonight in case I have questions? I'm going to go look for her."

"Okay," Katya said. "But Mrs. Castro, I really don't think you have anything to worry about. Ava's a good girl, and Xander—aside from his questionable taste in older women—is a pretty nice guy."

It wasn't Xander that Vanessa was worried about at the moment. She actually hoped her daughter was with him, and that she was safe.

Because if Ava wasn't, then where the hell was she?

THIRTY-NINE

Under the Clown Museum

Ava's head was pounding and she suspected her left shoulder was sprained, but her legs were working fine and so she kept moving. Carlos Jones was somewhere behind her. Whenever she turned around, she could see the little beam from his flashlight and was relieved he didn't have something like what her mother kept in the car—Vanessa Castro's Maglite was both a high beam and a weapon. Carlos Jones, lowly janitor and rapist at Wonderland amusement park, seemed only to have a flashlight the size of a pen, and thank god for that. In this instance, size mattered.

Her goal was to outrun the beam, which she wasn't sure she could do, considering she had no idea where she was going. She'd heard vague things about there being a tunnel or a dungeon underneath Wonderland, but she'd always assumed it was one of those urban legends, like *Candyman*.

Her iPhone, still in the pocket of her doll dress, had a flashlight app on it. But now her phone was dead, along with Ava's hopes of seeing anything in front of her. All she could do was keep one hand on the concrete wall and jog blindly. Every so often the wall ended and she was forced to go left or right, and logic dictated she would follow the draft of air. If there was air, there had to be a way out.

Carlos Jones's beam disappeared, and Ava stopped for a moment to catch her breath. Her hand remained on the wall, until she felt something crawl over it. Yanking her hand away, she shook it furiously, wanting desperately to scream, and knowing she couldn't. She forced herself to keep moving.

After another fifty steps or so, she saw a dim light up ahead and hesitated. She was hopelessly lost and wasn't sure what the light was from—it wasn't the janitor's tiny flashlight, but it could very well be light coming down from the supply closet/dressing room. It was entirely possible she'd gone in a circle and had ended up back at the staircase she'd fallen down. But then she realized the draft of air was coming from a different direction.

Ava decided to take her chances. She headed toward the light.

"Hello?" a voice said out of nowhere.

She almost screamed again, but caught herself just in time, and all that came out was a gasp. It wasn't Carlos Jones's voice, she was sure of it. This voice was younger, and hoarse, like sandpaper on sandpaper. And it didn't sound threatening. If anything, he sounded scared.

"Hello? Who's there?" the voice said again. "Hello? Are you there?"

Not knowing what else to do, Ava followed the sound. As soon as she saw him, she froze, her mouth falling open.

She took it in all at once, because it wasn't possible to process it piece by piece. Her eyes darted from one thing to the next in rapid succession. Cage, bars, prison cell, toilet bowl, sink, an old tube TV bolted to the upper corner of the cell, small bed, small mattress, food wrappers all over the floor, blond boy, face pale, eyes huge, dirty hair, dirty everything, wearing a Wonderland uniform.

She knew his face. She'd seen him before. But not like this.

Not like this.

"Help me," he said. His lips were as cracked as his voice. "My name is Blake Dozier. You have to help me get out of here. Please. *Please*."

FORTY

Vanessa had tried calling Xander Cameron's cell phone three times, but he wasn't picking up. She then called Nate Essex, pulling him off surveillance on Oscar Trejo's house. She told him to go to the Wonderland dorms to see if he could find the boy her daughter was supposed to be hanging out with. If they weren't there, maybe someone there would know where they were.

"Wake everybody up if you have to," Vanessa said. "It's my kid. If she's there, you have my permission to embarrass her on my behalf for scaring the shit out of me."

"Sure thing, Deputy," Nate said. "And don't worry, Oscar Trejo went to sleep right when he got home. He went straight upstairs, then all the lights went out. Pete'll keep watch. I only live three blocks away from here. I'll run home and grab my car and head straight to the dorms."

"Good man, Nate. Thanks."

"It's your daughter, Deputy," Nate said. "Whatever we need to do, we'll do."

She and Jerry had gone directly to the beach after Katya's, only to be informed that the bonfire party had ended at midnight on the dot, according the town employee whose job it was to clean up the mess. And no, he did not remember a girl fitting Ava's description being around.

"Sorry, but all those kids look the same to me," he said to Vanessa and Jerry. He could not have been more unhelpful.

Vanessa was struggling not to panic, but it was getting harder and harder. She might not have been so alarmed, except for the fact that all she'd done since moving her family to Seaside was work missing persons cases.

"Jerry, I'm going to lose my shit," Vanessa said. They were sitting in her unmarked trying to figure out their next move. Jerry's car had been left at Katya's. "If she's been taken—"

"She hasn't been," he said. "All the missing persons cases have been boys, fitting a very specific physical type—tall, blond, eighteen. Ava's fourteen, female, with dark hair. Whatever this is, it isn't that."

"Then what is it?"

"She's a teenage girl and she lied to you about her whereabouts. That's all. We'll find this Xander Cameron, and he'll tell us. If he doesn't know, we'll talk to every single person at Wonderland. We'll run her

phone records. We'll trace every move she made."
Jerry offered her a sympathetic smile. "And don't
forget, it's Miss Ava. She's far from a stupid girl. All
those crime shows she watches, all those horror
movies? They've made her savvier than most; she
knows the dangers out there. She'll be okay. We'll get
her home in one piece so you can ground her for the
rest of eternity, don't you worry, honey."

Vanessa's cell phone rang. It was Nate Essex.
"You found her?"

"Just Xander Cameron," the young officer said.
"He was in his dorm room, sleeping."

"Shit. Does he know where Ava is?"

"He says he doesn't, Deputy."

"Bring him into the department, anyway," she
said. "I want to question him."

"I figured you would, which is why he's sitting in
the back of my car," Nate said. "We'll meet you at
PD in ten minutes."

Nine minutes later, Vanessa was walking so quickly
into the department that even Jerry, with his long
stride, had to jog to keep up with her. Nate Essex had
stuck Xander Cameron in an interview room, and
was heading back to resume his surveillance of Oscar
Trejo's house.

"You want me to wait out here?" Jerry asked.
"I'm a civilian, after all."

"No," Vanessa said. "I need you."

He nodded, knowing nothing more needed to be

said. He followed her into the small room where Xander Cameron was waiting for them. The boy was half awake, slumped into the chair with his eyes mostly shut, his phone in front of him on the table. He sat up with a start when the door slammed shut.

"Am I in some kind of trouble?" Xander said, looking from Jerry to Vanessa and then to Jerry again. Her friend had subtly switched into cop mode even though his Seattle PD days were long behind him. He was standing differently, straighter somehow, and the expression on his normally cheerful face was unreadable. "The cop who brought me in said you were looking for one of my friends, but I already told him I don't know where she is. I gotta get back to the dorm, I got an early shift tomorrow." He stifled a yawn.

"Do you know who I am?" Vanessa asked.

"You're . . . a detective, or something." Xander's eyes dropped to her belt, where she'd clipped her gold badge. "The other officer said you were in charge."

"I'm Deputy Chief of Police Vanessa Castro." She took a seat across from him. Jerry remained standing. "I'm Ava's mother."

"Oh *hey*." Xander's face visibly brightened. "Yeah, she said you were with the police, I think that's so cool. And it's nice to meet you. I'm sorry, but I honestly have no idea where she is. We were supposed to meet at the Clown Museum, but when I got there, this guy told me that she'd gone home already."

"What guy?"

"The janitor, I think," Xander said. "I was surprised Ava even talked to him. I think she complained about him before, but he seemed nice enough, so I might have got them mixed up."

Vanessa looked at Jerry, the name coming to her a second later. "Carlos Jones. You sure you didn't find anything on him?"

"I did my standard check. Nothing came up." Jerry looked upset.

"Describe him to me," Vanessa said to Xander. "Be as detailed as you can."

"Um, let's see . . . he was short," Xander said. "Like five six, maybe five five. Very stocky, broad shoulders, muscular. Short dark hair, dark eyes, kind of had a gap between his two front teeth."

"Ethnicity?"

"I don't know. But he had a neck tattoo. A red rose with black leaves, and beside it was the name Nora. Written in script."

Vanessa pulled her keys out of her pocket and handed them to Jerry. "My computer login and password are on a sticky note inside the locked top drawer of my desk. The key's on the ring. The software is the same as what we used in Seattle."

"I'm on it." Jerry left the room.

"So Ava told you about the creepy janitor," Vanessa said. "And yet you believed him when he said Ava changed her plans and went home?"

"I . . ." Xander gestured helplessly. "He didn't seem creepy to me. I mean, she and I had kind of an argument recently, and we just started talking again, and I thought we were cool. But when the janitor said she went home, I thought maybe it was her way of telling me to get lost. I mean, that's something girls do. They get all, you know, passive-aggressive."

Vanessa sighed. Xander Cameron didn't strike her as the smartest kid in the world, but he was right about that.

"I'm guessing you argued about Bianca Bishop?" she said.

The kid's eyes widened. "She told you about that?"

"No, I heard it from another person."

"Awww, no, that's not supposed to get out." Xander sank into his chair. "Bianca's going to kill me. I wasn't supposed to tell anyone. I can't believe Ava would tell—"

"Watch what you say about my daughter," Vanessa snapped. "Remember why you're here. This isn't about you at all."

The ounce of patience she had for this young man, who was handsome and tanned and impossibly blond, was disappearing rapidly. He had the classic "Wonderland look," going by Glenn Hovey's definition, and a thought occurred to Vanessa then.

"How long have you been sleeping with Bianca Bishop?" she asked.

He looked mortified. "Since the beginning of the season."

"Who started it?"

"She did."

"Are you aware that Aiden Cole, also known as Homeless Harry, was someone she'd slept with, too?"

"What?" Xander frowned. "No, she didn't tell me that, but it explains why she was kind of upset the day they said who he was."

"Are you aware that there are three other Wonder Workers, all the same age as you, all with the same look as you, who've gone missing over the past eight years?"

"Well, I heard about the Wonder Wheel Kid . . ."

"Blake Dozier, yes. There's also Kyle Grimmie and Tyler Wilkins."

"Tyler?" Xander's head snapped up. "She mentioned someone named Tyler once."

"In what context?"

"Well, we were, you know . . . we had just finished." His cheeks reddened. "And she said I reminded her of someone named Tyler. Apparently we both made the same . . . noises. She thought it was cute. I didn't like that she said that. I didn't want to think about other guys she'd been with."

"Who else did she talk about?"

"I dunno, we talked about a bunch of different stuff," Xander said. "We talked about this guy who works with her in the office, who wants to leave to run a restaurant. She was kind of upset about that."

Oscar. "Go on."

"And there's this guy at the police department who pretty much does anything she says. They had a thing a long time ago, but he's still into her, will do anything for her."

Vanessa's heart skipped a beat. "Who? Carl Weiss? Earl Schultz?"

"No, it was someone who used to be a Wonder Worker. Danny something."

"Danny? I don't know of anyone named—" Vanessa stared at him. "*Donnie?*"

"That's it. Donnie," Xander said. "He worked at the park for a few summers. Apparently he was obsessed with her, took it hard when things ended, kept trying to do all kinds of weird stuff to get her attention. Every time something happened at the park, he'd make sure he was the cop on the scene, and I think she was telling me about him so that the same thing wouldn't happen to me. I mean, she said what we had was special, but I don't know if I believe her now, although the sex was amazing . . ."

He continued to talk, but Vanessa had stopped listening. Her mind was swirling as she tried to process it all.

Donnie? Detective Donnie Ambrose had been one of Bianca's special Wonder Workers? What did that even mean? He didn't even fit the profile . . . or did he? The young detective kept his hair clipped so short she'd never given much thought as to what his hair would have looked like longer. And Donnie hated the park. Donnie hated Bianca Bishop.

Didn't he? Or was Bianca Bishop the girlfriend he'd stayed in Seaside for?

None of this made sense.

The door to the interview room opened and Jerry popped his head in. "Need to talk to you."

"Can I go?" Xander said, looking hopeful.

"No." Vanessa followed Jerry out and shut the door behind her. She forced herself to focus on her friend. Whatever had happened between Donnie and Bianca Bishop would have to wait. Ava was the only thing that mattered right now. "What'd you find?"

Jerry handed her a printout. A black-and-white mug shot of a man fitting the description of Carlos Jones filled the top half the page, except his name wasn't Carlos Jones. This man's name was Albert Riggs. Short hair, dark eyes, rose neck tattoo with the name Nora in flowing cursive. He'd killed his mother when he was fourteen with a switchblade, and had spent four years in a psych ward until he was released at eighteen. He was the prime suspect in a series of violent rapes across Washington state and Oregon. His last known crime was two years ago, shortly before he'd started working at the park.

"This is a nightmare," Jerry said, echoing Vanessa's thoughts. "Every time I think Seaside can't be more full of fucked-up, scary, violent human beings, it just gets worse."

"We have to go to Wonderland." Vanessa's teeth were clenched so tight her jaw ached. Her daughter was in trouble, and it was taking every ounce of control she had to keep it together. She couldn't let herself fall apart. Ava needed her. She had to get to Ava. "It's the only place she could be. You bring your weapon?"

"Don't carry one anymore, though right now I wish I did."

"I have an extra thirty-eight special in the glove box." Vanessa forced herself to breathe and speak normally. "Got your name all over it."

FORTY-ONE

Under the Clown Museum

Blake Dozier stared at the younger girl. After days upon days of not seeing another human face, he wasn't sure if he was dreaming or hallucinating, or if maybe she was just a mirage that his brain had conjured up because he was so thirsty for another human being.

She was staring at him the same way, as if she couldn't grasp what she was seeing, either. He put a hand up, giving her a trancelike wave, and she lifted her hand and waved back.

And then she spoke.

"Hi," she stammered.

"Hello," he said. "Are you real?"

"Last I checked."

Not more than fourteen or fifteen, she had messy dark hair and huge dark eyes, and was wearing a gray hoodie over what looked like a doll dress, right down to the petticoat. Her face was all cracked, and it was scaring him shitless, but it didn't appear she was trying to scare him. She was like an antique porcelain doll come to life.

It was the hoodie that told him this was real. If he was dreaming, or hallucinating, she would have just been wearing the doll dress.

"Who are you?" she asked, sounding breathless, but before he could respond, her head cocked to the side, listening. "Oh god. Oh god, he's coming."

"Who is?" He continued to stare at her through the bars.

"Carlos Jones." She looked back over her shoulder. "The janitor."

The name meant nothing to Blake, but he could only assume that Carlos Jones was the man who'd snatched him and had been keeping him here.

"He tried to rape me and I fell down the stairs." A tear fell down her cheek, cutting a streak right through what he could now see was makeup. "I don't know how to get out of here."

They both heard footsteps approaching, and she looked around wildly, panicking.

"Hide," Blake said.

"Where?"

"There's a corridor over there." He pointed to the left of the dungeon. "Go there, crouch in the dark. I'll stall him."

"How—"

"Go *now*," he said.

She disappeared into the darkness, and a few seconds later, a man dressed in a gray coverall materialized. Blake could only presume this was Carlos Jones. Like the girl had said, he was a janitor, and Blake vaguely recognized him from the park, even though they'd never spoken to each other. Carlos Jones wasn't his captor. This man was much too short, and much too wide. But just because he wasn't the one who kidnapped Blake didn't mean he wasn't still a villain in his own right. He hoped the girl stayed out of sight.

"What the hell is all this?" Carlos Jones approached the bars of the dungeon slowly, looking both confused and suspicious. "What the fuck kind of sick—"

"Help." Blake kept one ear tuned to any sound that might emanate from the corner where the girl was hiding. "Help, please. I need you to let me out. I'm being kept here against my will. If you don't help me, he's going to kill me. I need you to help me escape and then we have to call the police right away. Hurry."

"No," Carlos Jones said, backing away. "No cops. Fuck that, no way. Whatever sick shit this is, I'm not getting involved."

He turned and started running back the way he came, his footsteps growing more and more faint until they could no longer be heard. Blake waited an additional ten seconds just to be sure.

"He's gone," he called out softly. "You can come out."

There was no response. Not even a sound. Blake's heart sank. Had she gone? Had she left him here? *Oh god, please still be there. Please.*

But then he heard rustling, like the sound of a petticoat rubbing against skin. She emerged from the darkness slowly, looking around, at him, at the cage, at the bars, and back to him again.

"What the *fuck* is this?" she said.

"Let me out and I'll tell you." He rattled the bars to keep her focused. "My name is Blake Dozier. Please, the key is on the wall right beside you. Please, please let me out. I have to get out of here."

"You're the Wonder Wheel Kid." She spoke softly, walking toward him. "That's why you look so familiar. Holy shit. You're not dead."

"What?" he said, not understanding.

"Your selfie," she said. "Of you on top of the Wonder Wheel. It went viral and everybody's been wondering what happened to you. They were starting to think you might be dead." She took the key off the wall. "I'm Ava. My mom is the deputy chief of police of Seaside, and she's been looking for you. Let's get you out of here."

She sounded confident, but her hands were shaking as she fumbled with the lock. Finally, she got the door open. She extended a hand and Blake stumbled as he reached forward to take it. The relief he felt was so powerful his knees almost buckled beneath him.

He felt the warmth of her palm, but before he could close his fingers around hers, he heard a loud snap. A sharp, hot, fierce pain emanated from somewhere in his midsection, and dropping her hand, he looked down in disbelief. A dark, wet spot was spreading fast over his purple Wonderland shirt.

The girl screamed as his knees finally gave out, and he collapsed to the floor of the dungeon.

It was cruel to have come so close to freedom only to die now, and the last thing he saw was the girl crouching over him, her face streaked with white makeup and tears, while his captor loomed over them both with a gun pointed toward them. His captor had never brought a gun with him before, at least not that Blake had seen, and he knew instantly that this wouldn't end well for the girl, either. She held his hand and touched his face, then turned and said something to the captor Blake couldn't quite make out. The dungeon was beginning to fade away.

Squeezing her hand with what strength he had left, he said the only word he could think of to say, the only word his brain seemed able to process.

"Run," Blake whispered, closing his eyes. It was so cold down here, colder than it had ever been. "Run."

FORTY-TWO

Vanessa and Jerry ran through the midway toward the Clown Museum, and if she hadn't been on the verge of complete and utter hysteria, she might have paused to think about how eerie Wonderland looked at this time of night. The Wonder Wheel lights were still on—those lights were always on—but there was not a soul other than themselves anywhere on park grounds that she could see.

Nate Essex and Pete Warwick would be here soon, along with Oscar Trejo, whom Vanessa had called personally. She explained what had happened with Ava, and he'd offered his assistance immediately. Despite what he'd done, she needed his expertise on where to look for Ava inside the park.

"I know every inch of Wonderland," Oscar had said to her on the phone. "We'll find her."

Donnie Ambrose, the detective who'd been so loyal and so anti-Wonderland from the beginning and who was likely the serial killer she'd been looking for, would have to be arrested by someone else. Vanessa had called for an APB on him, but all she cared about right now was finding her little girl. Ava was somewhere in this godforsaken park with a rapist who'd assumed someone else's identity, and who'd managed to go unnoticed at Wonderland for two whole years.

Until now.

She should have taken her daughter more seriously when Ava had first complained about Carlos Jones. She should have asked more questions about him, dug a little deeper. She'd been teaching Ava from a young age to always trust her gut, and the one time her daughter had, Vanessa had dropped the ball completely. Serial killer or no serial killer, her kid came first.

The Clown Museum, the attraction Ava was scheduled to work at all week, was the logical place to start. When the other officers arrived, they would all spread out.

She approached the museum as if seeing it for the first time, even though it had been here when she had worked at World of Wonder all those years ago. The entrance was a gaudy, massive plaster structure, designed to look like a clown's face, and guests entered through its wide, gaping mouth. The age of the attraction showed in the cracks and peeling paint, but somehow it only added to its creepiness.

A security guard was waiting for them right by the

clown's mouth. As they got closer, Vanessa saw that it was Rudy, the same security guy who'd helped out with the surveillance footage the day Homeless Harry's body had been dumped at the park.

"Deputy Chief." Rudy's eyes flickered to Jerry and then back to Vanessa again. "I have the keys to every door in this park if you need them. Oz told me to do whatever you ask."

"You can start by opening this door for us, Rudy. When we get inside, we'll all split up. Do you know Carlos Jones?"

"Not very well, I'm sorry to say." Rudy unlocked the door using a key attached to a giant ring. He stepped aside to let Vanessa and Jerry enter first. "He's always kept his head down, though once or twice a few of the female Wonder Workers complained that he stares a bit too much. No one's ever filed a complaint against him, though. Clearly we should have looked into it more."

"Yes, you should have. Turn the lights on, please."

"They are on." Rudy looked around. "It's always dim in here."

Swearing under her breath, Vanessa looked at Rudy and Jerry. The security guard seemed half as tall and twice as wide as her friend, but the expressions of grim determination on their faces were identical. "Spread out," she said to them. "Don't hesitate to use your weapon if it means saving my little girl's life."

"Got it." Jerry had grabbed an extra Maglite

from the trunk of Vanessa's unmarked and he switched it on. Vanessa switched hers on, too. Her gun was in its holster at her hip; Jerry's was tucked into the waistband of his jeans.

"All I got is my stick and a can of pepper spray," Rudy said, sounding ashamed. He turned on his flashlight. It was half the size of theirs and not nearly as bright. "They don't give us anything else."

"Then spray him and hit him as hard as you can," Vanessa said. "Rudy, you take the celebrity wax figures, and Jerry can take the Dollhouse. I'll take the clowns. Go."

The three of them disbursed, and Vanessa made her way quickly through the museum. It hadn't changed much in the twenty years since she'd been here. The wax clowns stared at her with their glassy eyes, and as she weaved her way through them, she looked for any sign of Ava. The light from her Mag flickered over every crevice and corner.

So help me god, if you've touched a hair on her head . . .

Two minutes later, she heard Jerry's voice echo through the silence of the museum. Vanessa's heart leapt into her throat, and she followed the sound until she found him. Rudy had beat her there, and they were standing by what looked like a utility or supply closet. The door was open.

"What is it?" Vanessa's heart was hammering as she approached. "Did you find her?"

"Rudy says this isn't normal." Jerry stepped aside so she could look into the supply closet.

It wasn't very big, and it appeared as though it had been converted into a dressing room of some sort. A row of clown and doll costumes hung from pegs along one wall, and there was a vanity table against the far wall. To the left was another door, which was also open. A second door inside a utility closet? That didn't seem to make any sense. Cold, drafty air was wafting out of it, and shattered pieces of mirrored glass were all over the floor. As Vanessa took a moment to process what she was seeing, a knapsack in the corner caught her attention.

It belonged to Ava. She would never have left her knapsack behind. This was the last place she'd been.

"What's through that door?" she asked Rudy.

"I don't know." The portly security guard looked genuinely baffled. "I've never seen it before."

Jerry walked over and shone his light into it. "I've heard rumors about an underground tunnel at Wonderland," he said. "Always thought it was an urban myth, something started by the kids to make the park seem cool. Looks like Miss Ava found it."

"When you guys get down the stairs, go left," a voice behind them said. They all turned to see Oscar standing there with Nate Essex and Pete Warwick. Vanessa nodded to him and Oz nodded back. "We'll go right. The tunnel is a bit of a maze and we don't know which way she went. It's faster if we split up."

FORTY-THREE

Under the Clown Museum

Ava could feel the life seeping out of Blake Dozier. His hand had gone limp in hers and his face was white. If he was breathing, she couldn't tell.

The man holding the gun was dressed all in black, a ski mask covering his whole face except for his eyes, which appeared dark in the dim lighting of the dungeon. He was taller than Carlos Jones had been, and leaner. Other than that, there was nothing about him that was distinguishing.

"Don't kill me." Ava's voice was cracked and hoarse from all the screaming she'd done. "I haven't seen your face. I don't know who you are. Please, just let me go."

"Stand up," he said.

She let go of Blake's hand and got to her feet, wobbling a little, and faced him. Instinctively, she put her hands up in the air, palms out. "Please," she said again. "I didn't mean to come here. I was trying to get away from someone who was going to hurt me, and I fell down the stairs. Just let me go, please."

"What's your name?"

She didn't recognize his voice, but he didn't sound old at all. She didn't want to tell him her name. Seaside was a small town, and everybody seemed to know who her mother was. If this man found out she was the daughter of the deputy chief, he would likely kill her so as not to take any chances that she might be able to identify him. He'd shot Blake without even hesitating. He was, clearly, the serial killer at Wonderland her mother was hunting.

"Marie." Ava gave him her middle name, which was the only name she could think of at the moment.

"What's wrong with your face?"

His question confused her, and then she remembered she was still in her doll costume. "It's makeup," she said. "I work here at the park. Upstairs. In the Clown Museum."

"I know who you are." He walked toward her, the gun comfortable and loose in his hand. "The makeup threw me, but as soon as you said Clown Museum . . . I've seen your picture. In your mom's office, on her desk. Your name isn't Marie. You're Ava Castro."

"No, my name is Marie." She started to cry, the sobs heaving up from her chest painfully.

He pulled off his mask, revealing a young, clean-cut

face and hair that was buzzed almost to the skull. He seemed weary and tired. "I guess I can take this off now. You're not going to be able to tell anybody anything, anyway. I'm sorry, Ava, but you're not getting out of here."

"No," she said, gasping for air. Hot tears were streaming down her face and every inch of her body began to tremble violently. It had nothing to do with the cold, and she couldn't control it, couldn't make herself still. The fear spread right to her bones, and then her gut, and she thought she might throw up. "No, please, I don't know anything. I don't even know who you are."

"I'm tired, Ava," he said. "I was going to stop, I really was. Blake was a mistake. I was trying to move Aiden's body. He escaped into the woods and I had to kill him there, but it was a few days before I could go back and get him, and there was no way to get him back down here except through the Clown Museum. Blake was pulling some stupid stunt on the wheel, which is just so typical for boys like him who think they run the world. He saw me. I had no choice but to take him."

Ava was still shaking so hard she could barely speak. "Please," she said. "Please don't hurt me."

"The irony is, I like your mom." His face crumpled for a second before he regained his composure again. "She took me under her wing, and I was learning so much from her. She made me believe I could turn it all around. She told me I could go to the FBI if I wanted to, that I could leave Seaside. She's nothing like Bianca. All Bianca did was play games with me.

Sometimes she wanted me, sometimes she didn't, and there were so many times I tried to break free of her, but couldn't. She'd always pull me back in. I thought when I made detective it would change things, that maybe she'd finally take me seriously, but nothing changed. To her I was always just a stupid Wonder Worker. I've wasted so much time on Bianca."

"She was seeing someone else." Ava's mind raced as she tried to understand what he was saying. He'd been involved with Bianca Bishop, too, that much was clear. Ava needed to keep him talking. It was the only hope she had of staying alive. "Bianca was seeing one of my friends. He's only eighteen."

"Bianca was seeing a lot of people. Always young, always blond, always the Wonderland look. I had that look once. I got too old for her." His voice hardened and he rubbed his head. "The things I've done for her. She doesn't even know the lengths I've gone to, the things I've done because I love her—" He stopped abruptly.

"What things?"

"It doesn't matter now," he said. "I can't undo it. I can't undo any of it. I wish your mom had been around back then. Your mom . . . she was nice to me."

"Then don't hurt her." Ava was desperate. She needed to reason with him, though she wasn't sure she could. His sense of right and wrong was completely warped, to say the least. "Hurting me will hurt her, don't you see that?"

"Get on your knees," he said.

"Please, I—"

"*Now*," he said.

She got on her knees. He was standing right above her, looking down. She turned her face up to his. "Please," she said one last time, and the shaking was so bad her teeth were chattering.

"I'm sorry," he said. And what was crazy was that he really *did* seem sorry.

He started to raise the gun, but then stopped when they both heard a noise. Seemingly out of nowhere, a thermos was rolling toward them. It was clear blue plastic, the kind that you put water in when you went hiking, and inside it was a mini Twix candy bar. It was the weirdest thing to see, and the noise it made as it rolled on the cement floor seemed loud inside the tunnel. It continued to roll until it stopped a few inches short of Ava's knee. She had no idea where it had come from, but it was just enough to distract the man, who was looking down at it, too.

Without hesitating, she grabbed for his gun with both hands, pulling on it as hard she could. If she was going to die, she might as well do it trying to save herself.

There was another loud snap—which she now knew was the sound of a gunshot—and Ava screamed.

FORTY-FOUR

Under the Clown Museum

"**A**va!" Vanessa screamed, racing through the tunnel as fast she as could. Behind her, Jerry and Rudy followed. "Ava! Goddammit, I don't know where the hell I'm going. Ava!"

"Deputy Chief!" she heard a male voice shout. It sounded like Nate Essex. "Deputy, go straight and make a left, then head toward the light!"

She did as she was instructed, and a minute later, she saw a flicker of light up ahead. Not slowing down even a bit, she ran toward it, Maglite in one hand, gun in the other. She took in the scene all at once.

Her daughter was on the floor, sobbing hysterically. Just in front of her, a man lay crumpled facedown, dressed entirely in black. He was completely still. Nate and Pete were standing over him, guns still cocked. Behind Ava was a jail cell of some kind, and another body could be seen lying on the cement floor, also still. Oscar stood in the corner, looking stunned by the whole thing.

Vanessa dropped her flashlight, holstered her weapon, and went straight to her daughter, scooping her up in her arms.

"It's okay," she said, holding Ava as tight as she could. Her daughter was trembling violently from head to toe, and she clung to Vanessa like she hadn't done since she was a toddler. "It's okay, I'm here. I've got you. You're okay. Shhh. Mommy's here. You're safe."

"I can't get a cell signal down here," Jerry said to Rudy, who seemed almost paralyzed by what was going on. "I need you to go back up and call an ambulance. Make sure they send at least two. I see two bodies." The security guard didn't move. "*Go*," Jerry said again, and Rudy finally snapped out of his trance.

Ava's crying slowed down a little, and she turned her face up to her mother. White, chalky makeup was flaking in little patches from her skin, and one of her false eyelash strips had come unglued and was hanging by a lash. "You're really here." She sounded as if she was afraid to believe it.

Vanessa plucked the dangling eyelashes off and kissed her daughter's clammy forehead. "I'm here. You're safe. They got him."

Ava nodded, burying her head in her mother's chest.

Looking up from where she was crouched, Vanessa said, "Is it Carlos Jones?"

Nate and Pete both shook their heads. "It can't be," Nate said. "He's too tall. We haven't turned him over yet."

Ava had calmed down, and she pulled back. "It's not Carlos Jones," she said, "Whoever it is, he knew you and you knew him. Go and do your job, Mom. It's okay."

Vanessa kissed her forehead again and squeezed her tighter. "This is my most important job. I'm fine right where I am." To Nate and Pete, she said, "Turn him over."

Jerry, after briefly squeezing Ava's shoulder, went over to see the body. Pete Warwick holstered his gun and bent down, rolling the man over onto his back. An audible gasp could be heard, confirming what Vanessa already suspected. She hadn't had a chance yet to tell anyone here about Donnie Ambrose, so it was a hell of a way for them all to find out.

"What the *fuck*?" Nate stepped back, his free hand flying toward his mouth. The hand holding the gun dropped to his side, and he looked like he was going to faint. "It's Detective Ambrose. Oh my god. Deputy Chief, I shot Donnie. Oh my god. *Oh no*."

"Nate—"

"I didn't know," Nate said again, looking down at

the dead man. On the floor, Pete Warwick looked equally stunned. "I swear to god, Deputy, I didn't know it was him. He was wrestling with your daughter and I saw the gun and I fired. I didn't even think—"

"Nate," Vanessa said, louder this time. The young officer looked over at her, visibly shaken, his eyes wide. "It was a good shoot. You did the right thing; you saved Ava's life. Donnie is the killer we're looking for. I found that out only an hour ago. He's been obsessed with Bianca Bishop since he was a Wonder Worker here, and he's the one who's been killing those boys."

"And he shot Blake," Ava said, starting to cry again. "I was trying to let him out, and he shot Blake."

"Blake's still alive," Jerry said. He was inside the cell, crouching down beside the boy, fingers pressed to his neck. "I'm getting a very faint pulse. Hang in there, buddy. Ambulance is coming. Hang in there."

Ava pulled away from Vanessa and ran over to Blake, getting right down on the floor with him. She reached for his hand. "I'll stay with him till the paramedics get here," she said.

Jerry looked over at Vanessa. She nodded her consent.

"I promise I won't let go of your hand this time," Ava said to the unconscious boy on the floor.

Vanessa let out a long breath and stood up, looking

around the dungeon, the one that nobody had ever thought really existed. Her gaze met Oscar's, and he shrugged helplessly, as if to say, *I'm sorry.* Somewhere down here were the remains of Nick Bishop and probably the other missing boys as well, but Vanessa had no intention of looking for their bodies right now. Not with her daughter here. Besides, they were already dead. It could wait for when they could get a proper crime scene team in place.

"Mom," Ava said. "There's another victim. I almost forgot. There's someone else here."

"I know, sweetie," Vanessa said. "We'll take care of it, don't worry."

"No, Mom, there's someone here who's *alive.* He's somewhere down there." With her free hand, Ava pointed toward the dark corridor just beyond where Oscar was standing. The conviction in her daughter's voice was unmistakable. "Whoever it is, he saved my life. He distracted the guy who almost killed me. I didn't see him, but I think it has to be one of the missing boys."

Almost right on cue, music began to waft out of the dark corridor and a flickering light could be seen. It wasn't just any song. It was the Wonderland jingle of all things, the one from the TV commercial that played on all the local stations about six times a day.

As if in a trance, Oscar began to head toward the music and the light. Concerned, Vanessa called out, "Oz, stay where you are," but the VP of operations either didn't hear her or was ignoring her. Pulling out her weapon once again, Vanessa was prepared to follow him, but a few seconds later, his voice could be heard clearly throughout the dungeon.

"Oh Jesus Christ," Oscar said, his voice breaking. "*Nicky.*"

FORTY-FIVE

It would take at least a week to process everything they'd found in the tunnel, but preliminary reports from the search team confirmed the remains of three more boys. Their bodies were in various states of decay, but one of the boys had an old army knapsack next to his remains, with a Devil's Dukes patch sewn onto the front. Vanessa's heart ached for Tanner. His words, expressing hope that his son was somewhere out there, alive and happy, had haunted her, and this wasn't the news she wanted to give him.

The second victim was likely Kyle Grimmie, and the third victim was a boy Oscar suspected Bianca had killed when she was only a teenager. However, nothing could be confirmed until thorough autopsies had been performed.

The sun wasn't even up yet, and the park was already in chaos. Half of Seaside PD was inside the midway, along with six ambulances and three fire trucks. Earl Schultz, unable to get in touch with

Vanessa for the past couple of hours, had heard the call come in over the radio that first responders had been dispatched to the park, with the possibility of at least two dead bodies and a possible gunshot victim. When Vanessa exited the Clown Museum with Ava, the chief of police was waiting for her.

"The security guard told me about your daughter," he said. "I'm glad she's all right."

She walked Ava over to the paramedics first to get checked out, then took her boss aside and filled him in on everything that happened. It was a lot to report, and the longer she talked, the more haggard Earl looked. When she finished, he heaved a long sigh.

"I should have retired last year. But I thought, nah, I'll hang in, what's one more year?" He looked around at the flashing lights and the stretchers carrying the bodies they were pulling out of the tunnel. "But this . . . this is not how I wanted to go out."

They watched as the paramedics finally brought Nick Bishop out into the light. He was strapped to a stretcher, but his face was uncovered, though they'd put dark sunglasses on him. Even wrapped in a blanket, it was clear how painfully thin he was from years of near-starvation and muscle atrophy. His hair had gone completely gray, the bones in his face sharp, his skin sallow.

He'd been unable to speak inside the tunnel when Vanessa tried to talk to him, as whatever head injuries he'd suffered seemed to have damaged that part of his brain. But he could write, and the note he'd scrawled into Vanessa's notebook said that Donnie had found him in the tunnel, still alive, the night he'd snatched Tyler Wilkins. Eight long years ago. There was so much more to ask him, but it could wait until he was in better health. Nick Bishop had saved her little girl's life, and for that, Vanessa would be forever grateful.

"Christ," Earl said. "Nick Bishop. *Alive*. If I wasn't seeing it with my own eyes . . ."

"He's in bad shape, Earl," she said. "He's been down there a long time."

"Why do you think he did it?" The police chief looked baffled. "Why would Donnie keep him there all these years?"

"I can only guess that it was for Bianca," she said. "Some kind of warped sense of love for her, or loyalty. Donnie was a Wonder Worker back then. In his mind, he was probably doing something good for the woman he loved."

"But Bianca believed she'd killed Nick, which was why she was pretending he was living in some other part of the world." Earl rubbed his face again. "I can't even wrap my mind around that."

Vanessa could only shrug. "All Bianca ever cared about was protecting the park. I'm sure it made sense to her. When I break the news to her later that her uncle is still alive, her reaction alone will tell us how much she really knew. At the very least, I've got her on attempted murder. She's done."

Vanessa checked on Ava again, and for the most

part, her daughter seemed okay. No physical injuries other than a few scratches and a small cut on the back of her head from where Carlos Jones had pushed her into the dressing room mirror. Jones—real name Albert Riggs—was long gone from Seaside, but Vanessa would find him if it was the last thing she did. Nobody touched her little girl and got away with it. Nobody.

One of the officers had offered to drive Ava home, but her daughter refused to leave. She wanted to stay close to her mother for the time being, and that was fine with Vanessa. Ava had asked about Blake, but all Vanessa knew was that he'd been flown to Harborview Medical Center. It was the state's only level-one trauma center, and he'd receive the best medical care possible. Her fingers were crossed that he'd pull through.

Even in the wee hours of the morning, news traveled at lightning speed. Wonderland's main entrance was jammed with reporters. The flashing lights of the police cars and ambulances were the only thing brighter than the midway, and by noon it would be all over the local news. By dinnertime, it would make national headlines.

Tanner Wilkins had bullied his way into the park with his usual charm, and the look on Vanessa's face when their eyes met told him everything he needed to know.

"It's not a hundred percent," she told him. "We won't be sure until the ME takes a look."

"But it's likely Tyler," he said.

"Yes." She touched his arm gently. "I'm so sorry, Tanner."

He nodded, moving away for a moment to compose himself. When he turned back, his face was filled with grief. Peace, Vanessa thought, would probably come much later for him, assuming it ever did.

"I guess I can leave Seaside now." Tanner's voice was thick.

"I think you should." She squeezed his arm. "Take Jenna, go on a vacation. You'll figure it out."

His grizzly face looked down at her. His eyes, always so bright blue, were sad. "Will you be here when I get back?"

"I'm not sure." It was the most honest answer Vanessa could give him. "But if I'm not, you'd better find me. My car might need servicing. Plus I'm a sucker for those free beers you promised. I'll even buy dinner."

Tanner managed a smile. "You hitting on me, Deputy?" Bending down, he kissed her cheek. "Thank you for everything you've done."

On his way out, he shook hands with Jerry, who offered his condolences and pulled him into a rough hug. Jerry then came over and slung a skinny arm around her. She put her arm around his waist and rested her head on his shoulder. She couldn't remember the last time she was this tired.

"Pretty crazy, huh?" he said.

"Sure you don't miss this?" Vanessa said. "Earl Schultz just told me he's retiring. They'll be looking for a new police chief."

"Nah, I'm good where I am," Jerry said. "And besides, I'm sure they'll ask you."

"I don't want it."

"Don't blame you." He sighed. "You think there's more bodies down there? Didn't you tell me you found a whole bunch of Wonderland ID cards in Glenn Hovey's bedroom?"

Vanessa shook her head. "Nate ran the other ID cards and from what we can tell, the rest are alive and well. My theory is that Donnie knew Hovey collected those ID cards, and he set him up by planting the cards of the boys he'd killed in with the rest of them. Glenn Hovey is weird, but I'm beginning to think that's true of everybody who's been at Wonderland a long time. I don't think Hovey killed anyone other than Jack Shaw, and from what I hear, he had good reason. How much time he'll serve for it, though, who knows."

"And the Dragon Lady?"

"Oh, she's going down," Vanessa said. "She tried to kill her uncle, and on some level she had to have known what Donnie was doing. All the Wonder Workers she'd slept with went missing, and she doesn't go to the police? Come on."

Ava came up to them and Vanessa put her other arm around her. The three of them stood staring at the Wonder Wheel, old and huge and majestic. The sun was just beginning to peek over the horizon, filling the early morning with a warm glow. The only thing missing was John-John. Her little boy was probably just waking up at his friend's house, safe and blissfully unaware of everything that had happened. It was too early to call over there now, but Vanessa couldn't wait to wrap her son in her arms and squeeze him till he squirmed.

"You know what, I'm going to stay till tomorrow," Jerry said. "Make sure you guys are okay. Plus I want to make sure you don't beat yourself up about Donnie." His voice softened. "You couldn't have known, honey. He hid it well."

"Too late." Vanessa sighed. "You know I need to kick my own ass righteously and properly before I can begin to forgive myself for missing that one."

"He liked you, Mom," Ava said. "He told me. If that makes you feel better."

It didn't, but she smiled at her daughter and pulled her closer.

"So what's next?" Jerry asked.

"Wonderland used to be the only good thing about Seaside, and now it's the worst thing about Seaside," Ava said. "I hate this place. I think we should move back to Seattle."

"That's a real possibility." Vanessa watched the commotion in the midway. "This town, it's too small, too corrupt, too tainted. Everything is fake. It looks like a postcard from the outside, but it's rotting on the inside. I don't want to raise my family here. Only problem is, I'll have to figure out what to do for work. I've burned all my bridges at Seattle PD."

"Yeah?" Jerry said. "Because if you're serious about coming back to Seattle, I could use a good partner. Isaac and Castro Investigations has a nice ring to it."

Vanessa couldn't help but laugh. It was a nice offer, but she couldn't imagine not being a cop. She'd been in law enforcement for sixteen years; the badge was all she knew.

In the distance, a familiar figure was walking toward them. It was Mayor Frank Greenberg, and when Ava saw him, she untangled herself from her mom and ran straight for him. He bent down and hugged her, lifting her up off her feet, and then his eyes met Vanessa's. Frank smiled at her tentatively. She smiled back, the weight of what they had done with John Castro both bridging and widening the gap between them.

"You know what," she said to Jerry. "I'll think about it."

And she would.

AUTHOR'S NOTE

Dear Reader,

As fiction writers love to do, I took reality and warped it a little bit for this story. Readers who are familiar with the Pacific Northwest region of the United States will notice that I've played around with geography, as I tend to do in all my books. For instance, there is a town called Seaside in Oregon, but there isn't one in the state of Washington. As far as I know, the fictional Seaside and the real Seaside are nothing alike.

There are several amusement parks throughout the world with the name Wonderland, including one just north of Toronto, where I grew up. However, Canada's Wonderland is nothing like the Wonderland I created for this story. It does not have a clown museum (and if it did, I would never, ever go in there), nor to my knowledge does it have an underground tunnel leading to a dungeon where bad things happen. The amusement park in this book is a mix of the real Wonderland I knew, the CNE (the Canadian National Exhibition, which is a huge fair in Toronto that happens every August), and my own demented imagination.

If you've read my earlier novels *Creep* and *Freak*, I hope you were as happy to see Jerry Isaac as I was. I had no idea he was going to show up in Seaside until I wrote the page where he is first mentioned. He definitely wasn't in the proposal I submitted to my editor before I started writing. Characters are surprising that way . . . or at least they are for me, as I don't outline my stories in advance. It's always awesome when old friends show up.

Speaking of old friends, if you're wondering whether Vanessa Castro stayed in Seaside or moved back to Seattle, and you haven't yet read a later novel of mine, *Little Secrets* . . . actually, what kind of thriller writer would I be if I spoiled it for you?

And now for one last thing: If you bought this book in 2023 or later, in ebook or mass market paperback, then you just read the reissued version of *Wonderland* . . . and I could not be more thrilled.

When *Wonderland* was first published in October 2015, it was released only as an ebook. So when I learned that it was going to be distributed in mass market paperback nearly eight years after its original publication (with a new cover, to boot!), I was elated. Of all my books, I've always felt *Wonderland* was the perfect story to be published in a lightweight, pocket-size print format. For many of us, the reading experience is tactile—there's something special about the feel of an actual book in your hands, the sound it makes when you turn the pages, the way the paper smells. As a writer, nothing fulfills me more than to see a book of mine all battered and worn, the cover bent, the pages dog-eared, with a coffee stain or two. While some of you are probably gasping in horror right now, I really do take a beat-up book as a huge compliment. To me, it's a sign of a book well-read, and hopefully well-loved.

While *Wonderland* will always be available as an ebook, I'm delighted that it now has a chance to reach readers who prefer to read in print, and who enjoy discovering their books in brick-and-mortar stores.

Whichever format you prefer, thank you for reading!

My warmest wishes,
Jennifer

ACKNOWLEDGMENTS

I started writing *Wonderland* when I was pregnant in 2013, and finally finished it in 2014, when my son was six months old. Back then, I was living in a different city in a different country. It's 2023 now, and we live in a suburb of Toronto, but reading the book over again instantly transported me back to Seattle and that very unique season of my life. It was exhausting being a new mom, and stressful being on a tight deadline (a date that I totally agreed to, in a fit of hormonal delusion). Looking back now, I can't believe I actually wrote a whole novel during the most sleep-deprived year of my life.

While I technically wrote this book alone, I had a lot of help with everything else in my life. I am so grateful to my husband, Darren Blohowiak, for being superdad and superhusband, and supereverything else I needed in order to complete this book. Our son is eight years old now, and Darren, you are still all those things. I couldn't do what I do without your support. Thank you, my love, now and always.

I've been with my agent, Victoria Skurnick, since the very beginning. Victoria, I wrote in my original acknowledgments that you are my navigator, arbitrator, negotiator, protector, and defender when it comes to all things publishing. That all remains true to this day, and then some. You are one of the sweetest, kindest, most generous people I know. I didn't just get published because of you. I have a career because of you. Thank you, thank you, thank you.

My editor for this book, Natasha Simons, was a joy to work with. Natasha, I'm not sure how you did it, but you managed to make the very tedious process of editing my own novel an almost painless endeavor (I'd say fun, but then you'd totally know I was lying). Thank you for believing in me and in *Wonderland*, and for taking my vision and making it better. I'm so glad we keep in touch. Mia Robertson, thank you so much for your help with this reissue, and everything you've done to give this book a second life. And to everyone else at Gallery Books and Pocket, thank you. It was a pleasure working with you wonderful folks for five years.

Mom, Dad, and John, thanks for being proud of what I do, and for all your encouragement. To my in-laws, the Blohowiaks, it's an honor to be part of your family, and thank you for all your support. A special shout-out to my aunt and uncle, Regina and Alex Perez, for being like second parents to me in so many ways. I love you guys.

I'm lucky to have had the same girlfriends for a few decades now. Annabella, Dawn, Lori, Shellon, Teri, and Micheleen, thank you for being there for the biggest moments of my life, and also for the tiny ones that happen every day. You're the greatest cheerleading squad a girl could ever ask for.

A special thank-you to my son's very first babysitter, McKenzie Nelson, for her tireless energy taking care of Mox while I was holed up in the office writing every day. Everyone in our neighborhood probably did think you were a teen mom, but that's only because Mox loved every moment he spent with you.

Someday, Maddox John, I hope you read this book and think it's cool you were growing inside me when I wrote it. I also hope you'll think it's cool to be named after a fictional serial killer—your mom has a warped sense of humor. I didn't know you were going to exist when I created Abby Maddox in my first two novels, but now it all makes sense. You are the reason for everything. Like the palm reader in Jamaica told me, you were coming. It was certain. And now here you are, and I couldn't love anything in the world more than I love you.